ALL AUNT HAGAR'S CHILDREN

ALSO BY EDWARD P. JONES

Lost in the City

The Known World

ALL
AUNT HAGAR'S
CHILDREN

Edward P. Jones

Amistad

An Imprint of HarperCollins*Publishers*

"Old Boys, Old Girls," "All Aunt Hagar's Children," "Adam Robinson Acquires Grandparents and a Little Sister" (as "Adam Robinson"), "A Rich Man," and in a slightly different form "Bad Neighbors" first appeared in *The New Yorker*. "The Devil Swims Across the Anacostia River" first appeared in *Grand Street*.

On page 50, "This Little Piggy" is from *Step It Down: Games, Plays, Songs and Stories from the Afro-American Heritage* (Athens: University of Georgia Press, 1972) by Bessie Jones and Bess Lomax Hawes.

This book is a work of fiction. References to real people, events, establishments, organizations, or locales are intended only to provide a sense of authenticity, and are used fictitiously. All other characters, and all incidents and dialogue, are drawn from the author's imagination and are not to be contrued as real.

HarperCollins books may be purchased for educational, business, or sales promotional use. For information please write: Special Markets Department, HarperCollins Publishers, 10 East 53rd Street, New York, NY 10022.

FIRST EDITION

Designed by Betty Lew

Library of Congress Cataloging-in-Publication Data

Jones, Edward P.
   All Aunt Hagar's children: stories / Edward P. Jones.— 1st ed.
      p. cm
   ISBN-13: 978-0-06-055756-0
   ISBN-10: 0-06-055756-7
      1. African Americans—Fiction. 2. Washington (D.C.)—Fiction.
I. Title.

   PS3560.O4813A77 2006
   813'.54—dc22   2006042746

06 07 08 09 10 ❖/RRD 10 9 8 7 6 5 4 3 2 1

To my sister
Eunice Ann Mary Jones-Washington
and

to the multitudes who came up out of the South
for something better, something different, and, again,

to the memory of my mother,
Jeanette S. M. Jones,
who came as well and found far less
than even the little she dared hope for

CONTENTS

ALL AUNT HAGAR'S CHILDREN

IN THE BLINK OF GOD'S EYE

That 1901 winter when the wife and her husband were still new to Washington, there came to the wife like a scent carried on the wind some word that wolves roamed the streets and roads of the city after sundown. The wife, Ruth Patterson, knew what wolves could do: she had an uncle who went to Alaska in 1895 to hunt for gold, an uncle who was devoured by wolves not long after he slept under his first Alaskan moon. Still, the night, even in godforsaken Washington, sometimes had that old song that could pull Ruth up and out of her bed, the way it did when she was a girl across the Potomac River in Virginia where all was safe and all was family. Her husband, Aubrey, always slept the sleep of a man not long out of boyhood and never woke. Hearing the song call her from her new bed in Washington, Ruth, ever mindful of the wolves, would take up their knife and pistol and kiss Aubrey's still-hairless face and descend to the porch. She was well past seventeen, and he was edging toward eighteen, a couple not even seven whole months married. The house—and its twin next door—was always quiet, for those city houses were populated mostly by country people used to going to bed with the chickens. On the porch, only a few paces from the corner of 3rd and L Streets, N.W., she would stare at the gaslight on the corner and smell the smoke from the hearth of someone's dying fire, listening to the song and remembering the world around Arlington, Virginia.

That night in late January she watched a drunken woman across 3rd Street make her way down 3rd to K Street, where she fell, silently, her dress settling down about her once her body had come to rest. The drunken woman was one more thing to hold against Washington. The woman might have been the same one from two weeks ago, the same one from five weeks ago. The woman lay there for a long time, and Ruth pulled her coat tight around her neck, wondering if she should venture out into the cold of no-man's-land to help her. Then the woman pulled herself up slowly on all four limbs and at last made her stumbling way down K toward 4th Street. She must know, Ruth thought, surely she must know about the wolves. Ruth pulled her eyes back to the gaslight, and as she did, she noticed for the first time the bundle suspended from the tree in the yard, hanging from the apple tree that hadn't borne fruit in more than ten years.

Ruth fell back a step, as if she had been struck. She raised the pistol in her right hand, but the hand refused to steady itself, and so she dropped the knife and held the pistol with both hands, waiting for something terrible and canine to burst from the bundle. An invisible hand locked about her mouth and halted the cry she wanted to give the world. A wind came up and played with her coat, her nightgown, tapped her ankles and hands, then went over and nudged the bundle so that it moved an inch or so to the left, an inch or so to the right. The rope creaked with the brittleness of age. And then the wind came back and gave her breath again.

A kitten's whine rose feebly from the bundle, a cry of innocence she at first refused to believe. Blinking the tears from her eyes, she reached down and took up the knife with her left hand, holding both weapons out in front of her. She waited. What a friend that drunken woman could be now. She looked at the gaslight, and the dancing yellow spirit in the dirty glass box took her down the two steps and walked her out into the yard until she was two feet from the bundle. She poked it

twice with the knife, and in response, like some reward, the bundle offered a short whine, a whine it took her a moment or two to recognize.

So this was Washington, she thought as she reached up on her tiptoes and cut the two pieces of rope that held the bundle to the tree's
branch and unwrapped first one blanket and then another. So this was
the Washington her Aubrey had brought her across the Potomac River
to—a city where they hung babies in night trees.

When Aubrey Patterson was three years old, his father took the
family to Kansas where some of the father's people were pros-
pering. The sky goes all the way up to God napping on his throne, the
father's brother had written from Kansas, and you can get much before
he wakes up. The father borrowed money from family and friends for
train tickets and a few new clothes, thinking, knowing, he would be able
to pay them back with Kansas money before a year or so had gone by.
Pay them all back, son, Aubrey's father said moments before he died,
some twelve years after the family had boarded the train from Kansas
and returned to Virginia with not much more to their names than bile.
And with the clarity of a mind seeing death, his father, Miles, reeled off
the names of all those he owed money to, commencing with the man to
whom he owed the most.

Aubrey's two older sisters married not long after the family returned
to Virginia and moved with their husbands to other farms in Arlington
County. They—Miles, the mother, Essie, and Aubrey—lived mostly
from hand to mouth, but they did not go without. Aubrey's sisters and
their husbands were generous, and the three of them, in their little house
on their little piece of land with a garden and chickens and two cows,
were surrounded by country people just as generous who had known the
family when they had had a brighter sun.

A little bit before Aubrey turned thirteen, it came to be that his
mother took to going off down the road most evenings. "Goin to set

with Miss Sally a piece," she would say of the old woman a half mile or so away. But her son learned that way before Miss Sally's cabin there lived a man in a shack with a busted door, and that was often where she stopped. If his father, a consumptive, knew, he never said. At first, before he closed his heart to her, Aubrey would stand on the porch and watch her go off, one of the yellow dogs following her until she turned and threw a stone at her. The other dog rarely moved from under the house. Aubrey would watch the road even after she had disappeared. "Whatcha you doin, son?" his father would ask from inside. "Come read me a few verses, maybe some chapters." His mother had taught him to read in Kansas when he was four. Her people were all book people.

They grew closer, the father and the son, in a way that had not been possible in Kansas, where each day's new catastrophe had a claim on their hearts. His father encouraged him to attend church. "It's but a little bit outa your whole life, son," Miles said, remembering how angry God must have been after he had awakened from his nap when the family was in Kansas. "And God has a long memory." His son was nearing fourteen then. So each Sunday morning, the boy, alone, would set off down the road, opposite the way to Miss Sally's, carrying the Bible inherited from his maternal grandfather, the same book he read from to his father about the trials and tribulations of the Jews thousands of years before the first black slave set foot in America.

Now Ruth Hawkins, whom Aubrey would one day marry, had four brothers born on one side of her and four brothers born on the other side, so men were no mystery to her, and they were not gods. She and Aubrey had played together as little bitty babies, though they had not remembered. But the old women all around Arlington remembered, and they liked to recite the short history of the two after Aubrey returned from Kansas. The old women would mingle after church, only steps away from the Praying Rock Baptist Church graveyard, leaning on walking sticks and on grandchildren anxious as colts to be out and away. "Come here, little bit," they would say to Ruth and Aubrey, seeing down the line that the two had a future together. "You member that time . . . ," and they would go on with a story about two playing infants that seemed to have no end.

At first, Ruth and Aubrey had nothing to say to each other after church, after the old women's talk had turned to something else and the two were free to go. He was always desperate to get back to his father, and she had a whole world of people and things to occupy all the moments of her days. Even her dreams were crowded, she told a friend. Then, in late August of 1899, Mrs. Halley Stafford, who, people said, had given her name to the comet, decided she had had enough and died in the bed she was conceived and born in. Representing her own family at the funeral, Ruth stepped up to the open grave with a handful of dirt and dust and let it sprinkle on Mrs. Stafford's coffin as it was lowered down into its resting place. The new preacher, with less than a hundred shaves to his name, kept repeating, "Dust to dust . . . Ashes to ashes . . ." The dirt flowed ever so slowly out of Ruth's hand, and in the slowness of the moments she began to feel as though she could count each grain as it all fell from her. She turned from the grave and looked at her mother, at her father, at her brothers, at everyone assembled about her, and all the while the dirt and dust kept flowing. After the funeral, she came up to Aubrey along the path that led to the road that would take him home. He stopped, and she walked a half circle or so around him, and he took off his hat and held it midway up his chest, hoping it would not be long off his head. Over her shoulders he could see departing people and buggies and wagons and horses and mules, stirring up heaps of dust. The sun behind her flowed soft yellow through the threads of her summer bonnet. "When you gonna ask my daddy when you and your daddy can take supper with us?" she said. He blinked. "I reckon . . . I reckon next week," he said, flinging out any words he thought would satisfy her. This was their longest conversation up to that moment.

"Could be the fire next time, come next week," Ruth said. He thought of his father carrying him at four years old on his shoulders along the flat roads of Kansas. In his bed that night, he realized that she had made that half circle so the sun would be out of her face and full on his.

Whenever they were together after that, her youngest brother, Harold, eight years old, accompanied them. More and more of the toys that had once belonged to his brothers were coming his way, so he was mostly a happy boy. Armies of wooden men, still vital after all those years of playing hands, were now his to command as he had always dreamed. In October and early November, before the cold came upon them, he would carry a platoon of soldiers in a small burlap sack as he walked several steps behind Ruth and Aubrey when they strolled a foot apart, hands to themselves, down to the creek. Harold would stamp down the grass and position the soldiers about the ground as the couple, giggling, skipped stones into the quiet water, or sat on what passed for a bank and saw who could kick up the biggest splash with their bare feet. The boy would lie back and tap the soldiers' heads against the face of the sun, putting fighting words in their mouths. In late February, after the cold took an early parting, his father told Harold it would be fine if the couple walked hand in hand, and the boy, on his own, increased the distance between himself and them by three paces and stopped singing the song he sang when he thought they were too close. Into March, into April, well beyond the planting season, he rested a squad of men in his lap while he played checkers with Aubrey's father in the front room that now doubled as the man's bedroom. And when he could not hear the mumble of the couple's conversation from the porch, the boy would excuse himself to Miles and go to the door, soldiers in both his hands. When he was satisfied that all was proper, he would go back to the game. He had already given names to all his men in the first days of his sister's courting, but in the time it took Ruth and Aubrey to grow comfortable with each other and then to move into love, Harold had more than enough time to rename them, enough time to promote a sergeant to colonel for saving a motherless kitten about to drown, to send a one-arm captain home to his family for sassing him.

Aubrey Patterson would go only twice down to the shack his mother shared with the man she had taken up with. She was an outcast to all the world, even more so than the man. Not even the postman went there.

The dawn he found his father dead, Aubrey first called him and waited. When he knew at last, he kissed his father's lips and his hands. Then, as he had done most mornings, he washed his father's face, combed his hair, and shaved him with the pearl-handled razor Miles's grandfather had purchased from a whore in Annapolis. He took off his father's nightclothes and put on the best clothes the man had owned, just as he would have if they were expecting company. Finally, he sat in a chair beside the man's bed and read a chapter of Genesis and two chapters of Psalms. Then he went down the road to the shack. "Case you wanna know, case you care . . . ," he began after he had shouted for his mother from the yard. All the way down there, he thought of his father, and all the way back, he thought of Ruth.

The second time he went to the shack, it was to tell his mother he was getting married. He and Ruth were in the wagon his father had left him. Ruth stayed in her seat as Aubrey got out and shouted for his mother as he had done the day his father died. In a few minutes they were gone, his mother this time not coming to the door. Essie Patterson, living in sin, disappeared out of his life. His oldest sister sent word to him when she died. "We gotta go to her," Ruth told him, two weeks after they started life in Washington. "We gotta go to her. She the only mother you ever had," which was something she would not be able to say about the baby in the night tree.

❄

They spent the first weeks of their marriage in his house. In between the lovemaking, they told each other things they had not been able, for any manner of reason, to say when they were courting. That third night ended with his confessing that he had once stolen a chicken. He had not started out to do it, he told her, but he was walking by Mr. Johnson's place and the chicken followed him down the road, and no matter what he did, the chicken would not go back home. Then God began to whisper to him, and those whisperings, along with his failing father at home, convinced him that Mr. Johnson could stand the loss of one chicken, a tough thing to eat as it turned out. She found it endearing that he could not tell the difference between God's counsel and the why-the-heck-not advice of the Devil.

About two in the morning that eighth night, Ruth, hearing that old night song, sat on the side of the bed and reached down in the dark for the slippers he had presented her. They were not where she thought she had put them and she settled for his boots. Outside in the warm, she let the flow of the song lead her about the place, lit by a moon that commanded a sky with not even one cloud. She walked all about, even near the dark of the night woods, for there was no cautionary story about wolves roaming in Virginia. An owl hooted and flew up, wings as wide as the arms of a scarecrow. It disappeared in the woods and Ruth turned back to the house. She would miss this little piece of a farm, but Aubrey's aunt, Joan Hardesty, had assured her that Washington was a good place to be. Joan had taken him aside in the moments after his father's funeral and told him there was always a place for him with her if he didn't think Virginia was good enough to give him a future. He had grown up knowing her as a dainty thing, famous for separating the different foods on her plate with toothpicks. Ruth, nearing the house, paused to admire the moon that had started out dusty orange at the horizon and had gotten whiter and whiter the more it rose. Paul Hardesty had married Joan not two months after first meeting her, and they had gone across the Potomac River to Washington, and the city had put some muscle on her. On the day of Aubrey's father's funeral, Joan had been a widow for more than a year, Paul having been killed by one of the first automobiles ever to go down the streets of Washington. The story of death by an automobile was such a novel one that white men told it in their newspapers. The white newspapers never mentioned that Paul was unable to run from the automobile because one of his legs was near useless, having been twisted and turned as the midwife pulled him from the womb.

"It grows on you," Ruth, at the funeral, remembered Joan saying of Washington, like a woman talking about a lover whose shortcomings she would just have to live with. "You just let it grow on you." In Washington Joan had found a special plate with compartments, and so never had to use toothpicks again to separate her food.

Ruth now came around the side of the house, stopped at the well, and pulled up the bucket and drank deeply. A married woman could dispense with the drinking cup. Aubrey's father was dead, and his mother less than a whore, so there was nothing much for him in Virginia anymore. He smiled when he said Ruth's name, and he smiled when he told people he was going to live in Washington, D.C. Ruth had no feeling for Washington. She had generations of family in Virginia, but she was a married woman and had pledged to cling to her husband. And God had the baby in the tree and the story of the wolves in the roads waiting for her.

"Ruth, honey?" Aubrey stood in the doorway. "Sweetheart, you hurtin or somethin?" The bucket had been returned and she had been watching the moon. "You all right, honey?" After your parents, Miles had advised Aubrey, nothing stands between you and unhappiness and death but your own true wife.

She turned from the path that led out to the road. "I'm fine as Sunday," she said. "I get this way sometimes. Specially when I'm happy." He came to her and she came to him.

"Thought maybe you was sleepwalkin. Knew a nice woman in Kansas who did that, useta go out and try to milk her cows till one of em kicked her one night."

"Not me. I'm wide awake. See my eyes." He laughed and put his arms around her. His arms were not trembling the way they had been the very first times. They stood there for a long time, time enough for the moon to hop from one tree across the road to another. The moon shone silver through all the trees, which the wife first noted to herself, then pointed to places on the ground for her husband to see—a shimmering silver all the more precious because it could be enjoyed but not contained. The moon was most generous with the silver where it fell, and even the places where it had not shone had a grayness pleasant and almost anticipatory, as if the moon were saying, I'll be over to you as soon as I can. "I'm gonna miss Virginia," Ruth said and yawned. Aubrey said, "I'll make it up to you. Sides, we be just cross the river. In a lotta places we can stand on the river and see Virginia." Sleep had escaped him now, but it was gaining on her, and at last he had to pick her up and carry her to bed. They were the children of once-upon-a-time slaves, born into a kind of freedom, but they had traveled down through the wombs with what all their kind had been born with—the knowledge that God had promised next week to everyone but themselves.

The feeling that the baby's mother might never come back started coming to Ruth three mornings after she had cut him down from the tree when she alone witnessed his umbilical cord dropping off. She held the blackened thing in the palm of her hand, a thing that was already turning to dust, and she realized her own mother must have done the same thing over and over again, with the children who would live and the ones who died before their first year. Fourteen days after she cut the infant down, she named him Miles, after Aubrey's father, who had treated her like a grown-up who always knew right from wrong. She did not consult Aubrey about calling the baby by his father's name—she just woke up that morning thinking it was a bit of bad luck for a child to be in the world and not be known by anything but "him" on a good day and "it" on a bad day. Aubrey said not a word when he heard her calling the baby Miles; they both had always known that was what they were to call their first son. It would not be untrue to say that it was a very long time before Aubrey stopped thinking that the baby's mother was returning, and for months and months he went all about Washington, even into Virginia, asking who might have lost a baby boy. He came from a land where human beings had a past as tangible as dirt, where even children with no parents or grandparents had laps they could cry into. But while his wife knew this, she also knew a body's world was held up only by a dime-store thread: Playing with three of her youngest brothers one day, she saw a brown bundle fall from the sky and hit the August corn with a *crack!* The children waited in the awful quiet after the fall, and after many seconds, a brown puppy poked most of its trembling body out of the cornfield, looked left, then right, like a well-taught child about to cross a road of danger. The puppy was clearly teetering between alive and dead, tattooed with the bloody marks of a hawk's talons on both haunches. Finally, satisfied it might now be safe, it wobbled its way in the direction of Harold.

Ruth and Aubrey had been two and a half months in Washington when the baby appeared, paid helpers in the various businesses Joan Hardesty ran out of the two-story houses at 1011 and 1013 3rd Street, N.W. She ran a little hotel at the 1011 address for colored people who were forbidden in the city's white hotels. She did laundry out back, and at the 1013 house people could buy supper five days a week and sit at the big table and enjoy their meal. The chickens in the back provided her with eggs, which had just gone up to three cents a dozen when the newlyweds arrived. People could also buy freshly killed chickens, though most of her customers preferred to take them home and wring the birds' necks themselves. There was a little blacksmith business, also in the back, but it had been failing since her husband was killed.

Ruth Patterson's first friend in Washington was forty-seven-year-old Sailor Willie, who rented a room from Joan at the 1013 address, where she herself lived, the place where she gave the big upstairs front room to Ruth and Aubrey. Joan had moved from that big room, where she had spent most of her married life, to the smaller upstairs one in the back after Paul was killed. Sailor Willie, Paul's second cousin, lived in the middle room, which was not big and not small and which looked out at the 1011 house. The view had never mattered to a man who had been all over the world, and it was mattering even less by the time Ruth and Aubrey arrived because his eyes were failing him. He was slowly becoming known as Blind Willie. He had made his living first as a merchant seaman and then as a whaler, and having spent so many years among men who smelled of the rotting flesh of whales, he loved to smell sweet all the day long. Before he came home from the sea for the last time, he had bought many bottles of a man's "evening water" in London, and he patted that on his face almost as soon as he was out of bed in the morning. He had had women all over Washington, before and after he retired from the sea, but as his light failed, these women began to see a chance to twist the heart of a man who had often twisted theirs, and they turned their backs on him. "Sailor Willie," they mocked, "want a nurse now that he turnin into Blind Willie. He sweet as sugar now, but I don't want none of that in my coffee." In the days before Ruth arrived, he had been going about the city to see some of the women, telling those who would open the door that he just wanted "to pay my respects." He actually wanted to say he was sorry, but the sea had not given him words for that, and what few meetings there were turned out badly. Two women he especially wanted to see had been avoiding him. One of them, Vi Sanchez, was dead, but he didn't know that, and the other, Melinda Barclay, had just been trying to hold on to what life she had left after Sailor Willie went away the second and last time.

In the days before she cut the baby from the tree, Ruth and Aubrey's time on 3rd Street was pleasantly exhausting. Joan was not a slave driver, but she wanted her money's worth from any who worked for her. Whenever the couple happened to meet up in some quiet corner in one of the houses, or in the barn out back, they clung to each other, kissing until they heard a noise. At night in their big front room, they would giggle and tickle each other, waiting until they heard the roar of Willie's snoring in the middle room. Then they made love, and when they were done, he would lick the sweat from her face, her chest. He was desperate to have a child, a son he could name for his father, who was with him always.

No one ever came to claim the baby, and before long Aubrey, no longer blessed with guiltless sleep because of the baby crying in the night, went the other way when he heard Ruth approaching those quiet corners. He began to devote even more time to trying to find who might have "lost" a baby boy. By February he was even knocking on the back doors of white people to find out, as he put it, if they had heard tell of someone who was in the family way and now was not but had no baby to show for it. By February, too, he was resenting Ruth for having so easily made a home for the baby with them in that big front room. From that first night she had put the baby in the wooden crib one of her older brothers had created, a small thing of absolute beauty with cherubs carved on the sides, cherubs doing everything from throwing balls to jumping rope to sitting on tree limbs. A cherub with closed eyes and upraised arms and wings unfurled sat with his fat crossed ankles on the crib's headboard. The crib had always been intended for their own first child, but now day after day Aubrey could see the orphan sleeping in it, his arms spread without a care in the world, his belly fat with milk Aubrey himself had taken from the humpbacked cow Joan rented to make the butter she sold.

It was in late April that he began to think that Ruth was not getting pregnant because her heart was too much with the orphan. ("Don't call him Miles," he had finally told her in March. "Don't call him nothin. Whoever come to get him will wanna give him back his real name, and the boy'll just haveta get used to bein called somethin else." Ruth had sighed, the same way she did in the old days when she was about to fall asleep.) And it was in April that he began to seek her out during the workday to take her wherever he found her alone. The force and frequency of his seed would overpower her heart's fondness for the tree baby. A guest came upon them in one of the upstairs rooms in the 1011 house and complained to Joan. "What kinda damn place yall think I'm runnin here?" she demanded of Ruth and Aubrey. "You can take that mess back to Virginia." All the while she spoke, she seemed about to cry, as if their doing it in broad open daylight like that was only a small part of what was troubling her.

When Aubrey took Ruth at night in their bed, he no longer waited to hear Blind Willie start to snore. In early May she screamed for the first time with the brutality of it. "I won't let you touch me no more if you keep hurtin me," she said one morning as she fed the orphan, the baby's eyes blinking sleepily, one hand raised to touch her mouth. "I'll do it right from now on," Aubrey said quietly, but his word lasted only three days. By the time Ruth got word in late May that her mother was ailing, she had not let him touch her in more than a week. They had quarreled all that week, mostly at night, and though Aubrey tried to contain his shouting, Blind Willie could hear them. He would knock on the wall. "Yall be good to one nother in there, you hear? Ain't no call for yall not bein good to one nother."

She took the orphan when she went to see about her mother, ignoring Aubrey when he asked what he should do when the baby's mother came back to get the child. In Virginia she found peace again, found she could shake off the unsettling way Washington had insinuated itself in her nerves, something that had happened long before she cut the baby down. She helped her father and brothers with the crops. Once her mother improved, the two took the orphan in the buggy and went all about Arlington, visiting people Ruth had not seen in many months. The world in Virginia kept telling her that marriage and Washington had been good for her. Ruth said yes, yes they had. She learned to tell people right away that Miles was not hers, that she had found him in a tree. Then people, the same people who said Washington had been good to her, would tsk-tsk and say what could anyone expect of a city with a president who was so mean to colored people. She slept with the orphan in the bed she had slept in before her marriage. The baby slept holding tightly to her nightgown. May became June, and then before she could turn around, it was July.

Aubrey sent her a letter:

> *My dear Wife,*
>
> *I write with all hope that your dear Mother is taking well once again. I have prayed for Her. I have prayed for You and I have prayed for the Life We have tried to make for ourselves here in the City.*
>
> *I do not sleep because You are not beside me. I work but I am not happy because I know that I cannot find You quick as I could before You left for your sick Mother and Virginia. I want more than living tomorrow to come to get You before the second day of August, 1902. Please know that I write these words with my Heart true in every word. I will come out to get You.*
>
> *To my loving Wife Mrs. Ruth Patterson*
> *From Your true and one Husband*
> *Mr. Aubrey Patterson*

She read the letter a dozen times the day she received it. That night, after the house was quiet and the baby fast asleep, she went outside, not so much because of the song—though it played on still—but because standing in the yard might bring Aubrey quicker than the second of August.

He came and stayed with her and her family for three days. For some reason he seemed surprised to see the baby, as if he had expected it to have simply disappeared over time. He thought the baby twice as large as he had been before leaving Washington. The same size might have been the most he could ever hope for, but to have blossomed, to appear twice its size, was a blow to the heart. But he said nothing.

While Ruth was away, Joan had increased Aubrey's pay to $2.50 a week. Had he been asked the day he held the new pay in his hand, he would have said that he was now a Washingtonian. Virginia was way over there somewhere in the past. He would not have returned to Virginia to be a man for anything in the world except the resurrection of his father. The only thing that could make his living perfect was Ruth's return. There was a terrible part of him that resented her for being absent for so long, though he could understand about her mother. A woman on I Street owed Joan some money, and she sent Aubrey to collect it. The woman opened her door to invite him in, and he sensed that she wanted to give more than the money. He hesitated, looked all the way up and down I Street, where no one knew him or his business. His father had said once that even if he were ten thousand miles from any human being, he must still sit and eat at his table with a knife and fork and use his eating manners the way he had been taught. So he told the woman that if she didn't have the money that day, he would just tell his aunt. And he banked his pay, every penny except that used to buy sweets, which he could not live without.

Also while Ruth was away, Joan hired Earl Austin, a man only four months up from Georgia. Suffering headaches in Georgia, Earl had gone to a root doctor, and the woman, after having Earl spit on a plate painted black, had diagnosed, "Your wife ain't your wife no more." Free of headaches but with a heart sliced up, he fled the state after catching his wife in their marriage bed with a man still in his hat and socks and then beating the man for nearly an hour and leaving him for dead in his wife's spring garden. He knew how to blacksmith, he had told Joan when seeking a job, and he could even sew and crochet if that would put food in his belly. He did not say that he had seen her one day walking down K Street and had followed her all the way back to 3rd Street. He did not say that he was quitting a good porter job at the Ebbitt House just to be near her, that he had been seized that day on K Street by an emotion that overwhelmed and confused him. He did not say that he would have worked for free or that he knew that even in a thousand years he had no hope of reaching the heart of a woman like her, one with money and property.

Ruth and Miles came back.

Aubrey thought that if he made his wife's life as easy as possible in Washington, her body would consent, and she would at last become pregnant. With Earl around and the baby needing to be watched as he began to explore more and more of his world, Ruth had about a third less work than before she went home to Virginia. And so she took Aubrey to her at night, eager, happy to be back, and he returned to her body, a man in love, in awe, in fear. Washington survived the blazes of August. September was warm, quite acceptable to Joan's guests not from the South. Much of October was fiercely cold, but November was like September all over again.

Like a thick window shade being pulled down in the brightness of day, the world was darkening for Blind Willie. By Ruth's return, he was accepting his new nickname, but he joked it was unfair to be called blind even before he was fully so. "I think I should be just Half-Blind Willie. Next thing you know," he said to Ruth one evening as everyone lingered after a pork chop supper, "they'll wanna put me in the ground when I'm only half dead."

He and Ruth, with Miles, went about the city in the afternoons of November in a wagon pulled by a mule that was good for short trips about the city but would have died, or simply refused, if forced to try anything longer. Born and raised in Washington, Willie told Ruth he wanted to show her the places of his childhood before his eyes took the places away. The truth is that he needed a companion as he went about trying "to pay his respects" to the women he had known. He saw his blindness as a kind of death. By November he had learned that Vi Sanchez was dead, but Melinda Barclay was still managing to avoid him. Her neighbors kept telling him she was off on a trip around the world. Ruth enjoyed being with him. She believed that Miles was going to grow up in Washington, so he may as well learn about it early. And Willie had an endless amount of stories, about the sea, about whales, about foreign countries, about love in Africa and Brazil. That all of Washington seemed to know him reminded her of how well known she was in Virginia. The old people in Washington called him William, for that, they would say, was the name his mother gave him, and it should be good enough for everybody else. With plenty of rest for the mule along the way, he and Ruth would go as far as Georgetown some days, picnicking and fishing at the river's edge.

At last, after months and months, two days before the end of November, Melinda opened the door to her home at 8 Pierce Street, N.W. Her face said nothing when she saw Willie. Indeed, she looked over his shoulders and around him, as if she had been expecting someone who had never caused her pain. She sighed with disappointment. Willie was surprised at how happy he was to find her, and he thought right away of the letter—only the third one of his life—he had written her that last time two years before, a letter labored over only days before he decided to retire from the sea. He wrote in the letter that he would miss her cooking, that it was the hardest thing in the world to go back to the ship's food. He had started the letter in the middle of the Atlantic Ocean and finished it before the ship saw England, but he had not mailed it. He wrote in the letter that he knew a dressmaker in Paris and he would have her make Melinda something out of this world.

"Oh, Melinda," Willie said now in the doorway, "you don't know how happy I am to find you at home."

"Willie."

"I been lookin for you, Melinda."

"I been away, Willie. Way away. Didn't folks tell you?" She had now stepped back. Her hair was made up quite prettily, as if for some party. "I heard bout whas happenin to you and it's a shame. To be blind."

Willie looked around at Ruth and Miles in the wagon.

"You should get back to em," Melinda said and made to close the door. He saw the darkening figure of the door and raised his hand to stop it from closing. "Please, Melinda. Please, darlin." She stopped the closing and sighed once more. "Thas Ruth and little Miles. She my landlady's niece. Her . . . her niece-in-law." He turned around to look at Ruth as if to make certain he had gotten right her relationship to Joan. There had been a woman in Brazil who had understood very little English and who just nodded at everything he said, even when he told her he was coming back with a ring that would weigh her hand down.

"I have somewhere to go, Willie," Melinda said. "You might have to come back some other time."

Ruth could not hear their words from the wagon, but she sensed the distress in Willie, in the way his head hung a little bit. Miles was in her lap, playing with the reins.

"Now, Melinda, please wait a little bit," Willie said. His head was turned slightly to the side, for there out of the corners of his eyes was where most of the last of his sight resided. A stranger walking by would have seen him talking to the side of Melinda's house.

She did a dismissal with her teeth. "You promised me a letter, Willie. Just some plain letter that a child could manage. Just a plain old letter."

"I know I did, Melinda."

"And you know what else," she said, opening the door just an inch or so more. "That damn necklace fell apart on me, do you know that? But I can understand fallin apart. Everything does that. It woulda been nice to know it was gonna happen. It woulda been nice to know that it never come from the king of Haiti. I didn't mind the fallin apart. Just the lyin."

"I know," Willie said, not even remembering the necklace. "I shouldna said that. There ain't been no king in Haiti for a lotta years."

"It ain't the necklace. I got all the necklaces I could ever need."

"I'll get you something else, and I mean that," Willie said.

They did not speak for a time, until Miles squealed when he dropped one of the reins.

"Yall may as well come in," Melinda said. "Yall may as well do that. You make my house look poor standin out there like that."

On the morning of the third night Willie was with Melinda, he felt someone tap him lightly on the left side of his head. He woke and found it curious because Melinda was sleeping on his right side. In the half-darkened room he sat on the side of the bed and waited for his eyes to adjust. Finally, he held his hand before his face, moved it back and forth. Melinda was sleeping quietly, like a little girl, the way she had always done. He put his hand in his lap. "Oh, shoot," he said at last. "I'm all the way blind." He said it with no more emotion than a man might say he was late for something of little consequence after seeing his clock had stopped. He had hoped for a few months more.

He dressed with as little noise as possible and went down and out her door. He closed the door behind him and stood in his first morning hearing the sound of the closing door echo in his head. He went out the gate, making sure to shut it tight behind him. A neighbor's smelly dog liked to come in her yard and sleep under the porch. Willie took three tentative steps away from Melinda's house. A rooster crowed and Willie was emboldened. He put his right hand out in front of him, and the left hand he held out to the side where the homes were. He remembered that once he had come out of a woman's house in Northeast on just such a crisp morning and had gone three blocks in the wrong direction before he realized just what woman he had been with. He reached the end of Pierce Street and went down 1st. The slight dip was a surprise, something that had certainly not been there in all the years he had had eyes. He made his way home, to 3rd Street, and with all his steps he spelled out her name. William had never been a good speller in school, and Sailor Willie had been even worse, so Blind Willie made his way to Joan's repeating M-I-L-I-N-D-A.

Late the next day Ruth got word that her mother was again ill. Aubrey sulked all the rest of the day, slept on the edge of their bed that night, and twisted and turned as loudly as he could. He sulked most of the next day as well, until Ruth left with Miles. She was gone nearly two weeks, until days before Christmas. He did not touch her again until well after Christmas. He stopped while inside her, dropped all his weight on her, and then, after she began complaining, rolled away.

One day in early January, he saw her talking to Earl in the kitchen of the 1013 house and suspected something. How, he wondered, as he stepped between them to get to the coffeepot, could he trust any child out of her to be his? He poured his coffee and before taking the first sip told Earl to go tidy up the chicken coop.

"You didn't have to say that to him like that," Ruth said to her husband after Earl left.

"Say it what way?" her husband said, holding his cup in both hands.

"Mean like that. He a good man. Earl don't trouble nobody less they trouble him." With winter, there were fewer guests in the 1011 house and Joan had allowed Earl to stay in the back room upstairs. "Ain't no call for bein mean like that, Aubrey." One morning Earl had raised his shade and saw Joan across the way in 1013, her back to him, looking in her mirror as she fixed her hair. He thought his heart would run away from him.

"Why you takin up for somebody against your own legal husband?" Aubrey knew as soon as he had said them that the words made no sense, but once they were out there in the kitchen where two pots were cooking supper, he could do no more than support them. "Ain't no call for you to do that, thas what I say." Joan had turned from the mirror and saw Earl watching her that morning.

"You could be nicer to everybody, Aubrey, thas all I'm sayin. Earl, Willie, you could be nicer." As Earl watched Joan, he saw himself exiled back to Georgia, but rather than turning away, Joan had stepped to the window and stuck the second hatpin down through her hat and into her hair and never took her eyes from him. Earl lowered his head until his eyes fell on his shoes. He raised his hand Good Morning and left the window.

"I'm as nice as I need be," Aubrey said, wanting no more of the coffee. "Seem to me that the crime round here is you bein too nice. If I ain't bein nice, you sure makin it all up for me."

What he was saying finally came to her, and it pounded into her heart. "It don't cost one penny to be nice to people, Aubrey. It don't hurt a soul one bit." She wanted to cry, but the baby was asleep upstairs, and it would not have done for him to awaken and find her in distress. The orphan cried at the least little thing. Ruth stepped away to go upstairs.

There came to be nothing to talk about between them. He often pointed to something when he wanted her to do anything. At the dining table, with Joan and Willie and Earl and any guests, they sat as far from each other as they could. Willie was usually the life of the table, with a story about any subject someone could name. Say "speck of sand," for example, and he would regale with a story about an Abyssinian pirate who was caught at his lair near the sea and died wiggling with the hangman's rope around his neck, wiggling with the pain of the rope and the discomfort of the sand that had blown into his eyes. The pirate had lived most of his time on the sea, but he had detested sand all his days. Ruth liked everything Willie said, but her pleasure would dissolve when she would look across the table and find an unsmiling Aubrey staring hard at her, his arms folded.

One day she came into the room after hearing the baby whimpering on the pallet she had made for him. He was now too big for the crib and she had put it out in the barn. Aubrey was kneeling down, holding one of the baby's legs. "What he want?" she said. "I don't know," Aubrey said. "I didn't ask him and he didn't tell me."

He released the leg after she knelt down to the baby. He stood up and left. The child was wet, as it turned out. He was smiling. As she changed him, she kept hearing the sound of his whimpering before she had entered the room. Had the child been quiet or asleep when she found Aubrey over him, it would not have mattered. But the whimpering said so much to her, becoming as she stood up with him in her arms not even whimpering anymore but a long and painful cry.

She did not let Miles out of her sight after that. She carried him about in her arms. Or, when there were jobs that required both hands, she toted him on her back, having fashioned a pouch out of a blanket that he could lie in comfortably. She made the pallet beside the bed bigger and slept there with Miles. That was mid-January.

Willie woke in the night toward the end of January and remembered once again that he had promised Melinda to make up for the necklace from the king of Haiti. There had been nothing between them since the morning he went blind and left her asleep in bed. He felt he had enough money saved up from the sea to provide for his room and board at Joan's for the rest of his days. He would not trouble anyone else. He had at first thought that he and Ruth would pick out something for Melinda in some Washington store that would treat colored customers with respect. He would have Ruth or someone else take the jewelry to

Melinda, for he would not want her to think he wanted something by taking it himself.

He got up that January night and opened the trunk that had been all around the world with him, a trunk big enough to be a man's coffin. In one corner there was a brooch, wrapped in two handkerchiefs, a brooch that he had not thought about for a long time. It was a cameo of a long-necked woman looking to the left. He had bought it in Marseilles, from a man with only nubs for hands. Intending it as a present for his mother. Twelve American silver dollars. But when he returned home he found that his mother had been dead a little more than two weeks, and he had put the brooch away, vowing not to think about it again. But he owed Melinda something wonderful.

Melinda said nothing when Ruth took the brooch to her. She invited her in. The baby, in a wooden carriage Earl had found in an alley and made over, had fallen asleep. It was early afternoon, a Saturday. Ruth declined to go in, saying she best get back, and Melinda walked her to the corner, to 1st Street. Ruth said, "He told me to tell you to enjoy every time you wear it. He wants you to be happy with it." The next morning Melinda was standing outside their home as the group at 1011 and 1013 prepared to go off to church. They came through the gates of the houses and Melinda touched Blind Willie's shoulder. He could tell it was not one of the people he had come out of the house with.

"Who?" he asked.

"Me," she said. She unwrapped the fingers of one of his hands and placed the brooch, now in one of her own handkerchiefs, in the center of the hand. He knew right off what it was.

"I want you to have it," he said. "I honestly did." Everyone else walked away a piece, up toward L Street.

"Why you treat me like this? What bad thing did I do you, William?"

"Nothin, you know that."

"If I done nothin, then good. Then your and my books been set straight if I never done nothin bad to you. I never want your things. Not a one." He heard her walk away.

"Melinda, please . . ." He took a step, fearful now of falling, holding the fence as best he could with the hand she had put the brooch in. "Melinda, please please, darlin. Please, darlin." He held his hand out to her, but he began to cry and so had to take that hand and cover his eyes. Ruth, with Miles in his carriage, considered going to him. Willie said, "I meant you no bad thing. Only my kind of love, such as it is." Melinda looked at Ruth, at Miles's hands and feet rising and falling in the carriage, and then she slowly turned around. Everyone in the group going to church started to walk away and they did not stop. It was not very cold considering it was January, but for days there had been talk of snow.

That Sunday the preacher gave his first sermon since returning from South Carolina from burying his mother, who died two days short of her seventy-ninth birthday. He had buried his father three years before, he reminded his congregation, and now "the whole fortress" between him and death was gone because he was their oldest child.

"On that long train ride back here, back to what's gotta be called home now cause Mama and Papa made my home down there and that home ain't really home no more, all the way back up here I kept thinkin how afraid I shoulda been. But I wasn't. I didn't have a crumb's bit of fear," he said, and his people said, "Amen."

"I'm next in that long death line that started with our Daddy Adam. And with Mama Eve. O Mama Eve, we forgive you for pickin that fruit and bitin into it with not a care for all of us what was to come after you and face death. Yes, we forgive you. We forgive, Mama Eve." And his people said, "Yes, we forgive." In that church row Ruth sat at one end with Miles on her lap, and Joan was at the other end. Aubrey sat next to Ruth and Earl sat next to him. Between Earl and Joan there were two guests from 1011, a medical doctor and his wife up from North Carolina. The wife had not even finished the North Carolina Normal School for Colored Girls, but her husband insisted on calling her "Doctor," at times in a very endearing way, punctuated with a touch of his fingers on her wrist. Before their visit to Washington had ended, everyone else was addressing her as "Doctor" as well.

"I tell ya," the preacher said. "I wanna tell yall that the wind was blowin the day we buried my mother down in South Carolina and I looked over at all the empty spaces that was to the right of where they laid her, all the empty spaces all the way to that little baby iron fence, and I said to myself, 'What's the use of goin back to Washington? What's the use? Why not go back to that little house you was raised in and sit on the porch and wait on Papa Death?'"

"Oh, Jesus," the people said. "Oh, my Jesus."

"I tell ya I just stood there watchin the wind rock that baby iron fence of that cemetery and I musta stood there too long, cause my own baby girl pulled on my arm and said, 'Daddy? Daddy?' Her little boy had hold of her frock and the wind stopped and they was fillin in the place where they put my mama. I blinked right then and there. I just blinked and I could see that day I first held her little baby boy and the way he squirmed like I wasn't holdin him right and all that hair on his head like he was a full-grown boy and I could see me again blowin on all that hair till he stopped squirmin and got to knowin I didn't mean him a pip's worth of injury. I tell ya I just blinked and God asked me what was I afraid of." The people said, "I know He did." "And the wind started back and God asked me the same question and I didn't have an answer. Cause there ain't no answer when you get down to the marrow of the marrow, and He knowed that when He asked me. God does that to us, you know?" "He does that," the people said. "I blinked again and I could see myself goin home on that train, goin home to Washington and havin yall tell me I was home. And I wasn't afraid comin out that churchyard where every tombstone had a name I could tell you a hundred stories about and I wasn't afraid goin back to that little baby house and hearin people say what a good and steady woman my mama was, through rain and sunshine and any bad weather she was a good human bein my mama was, and how heaven was lucky to have her and I wasn't afraid comin back home, comin back to yall in Washington. I tell ya I just blinked and it was all laid out to me."

Miles had fallen asleep in Ruth's lap. She was crying as she listened to the preacher. Aubrey had placed a hand on the baby's leg. Ruth picked up Miles and rested his head on her shoulder and Ruth's husband's hand fell away. It was far less cruel to do it that way than remove Aubrey's hand.

"So we forgive you, Mama Eve. God did that for you, so how can we do less? I stand next in the long death line under that eternal gaze of a just and fair God who just blinked, just blinked a few times, I tell ya, and in that little bit of blinkin my mama had lived her seventy-nine good years. Just a blink in God's eye. But O what a wondrous blink!"

Ruth thought to tell her husband that her mother was ill once more, but she was old enough now to know that God would not be pleased with such a lie and might well punish her by hurting her mother and others she loved. So she told her husband simply that she was going home. Aubrey himself took it to mean sickness in the family and said nothing to her.

Earl took her back to Virginia. The weather was cold, the baby wrapped in three blankets. The week before, Earl had seen the man he had beaten in Georgia walking without a care in the world up New Jersey Avenue toward New York Avenue. He lost sight of the man and figured he had been a ghost. He and Ruth and Miles reached Georgetown about noon. Just before they touched the Aqueduct Bridge to Arlington, Earl asked Ruth, "You think if a man does a great sin, he has a right to any happiness after that?"

She had been home a week when Aubrey decided to go out to Virginia, having awakened one morning and heard only the sound of a solitary heartbeat in their bedroom. He borrowed a sorrel mare from a friend with a large stable on I Street. He left two hours after breakfast and about eleven was a little more than a mile from the place where he and Ruth had spent their first married days. A light snow began, and he apologized to the horse. He did not know why, but he got off the horse less than half a mile before his father's house, where he had been told two days before she was living. He tied the horse to a magnolia tree and walked the rest of the way. There was a handful of trees just before the path that led down to his father's place, and he stopped at the edge of those trees and looked down at Ruth. She could have seen him if she had looked up, but something told Aubrey that she would not. Farther down the road, where his mother's lover had lived, all the land now belonged to Ruth's brothers.

Miles was strapped to her back, his arms flailing as he played with cherubs only he could see. Aubrey looked down at his boots, at the way the wind dusted the snowflakes over them. He did not remember what snow there had been last winter, so this could well be the baby's first snow. He recalled the dimples on the back of the baby's hand when it was outstretched over the green blanket. The dimples Ruth loved to kiss.

Ruth was chopping wood. She cut pieces and threw them around to a pile just behind her. She was accompanied by two massive dogs, as large as wolves, descendants of the brown dog that had fallen from the sky into the August corn. She had taught one of the dogs to take wood up to the porch, where it dropped it in an untidy pile and returned for more. The other dog took pieces from the porch pile into the house. After some minutes, the first dog stopped and looked up at Aubrey. It waited for Aubrey to make some gesture to signal his intent. It turned once or twice as if to make certain that the other dog saw Ruth's husband as well. Finally, the first dog went back to work. The day Earl took

Ruth to this place, she had answered his question, "Every last one of us is a sinner, Earl, but we all got some right to peace and happiness till the day we die."

The snow stopped. Aubrey saw the gray smoke rising from the chimney with great energy, and it was, at last, the smoke, the fury and promise of it, the hope and exuberance of it, that took him back down to the horse.

In his mind, Ruth's husband shrugged. He was learning to put the events of his young life on a list according to where they stood with his father's death, which was at the top. He had at first put his mother's death at number ten, even though numbers five to nine were blank. But over the months, as he had remembered her touch, her mama words, he put her dying at number two. He did not know where to put the end with his wife.

The snow came up again and he turned onto the main road that would lead all the way down through Arlington to the bridge. Ruth's husband patted the horse's neck to reassure her that she was capable of the snow journey, that the snow would not amount to much. The horse's mane was in a tangle, and as he made his way through the new snow, he busied himself with trying to untangle it. But it was a hopeless task, and he patted the neck again, told the horse he would do a proper job with a soft brush before he returned her to her owner. The dank smell of the horse rose up and held fast like a stalled cloud before his face. Ruth's husband smiled and told the horse he forgave her.

In less than a mile, the snow came up fierce and he considered stopping for the night at the Landrys. But within sight of their place, the snow returned to a gentle falling, and he passed the Landrys and their hearth and its promise and continued on. He and the horse were alone on the road, and it occurred to him that all the world might know something about the weather to come that he should know, something that maybe he, no more a country boy, had learned and forgotten. In another mile, the snow took a turn toward bad again. Ruth's husband stopped and tied his scarf around his head and pulled the hat tight on top of that. They went on. They came through a small forest virtually empty of snow and he pulled the coat tighter, and as they emerged from the forest, Washington appeared before him, a long grayness shimmering between the snowflakes across the Aqueduct Bridge, across the quiet Potomac.

He halted at the mouth of the bridge, the land of Washington, D.C., spread out forever and ever before him. He ran his hand over his meager mustache and the beginnings of a beard. He wiped the snow from them and thought what a wasted effort it was since there was more snow to come. The horse raised her head high, then a bit higher, perhaps knowing something the man did not. Ruth's husband could hear voices now, and he shuddered. He turned in the saddle to see the southern road so many would travel on to reach that land just across the river. He saw nothing but the horse tracks in the snow, growing fainter with each second as more and more snow covered them. The voices hushed. His boots touched the horse's sides ever so gently. The horse stepped onto the bridge to Washington, her white breath shooting forward to become one with the white of the snow. Ruth's husband patted her neck. The top button on his coat came loose again and he rebuttoned it, thankful that his hand had not yet stiffened up. His heart was pained, and it was pain enough to overwhelm a city of men.

SPANISH IN THE MORNING

In the days before I first started kindergarten, the men in my life came from here and there to bring me things and more things, as if, my mother was to say, I was going away and never coming back. In mid-August, my mother's baby brother came down from his life in Philadelphia and went with the girlfriend of the moment, the one who would break his heart, to buy "some quality" at Garfinckel's, a department store that had Negroes arrested if they tried to shop there. While the girlfriend could have passed for white among white people, black people knew their own kind. My uncle, in the darkest of his summer suits, walked two or so paces behind her up and down Garfinckel's aisles, carrying two small boxes, wrapped and empty, a made-up chauffeur's cap setting ever so straight on his chemist's head. They were enveloped in youth and lived for games like that. My uncle giggled at one point, excited by it all, and his girlfriend, to halt her own giggling, turned and asked in a voice cultivated at Spelman College, "Is there something you want to share with us all, Rufus?" And she waved her arm as dramatically as she could, and all the white people near them turned to see one of their own take charge. My grandparents did not name him Rufus. My uncle bought me nine exquisite dresses and had me model each one for him and his girlfriend before they returned to Philadelphia.

The days took me closer to my first day of school, and the men in my life continued to come to me. My uncle Cyphax, who couldn't seem to stay out of jail, came in the night when we were all asleep and left three pairs of shoes at our front door, and tucked in the box of each pair was a receipt from Hahn's. "I have to fly," he wrote in a note to me, "but I will see you before the end of the first lesson." My grown cousin Sam and his family came with a bag of various items, including a ruler that changed colors depending upon the light falling on it and a composition book of about a hundred pages. On a few of the pages Sam had drawn some of the men in my life. "You can do school work on the rest," he said and winked. At three months old, I had sat at his wedding on my mother's lap in the second row of the drafty church on Minnesota Avenue.

Five days before I started school, my mother's father, a widower of seven months, came and had three beers and had to stay the night on our couch. "I got a little beside myself yesterday," he confessed to me the next morning before counting out and handing me five one-dollar bills. I held my hands out for the money and thought of the first memory of my life—my grandfather playing little piggy on my toes when I was four weeks old. At eight months old, I sat again on my mother's lap at her mother's funeral. And at one year and two months, I sat at another church when my grandfather married his second wife, who was to die in less than a year.

Finally, the night before school started, three hours before sunset, my father's father came and tapped twice, as always, on our door. My parents had long ago offered him a key, as he lived less than a block away, but he always said he wanted a key to no man's home but his own. My father's father gave me a wooden pencil box he had paid a man fifty cents to carve my name into. And he gave me a red plastic transistor radio. My seven-year-old cousin, who had learned to read at three years old, would later dismiss the radio as junk because it was made in Japan. But I never cared. "Don't take it to school, sugar," my grandfather said that evening.

"I already put the batteries in, but you can't take it to school." I pulled out the silver antenna and looked up at him. Perhaps for months and months I had never taken the idea of school very seriously. The idea now stepped before me and for a moment seemed to blot just about everything out of my head, the whole summer, all the playing, my happy life. *I was going to school.* I turned the radio on. The music burst out and bounced about the room. The radio would work well for a very long time, but toward the end of its life, I had to practically stand on my head to get station WOOK to come in clearly.

I was the first of my parents' three girls, inheriting from my mother her wide blossom of a nose and the notion that the universe could be lassoed and tamed. She came from a long line of Washingtonians who saw education as a right God had given their tribe the day after he gave Moses the Ten Commandments.

I inherited from my father the tendency to sleep on my side with one folded arm under my head and the other hand nestled between my thighs. I inherited from him the notion that the soil in D.C. was miraculous, that it would grow anything, even a rubber tree and oranges, which was what he managed to do. But the oranges were no bigger than cherries and they had hair and my mother would not let her girls touch them.

But this is about my father's father. And me. And all of them.

My grandfather got as far as the second grade. "One and a half," he would say and raise two fingers and bend one finger over. He spent most of my father's first years as a shadow to his son. My father, at six, seven, eight years old, would turn a dusty corner in some road and happen upon a noisy crowd of men trudging to the fields in that place five miles outside of Columbia, South Carolina, men who laughed when my father asked if they had seen his father. My father would wake in the darkest part of the night and hear his father snoring somewhere in their cabin, only to find him gone in the morning. Sometimes, before morning hit, my father, hungry for the man, would rise and stand before the bed my grandfather shared with my grandmother, and she would wake and at first think her son was her father's ghost. And there were nights, too, when my father would watch my grandfather in a piss and drunken sleep on the floor just inside the open front door, the last place he had fallen once he had crawled home. If my father touched him there in the doorway, my grandfather would groan, responding to the life in his dreams— perhaps a fist coming at him, or the candlelight reflecting off a third jar of moonshine, or the sliver of the thigh of a woman not his wife as she telegraphed something while crossing her legs.

In my father's eighth year, my grandmother turned her back on all the life she had known and took my father and his two sisters to Washington, where, South Carolina old folks said, people threw away their dishes after every meal because it was cheaper to buy new ones. Three months after they left, my grandfather woke soaked in dew a few feet from train tracks, having spent the night with two quarts of a cloudy brew he had bought off a stranger who said he was from Tennessee "where good likker was born." Before he woke, my grandfather had been dreaming that a child was sticking an especially long hatpin in his right leg as he weeded a section of his collard green patch in a cruel rain. Awake at the train tracks, he tried to move that right leg but found it twisted in an awful way, so twisted, as he later learned, that only the hands of God could untwist it. He laid his head back down. He could hear a train, but his mind could not tell him if the train was coming or going. My grandfather raised his head as best he could and managed to turn it to the right, to where the sun was coming from. He saw a boy no more than five years old eating crab apples. The boy raised his hand Hello. The sun told my grandfather it was not yet seven in the morning.

He knew that a drink would tell him five minutes this way or that exactly what time it was. The boy was steady watching him. He ate the apples whole, core and all. Not long before he told the boy to go get help, my grandfather asked him why he had not awakened him, and the boy told him he had been taught never to wake a sleeping man. With each syllable of the boy's words, the pain in his leg grew.

When it came time for me, my parents' first girl, to go out beyond their gate that kept the world at bay and begin school, they chose Holy Redeemer, a Catholic school that was down L Street where we lived, up 1st Street, and all the way down Pierce Street to the corner of New Jersey Avenue. My father had wanted me to go to Walker-Jones Elementary. The phrase "a stone's throw" was made for how close Walker-Jones was to us—less than a hundred feet diagonally across the intersection of L and 1st Streets, close enough for him to stretch and stretch and stretch an arm across the traffic of the intersection into some classroom and tug at one of my plaits or tweak my nose when the teacher's back was turned. Going there, in some ways, would have been almost like never going beyond the small world of my yard.

But my mother wanted her children to be educated by nuns and priests all dressed in black, the way it had been done down through the generations with her people. Taught by people who had a firm grasp of how big and awful the world could be. My father said she was way too impressed with the fact that the nuns had taught her Spanish, and my mother reminded him that the first things she had ever said to him had been in Spanish. Before noon, Spanish was just about all my mother ever spoke to my father and my sisters and me. There was no Miss La-De-Da to it, no putting on airs, just Spanish in the morning. No one in her life spoke Spanish, but she went on and on, conversing in Spanish for long periods with some imaginary person, or conjugating verbs, staying sharp for that day some woman from Mexico, lost and without a word of English, might knock on her door and ask for help.

That first day of school, my father took off from being a postman, and he and my mother walked me up to Holy Redeemer. Registration was a rather quick process, and before long they were bending down and telling me that they would see me in a little bit. Then they were gone, but I got the notion that they were just outside the school, standing on New Jersey Avenue or Pierce Street, waiting for me to finish or for me to tell them that I had had enough and wanted to go home.

I found myself in a kindergarten room with some eighteen other children and a teacher who was not a nun and whose eyebrows came together in a hypnotic "V." We, including our teacher, were all colored. Not long after the door was closed, a boy at our little table of four began crying. The teacher could not comfort him, but she did manage to get him down to a whimper in that first hour. I felt strangely at peace sitting next to him, as if I had done no more than move from one room in my house to another. I, too, tried to comfort him, placing my hand on his shoulder. But he looked at me as if I were part of why he had to cry. In the end, he cried so much that a nun, a white woman encased in her habit, appeared and took him away. I did not see the boy again, but whenever I thought of him, I imagined him going on to a grand life at another school where they did wonderful things he did not have to cry about.

That first day my parents were waiting for me at noon. Back at home, my father's father was with my two sisters and Sadie Cross, my mother's best friend from across L Street. Sadie was married to One-Eye Jack, whose left eye had been shot out across the D.C.–Maryland line by a Prince George's County policeman as Mr. Jack innocently changed a flat tire when I was six months old. Late that night he was shot, several of his friends gathered in my father's kitchen, cursing white people. My father had me resting on his shoulder, and he kept telling me that it would be nice if I went to sleep like a good little baby was supposed to. Within two weeks of Mr. Jack being shot, the policeman's Laurel lawyer and the Prince George's County government people sent Mr. Jack separate letters designed to head off anything legal Mr. Jack might consider. The lawyer's letter, with the law firm's name embossed in gold letters across the first page, was two pages, double-spaced, and it related how

Mr. Jack, kneeling on the ground as he fixed the tire in Mitchelville, had in fact threatened the policeman's life. Mr. Jack had not only threatened the man's life, the letter said, but the life of the policeman's wife, at home asleep in her bed in Rockville. Had Mr. Jack killed the policeman, the letter said, life as the wife then knew it would cease to be. The policeman had no children but nevertheless Mr. Jack had endangered them and all the policeman's generations to come for hundreds of years, because if the policeman had been murdered by Mr. Jack, none of those people would ever be born. Back at home, we celebrated my first day of school in the backyard with a feast my grandfather and Miss Sadie had prepared, including some fruits and vegetables my father had grown and which my mother allowed her girls to eat.

When the meal was done, my grandfather stood me before him as he sat and took my hands in his. "They treat you okay up there?" he asked. Anyplace he ever mentioned was always "up there."

I nodded. He started to count the fingers on both my hands, five pigs on one hand, five pigs on the other. Before I left that morning he had had me knock three times on his wooden leg for good luck. "You still got all your toes, too, I guess," he said now and smiled. "The nuns can sell a little girl's fingers and toes for a lotta money up there at the K Street market." He picked me up and sat me on his left leg, his good leg.

"Now *my* teacher," he said, "was a mean old colored man who had the Devil in him." I was still in one of the dresses my uncle from Philadelphia had bought me, though the dress was now covered with a towel tied around my neck. My youngest sister was asleep across my father's lap, and my mother had put her middle child down inside for her nap. Miss Sadie was sitting next to my father. Her son was nine, a boy with thick eyeglasses who lived for books. He was a good son, named Jack after his father, and all the world praised him.

I told my grandfather about my new teacher.

"She's no kin to that teacher of mine, I can tell you that," my grandfather said. "Oh, how my teacher did have the Devil in him. And you know what? If you gave him a wrong answer, he'd take his pitchfork and bring it down on your desk, them that had a desk. Put holes in the thing and made it hard to write your lessons." My grandfather's right leg was made of the same wood used for coffins down in his part of South Carolina. "Itty-bitty holes in the desk. You'd be writin, 'The grass is green,' and just when you got to the green part, your pencil would sink down in one a them pitchfork holes." My grandfather stretched out his wooden leg. We were mostly in the shade of the afternoon, but a bit of the sun covered his wooden foot in his well-shined shoe.

For the three weeks I was in Holy Redeemer's kindergarten, my mother always picked me up at noon, as kindergarten was only half a day. She usually left my two younger sisters at home with Miss Sadie. Sadie's son Jack went to Walker-Jones and would come to our house for his lunch. Sometimes, on the nicest days, my mother would put her youngest, Eva, in the carriage and have her middle girl, Delores, walk alongside. Delores, at three, was picking up bits and pieces of Spanish from my mother and the two of them would gabber in what a stranger to Spanish would have thought was real conversation.

It was on a particularly fine day in late September that I waited in the playground for my mother, standing near the kindergarten door, mildly interested in the children from the upper grades running and ripping about. My own classmates and the teacher had all gone. My mother had never been late before, and because of the world my parents had made for me, I was not afraid.

About one o'clock, the nuns had each class line up. All the children were in uniform, the girls in blue jumpers and white blouses, the boys in blue pants and white shirts. The school was in the shape of an upside-down "L," with my kindergarten door at one end and the door to all the other grades at the other. In moments, everyone had gone through the other door and I was alone in the playground.

I sat down on the bench under the kindergarten windows, still not at all worried. Somewhere in our world my mother was making her way to me, with or without her other two children. And as time moved on past one o'clock, as I edged toward concern, she was joined in my mind by my father and then by both my grandfathers and my mother's people and all my father's people, all of them coming to get me. So I hummed, and then I made up a song about that lady in Mexico who spoke Spanish in the morning the way my mother did. The lady in Mexico was standing in the road with her hand shading her eyes, watching her children skip toward her.

A little after one thirty a priest came from the other end of the playground, hurrying to the door to the rest of the school. Midway he happened to look toward me. He paused, no doubt surprised to see a child alone in the playground. Kindergarten children did not wear uniforms. The priest raised his hand Hello. I raised my hand Hello and after a moment the priest went on.

I was getting worried. I grew bored with singing and started to count the birds flying over. In one category, the pretty princesses' category, I put the birds that I saw land in the trees, and in another category, the evil witches' category, I put the birds that never landed. I could see my father and mother and the dozens and dozens of people in my life waiting at a traffic light, still on their way to me. The red light took too long and they looked both ways and did what I was warned never to do—they crossed against it. The birds stopped flying and I took to inspecting the hem of my dress.

It was more than twenty minutes before the priest came out the door and started back across the playground. He paused midway again, looking at me. He turned and went back through the door and soon returned with a nun. The nun motioned for me to come to them, and in the time it took for a bird to fly over, it was decided between them that I should wait for my tribe in that nun's first-grade class.

The nun was white, and except for the wooden beads clucking at her side, she moved silently down the hall. I heard singing and talking children in the classrooms as we walked. I heard nothing from her class as we approached, and when we entered, all the faces turned to us. My unease was extreme because now I was so far from the spot upon which my mother had ordered me to stay put. But I said nothing. In four rows, front to back, the class had twenty-two or so students, and they were all colored. I alone had no uniform but was arrayed in a yellow Garfinckel's dress. I was given the penultimate seat in one of the middle rows. Sister began the lesson where she had left off, and I, needing to be elsewhere, watched the clock in the front of the room because it was easier than looking at heads and a room and a nun I would not see again.

B efore they left South Carolina for Washington when my father was eight years old, my grandmother kept reminding him and his sisters not to waste time. "Time's a wastin," she would say if they lingered in packing in the days before they left that Monday morning. It had been more than a week since they had last seen my grandfather. They heard rumors that he was about, around, but while my father would go in search of him, my grandmother set about discarding her old life as if her husband was not in the world. Her decision to leave South Carolina had come three weeks before they left, when my grandmother awoke alone in her bed and pulled back the covers and looked down at how still perfectly made up was the place where her husband should have been sleeping. Something in the very perfection of his place in the bed told her that she did not love my grandfather anymore. That particular morning my grandfather was asleep on some fallen magnolia leaves in a little forest not far from their cabin, where he had dropped in the night on his way home. The second my grandmother pulled back the bedcovers, her husband raised his head, as heavy as John Henry's anvil, and for several moments he tossed off the aftermath of his drunkenness, because his world had shuddered and he had been disturbed in his sleep and did not know why.

"Time's wastin. Time's wastin." She gave away what furniture she could not sell, gradually leaving the cabin empty of everything but my grandfather's clothes, such as they were.

My father had no heart for any of it, for leaving their old piece of a home and his shadow of a father. He moped, he refused to put things in the heavy pasteboard suitcases my grandmother had collected. He said bad words and did not care if his mother heard him.

The evening before they left, my grandmother sat on the last chair they possessed, counting the money a man had given her for their chifforobe. For the seventh time that evening, my father shuffled by her, cursing under his breath. His mother grabbed his arm, startling him. "Ain't I told you bout that?" she screamed. "Ain't I?" His sisters came in from outside and stood watching.

"I ain't goin no D.C.," my father said. There was a good reason why my grandmother would sometimes see his face in the near darkness and think it her father's ghost.

My grandmother took his shirt in both hands and lifted him up on his tiptoes, the way a strong man might do a lesser man.

"I'll run away from that D.C. and come back down here to Daddy." My father began to cry.

My grandmother considered his face, his body. "I'll catch you," she said at last, her face so close to his that he had no choice but to breathe the air she expelled. "No matter what, I'll catch you." She raised him up higher with one hand and slapped him. She waited while his whole body registered what she had done, then she slapped him twice more. "I'll catch you and tie you to a bed till you a grown man. And every day I'll beat you. Beat all the black off you, boy. Beat you every day of your no-count life." She released my father, and he crumpled to the floor. My aunts had not moved from the doorway. My grandmother stood up. She took the money she had been counting off the table and put it in her bosom as she stepped over my father.

When I was two and a half years old, my father sat me on his lap and we spent part of an afternoon going through his *Life* magazines. In one there was an article on proletarian art in the Soviet Union. In my imagination my grandmother and my father and my aunts were to become like the statue in a picture in that article. There was a road that southern people took to get to Washington, and on that road there were the four of them. My grandmother had one hand pointing ahead. She wore a bonnet and a long pioneer-woman dress. My two aunts, each carrying a bundle, were looking to where she was pointing, and their hands were shading their eyes like that lady in Mexico waiting for her children. One of my father's hands was in my grandmother's hand, lest he run away, and his other hand was pointing back, a boy frozen in photograph-gray.

I was never to return to kindergarten. Gradually, as I waited for my mother that first day in Sister Mary Frances Moriarty's first-grade class, I took my eyes from the clock because the slowness of the minute hand was beginning to hurt my heart. I looked about without moving my head. Sister was printing the letter "P" on the blackboard. Taking up her pointer from the tray at the board, she turned and pointed at the beginning of the line of letters. The students began to recite the alphabet. At the letter "D," I joined in. I had nothing better to do. My father had taught me the alphabet when I was two. On a blackboard of a million words, I could pick out my name.

At the letter "H," Sister Mary Frances looked at me, the third-week kindergarten student. At "J," she told the class to hush. She aimed the pointer at me. "Only you," she said, and pointed to the letter "A." I recited the alphabet as she pointed. When she came to "P," the last one she had printed, we stopped. There were cards of the whole alphabet along the top of the board, and I raised my hand up to the letter "Q," which was a foot or so to the right of the clock. I pointed to each letter all the way to "Z." I was tempted to do more, to point all about and name them out of order, the way my father had taught me. For my father, the letter "M," for example, had no life if it only existed between "L" and "N."

Sister returned the pointer to the tray. Whatever she was thinking, it was not on her face. She came down the aisle toward me, her hands behind her back, her beads gently swaying. The door opened, and I saw Miss Sadie with Mother Superior, the principal. Sister went to them. Miss Sadie's eyes found me and she raised her hand Hello. I raised my hand Hello. The nuns were saying something to Miss Sadie but her eyes never left me. The wife of One-Eye Jack had no time for white people.

"They treat you right?" she asked as we walked home. She told me that after my sister Delores had fallen off the couch, and a big knot had appeared on her forehead, my mother had run up with her and Eva both in the carriage to Sibley Hospital on Pierce Street. Knots on the body terrified my mother, and she had momentarily forgotten about me waiting for her at school. "They treat you right?" Miss Sadie asked again after we had turned off 1st Street onto L.

S ister Mary Frances had seen something, and so kindergarten, she told my mother the next morning, would not be enough for me. First grade and even second grade might not even be enough. My mother was happy, but my father saw something he didn't like in my skipping a grade only three weeks after I started school. "Watch out when white folks wanna do somethin for you, cause it ain't gonna be pretty," he said as they talked in bed after my sisters and I were asleep. My mother prevailed.

They gave me two weeks to get a uniform, and so good-bye to all my Philadelphia uncle's beautiful dresses. I was given the same seat of that first afternoon. I learned that my seat had once belonged to a boy who was gone now. I had the seat in front of a boy named Lawrence Wilson. I was to the left of Sylvia Carstairs, who liked to look at me and flutter her eyelashes as if imparting some coded message. "You wanna be my best friend?" Sylvia whispered my third day in first grade. I had no great mission in life at that point, and so I nodded. "Friends for life, right?" she whispered and flashed the eyelashes. I had the seat to the right of Herman Franks, who quietly hummed all the day long. I was behind Regina Bristol, who had the darkest and the most perfect skin of anyone I had ever known. Angels in my dreams had such skin.

"You know what?" Sylvia said not long after we became friends for life. We were jumping rope with three other girls at recess, and Sylvia was standing beside me as I turned the rope, waiting for one girl to miss so Sylvia could get a go. She was whispering, the way she did in class. "Regina got a boyfriend." I looked Sylvia full in the face as the news settled over me. My father liked to call himself my mother's boyfriend, but a boy, not a man, as a boyfriend was quite new to me. "Am I still your boyfriend?" my father would ask my mother, putting his lips to her neck as she stood at the stove. Sylvia pointed to a boy who was playing tag. In class, that boy sat two seats up and to the left of me. He, like most of the children in class those first days, was only a uniform. Now, as Sylvia whispered, he started to exist whole and unto himself. He was skinnier than the son of One-Eye Jack and not half as handsome as Regina was beautiful. On a purple shelf in my imagination, Regina and her tag-playing boyfriend took their places and stood straight, holding hands, like two figures plucked from a wedding cake. "I think they gon get married one day," Sylvia said. The girl jumping rope had been going for a little more than two minutes. "My boyfriend forever," my mother would say at the stove and turn to kiss my father. I could see Regina across the way on the kindergarten bench, her legs crossed, her arms folded, talking to another girl. Then, as if to emphasize what Sylvia was saying about them, the boyfriend stopped playing tag and waved vigorously and desperately to Regina as if from far, far away. Finally, Regina raised her hand to him and lowered it quickly and went back to talking. "See,"

Sylvia said. "They gon get married in a big church," and she raised her arms to indicate the bigness of the church.

I chanted with the other girls as the jumping girl went on through the third minute:

I'm happy, you're happy

At last, the jumping girl stumbled and Sylvia moved to take her place. The girl took the rope from me, and I waited my turn. Sylvia jumped high, higher than all of us. We had good sun that day. Regina uncrossed and then recrossed her legs, keeping her knees very much together, the way a woman of the world did without thinking. The girl she was talking to seemed to have something important to say, and that girl punctured the air with her forefinger to make certain Regina got her point.

I'm happy, you're happy
Go tell Mama, go tell Pappy

We went on in the different suns down through September and up into the days of October. My father's corn that fall was not what he would have liked, but the peaches from the small tree in the northeast corner of the backyard did well by him. My mother sliced up some and put cream on them and allowed me and Delores to eat them. She had enough left over to make a cobbler for my father's father.

Aside from the days at school, my life was not different in ways I noticed. My sister Delores, though, had become emboldened while I was away and seemed to think that all the toys I possessed belonged to her. I would come home from school and most of my things would be in her toy box. The only weapon I had was to tell her that I was going to school and she was not. Saying this to her made her blink to the verge of tears, and she would go out of our room and I would be free to reclaim my things.

Three years after my grandmother and my father and my aunts arrived in Washington, my grandmother—in the year she bought her first tourist home to house black travelers not allowed in white hotels—married a man who had never taken a drink in his life. He had three filling stations, one in Northeast and two in Northwest, and he had a big house in Anacostia that stood strong against the wind. With all his soul, this man wanted my father to see him as his father and to love him, but my father would have none of that. Then my father, at seventeen, began to change. He had witnessed the man bathing and feeding and caring for my grandmother that year she took a horrible sick; it was too late, for the man, Grandpa Peter, having suffered year after year in my father's awful light, had tried to save himself by closing his heart to my father.

My father's father had found his way to Washington in an April when my grandmother was still yet a newlywed. My grandfather arrived with his new wooden leg; his whole being was wobbly those first days in Washington, for he had not had a drink in five months. He sent word to let his children know where he was, and he made a life shining shoes. My father, eleven years old, walked the miles to the hotel lobby where my grandfather worked, but my aunts did not go to their father for a long time, and when they did, Grandpa Peter, their stepfather, drove them.

That second Monday in October the hands on the clock had just settled into being eleven o'clock when Mother Superior, the principal, opened the door and looked at Sister Mary Frances. Sister pointed at Regina Bristol and then to the boy the whole class knew as her boyfriend. The boy rose first, then Regina rose, slowly. She put the two pieces of paper on her desk together and slid them up to the corner opposite the well where the ink bottle would have gone, though Sister had not told her to do that. The four of them, the nuns and the children, left, with Sister closing the door behind them and looking sternly at us before she did. We heard them go through the nearby door that led to the stairs going up. They must have stopped in the stairwell because we did not hear them ascending. After a long, long bit of time we heard a slap, then silence. There was another slap, and there quickly followed a wail from Regina. They all returned shortly, the boy quiet and Regina crying, and Sister took up where we were before Mother Superior had opened the door.

I said nothing about it to my parents, but a fear took hold of me throughout all the school days, even though Sister Mary Frances continued to look at me with eyes that said In-You-I-Am-Well-Pleased. Regina and the boy were still together on that purple shelf in my imagination, but they were sitting now, hands casually in their laps, sitting as if they were getting tired of waiting. At home in my bed I dreamed of school. I went there in my dreams, but the door was always locked.

That Thursday following the Monday after the slaps, minutes after our snack, I stood to answer a question, an answer that would earn me a gold star. I sat down, and as I listened to others answer, I looked at the backs of Regina and the boy who would not be her boyfriend ever again, their heads turning left or right depending upon which of our fellow pupils was speaking. I thought how easy it would have been for him to turn and make a face at her, the way he used to do. I studied the back of Regina's head, the way the dark perfect skin of her neck flowed down from her yellow-ribboned hair, down, down beneath her collar. It was such a vulnerable neck. Then, though Sister had not spoken to me, I rose as if a question had been put to me. I looked around as I stood and held tight to my desk, for my head had begun to swirl. I began to sit down again, but stopped, not knowing which way to go, back down or back up. I looked at Regina's neck and felt a great flood overwhelm me.

It was, I learned later about myself, as if my heart, on the path that was my life, had come to a puddle in the road and had faltered, hesitated, trying to decide whether to walk over the puddle or around it, or even to go back.

I woke in my bed that Thursday, and it was dark outside. Dr. Jackson, one of my mother's cousins, had come over from Myrtle Street. He was sitting on the side of the bed, holding my hand and looking down at me as if I, now that I was awake, could tell him the why of it all.

"How you feelin, sweet of my heart?" he said. He was married to a woman taller than he was and they lived with their five children in a gingerbread brown house.

"Fine," I said. He helped me sit up. I was wearing my pajamas. My father, in his postman's uniform, was standing behind Dr. Jackson. He was holding my sister Eva. My mother was at the foot of the bed. My sister Delores was also at the foot of the bed, and I could just barely see the top of her head and her eyes. Seeing them all, I thought, "My room can't hold all these people. It will bust."

Dr. Jackson placed my hand at my side. His tools were beside him on the bed. He took up the stethoscope, and after he had listened to my heart, he put all his tools in his bag on the table next to my bed. He stood and commanded me to sleep. As they all left the room, I heard him say that he could find nothing wrong, but I may have dreamed those words later that night, just as I dreamed that I had knocked at the school door:

I stepped away from the locked school door and went alone back down to L Street, but rather than go home, I knocked at our next-door neighbors'. Mr. and Mrs. Lewis lived there. He had been in the merchant marines all his life and had saved a lot of money for his retirement so he could take Mrs. Lewis around the world as many times as she wanted. But not long after he left the sea for good, he had a massive stroke and now lived his days in a wheelchair that his son and my father could not get to stop squeaking. In my dream Mr. Lewis came to the door, talking and standing on his two legs the way I remembered when I was just an infant, no more than two months old. He took me into the backyard that he had given over to my father so my father could have more space to grow things. Mr. Lewis served me a fruit salad with the hundreds of fruits my father had grown. We were joined by my father's father and Grandpa Peter and my Philadelphia uncle, One-Eye Jack, and a hundred others. My uncle Cyphax was there, once more out of jail, and he kept winking and raising his finger to his lips for me not to tell his secret. It became crowded in the yard, and I couldn't see all the rest of the men in my life. I kept telling Mr. Lewis that I had to knock on the school door again. "Wait," he said. "Just wait. Wait till the bell rings."

I woke very late that Thursday night, and after adjusting my eyes to the darkness, I saw my father in a rocking chair across from the bed. He was arguing with someone in his sleep.

When I awoke the next morning I saw my father still in the chair. But when I sat up and cleared the sleep from my eyes, I saw that it was not my father but my father's father. He was staring at me as if that was all he had to do in his life. I had never once seen my grandfather above our first floor. I had not thought that his wooden leg would allow him to climb the stairs.

"They didn't treat you so good up there, huh?" he said. He was wearing a suit and a tie and his hat was propped on his wooden knee.

I shook my head No. I wasn't yet able to do words because I still could not believe he had managed the stairs.

"Well, never you mind," he said. "Maybe you don't have all the luck you need." He leaned forward in the rocking chair. "Here—" He pointed to his wooden leg before lifting his hat. "Get you some good luck." I leaned over and tapped three times on the wooden knee. "Better get three more just to make sure." I tapped again. "There be boogeymen everywhere."

He leaned back. "Now your mama and your daddy say you don't never have to go back to that school. You can go just cross the street," and he thumbed over his shoulder in the direction of Walker-Jones Elementary some one hundred feet away. "Go just cross that street and be safe and happy as you would be in that front yard." And just like that, the idea of going there seized me. Miss Sadie's son went there, most of my friends in our neighborhood went there. It was only a few steps away, while Holy Redeemer was way out in the world.

My grandfather got to his feet. "Your mama gon come with some food directly." I nodded. "I best get on. Don't wanna suck up all your air. But I'm gonna come back to you tomorrow." After he was full on his feet, he looked a moment at me and ran his hand around the brim of his hat and then placed it atop his head.

The next morning I came out of sleep to a thump on one of the bottom stairs. My father cleaned those steps until they shined like crystal. There was another thump. I sat up and began to realize what the sound was. I waited and wiggled my toes under the covers. "This little piggy wants some corn. This little piggy says, 'Where you gon get it from?' This little piggy says, 'Outa Massa's barn . . .'" When I was done with that foot, I started on the other. There came a thump. "This little pig says, 'Run go tell!'" I came to the end on that foot and raised my left hand to my forehead. A Band-Aid covered the wound I suffered when I fell at my desk. There was another thump. I thought about the scab that would form and wondered if I would have a scar as big as the one on a boy I knew who had gotten hit in the forehead with a sharp rock. Children called him Rock Head because he had managed to live. Would people now call me Miss Rock Head, or would they have to come up with another name? There was a thump. "This little pig says, 'Twee,

twee, twee, I'll tell old Massa, tell old Massa!'" Finally, all the thumps stopped, but my grandfather did not appear. I learned much later that he stood in the hall in those moments after the climb, straightening his tie and wiping the sweat from his face, preparing to come in.

Sister Mary Frances rearranged our seating, and I found myself in the last aisle, next to a window. In the curious alphabet of our lives, I sat behind Herman Franks. He continued on with his quiet humming. He would smell a mimeographed page, and he would hum. He hummed to scratch his head. He hummed to hear the song of a bird drifting into the room. The boy, the boyfriend, was gone when I returned, and I never saw him again. The curious alphabet of our lives still placed Sylvia Carstairs, my best friend for life, beside me. "Welcome back," Sister Mary Frances said to me that first morning. "Welcome back." I had not yet been taught what to say in such situations, and so I said nothing. In the curious alphabet of our lives, Regina Bristol was one seat down from the front of the class, still in one of the middle aisles. Sometimes, in those days of being back, I would lose myself and watch the orange leaves and the red leaves and the gold leaves snowing down along Pierce Street. By then, by late October, my wound was healing as best it could, and our class was down to nine boys.

RESURRECTING METHUSELAH

At about the same time Sergeant Percival Channing was finishing his business with the prostitute in the Half Moon Hotel on General Douglas MacArthur Boulevard in Okinawa, his daughter—thousands and thousands of miles away in Northeast Washington, D.C.—managed to find rest at the very end of the second night of no more sleep than a minute here and a minute there. The girl was in the last stages of a fever brought on by a sore throat, and while the pediatrician had said there was nothing to worry about, "just another passage through childhood," the girl's mother, who had become pregnant with her daughter three months before she was to enter nursing school, knew children throughout the world had died before they could negotiate such passages. So her fear did not abate when her child closed her eyes and found peace, and the mother continued sitting near the edge of her seat in a plain wooden chair built to last 142 years before that night by a man who had been a slave. The chair, now with year-old cushions from Hecht's, had been given to her and Sergeant Channing as a wedding present. Seeing her child go away into sleep, however, the mother did allow her mind to drift somewhat, and she tried to remember just what time it was in Okinawa, whether the difference between the two cities was ten or eleven or twelve hours.

What the sergeant her husband did with the prostitute, he had not done with the mother of his child in nearly six months, and he would not do it ever again. Neither the sergeant nor his wife knew this as their only child turned in exhaustion onto her right side and entered a dream where Methuselah was waiting, not centuries old, not even a man, but waiting as a little girl who merely wanted to play.

The prostitute—Sara Lee, though she had been born and was still known to those who mattered as Keiko Hamasaki—called Sergeant Channing "passion capitain" as he lifted himself up with a grunt and left her body, and both of them, drunk and drugged, slept side by side for a very long time as the moon and the sun came and went. When Sara Lee finally lifted herself up on her elbows and shook her head, feeling the desire for a cigarette and for food, she did not know the time, for the year-old clock provided by the management of the Half Moon Hotel had worked only for the first month of its life and Sara had never owned a watch. The American military people in Okinawa had nicknamed her "My Time Is Your Time" because that was often what she said to them within minutes after meeting them. Sergeant Channing, still dead to the world beside her, had forgotten his own watch, and it had wound down back in his room on the base.

Sara Lee reached over the sergeant to get to his pack of cigarettes and three-dollar lighter on the small bedside table, and in reaching she had to support herself with one hand on the sleeping man's chest. Sara Lee weighed next to nothing. Still, the sergeant's eyes shot open and he screamed in such agony there in the third-floor back room that the Half Moon Hotel clerk down at the front desk could hear him, but the clerk did not let on and he continued talking to the corporal and his "Betty Crocker" as the latter two begged for a cheaper room.

"What the fuck you doin to me?" Percival Channing shouted to Sara Lee.

"No thing, passion capitain. No thing. Just a little bit cigarette. Just a little bit." She knew perfect English, but she had learned with her first two Americans that they did not want perfection in the women they whored with.

Percival sat up and felt as if he were about to vomit. He covered his chest with one hand, not yet feeling the lump, and with the other hand he grabbed again and again at the air as though something out there might give him relief, if only by a few degrees. He leaned forward, still grabbing, and in the end he struggled out of bed and limped to the open window, where he bent down and gulped in the pitiful Okinawa air. "Jesus Christ! Jesus, what the fuck!"

Sara went to him and rubbed his back, repeating the profanity Percival had just spoken. He raised himself up from the window, feeling slightly better the closer he got to standing fully upright. He was crying, because it had been just that much pain. He turned to Sara and she held his shoulder. "What the fuck did you do to me, Betty? You stab me or what?"

"No stab, passion capitain. Just a little bit cigarette." She had thought heart attack almost immediately, but the Americans were know-it-alls, and she felt it best that Sergeant Channing should come to his own diagnosis. Sara continued touching his shoulder as his breathing achieved some regularity. After he had rubbed the tears from his eyes, he put his right hand to his chest, now only half expecting a wound and flowing blood, and there, just below the right nipple, right where his heart would have been if a man's heart were on that side, he felt the lump. He thought it her doing, a little Asian voodoo, but when he looked into her eyes and saw something far from a woman capable of harm, a great part of him thought some shit had descended upon him from being in the man's army, from being in a foreign land among people who named themselves after food products. And a very, very tiny part of him thought that his body, long a thing of wonder chiseled after hundreds and hundreds of races on American high school and college tracks, had come to fail him somehow.

"Just let me get to that bed," Percival said, and Sara agreed with him that everything in the world got better after a little food and a long nap.

The sergeant's wife, Anita Hughes Channing, had, even before her child's illness, begun to think that the school her daughter attended was not the best place for her. She knew that most of the teachers and administrators at the New Day Arising Christian School had their hearts in the right place, but Anita, a lapsed Catholic, had concerns about her child's new teacher, a forty-seven-year-old man with seven children, a good and passionate man who had found religion when he was forty years of age. Perhaps too much goodness and passion might be too much for nine-year-old Bethany. Anita had picked New Day Arising because it was only blocks down from her D.C. government job at a nearly forgotten outpost on Minnesota Avenue in Northeast and because she thought her daughter should have some religion in her life, since they did not regularly attend church. What religion Bethany did get before New Day Arising had come from Sunday mass at St. Augustine's on 15th Street when she visited Anita's parents who lived in an apartment a block from Scott Circle on 16th. At mass, safe between her grandmother and grandfather, the child all but ignored the priest, but concentrated, Sunday after Sunday, on the Stations of the Cross.

Through the second and third grades, Bethany's teachers had been fine, exactly what her mother had wanted. The school had a reputation for, as its four-page brochure proclaimed, serving up education as the main course, with religion as the appetizer and the drink and the dessert. The latter three were there and they had importance, but they weren't the entrée, they weren't the whole of the school's reason for being. Bethany's fourth-grade teacher, Methuselah Harrington, accepted this when he was hired; he even signed a vague pledge to that effect minutes after he filled out tax forms in the school's office two weeks before school started. But Methuselah, "a reformed and wanton scoundrel," knew well what religion had done for him and for his own children, and he was determined that every black child he had any influence on would know that salvation as well. He was never to do anything so outrageous as to violate the pledge, to put religion at the center of the meal, but in the middle of a child answering an arithmetic question or as a child was reading something quite secular, he would ask the boy or girl, "Who will save you from the pains of perdition?" or "Who will favor you with everlasting life?"

The answer to those questions earned gold stars. Nothing was given for a correct arithmetic answer or for a splendid reading of a passage about some family's summer trip to the sea with Grandmother and Grandfather. In early October, a week before Bethany became ill, Methuselah brought in a poster and taped it to the wall under the clock and opposite the windows. It was not a big poster, certainly smaller than the map of the United States to its left, and more or less the same size as the pictures to the right of Malcolm X and Sojourner Truth and Martin Luther King Jr. But the poster, an elongated thing that reminded Bethany and her friend Jessica of a scroll, held the children's attention because at the top of it were the words "The Life of Methuselah." The children had been told on the first day of school that they could call their teacher "Mr. Harrington" or "Mr. Methuselah"; being children, they chose something different from what the other kids did with their teachers, and Bethany and her classmates called him by his first name. And being children, they found it hard not to relate the man named Methuselah on the poster with the teacher Mr. Methuselah who led them in the Lord's Prayer every morning and who told them how the people in Lapland lived day to day amid snow and reindeer and darkness a good part of the year.

The poster showed Methuselah—always in brown sandals and a brown biblical robe similar to what the kids always saw Jesus wearing— first as a crawling baby, then a boy, a teenager, a man, et cetera, until he was a ninety-year-old man, a rather spry-looking fellow still full of life with his legs apart and his hands at his hips as though ready for any demon the Devil would toss his way. But at ninety-one, Methuselah seemed to be faltering, head bent, arms sluggishly at his sides, his robe not as well cared for as in earlier pictures. Jesus stood behind him at ninety-one and was touching the top of the man's head. From there on, at one hundred, at two hundred, and all the way to nine hundred, Methuselah was spry again. At nine hundred and one, he had wings and a halo, and aside from those things, he didn't look any different than he had throughout the centuries. The children in Bethany's class didn't yet know a whole lot about the difference between the Old and New Testaments, and the teachers and administrators who went in and out of Methuselah's class never paid the poster much attention. Only the janitor saw that Jesus Christ had wandered over from the New Testament into the Old, but New Day Arising didn't pay her to tell anyone about an impossibility.

Bethany Channing woke a little after one in the afternoon, and her fever and sore throat were gone and she was very hungry. She called for her mother and then for her father, forgetting for the moment that the sergeant—according to how she measured on the globe next to Mr. Methuselah's desk—was nearly two hands away from that little star that was Washington, D.C. She called for her mother again, and as the child edged toward the side of the bed, she looked down to see Anita covered with a blanket and asleep on the floor. Nothing in days and days had made her happier than to see Anita that way. She thought to lean down and kiss her mother but hunger pulled the child to the other side and Bethany got up and went to the kitchen to fix a breakfast of cold cereal and a croissant splattered with marmalade.

Anita found her child sitting at the table with the bowl at her mouth, drinking the last of the cereal's milk. The mother herself had become ill at about eleven years old, bones aching, headaches that tossed her mind from one shore to another. She suffered along for years and years, better sometimes and other times too ill to even get out of her bed. No doctor knew what was wrong, and most of them told Anita's parents that the best that could be done was to keep her comfortable. The parents, not knowing from where the harm came, forbade so many things, from stuffed animals to sweets to Anita's friends with colds and small cuts on faces and hands. They sensed that what all the doctors were leaving off was that she should be comfortable because the end was not far away. Her mother stopped working in Anita's eleventh year because, as she told her husband, if her child was to die, she did not want her to pass away alone. Anita's mother had three years of college, and she taught her daughter what little she had learned during those times the girl was capable of learning. Her father took a second job in the evenings, and the family, which included a younger brother, stayed near the bottom of the middle class, a few paychecks from the lower class in which the parents had been raised and which they had thought they would not have to see again.

Anita waited until Bethany had downed the last of the milk and the girl, seeing her mother, did a little dance as she sat, her feet tapping the floor, her shoulders twisting from side to side as she moved her arms up and down. The mother's childhood had more or less stopped with the illness no doctor could diagnose. Her friends came by off and on during the first year, but in time, as she failed to recover fully, most of them went back to their own childhoods and forgot the girl whose mother had made a permanent pallet beside her bed.

"You went away there for a time," Anita said to Bethany and kissed her forehead because the girl's cheeks were covered with marmalade.

"Huh huh." The child could not remember very much about the last two days, but she did recall that last dream before waking, and in it she was still playing with the girl the dream told her was named Methuselah. "Me and Methuselah had a good time playing." Anita took little note of what the child was saying, but she would weeks later, halfway between Veterans Day and Thanksgiving.

"How bout a day at the playground and then at the movies and then going to see Granddad and Grandma? How bout it?"

Bethany rubbed her hands together and did the dance again. In her nineteenth year, Anita's illness disappeared and she was never sick again, not even a half day of sniffles. She tried to get a diploma based on what her mother had taught her, but the D.C. school people shook their heads and said it was either work for a high school equivalency diploma in the evenings or go to the regular high school. Though she had failed two grades during her sickness and though all her friends had gone on, she nevertheless decided to become a regular student. She was about two years older than most of the students in the senior class at Cardozo High School, but she was alive and well and hopeful about what was to come, and that mattered most. And then Percival, a star of track and field, saw her in the school library one day where he was conversing with friends. She had spent her teens not knowing the company of boys not her brother or cousins. Now, one of those people she knew little about came across the room and closed the book she was about to take out and told her that her feet must be tired because she had been running through his mind all day. Not even a twelve-year-old would have accepted that, but she had never really been twelve or thirteen or fourteen, except in a way that would not count in the real world. Later, when she liked to tease him, he became "a star of field and stream."

"I had such hopes for you," her father was to say before her senior year was done. He was in tears, and father and daughter were alone in the living room, a lamp with a flickering sixty-watt bulb across the way. "I had such very big hopes for you." She was never to be a nurse, but in her file the D.C. government people kept at the District Building, they said glowing things about her year after year in her job as a manager at that almost forgotten outpost in Northeast. Her father would never completely forgive Anita, and that created an opening through which Percival Channing could step into all the way. With marriage, she called herself Anita Hughes Channing, but it was always "Channing" she was most proud of, and the name she emphasized. Her father warmed a bit, though, because Bethany became more important than anyone, but he was never the same man who read to his chronically ailing daughter before going off, renewed, to that second job.

S ergeant Channing found he could ignore the lump in his chest because most of the time it did not bother him, but one morning one and a half weeks after the episode with Sara Lee, he could barely get out of bed.

One of the doctors at the base, Captain Jerome Henderson, touched the lump as Percival sat on the examining table, and when the sergeant winced and shrunk away, the physician's eyes widened and he said, most quietly, "Hmm. . . ." The doctor was a smoker, and throughout the examination Percival kept thinking that whatever brand of cigarettes the doctor smoked, it wasn't Marlboro. After two X-rays and three vials of blood were taken, Captain Henderson sent the sergeant away with two prescriptions for painkillers and an order to return in three days. The doctor saw dozens upon dozens of soldiers each day, most of them for no more than five minutes, and so while very few faces stuck in his memory, he recognized the sergeant's right away, for Percival was only the second case of male breast cancer the doctor, at fifty-five, had seen in his life. What a wonder is man, he had thought the day before as he looked at Percival's X-rays and then, for the third time, read the blood results. What a Godawful wonder is man. . . .

The sergeant smiled when the captain told him what he had found. Percival knew the quality of doctors and equipment the army people had. He was again sitting on the examining table, this time still in his uniform. Percival, chuckling, pointed down at his crotch. "Doctor, no disrespect, sir, but you have noticed what we have down there."

"I never take an inordinate, unprofessional interest in anyone's 'down there,'" the captain said. He should have been a major, but he often said mean words to people he shouldn't have said.

"But breast cancer, Doctor, I mean, you know, come on, thas for women."

"Sergeant," the captain said, his arms folded and standing but two feet from Percival, "there is one thing you have in common with the billions of women on this earth—you all have breasts. Ask some old man. Ask any private you know." He turned to the opposite table of cotton swabs and tongue depressors and opened the folder that was the Army medical life of Sergeant Channing and wrote two lines, underlining three words on the first line. When he turned back, the captain had the same serious look. "This isn't some strike against your masculinity, Sergeant. I promise."

"But breast cancer, Doctor. I mean, of all the things to get." Percival, in seconds, had accepted what was, and now he was beginning to think that had he not done this or that with some bitch in some foreign city, he'd still be fine. Someone, while he was stationed in Germany, had told him to be careful because at the end of the day foreign cunt was very different from American cunt. The foreign had "properties," that forgotten someone had said. The doctor placed a hand on his shoulder. Whatever breast cancer was, Percival was thinking, it was not in the same family as all other cancers. It wasn't the lung thing, which he could have understood, given the thousands of Camels he had smoked. It wasn't even the blood thing. When the doctor asked if there were people in his family with breast cancer, he said no because he had truly forgotten.

"This isn't the end of the world," the captain said. "It's a new day now, and that wouldn't have been the case a time ago." The sergeant got off the table, though he had not been told to. "I need you back here in two days, Sergeant. Two days, and if you don't show, I'll have the MPs after your ass."

The chemicals they gave him were to do nothing except, as he was to think later at Walter Reed, make the cancer mad. They gave him many brochures about those chemicals, and one evening in that hospital in Okinawa, as he waited for Anita to arrive from Washington, he looked up from reading one of the brochures and thought not about his wife or his daughter, but about a race he had when he was a junior at Cardozo, a race that ultimately came down to him and some no-account from Coolidge High. After he crossed the finish line first, he wanted to show to all who were watching what a big man he could be, so he took Coolidge's extended hand in both of his. He didn't bother to listen to anything Coolidge was saying, but simply offered a perfunctory "Good race" that should have handled anything Coolidge said. He lowered his eyes back to the brochure. Didn't that kind of sportmanshit count for something? The brochure had pictures of only healthy women; it did not seem to have heard of men with breast cancer. Didn't giving a whore an extra ten dollars count for something? Didn't the big whoever see that it all came out the same? Why should ten ones count for less than two fives? "I heard your mother wasn't well," Coolidge had said. "I want you to know I'm praying for her." "Good race, man."

For weeks following Bethany's recovery, Anita tried recalling a few lines from *Porgy and Bess* about Methuselah. She, at thirteen, had watched the musical that first time one Sunday night on television with her mother while her father and brother had gone to a movie. Anita sat with her legs on the couch and her mother was at the other end, Anita's blanketed feet in her lap. Each time Sidney Poitier appeared, they pretended to swoon. She knew that the lines she wanted to remember began with *What's the use,* but she couldn't get hold of any words beyond that. *What's the use . . . What's the use . . .* She had failed to find the tape of the musical's songs. Maybe she had left it in Germany. Maybe she had lost the tape on the way to Germany, or on the way back. *Sprechen see what I mean . . . What's the use . . .*

Her great fear was that her daughter would become her and live some of her best young days in bed and on the couch. The whole world was out there and she wanted Bethany to know every molecule of it, but blood was blood, and in her own blood floated molecules that were up to no good. The whole world was why she had said yes to going to Germany when the army people stationed Percival there. Corporal Channing. But the days and nights had been long with him not there, and when he was there, the days and nights were even longer. *What's the use . . .* So back home to Washington, though one good thing was that Bethany had absorbed German in their two years there, could speak it as well as any German child born to it. *Sprechen see what I mean . . .* The New Day Arising Christian School had no one who spoke German, so Anita had had to hire a Catholic University graduate student to keep the language alive in the child, though Bethany could barely remember life in Germany. She did know that when she measured the distance on Mr. Methuselah's globe, the country was two whole hands from the little star that was Washington, D.C.

"Mama, what did Mama Channing die with?"

They were in the car and they were returning from the National Arboretum. It was Friday afternoon, a time she had begun to give only to her child. One more report to the District Building had been written from the Northeast outpost before she left work early.

"Mama, what did Mama Channing die with?" the child asked again.

"Why?" Anita said. She looked at her daughter in the rearview mirror, then at the tiny statue of Saint Christopher with its magnetic base on the dashboard.

"Mr. Methuselah wants us to write down what age our grandparents was when they died, and if they're alive now, how old they are."

"What kind of assignment is that, honey?" Saint Christopher never moved, no matter how bumpy the road.

"I don't know. It's Mr. Methuselah's assignment. So what age did Mama Channing die?"

"I'll have to find out. I don't know it off the top of my head."

"So everybody else is alive, all my other grandparents?"

"You know that already."

"So what about great-grandparents? Their ages when they died, since they're all dead?"

"Bethany!" The child sometimes talked in her sleep, and when she did, the words were sometimes German. "Bethany!"

"It's not me, Mama. It's Mr. Methuselah. You know what? He said we could all live forever as long as we first accepted Jesus. He said we could resurrect what was in that other Methuselah. He said we could be better than the other Methuselah. He was only nine hundred years old, but we could live as long as we wanted. And Reggie said could we live till one hundred cause his grandfather died when he was like only ninety-nine, and Mr. Methuselah said we could live ten times one hundred. And Reggie said could we live till five thousand years, and Mr. Methuselah said yes, as long as we accepted Jesus and everything He stood for." Anita had taken to marking off the days after the child's recovery. She had forgotten to do it that morning because the fever and sore throat were getting further and further away. "So I need all the dates for Monday." She said nothing for a while, and Anita looked at her again in the mirror. "I guess, like . . ." They were on New York Avenue, having passed North Capitol Street. Sixteenth Street where her parents lived was far ahead.

"Guess what?" Two thousand fucking bucks a year to scare a child. . . .

"I guess Mama Channing didn't accept Jesus."

"Your grandmother accepted Him more than anyone I know, Bethany. Don't let anyone tell you any different."

"Well, she's not here. She didn't live till a hundred. She probably didn't even live till ninety-nine. Mr. Methuselah said we're lucky cause Jesus doesn't go everywhere. He's not in Lapland. He's never going to Lapland."

"He's everywhere people need Him, Bethany."

"Maybe not in Lapland. They don't need Him in Lapland."

At 7th Street, Anita made a right and soon turned left so she could go down Massachusetts Avenue. Ah yes, she thought as she looked at the fish symbol on the bumper sticker on the car ahead. Ah yes . . .

What's the use a livin
When nobody's givin
    To a man who's nine hundred years old . . .

That Sunday evening on the couch, she had not known what the singer was meaning until her mother started giggling just after the word "givin," and then she knew very well.

I have this cancer shit. I have this cancer thing." He did not say "breast," and he would not until he was in Washington, at Walter Reed. "They're sayin good things and whatnot, but I don't know. . . ." Given the distance between them, the connection was not altogether bad, unlike many other times. Given the ten or twelve hours between them. The connection had always been good to Germany.

"Percy . . . I'm sorry. I'm so sorry."

"Yeah, well." He sounded weak, she thought, but maybe what the telephone gave in the clarity of words, it took back in other ways. "I was wonderin if yall could come see me. You and Bethany. They say family is important with this kinda thing."

"I know it is, but . . ."

"Try, all right. Try."

"Okay, but if not Bethany, then I'll make it." Until she landed in Los Angeles, with Honolulu still to come, she would not think to ask what type of cancer. "Give a try . . . ," Percival said. She felt the conversation ending, and she was trying to think of what one was supposed to say. She knew there was something to be done in such situations, for she had seen it done before, though she could not remember if she had read it in a book or seen it in a movie or a parent had told her. And then, only seconds before the conversation ended, she remembered. "Percy, I love you."

"Yeah. Okay. Me, too."

It was evening for her, her child safe and healthy and asleep, and there in the armchair, her feet on the ottoman, she closed her eyes and began praying for Sergeant Percival Channing. Her first prayers for anything in a long time. There was a saint Catholics prayed to when there was illness, but she could not remember the name, could not recall if it was a man or a woman. Maybe Saint Methuselah. She continued on with a second Lord's Prayer. In the middle of it, she realized she had forgotten what the father of her child looked like. She thought there was a picture next to the armchair, but she was wrong. It was across the room, too far away to make it out clearly, and she was quite comfortable where she was. But perhaps a husband with cancer was worth a trip across the room. A journey of a few steps. Hear our prayer Saint Christopher as we make this journey. In the morning she began to see the trip to Okinawa, and his illness, as a way for them to reestablish something. "I'll be all that you need. I'll be a parent," Percival had said after she, two months pregnant, knew that her father was drifting away from her. "Watch. You'll see."

Anita came out of the Honolulu Hilton and turned toward the sun. She did not yet know if she wanted to swim, but it would take her no time to return and change into a swimsuit. The airplane to Okinawa was in the morning. There were shops for the several blocks down to the beach, and she took her time and paused before all the windows. If there was something especially grand, there was no point in waiting until Okinawa for a present for her child. Indeed, two or three gifts would not be a problem for a little girl who was far from spoiled, who was turning out quite nicely.

About midway up the first block, there was a pawnshop, and she stood before a display of items for sale, things pawned but never redeemed. While everything she saw was in good condition, nothing seemed of her time, the present day. On a small red pallet on a stool nearest the window, some ten Morgan silver dollars in plastic packages had dates ranging from 1879 to 1924. Her father and grandfather had had small collections of such coins, and while she had been familiar with them growing up, had even played with those her father had, the money on the other side of the glass seemed from a place quite alien to her. Still, her father might like one, but she could not recall dates he did and did not have, and so she continued on.

In the third block, where she could hear clearly the sound of the sea coming to the shore and going back out, there was a candy shop. A SWEET OLD TIME, the many-colored letters said in a half circle on the window. She went in, thinking of the candy from childhood, the kind of sweets she had enjoyed for only a handful of pennies. Kits. Squirrel Nuts. Sugar Daddy. Sugar Mama. And the little Sugar Babies. She did not think they made that stuff anymore, and that was a shame because she had good memories of those treats, and it would have been nice for her daughter to know a part of what had been her childhood. But she was curious. "Welcome back," a recorded child's voice sang when Anita opened the door. "Welcome back to a sweet old time."

The shop was nearly empty except for a man who was standing with his hands behind his back in front of the display case near the door. He seemed to be trying to decide what to buy. The man turned and said good morning, and Anita nodded and said good morning. "Welcome to my humble shop," he said. The man, about her age, was mostly Asian, but, as she had noticed with many in Hawaii, he seemed a mixture of a good deal more; he could even have been partly black. "Let me know if I can be of service," he said as Anita went to the first case. It had no more than an enormous variety of jelly beans, but in the second case she saw behind the glass a feast of that old-fashioned candy and she beamed at the man, and he beamed back, as if she and he had shared the same things from the same store once upon a time. "I get that look all the time," he said. She leaned forward slightly and saw just about everything she could remember. The same girl on the Mary Jane wrapping, that candy of no more than an inch with the surprise nutty mixture buried within the hard outside. Necco wafers were there. She and her brother and their cousins, Catholics all, had played priest and churchgoers with that candy. "Don't chew it. It's the host, stupid. You not sposed to chew." "I gotta chew. You want me to get sick or somethin?"

She bought two bags of various pieces, a large bag for Bethany and a smaller one she could enjoy going to Okinawa and then on the way back home.

"I thought all of this was a dying art," she said to the man as she paid for her purchase. It wasn't penny candy anymore.

"I thought so, too," the man said, "until I found this company in Wisconsin that caters to people like us." He tied each bag with a red bow. "I have colored string as well," he said, "but that is for the men who come in and remember, too."

The child sang again after she opened the door. *Welcome back to a sweet old time.* She took off her sandals at the entrance to the beach. She hadn't had breakfast, and though she knew better, she decided that her breakfast would be candy on the beach. It was a good thing Bethany wasn't with her. A few yards from the sea, she set down the sandals and the larger bag on the sand and began to open her bag, her mouth watering and her fingers failing to untie the bow. She tried biting it loose, but the simple bow held tight. She then tried rolling it up to the top of the bag where she might just pull it away. That failed as well, and she found herself smiling. "Serves you right, you little penny ninny. What kind of an example are you to your child, eating candy on an empty stomach at ten-thirty in the morning? And in Hawaii. Shame shame, everybody knows your name."

At last she bit a tiny hole into the bag itself and into the opening she stuck a finger and made an even larger hole. She pulled out one Mary Jane, marveled at the familiar black and red and light brown wrapping. She popped it into her mouth. There was at first nothing but an overwhelming sugariness, and even after a flavor of some kind seeped through the sugar, it did not last, and it was not as she remembered. She tried other kinds of candy, and it was the same, a bunch of something she could not remember ever knowing.

Back in the shop, the man raised his head and seemed initially surprised to see her again, but long before the recording stopped, the surprise disappeared from his face. There were five children before that second case, and each was pointing at this or that piece. A man and a woman stood back, quietly conversing. As he waited for the children to make up their minds, the proprietor said, "Back for more?"

"No," Anita said. "It doesn't taste right. Maybe it's old, or moldy, or something. It tasted funny." The children were not even aware of her, but the two adults were listening.

"Well, it's new. I just opened a brand-new shipment of everything last evening. See," and he reached into the case and brought out different pieces and gave them to the children. "See." The children unwrapped and ate, and they all showed happy faces and looked with some amazement at each other as they chewed. "See, just in from Wisconsin."

Anita left. At the end of that third block, she took the candy piece by piece out of her bag, looked at the wrappers that she knew so well, and dropped them one by one into a trash can, which told her in letters of pink leis to KEEP HONOLULU CLEAN. Someone had told her that the military airplane would take four or five hours to get her to Okinawa. "Depending," the person had said, but never said depending upon what. She crossed to the next block. The other candy would be fine for Bethany. Her discarded bag of stuff had cost $5.25. When she was a girl, it would have been no more than a quarter. And the trip back from Okinawa—another four or five hours. Depending . . .

In the first block, just before the pawnshop, she realized that even an hour of a perfect trip to Okinawa would now be too much. The desk clerk at the hotel told her she knew of a flight in seven hours that would take her to Los Angeles, but Mrs. Channing would have to go first to Chicago, rather than directly to Washington, and Anita told her that would be fine. The clerk said she would make the arrangements, and before Anita left the desk, she asked about sending a telegram, and the clerk said someone would call her room to make those arrangements.

On the elevator, she began to feel that she had slept through something and now that she was awake, she had to make do with what she now had.

The military people had one of their airplanes take the sergeant from Okinawa to Hawaii, and there he waited a day and a half for another to fly him to a base in California. The doctor who was a captain in Okinawa wanted him to rest as much as possible for the journey to Washington. Two days after getting to California, the military people flew the sergeant and fifteen other sick people to a base just outside Washington. There were files on all of these sixteen people, and in each one, from Okinawa to Washington to Germany, somebody had stamped on the first page of each file the red word INACTIVE. The army doctor had told the sergeant that Washington could do for him what Okinawa did not have the equipment to do. "Watch. You'll see," the doctor said. A fleet of twelve ambulances and military medical personnel left the base just after sundown and transported the sixteen men and women to Walter Reed Army Hospital on 16th Street. And there the sergeant's daughter and his wife, who was already on her way to not being his wife, came to see him in his bright room on the third floor. They arrived on a Saturday, not even three weeks after the military people had torn into his body and cut away nearly a fourth of his chest. The pain drugs eased the crush of misery after that, but not thoroughly, and in his dreams the sergeant always lost a fight against a sexless monster that clawed him apart. It was the only dream he would have for a very, very long time.

The visit was quite brief, with most of it taken up with Bethany standing between her father's legs as he sat in a chair two feet from his bed. Anita stood at the window. She could see how the sergeant had withered, could see what was missing. While the room was bright, it faced nothing more than the roof of the second floor. He was in the brown pajamas and bathrobe and slippers his father had brought him. At the last minute, Anita had thought to bring him the same things, only in blue, but she was too late with hers, and he was never to wear them. She had forgotten that blue was a color he did not like.

The mother and her child both kissed his cheek and left him in the chair as he admired the book of poems Bethany had brought. As the two neared the elevator, Anita turned and found him following them. He said he might walk out with them because he hadn't seen the sun in a while. His daughter held his hand all the way.

Out in the sun, Percival slowed and went to the nearest bench. The woman and the child stood for a bit until Anita thought they had waited long enough. They kissed his cheek again.

Once in her car, she considered going around the parking lot and passing the sergeant on the bench so that he might get one more look at their daughter. There seemed an extremely long line of cars passing behind her, and she waited in the parking space.

"Mama, Mr. Methuselah wants us to do a project by the end of next week," Bethany said.

"Oh?" Anita said. "What is it this time? More grandparent stuff?" After the tenth car passed behind her, she wondered why everyone had decided to leave at once.

"No, we're done with that." Anita stopped watching the passing cars and looked at her daughter's face in the rearview mirror. There was a public school near her parents, a good school she had heard about from her sister-in-law. "He wants us to write a paragraph about what we would say to people who might not know Jesus and don't even know they could live till five thousand years." On some days, she could see Percival's mother's face in her child; on other days, she could see her own father. He, too, was dying, just as Percival might be. "What would we say to the poor Lapland people, you know? What would you say to em, Mama? Gimme a hint." She had seen Methuselah several times, and each time he seemed only steps from his own grave.

Anita began inching out of the space. Through trial and error, she had learned many things about the world, about her husband, and one of them was that he would be waiting, for such was the way of many men whose lives had taken a cut to the bone. As she came out of her parking space, she again saw her daughter's face in the rearview mirror, bright and hopeful with all the life any parent could ever hope for, and she began looking for an exit that would not take her back that way to the sergeant and his bench. Waiting to go on to 16th Street, she did not know whether she wanted left or right. Perhaps it might be good to go left, into Maryland. There was a street, a curious side street in Bethesda, that she had seen one busy, crowded day as she took Wisconsin Avenue into Maryland, and she had told herself that one day she and Bethany would explore that most inviting street and not even care that much if they got lost. What time could be better than today? What time could be better than what might be the last day of five thousand years?

OLD BOYS, OLD GIRLS

They caught him after he had killed the second man. The law would never connect him to the first murder. So the victim—a stocky fellow Caesar Matthews shot in a Northeast alley only two blocks from the home of the guy's parents, a man who died over a woman who was actually in love with a third man—was destined to lie in his grave without anyone officially paying for what had happened to him. It was almost as if, at least on the books the law kept, Caesar had got away with a free killing.

Seven months after he stabbed the second man—a twenty-two-year-old with prematurely gray hair who had ventured out of Southeast for only the sixth time in his life—Caesar was tried for murder in the second degree. During much of the trial, he remembered the name only of the first dead man—Percy, or "Golden Boy," Weymouth—and not the second, Antwoine Stoddard, to whom everyone kept referring during the proceedings. The world had done things to Caesar since he'd left his father's house for good at sixteen, nearly fourteen years ago, but he had done far more to himself.

So at trial, with the weight of all the harm done to him and because he had hidden for months in one shit hole after another, he was not always himself and thought many times that he was actually there for killing Golden

Boy, the first dead man. He was not insane, but he was three doors from it, which was how an old girlfriend, Yvonne Miller, would now and again playfully refer to his behavior. *Who the fuck is this Antwoine bitch?* Caesar sometimes thought during the trial. *And where is Percy?* It was only when the judge sentenced him to seven years in Lorton, D.C.'s prison in Virginia, that matters became somewhat clear again, and in those last moments before they took him away, he saw Antwoine spread out on the ground outside the Prime Property nightclub, blood spurting out of his chest like oil from a bountiful well. Caesar remembered it all: sitting on the sidewalk, the liquor spinning his brain, his friends begging him to run, the club's music flooding out of the open door and going *thumpety-thump-thump* against his head. He sat a few feet from Antwoine, and would have killed again for a cigarette. "That's you, baby, so very near insanity it can touch you," said Yvonne, who believed in unhappiness and who thought happiness was the greatest trick God had invented. Yvonne Miller would be waiting for Caesar at the end of the line.

He came to Lorton with a ready-made reputation, since Multrey Wilson and Tony Cathedral—first-degree murderers both, and destined to die there—knew him from his Northwest and Northeast days. They were about as big as you could get in Lorton at that time (the guards called Lorton the House of Multrey and Cathedral), and they let everyone know that Caesar was good people, "a protected body," with no danger of having his biscuits or his butt taken.

A little less than a week after Caesar arrived, Cathedral asked him how he liked his cellmate. Caesar had never been to prison but had spent five days in the D.C. jail, not counting the time there before and during the trial. They were side by side at dinner, and neither man looked at the other. Multrey sat across from them. Cathedral was done eating in three minutes, but Caesar always took a long time to eat. His mother had raised him to chew his food thoroughly. "You wanna be a old man livin on oatmeal?" "I love oatmeal, Mama." "Tell me that when you have to eat it every day till you die."

"He all right, I guess," Caesar said of his cellmate, with whom he had shared fewer than a thousand words. Caesar's mother had died before she saw what her son became.

"You got the bunk you want, the right bed?" Multrey said. He was sitting beside one of his two "women," the one he had turned out most recently. "She" was picking at her food, something Multrey had already warned her about. The woman had a family—a wife and three children—but they would not visit. Caesar would never have visitors, either.

"It's all right." Caesar had taken the top bunk, as the cellmate had already made the bottom his home. A miniature plastic panda from his youngest child dangled on a string hung from one of the metal bedposts. "Bottom, top, it's all the same ship."

Cathedral leaned into him, picking chicken out of his teeth with an inch-long fingernail sharpened to a point. "Listen, man, even if you like the top bunk, you fuck him up for the bottom just cause you gotta let him know who rules. You let him know that you will stab him through his motherfuckin heart and then turn around and eat your supper, cludin the dessert." Cathedral straightened up. "Caes, you gon be here a few days, so you can't let nobody fuck with your humanity."

He went back to the cell and told Pancho Morrison that he wanted the bottom bunk, couldn't sleep well at the top.

"Too bad," Pancho said. He was lying down, reading a book published by the Jehovah's Witnesses. He wasn't a Witness, but he was curious.

Caesar grabbed the book and flung it at the bars, and the bulk of it slid through an inch or so and dropped to the floor. He kicked Pancho in the side, and before he could pull his leg back for a second kick Pancho took the foot in both hands, twisted it, and threw him against the wall. Then Pancho was up, and they fought for nearly an hour before two guards, who had been watching the whole time, came in and beat them about the head. "Show's over! Show's over!" one kept saying.

They attended to themselves in silence in the cell, and with the same silence they flung themselves at each other the next day after dinner. They were virtually the same size, and though Caesar came to battle with more muscle, Pancho had more heart. Cathedral had told Caesar that morning that Pancho had lived on practically nothing but heroin for the three years before Lorton, so whatever fighting dog was in him could be pounded out in little or no time. It took three days. Pancho was the father of five children, and each time he swung he did so with the memory of all five and what he had done to them over those three addicted years. He wanted to return to them and try to make amends, and he realized on the morning of the third day that he would not be able to do that if Caesar killed him. So fourteen minutes into the fight he sank to the floor after Caesar hammered him in the gut. And though he could have got up, he stayed there, silent and still. The two guards laughed. The daughter who had given Pancho the panda was nine years old and had been raised by her mother as a Catholic.

That night, before the place went dark, Caesar lay on the bottom bunk and looked over at pictures of Pancho's children, which Pancho had taped on the opposite wall. He knew he would have to decide if he wanted Pancho just to move the photographs or to put them away altogether. All the children had toothy smiles. The two youngest stood, in separate pictures, outdoors in their First Communion clothes. Caesar himself had been a father for two years. A girl he had met at an F Street club in Northwest had told him he was the father of her son, and for a time he had believed her. Then the boy started growing big ears that Caesar thought didn't belong to anyone in his family, and so after he had slapped the girl a few times a week before the child's second birthday she confessed that the child belonged to "my first love." "Your first love is always with you," she said, sounding forever like a television addict who had never read a book. As Caesar prepared to leave, she asked him, "You want back all the toys and things you gave him?" The child, as if used to their fighting, had slept through this last encounter on the couch, part of a living room suite that they were paying for on time. Caesar said nothing more and didn't think about his eighteen-karat-gold cigarette lighter until he was eight blocks away. The girl pawned the thing and got enough to pay off the furniture bill.

Caesar and Pancho worked in the laundry, and Caesar could look across the noisy room with all the lint swirling about and see Pancho sorting dirty pieces into bins. Then he would push uniform bins to the left and everything else to the right. Pancho had been doing that for three years. The job he got after he left Lorton was as a gofer at construction sites. No laundry in the outside world wanted him. Over the next two weeks, as Caesar watched Pancho at his job, his back always to him, he considered what he should do next. He wasn't into fucking men, so that was out. He still had not decided what he wanted done about the photographs on the cell wall. One day at the end of those two weeks, Caesar saw the light above Pancho's head flickering and Pancho raised his head and looked for a long time at it, as if thinking that the answer to all his problems lay in fixing that one light. Caesar decided then to let the pictures remain on the wall.

Three years later, they let Pancho go. The two men had mostly stayed at a distance from each other, but toward the end they had been talking, sharing plans about a life beyond Lorton. The relationship had reached the point where Caesar was saddened to see the children's photographs come off the wall. Pancho pulled off the last taped picture and the wall was suddenly empty in a most forlorn way. Caesar knew the names of all the children. Pancho gave him a rabbit's foot that one of his children had given him. It was the way among all those men that when a good-luck piece had run out of juice, it was given away with the hope that new ownership would renew its strength. The rabbit's foot had lost its electricity months before Pancho's release. Caesar's only good-fortune piece was a key chain made in Peru; it had been sweet for a bank robber in the next cell for nearly two years until that man's daughter, walking home from third grade, was abducted and killed.

One day after Pancho left, they brought in a thief and three-time rapist of elderly women. He nodded to Caesar and told him that he was Watson Rainey and went about making a home for himself in the cell, finally plugging in a tiny lamp with a green shade, which he placed on the metal shelf jutting from the wall. Then he climbed onto the top bunk he had made up and lay down. His name was all the wordplay he had given Caesar, who had been smoking on the bottom bunk throughout Rainey's efforts to make a nest. Caesar waited ten minutes and then stood and pulled the lamp's cord out of the wall socket and grabbed Rainey with one hand and threw him to the floor. He crushed the lamp into Rainey's face. He choked him with the cord. "You come into my house and show me no respect!" Caesar shouted. The only sound Rainey could manage was a gurgling that bubbled up from his mangled mouth. There were no witnesses except for an old man across the way, who would occasionally glance over at the two when he wasn't reading his Bible. It was over and done with in four minutes. When Rainey came to, he found everything he owned piled in the corner, soggy with piss. And Caesar was again on the top bunk.

They would live in that cell together until Caesar was released, four years later. Rainey tried never to be in the house during waking hours; if he was there when Caesar came in, he would leave. Rainey's name spoken by him that first day were all the words that would ever pass between the two men.

A week or so after Rainey got there, Caesar bought from Multrey a calendar that was three years old. It was large and had no markings of any sort, as pristine as the day it was made. "You know this one ain't the year we in right now," Multrey said as one of his women took a quarter from Caesar and dropped it in her purse. Caesar said, "It'll do." Multrey prized the calendar for one thing: its top half had a photograph of a naked woman of indeterminate race sitting on a stool, her legs wide open, her pussy aimed dead at whoever was standing right in front of her. It had been Multrey's good-luck piece, but the luck was dead. Multrey remembered what the calendar had done for him and he told his woman to give Caesar his money back, lest any new good-fortune piece turn sour on him.

The calendar's bottom half had the days of the year. That day, the first Monday in June, Caesar drew in the box that was January 1 a line that went from the upper left-hand corner down to the bottom right-hand corner. The next day, a June Tuesday, he made a line in the January 2 box that also ran in the same direction. And so it went. When the calendar had all such lines in all the boxes, it was the next June. Then Caesar, in that January 1 box, made a line that formed an X with the first line. And so it was for another year. The third year saw horizontal marks that sliced the boxes in half. The fourth year had vertical lines down the centers of the boxes.

This was the only calendar Caesar had in Lorton. That very first Monday, he taped the calendar over the area where the pictures of Pancho's children had been. There was still a good deal of empty space left, but he didn't do anything about it, and Rainey knew he couldn't do anything, either.

The calendar did right by Caesar until near the end of his fifth year in Lorton, when he began to feel that its juice was drying up. But he kept it there to mark off the days, and, too, the naked woman never closed her legs to him.

In that fifth year, someone murdered Multrey as he showered. The killers—it had to be more than one for a man like Multrey—were never found. The Multrey woman who picked at her food had felt herself caring for a recent arrival who was five years younger than her, a part-time deacon who had killed a Southwest bartender for calling the deacon's wife "a woman without one fuckin brain cell." The story of that killing—the bartender was dropped headfirst from the roof of a ten-story building—became legend, and in Lorton men referred to the dead bartender as "the Flat-Head Insulter" and the killer became known as "the Righteous Desulter." The Desulter, wanting Multrey's lady, had hired people to butcher him. It had always been the duty of the lady who hated food to watch out for Multrey as he showered, but she had stepped away that day, just as she had been instructed to by the Desulter.

In another time, Cathedral and Caesar would have had enough of everything—from muscle to influence—to demand that someone give up the killers, but the prison was filling up with younger men who did not care what those two had been once upon a time. Also, Cathedral had already had two visits from the man he had killed in Northwest. Each time, the man had first stood before the bars of Cathedral's cell. Then he held one of the bars and opened the door inward, like some wooden door on a person's house. The dead man standing there would have been sufficient to unwrap anyone, but matters were compounded when Cathedral saw a door that for years had slid sideways now open in an impossible fashion. The man stood silent before Cathedral, and when he left he shut the door gently, as if there were sleeping children in the cell. So Cathedral didn't have a full mind, and Multrey was never avenged.

There was an armed-robbery man in the place, a tattooer with homemade inks and needles. He made a good living painting on both muscled and frail bodies the names of children; the Devil in full regalia with a pitchfork dripping with blood; the words "Mother" or "Mother Forever" surrounded by red roses and angels who looked sad, because when it came to drawing happy angels the tattoo man had no skills. One pickpocket had had a picture of his father tattooed in the middle of his chest; above the father's head, in medieval lettering, were the words "Rotting in Hell," with the letter "H" done in fiery yellow and red. The tattoo guy had told Caesar that he had skin worthy of "a painter's best canvas," that he could give Caesar a tattoo "God would envy." Caesar had always told him no, but then he awoke one snowy night in March of his sixth year and realized that it was his mother's birthday. He did not know what day of the week it was, but the voice that

talked to him had the authority of a million loving mothers. He had long
ago forgotten his own birthday, had not even bothered to ask someone in
prison records to look it up.

There had never been anyone or anything he wanted commemo-
rated on his body. Maybe it would have been Carol, his first girlfriend
twenty years ago, before the retarded girl entered their lives. He had
played with the notion of having the name of the boy he thought was his
put over his heart, but the lie had come to light before that could happen. And before the boy there had been Yvonne, with whom he had lived
for an extraordinary time in Northeast. He would have put Yvonne's
name over his heart, but she went off to work one day and never came
back. He looked for her for three months, and then just assumed that
she had been killed somewhere and dumped in a place only animals
knew about. Yvonne was indeed dead, and she would be waiting for him
at the end of the line, though she did not know that was what she was
doing. "You can always trust unhappiness," Yvonne had once said, sitting in the dark on the couch, her cigarette burned down to the filter.
"His face never changes. But happiness is slick, can't be trusted. It has
a thousand faces, Caes, all of them just ready to re-form into unhappiness
once it has you in its clutches."

So Caesar had the words "Mother Forever" tattooed on his left bicep.
Knowing that more letters meant a higher payment of cigarettes or
money or candy, the tattoo fellow had dissuaded him from having just
plain "Mother." "How many hours you think she spent in labor?" he asked
Caesar. "Just to give you life." The job took five hours over two days,
during a snowstorm. Caesar said no to angels, knowing the man's ability
with happy ones, and had the words done in blue letters encased in red
roses. The man worked from the words printed on a piece of paper that
Caesar had given him, because he was also a bad speller.

The snow stopped on the third day and, strangely, it took only another three days for the two feet of mess to melt, for with the end of the
storm came a heat wave. The tattoo man, a good friend of the Righteous

Desulter, would tell Caesar in late April that what happened to him was his own fault, that he had not taken care of himself as he had been instructed to do. "And the heat ain't helped you neither." On the night of March 31, five days after the tattoo had been put on, Caesar woke in the night with a pounding in his left arm. He couldn't return to sleep so he sat on the edge of his bunk until morning, when he saw that the "e"s in "Mother Forever" had blistered, as if someone had taken a match to them.

He went to the tattoo man, who first told him not to worry, then patted the "e"s with peroxide that he warmed in a spoon with a match. Within two days, the "e"s seemed to just melt away, each dissolving into an ugly pile at the base of the tattoo. After a week, the diseased "e"s began spreading their work to the other letters, and Caesar couldn't move his arm without pain. He went to the infirmary. They gave him aspirin and Band-Aided the tattoo. He was back the next day, the day the doctor was there.

He spent four days in D.C. General Hospital, his first trip back to Washington since a court appearance more than three years before. His entire body was paralyzed for two days, and one nurse confided to him the day he left that he had been near death. In the end, after the infection had done its work, there was not much left of the tattoo except an "o" and an "r," which were so deformed they could never pass for English, and a few roses that looked more like red mud. When he returned to prison, the tattoo man offered to give back the cigarettes and the money, but Caesar never gave him an answer, leading the man to think that he should watch his back. What happened to Caesar's tattoo and to Caesar was bad advertising, and soon the fellow had no customers at all.

Something had died in the arm and the shoulder, and Caesar was never again able to raise the arm more than thirty-five degrees. He had no enemies, but still he told no one about his debilitation. For the next few months he tried to stay out of everyone's way, knowing that he was far more vulnerable than he had been before the tattoo. Alone in the cell, with no one watching across the way, he exercised the arm, but by November he knew at last he would not be the same again. He tried to bully Rainey Watson as much as he could to continue the facade that he was still who he had been. And he tried to spend more time with Cathedral.

But the man Cathedral had killed had become a far more constant visitor. The dead man, a young bachelor who had been Cathedral's next-door neighbor, never spoke. He just opened Cathedral's cell door inward and went about doing things as if the cell were a family home—straightening wall pictures that only Cathedral could see, turning down the gas on the stove, testing the shower water to make sure that it was not too hot, tucking children into bed. Cathedral watched silently.

Caesar went to Cathedral's cell one day in mid-December, six months before they freed him. He found his friend sitting on the bottom bunk, his hands clamped over his knees. He was still outside the cell when Cathedral said, "Caes, you tell me why God would be so stupid to create mosquitoes. I mean, what good are the damn things? What's their function?" Caesar laughed, thinking it was a joke, and he had started to offer something when Cathedral looked over at him with a devastatingly serious gaze and said, "What we need is a new God. Somebody who knows what the fuck he's doing." Cathedral was not smiling. He returned to staring at the wall across from him. "What's with creatin bats? I mean, yes, they eat insects, but why create those insects to begin with? You see what I mean? Creatin a problem and then havin to create somethin to take care of the problem. And then comin up with somethin for that second problem. Man oh man!" Caesar slowly began moving away from Cathedral's cell. He had seen this many times before. It could not be cured even by great love. It sometimes pulled down a loved one. "And roaches. Every human bein in the world would have the sense not to create roaches. What's their function, Caes? I tell you, we need a new God, and I'm ready to cast my vote right now. Roaches and rats and chinches. God was out of his fuckin mind that week. Six wasted days, cept for the human part and some of the animals. And then partyin on the seventh day like he done us a big favor. The nerve of that motherfucker. And all your pigeons and squirrels. Don't forget them. I mean really."

In late January, they took Cathedral somewhere and then brought him back after a week. He returned to his campaign for a new God in February. A ritual began that would continue until Caesar left: determine that Cathedral was a menace to himself, take him away, bring him back, then take him away when he started campaigning again for another God.

There was now nothing for Caesar to do except try to coast to the end on a reputation that was far less than it had been in his first years at Lorton. He could only hope that he had built up enough goodwill among men who had better reputations and arms that worked a hundred percent.

In early April, he received a large manila envelope from his attorney. The lawyer's letter was brief. "I did not tell them where you are," he wrote. "They may have learned from someone that I was your attorney. Take care." There were two separate letters in sealed envelopes from his brother and sister, each addressed to "My Brother Caesar." Dead people come back alive, Caesar thought many times before he finally read the letters, after almost a week. He expected an announcement about the death of his father, but he was hardly mentioned. Caesar's younger brother went on for five pages with a history of what had happened to the family since Caesar had left their lives. He ended by saying, "Maybe I should have been a better brother." There were three pictures as well, one of his brother and his bride on their wedding day, and one showing Caesar's sister, her husband, and their two children, a girl of four or so and a boy of about two. The third picture had the girl sitting on a couch beside the boy, who was in Caesar's father's lap, looking with interest off to the left, as if whatever was there were more important than having his picture taken. Caesar looked at the image of his father—a man on the verge of becoming old. His sister's letter had even less in it than the lawyer's: "Write to me, or call me collect, whatever is best for you, dear one. Call even if you are on the other side of the world. For every step you take to get to me, I will walk a mile toward you."

He had an enormous yearning at first, but after two weeks he tore everything up and threw it all away. He would be glad he had done this as he stumbled, hurt and confused, out of his sister's car less than half a year later. The girl and the boy would be in the backseat, the girl wearing a red dress and black shoes, and the boy in blue pants and a T-shirt with a cartoon figure on the front. The boy would have fallen asleep, but the girl would say, "Nighty-night, Uncle," which she had been calling him all that evening.

An ex-offenders' group, the Light at the End of the Tunnel, helped him to get a room and a job washing dishes and busing tables at a restaurant on F Street. The room was in a three-story building in the middle of the 900 block of N Street, Northwest, a building that, in the days when white people lived there, had had two apartments of eight rooms or so on each floor. Now the first-floor apartments were uninhabitable and had been padlocked for years. On the two other floors, each large apartment had been divided into five rented rooms, which went for twenty to thirty dollars a week, depending on the size and the view. Caesar's was small, twenty dollars, and had half the space of his cell at Lorton. The word that came to him for the butchered, once luxurious apartments was "warren." The roomers in each of the cut-up apartments shared two bathrooms and one nice-sized kitchen, which was a pathetic place because of its dinginess and its fifty-watt bulb, and because many of the appliances were old or undependable or both. Caesar's narrow room was at the front, facing N Street. On his side of the hall were two other rooms, the one next to his housing a mother and her two children. He would not know until his third week there that along the other hall was Yvonne Miller.

There was one main entry door for each of the complexes. In the big room to the left of the door into Caesar's complex lived a man of sixty or so, a pajama-clad man who was never out of bed in all the time Caesar lived there. He *could* walk, but Caesar never saw him do it. A woman, who told Caesar one day that she was "a home health-care aide," was always in the man's room, cooking, cleaning, or watching television with him. His was the only room with its own kitchen setup in a small alcove—a stove, icebox, and sink. His door was always open, and he never seemed to sleep. A green safe, three feet high, squatted beside the bed. "I am a moneylender," the man said the second day Caesar was there. He had come in and walked past the room, and the man had told the aide to have "that young lion" come back. "I am Simon and I lend money," the man said as Caesar stood in the doorway. "I will be your best friend, but not for free. Tell your friends."

He worked as many hours as they would allow him at the restaurant, Chowing Down. The remainder of the time, he went to movies until the shows closed and then sat in Franklin Park, at 14th and K, in good weather and bad. He was there until sleep beckoned, sometimes as late as two in the morning. No one bothered him. He had killed two men, and the world, especially the bad part of it, sensed that and left him alone. He knew no one, and he wanted no one to know him. The friends he had had before Lorton seemed to have been swept off the face of the earth. On the penultimate day of his time at Lorton, he had awoken terrified and thought that if they gave him a choice he might well stay. He might find a life and a career at Lorton.

He had sex only with his right hand, and that was not very often. He began to believe, in his first days out of prison, that men and women were now speaking a new language, and that he would never learn it. His lack of confidence extended even to whores, and this was a man who had been with more women than he had fingers and toes. He began to think that a whore had the power to crush a man's soul. "What kinda language you speakin, honey? Talk English if you want some." He was thirty-seven when he got free.

He came in from the park at two forty-five one morning and went quickly by Simon's door, but the moneylender called him back. Caesar stood in the doorway. He had been in the warren for less than two months. The aide was cooking, standing with her back to Caesar in a crisp green uniform and sensible black shoes. She was stirring first one pot on the stove and then another. People on the color television were laughing.

"Been out on the town, I see," Simon began. "Hope you got enough poontang to last you till next time." "I gotta be goin," Caesar said. He had begun to think that he might be able to kill the man and find a way to get into the safe. The question was whether he should kill the aide as well. "Don't blow off your friends that way," Simon said. Then, for some reason, he started telling Caesar about their neighbors in that complex. That was how Caesar first learned about an "Yvonny," whom he had yet to see. He would not know that she was the Yvonne he had known long ago until the second time he passed her in the hall. "Now, our sweet Yvonny, she ain't nothin but an old girl." Old girls were whores, young or old, who had been battered so much by the world that they had only the faintest wisp of life left; not many of them had hearts of gold. "But you could probably have her for free," Simon said, and he pointed to Caesar's right, where Yvonne's room was. There was always a small lump under the covers beside Simon in the bed, and Caesar suspected that it was a gun. That was a problem, but he might be able to leap to the bed and kill the man with one blow of a club before he could pull it out. What would the aide do? "I've had her myself," Simon said, "so I can only recommend it in a pinch." "Later, man," Caesar said, and he stepped away. The usual way to his room was to the right as soon as he entered the main door, but that morning he walked straight ahead and within a few feet was passing Yvonne's door. It was slightly ajar, and he heard music from a radio. The aide might even be willing to help him rob the moneylender if he could talk to her alone beforehand. He might not know the language men and women were speaking now, but the language of money had not changed.

It was a cousin who told his brother where to find him. That cousin, Nora Maywell, was the manager of a nearby bank, at 12th and F Streets, and she first saw Caesar as he bused tables at Chowing Down, where she had gone with colleagues for lunch. She came in day after day to make certain that he was indeed Caesar, for she had not seen him in more than twenty years. But there was no mistaking the man, who looked like her uncle. Caesar was five years older than Nora. She had gone through much of her childhood hoping that she would grow up to marry him. Had he paid much attention to her in all those years before he disappeared, he still would not have recognized her—she was older, to be sure, but life had been extraordinarily kind to Nora and she was now a queen compared with the dirt-poor peasant she had once been.

Caesar's brother came in three weeks after Nora first saw him. The brother, Alonzo, ate alone, paid his bill, then went over to Caesar and smiled. "It's good to see you," he said. Caesar simply nodded and walked away with the tub of dirty dishes. The brother stood shaking for a few moments, then turned and made his unsteady way out the door. He was a corporate attorney, making nine times what his father, at fifty-seven, was making, and he came back for many days. On the eighth day, he went to Caesar, who was busing in a far corner of the restaurant. It was now early September and Caesar had been out of prison for three months and five days. "I will keep coming until you speak to me," the brother said. Caesar looked at him for a long time. The lunch hours were ending, so the manager would have no reason to shout at him. Only two days before, he had seen Yvonne in the hall for the second time. It had been afternoon and the dead lightbulb in the hall had been replaced since the first time he had passed her. He recognized her, but everything in her eyes and body told him that she did not know him. That would never change. And, because he knew who she was, he nodded to his brother and within minutes they were out the door and around the corner to the alley. Caesar lit a cigarette right away. The brother's gray suit had cost $1,865.98. Caesar's apron was filthy. It was his seventh cigarette of the afternoon. When it wasn't in his mouth, the cigarette was at his side, and as he raised it up and down to his mouth, inhaled, and flicked ashes, his hand never shook.

"Do you know how much I want to put my arms around you?" Alonzo said.

"I think we should put an end to all this shit right now so we can get on with our lives," Caesar said. "I don't wanna see you or anyone else in your family from now until the day I die. You should understand that, mister, so you can do somethin else with your time. You a customer, so I won't do what I would do to somebody who ain't a customer."

The brother said, "I'll admit to whatever I may have done to you. I will, Caesar. I will." In fact, his brother had never done anything to him, and neither had his sister. The war had always been between Caesar and their father, but Caesar, over time, had come to see his siblings as the father's allies. "But come to see me and Joanie, one time only, and if you don't want to see us again, then we'll accept that. I'll never come into your restaurant again."

There was still more of the cigarette, but Caesar looked at it and then dropped it to the ground and stepped on it. He looked at his cheap watch. Men in prison would have killed for what was left of that smoke. "I gotta be goin, mister."

"We are family, Caesar. If you don't want to see Joanie and me for your sake, for our sakes, then do it for Mama."

"My mama's dead, and she been dead for a lotta years." He walked toward the street.

"I know she's dead! I know she's dead! I just put flowers on her grave on Sunday. And on three Sundays before that. And five weeks before that. I know my mother's dead."

Caesar stopped. It was one thing for him to throw out a quick statement about a dead mother, as he had done many times over the years. A man could say the words so often that they became just another meaningless part of his makeup. The pain was no longer there as it had been those first times he had spoken them, when his mother was still new to her grave. The words were one thing, but a grave was a different matter, a different fact. The grave was out there, to be seen and touched, and a man, a son, could go to that spot of earth and remember all over again how much she had loved him, how she had stood in her apron in the doorway of a clean and beautiful home and welcomed him back from school. He could go to the grave and read her name and die a bit, because it would feel as if she had left him only last week.

Caesar turned around. "You and your people must leave me alone, Mister."

"Then we will," the brother said. "We will leave you alone. Come to one dinner. A Sunday dinner. Fried chicken. The works. Then we'll never bother you again. No one but Joanie and our families. No one else." Those last words were to assure Caesar that he would not have to see their father.

Caesar wanted another cigarette, but the meeting had already gone on long enough.

Yvonne had not said anything that second time, when he said "Hello." She had simply nodded and walked around him in the hall. The third time they were also passing in the hall, and he spoke again, and she stepped to the side to pass and then turned and asked if he had any smokes she could borrow.

He said he had some in his room, and she told him to go get them and pointed to her room.

Her room was a third larger than his. It had an icebox, a bed, a dresser with a mirror over it, a small table next to the bed, a chair just beside the door, and not much else. The bed made a T with the one window, which faced the windowless wall of the apartment building next door. The beautiful blue-and-yellow curtains at the window should have been somewhere else, in a place that could appreciate them.

He had no expectations. He wanted nothing. It was just good to see a person from a special time in his life, and it was even better that he had loved her once and she had loved him. He stood in the doorway with the cigarettes.

Dressed in a faded purple robe, she was looking in the icebox when he returned. She closed the icebox door and looked at him. He walked over, and she took the unopened pack of cigarettes from his outstretched hand. He stood there.

"Well, sit the fuck down before you make the place look poor." He sat in the chair by the door, and she sat on the bed and lit the first cigarette. She was sideways to him. It was only after the fifth drag on the cigarette that she spoke. "If you think you gonna get some pussy, you are sorely mistaken. I ain't givin out shit. Free can kill you."

"I don't want nothin."

"'I don't want nothin. I don't want nothin.'" She dropped ashes into an empty tomato-soup can on the table by the bed. "Mister, we all want somethin, and the sooner people like you stand up and stop the bullshit, then the world can start bein a better place. It's the bullshitters who keep the world from bein a better place." Together, they had rented a little house in Northeast and had been planning to have a child once they had been there two years. The night he came home and found her sitting in the dark and talking about never trusting happiness, they had been there a year and a half. Two months later, she was gone. For the next three months, as he looked for her, he stayed there and continued to make it the kind of place that a woman would want to come home to. "My own mother was the first bullshitter I knew," she continued.

"That's how I know it don't work. People should stand up and say, 'I wish you were dead,' or 'I want your pussy,' or 'I want all the money in your pocket.' When we stop lyin, the world will start bein heaven." He had been a thief and a robber and a drug pusher before he met her, and he went back to all that after the three months, not because he was heart-broken, though he was, but because it was such an easy thing to do. He was smart enough to know that he could not blame Yvonne, and he never did. The murders of Percy "Golden Boy" Weymouth and Antwoine Stoddard were still years away.

He stayed that day for more than an hour, until she told him that she had now paid for the cigarettes. Over the next two weeks, as he got closer to the dinner with his brother and sister, he would take her cigarettes and food and tell her from the start that they were free. He was never to know how she paid the rent. By the fourth day of bringing her things, she began to believe that he wanted nothing. He always sat in the chair by the door. Her words never changed, and it never mattered to him. The only thanks he got was the advice that the world should stop being a bullshitter.

On the day of the dinner, he found that the days of sitting with Yvonne had given him a strength he had not had when he had said yes to his brother. He had Alonzo pick him up in front of Chowing Down, because he felt that if they knew where he lived they would find a way to stay in his life.

At his sister's house, just off 16th Street, Northwest, in an area of well-to-do black people some called the Gold Coast, they welcomed him, Joanie keeping her arms around him for more than a minute, crying. Then they offered him a glass of wine. He had not touched alcohol since before prison. They sat him on a dark green couch in the living room, which was the size of ten prison cells. Before he had taken three sips of the wine, he felt good enough not to care that the girl and the boy, his sister's children, wanted to be in his lap. They were the first children he had been around in more than ten years. The girl had been calling him Uncle since he entered the house.

Throughout dinner, which was served by his sister's maid, and during the rest of the evening, he said as little as possible to the adults—his sister and brother and their spouses—but concentrated on the kids, because he thought he knew their hearts. The grown-ups did not pepper him with questions and were just grateful that he was there. Toward the end of the meal, he had a fourth glass of wine, and that was when he told his niece that she looked like his mother and the girl blushed, because she knew how beautiful her grandmother had been.

At the end, as Caesar stood in the doorway preparing to leave, his brother said that he had made this a wonderful year. His brother's eyes teared up and he wanted to hug Caesar, but Caesar, without smiling, simply extended his hand. The last thing his brother said to him was, "Even if you go away not wanting to see us again, know that Daddy loves you. It is the one giant truth in the world. He's a different man, Caesar. I think he loves you more than us because he never knew what happened to you. That may be why he never remarried." The issue of what Caesar had been doing for twenty-one years never came up.

His sister, with her children in the backseat, drove him home. In front of his building, he and Joanie said good-bye, and she kissed his cheek and, as an afterthought, he, a new uncle and with the wine saying, *Now, that wasn't so bad,* reached back to give a playful tug on the children's feet, but the sleeping boy was too far away and the girl, laughing, wiggled out of his reach. He said to his niece, "Good night, young lady," and she said no, that she was not a lady but a little girl. Again, he reached unsuccessfully for her feet. When he turned back, his sister had a look of such horror and disgust that he felt he had been stabbed. He knew right away what she was thinking, that he was out to cop a feel on a child. He managed a good-bye and got out of the car. "Call me," she said before he closed the car door, but the words lacked the feeling of all the previous ones of the evening. He said nothing. Had he spoken the wrong language, as well as done the wrong thing? Did child molesters call little girls "ladies"? He knew he would never call his sister. Yes, he had been right to tear up the pictures and letters when he was in Lorton.

He shut his eyes until the car was no more. He felt a pained rumbling throughout his system and, without thinking, he staggered away from his building toward 10th Street. He could hear music coming from an apartment on his side of N Street. He had taught his sister how to ride a bike, how to get over her fear of falling and hurting herself. Now, in her eyes, he was no more than an animal capable of hurting a child. They killed men in prison for being that kind of monster. Whatever avuncular love for the children had begun growing in just those few hours now seeped away. He leaned over into the grass at the side of the apartment building and vomited. He wiped his mouth with the back of his hand. "I'll fall, Caesar," his sister had said in her first weeks of learning how to ride a bicycle. "Why would I let that happen?"

He ignored the aide when she told him that the moneylender wanted to talk to him. He went straight ahead, toward Yvonne's room, though he had no intention of seeing her. Her door was open enough for him to see a good part of the room, but he simply turned toward his own room. His shadow, cast by her light behind him, was thin and went along the floor and up the wall, and it was seeing the shadow that made him turn around. After noting that the bathroom next to her room was empty, he called softly to her from the doorway and then called three times more before he gave the door a gentle push with his finger. The door had not opened all the way when he saw her half on the bed and half off. Drunk, he thought. He went to her, intending to put her full on the bed. But death can twist the body in a way life never does, and that was what it had done to hers. He knew death. Her face was pressed into the bed, at a crooked angle that would have been uncomfortable for any living person. One leg was bunched under her, and the other was extended behind her, but both seemed not part of her body, awkwardly on their own, as if someone could just pick them up and walk away.

He whispered her name. He sat down beside her, ignoring the vomit that spilled out of her mouth and over the side of the bed. He moved her head so that it rested on one side. He thought at first that someone had done this to her, but he saw money on the dresser and felt the quiet throughout the room that signaled the end of it all, and he knew that the victim and the perpetrator were one and the same. He screwed the top on the empty whiskey bottle near her extended leg.

He placed her body on the bed and covered her with a sheet and a blanket. Someone would find her in the morning. He stood at the door, preparing to turn out the light and leave, thinking this was how the world would find her. He had once known her as a clean woman who would not steal so much as a needle. A woman with a well-kept house. She had been loved. But that was not what they would see in the morning.

He set about putting a few things back in place, hanging up clothes that were lying over the chair and on the bed, straightening the lampshade, picking up newspapers and everything else on the floor. But when he was done, it did not seem enough.

He went to his room and tore up two shirts to make dust rags. He started in a corner at the foot of her bed, at a table where she kept her brush and comb and makeup and other lady things. When he had dusted the table and everything on it, he put an order to what was there, just as if she would be using them in the morning.

Then he began dusting and cleaning clockwise around the room, and by midnight he was not even half done and the shirts were dirty with all the work, and he went back to his room for two more. By three, he was cutting up his pants for rags. After he had cleaned and dusted the room, he put an order to it all, as he had done with the things on the table—the dishes and food in mouseproof canisters on the table beside the icebox, the two framed posters of mountains on the wall that were tilting to the left, the five photographs of unknown children on the bureau. When that work was done, he took a pail and a mop from her closet. Mice had made a bed in the mop, and he had to brush them off and away. He filled the pail with water from the bathroom and soap powder from under the table beside the icebox. After the floor had been mopped, he stood in the doorway as it dried and listened to the mice in the walls, listened to them scurrying in the closet.

At about four, the room was done and Yvonne lay covered in her unmade bed. He went to the door, ready to leave, and was once more unable to move. The whole world was silent except the mice in the walls.

He knelt at the bed and touched Yvonne's shoulder. On a Tuesday morning, a school day, he had come upon his father kneeling at his bed, Caesar's mother growing cold in that bed. His father was crying, and when Caesar went to him his father crushed Caesar to him and took the boy's breath away. It was Caesar's brother who had said they should call someone, but their father said, "No, no, just one minute more, just one more minute," as if in that next minute God would reconsider and send his wife back. And Caesar had said, "Yes, just one minute more." *The one giant truth . . .* , his brother had said.

Caesar changed the bedclothing and undressed Yvonne. He got one of her large pots and filled it with warm water from the bathroom and poured into the water cologne of his own that he never used and bath-oil beads he found in a battered container in a corner beside her dresser. The beads refused to dissolve, and he had to crush them in his hands. He bathed her, cleaned out her mouth. He got a green dress from the closet, and underwear and stockings from the dresser, put them on her, and pinned a rusty cameo on the dress over her heart. He combed and brushed her hair, put barrettes in it after he sweetened it with the rest of the cologne, and laid her head in the center of the pillow now covered with one of his clean cases. He gave her no shoes and he did not cover her up, just left her on top of the made-up bed. The room with the dead woman was as clean and as beautiful as Caesar could manage at that time in his life. It was after six in the morning, and the world was lighting up and the birds had begun to chirp. Caesar shut off the ceiling light and turned out the lamp, held on to the chain switch as he listened to the beginnings of a new day.

He opened the window that he had cleaned hours before, and right away a breeze came through. He put a hand to the wind, enjoying the coolness, and one thing came to him: he was not a young man anymore.

He sat on his bed smoking one cigarette after another. Before finding Yvonne dead, he had thought he would go and live in Baltimore and hook up with a vicious crew he had known a long time ago. Wasn't that what child molesters did? Now, the only thing he knew about the rest of his life was that he did not want to wash dishes and bus tables anymore. At about nine-thirty, he put just about all he owned and the two bags of trash from Yvonne's room in the bin in the kitchen. He knocked at the door of the woman in the room next to his. Her son opened the door, and Caesar asked for his mother. He gave her the hundred and forty-seven dollars he had found in Yvonne's room, along with his radio and tiny black-and-white television. He told her to look in on Yvonne before long and then said he would see her later, which was perhaps the softest lie of his adult life.

On his way out of the warren of rooms, Simon called to him. "You comin back soon, young lion?" he asked. Caesar nodded. "Well, why don't you bring me back a bottle of rum? Woke up with a taste for it this mornin." Caesar nodded. "Was that you in there with Yvonny last night?" Simon said as he got the money from atop the safe beside his bed. "Quite a party, huh?" Caesar said nothing. Simon gave the money to the aide, and she handed Caesar ten dollars and a quarter. "Right down to the penny," Simon said. "Give you a tip when you get back." "I won't be long," Caesar said. Simon must have realized that was a lie, because before Caesar went out the door he said, in as sweet a voice as he was capable of, "I'll be waitin."

He came out into the day. He did not know what he was going to do, aside from finding some legit way to pay for Yvonne's funeral. The D.C. government people would take her away, but he knew where he could find and claim her before they put her in potter's field. He put the bills in his pocket and looked down at the quarter in the palm of his hand. It was a rather old one, 1967, but shiny enough. Life had been kind to it. He went carefully down the steps in front of the building and stood on the sidewalk. The world was going about its business, and it came to him, as it might to a man who had been momentarily knocked senseless after a punch to the face, that he was of that world. To the left was 9th Street and all the rest of N Street, Immaculate Conception Catholic Church at 8th, the bank at the corner of 7th. He flipped the coin. To his right was 10th Street, and down 10th were stores and the house where Abraham Lincoln had died and all the white people's precious monuments. Up 10th and a block to 11th and Q Streets was once a High's store where, when Caesar was a boy, a pint of cherry-vanilla ice cream cost twenty-five cents, and farther down 10th was French Street, with a two-story house with his mother's doilies and a foot-long porcelain black puppy just inside the front door. A puppy his mother had bought for his father in the third year of their marriage. A puppy that for thirty-five years had been patiently waiting each working day for Caesar's father to return from work. *The one giant truth . . . Just one minute more.* He caught the quarter and slapped it on the back of his hand. He had already decided that George Washington's profile would mean going toward 10th Street, and that was what he did once he uncovered the coin.

At the corner of 10th and N, he stopped and considered the quarter again. Down 10th was Lincoln's death house. Up 10th was the house where he had been a boy, and where the puppy was waiting for his father. A girl at the corner was messing with her bicycle, putting playing cards in the spokes, checking the tires. She watched Caesar as he flipped the quarter. He missed it and the coin fell to the ground, and he decided that that one would not count. The girl had once seen her aunt juggle six coins, first warming up with the flip of a single one and advancing to the juggling of three before finishing with six. It had been quite a show. The aunt had shown the six pieces to the girl—they had all been old and heavy one-dollar silver coins, huge monster things, which nobody made anymore. The girl thought she might now see a reprise of that event. Caesar flipped the quarter. The girl's heart paused. The man's heart paused. The coin reached its apex and then it fell.

ALL AUNT HAGAR'S CHILDREN

On what was to have been one of my last days in Washington, my mother, my aunt, and murdered Ike's mother came up to the second-floor office I had been sharing with Samuel Jaffe. This was three weeks after Sam had gone to Israel, and a little more than nine months since I'd left the Korean War. When the big front door downstairs opened and shut, it shook the windows of our building on F Street, and as the three women came in I watched the giant window in our office do a quick, awful shaking, then slowly come to rest. I heard the three coming up the stairs and learned seconds later that it was murdered Ike's mother who was wearing those heavy black old-lady shoes, which made the loudest sound as the women clumped their way up to me. This was two months since I'd told Sheila Larkin as kindly as I could that she and I were finished. *"So, you have your way with this woman and now you tellin her to just disappear?"* The three women were all the while talking, talking as easily as if they were sitting around over coffee and sweet rolls in one of their living rooms, the way they had no doubt been doing since before I was even a consideration in my mother's eye. Then they were standing in my doorway, the three of them. I turned from the giant window showing me a beautiful day on F Street and faced them. I put down the box I was holding and brushed myself off; a man like me does not greet the woman who brought him into the world while holding a box of dusty belongings from an undistinguished life. This was a little more than a month since the white woman had died right in front of my eyes. *"No, Sheila baby, that ain't what I'm sayin at all."*

"Talked to Freddy, and he told me say hi," my mother said. My older brother was studying to be a lawyer. She offered her cheeks and I kissed them, her face wrinkle-free. "I'm guiltless," she once said to me. Her dark cheeks were lightly rouged. As a rule, my mother wasn't demonstrative. She lived in a sphere all her own, where few things could intrude and hurt her anymore. She always let Freddy and me in, but she kept her eye on the door while we visited, lest we say something wrong and she had to show us out. I got a letter from Freddy three weeks after I hit Korea: "You'd best return alive or Mama will never be the same. She can't stop crying." I spent many Korean months trying to reconcile the mother to beat all mothers of my childhood with the mother in Freddy's letters who was mourning me.

I touched my mother's elbow and stepped around her to Aunt Penny. I kissed her cheek. She and Uncle Al owned a grocery store at 5th and O Streets, N.W. As children, Freddy and I had all the sweets boys could want. "Love ya," Aunt Penny said. The three women were all wearing gloves on that warm day; theirs may have been the last generation of Negro women to go about the world in such a way. "Here, Aggie," my aunt said, turning to Miss Agatha. I hugged Miss Agatha. I hadn't seen her for months, though we had talked soon after I returned from Korea, when I made the obligatory visits in my uniform to family and friends: a Negro had gone off to the man's war and survived to tell about it to all who had prayed for him. Miss Agatha's only child had been murdered while I was in Korea, and Freddy had sent me the articles from the *Daily News*. Ike Appleton had always gone for bad. He beat me bloody when I was in junior high school, and Freddy found him and whipped him just as bad, and after that I never had any trouble from Ike. The articles had a picture of Ike in his high-school-graduation cap.

Miss Agatha's face had enough lines for all three women—someone had come up behind Ike as he sat over supper and blown his brains out.

"You look well," Miss Agatha said. "Maybe workin downtown mongst white folks grees with you." When I was eight, I went to some boy's birthday party and spent days telling Freddy about the good time I'd had and about all the boss gifts the boy had received. On the third day of all that talking, my mother, unsmiling, said to me, "Remember, every happy birthday boy is headed for his grave."

I asked Miss Agatha, "How you been?"

"Fine. In my way."

My mother came around me. I knew she had been behind me, taking the measure of me and the room, finding something she could use against me. She took off her gloves, slowly, one long finger after another. "She's here to ask for your help," my mother said. "Aggie thinks you know things. It ain't for me to tell her different." I looked at her. "She thinks her way." Any day now, I was due to go off to Alaska to hunt for gold with a war buddy. ("I didn't think white people let Negroes into white Alaska," my mother said when I mentioned my plans.) The "favor" thing sounded like a big obstacle between me and gold and cars and clothes and more women than I could shake a dick at, as my buddy had put it. I was ready for a new place; I was a veteran of Washington, D.C., and there was nothing else for me to discover here. And I wanted to get far away, because I thought it might help me to stop thinking about that dead white woman. *"A moll is gav vain ah rav und ah rabbit sin,"* the woman had said as she was dying. The night before, I dreamed I had been able to save her. She had gotten up off the streetcar tracks and walked away. "A favor. We don't ask for much," my mother was saying.

That could be true about women. Even Sheila Larkin had said it that last time, when I told her we were finished: "God knows I don't ask for much from you, man." Maybe in Alaska I could learn something new about women and become a different kind of veteran. My mother opened her pocketbook and dropped her gloves into it and, while looking at me, one of her two living children, snapped it shut. That sound was all the room had.

"They killed my Ike," Miss Agatha said, as if I needed to be reminded. He was one of only sixty-six people murdered in D.C. that first year I was away. "Near bout two years gone by, and they ain't done any more than the day it happened."

"If they are doin somethin, they keepin it secret," Aunt Penny said. "One more colored boy outa their hair. It's a shame before God, the way they do all Aunt Hagar's children."

"Penny," my mother said, "don't get worked up now." My mother was the youngest of them, Miss Agatha the oldest by at least five years. When the three were girls in Alabama, a white man had set out after Miss Agatha as they walked home from school. The man tried to drag her into the woods and have his way with her. My mother and my aunt picked up rocks and beat the man down to the ground until he was no more than an unconscious lump. In the woods, when it was done, the girls held each other and cried, half out of their minds, afraid of what the world was going to do to them. They were barefoot. The man lay in the woods for three days, covered with tree bark and leaves, half in life, half in death. He was not a rich man, but he was white. So when the law discovered him, dead or alive, it would do everything to find out what had happened to him.

I got a chair for Miss Agatha. Once seated, she pulled out her hatpins and took off her hat, a modest thing with a veil pulled back over it, black like her dress and black like her old-lady shoes with Cuban heels. A woman's boy child deserved more than one year of mourning.

"I have waited and I done called the police," Miss Agatha said. "I just wanna know who hurt my boy so I can put my mind to rest. I'll leave the punishin up to God. But I must know. I even talked to a colored policeman at Number 2. You'd think a colored policeman would help me."

"Trust what they do, Aggie, not the color of their skin, is what I say," Aunt Penny said. "You put a Negro workin round white folks and he starts forgettin."

"Miss Agatha, I'm no detective," I said, looking first at her and then at my mother. I had been in the military police in Korea, doing nothing. Lording it over some Southern cracker for a bit. Helping drunks back to their tents and thinking myself blessed if I didn't get puked on. But murder was a dance on the more complicated side of life. And I, a veteran hearing Alaska singing, didn't want to ask any big questions and didn't want anybody asking me any big questions. I was twenty-four and just starting to dance away on the easy side—a little soft-shoe here, a little soft-shoe there.

"You know a lot more than them fools at Number 2," Aunt Penny said. Working in Sam Jaffe's office, I wanted to say, wasn't the same as finding a killer. Sam, a lawyer, did some private detective work, and I sometimes went along with him when I wasn't filing. But mostly I just filed. A veteran doing ABCs.

"You the only thing close to the law we got," my mother said. "Talk to Aggie. Listen to what she got to say. You know her. She was there when I birthed you."

"Whatever you can do would be good," Miss Agatha said. "It all just worries the heart so much. It worries the mind. I can't sleep at night. A few crumbs of why would be better than what I'm gnawin on now." She took off one glove and put her hand over mine. Flesh must meet flesh, my mother had taught her sons. Never shake hands with your glove on. Miss Agatha's husband had died of a stroke four years ago. She was wearing her wedding ring, and it was shiny and unmarred.

"He'll help us, Aggie. Don't worry bout that," Aunt Penny said, putting both hands on Miss Agatha's shoulders. "They gonna pay, whoever did it." Since Sam had left for Israel on business, I'd been leaning back in my chair facing that giant window onto F Street and imagining returning to Washington with Alaska gold. I saw myself walking down M Street, strutting about New York Avenue, my pockets bulging with nuggets, big pockets, big as some boy's pockets fat with candy—your Mary Janes, your Squirrel Nuts, your fireballs.

I t was my mother who came up with the idea of the three of them leaving Alabama. It was late evening of the day she and my aunt had beaten the white man. He still lay in the woods, alone except for what animals came, sniffed, and walked over him. All the Negroes who had any business knowing knew what had happened, but not a white soul knew. At first, the Negroes understood, the law would be thinking the culprit was a stranger from someplace else; it was a nice world the law and its people thought they had in Choctaw, Alabama, and coloreds in that place didn't do bad things to white people, whom the law was built to protect.

The families of the three girls were sitting and standing around the parlor in Miss Agatha's house. She was in her father's arms on the settee. The youngest children were being fed in the kitchen. My grandfather, arms crossed and leaning in the doorway, said that the men in that room should go out and kill the white man if he wasn't dead already. "Finish him for good," he said. "I'll kill him with my own hands and be done with it."

No one said anything for some time. One boogeyman erased forever from a child's life was tempting, and in the quiet their hearts reached for it. But everyone in that room feared God and wanted one day to sit in the aura of his majesty. And they wanted to be able to sit there in the happy company of my grandfather. That could not happen if he came before God with murder on his hands.

"Morris, we won't have no talk of that," my grandfather's mother said eventually. She was sitting at the back of the room in a cane-bottomed chair, leaning over because she breathed best that way. She was not fifty years out of slavery. She was five years from death. She had seen death following her for more than three years. *"Do it or leave me be."*

"Then what kinda talk is we gonna have, Mama?"

"Not none of my son goin out and killin somebody in cold blood." My grandfather's mother raised her head and looked at her son. Her walking stick, with a series of snakes carved into it, was across her lap. Someone had sent for the preacher, but he hadn't arrived. He was a drinking man and Sunday was the only day he could be counted on. Miss Agatha had been attacked on a Wednesday.

My grandfather smiled. "In hot blood, then, Mama. I'll kill him in hot blood."

"Do nothin, Morris," my grandfather's mother said. "You can't kill in Aggie's name. What would become of her? Ask yoself that, son. What would become of Aggie? What would become of your own chirren if you had your way with him? What would come of Penny and Bertha if you killed that man?"

A*moll is gav vain ah rev und ah rab-bit sin,"* I said as I listened to the three women go back down the stairs. I watched them walk the few steps to 8th Street and turn the corner, heading to Kann's Department Store. It was the Sabbath, so Sam's wife, Dvera, was not upstairs in the back office. She and I rarely spoke, and I had never been up to the third floor. She made me nervous, moving about in her silence with those fat ankles.

I called my brother, whom Sam had encouraged to become a lawyer. He might know where I should start to look for a murderer. His wife, Joanne, told me he was out. Joanne was pregnant. A root worker had had Joanne throw ten hairpins up in the air and have them fall on one of Joanne's head scarves. Examining the pattern of the fallen pins, the root worker predicted that Joanne would be having twin girls. The news excited my mother like nothing else I'd seen. I didn't care. I was not a man to suffer the company of children. Joanne said, "I'll have Freddy get in touch." "No," I said. "I guess it can wait." Lying naked in her bed beside me, Sheila Larkin had said two months ago, "I'll wait for you until you return from Alaska, man. I'll wait."

At about four, I closed the office and drove to Mojo's in my Ford, the only meaningful thing I had bought with my army money, taking the route I thought would best help me to avoid Sheila Larkin. I had been very successful in avoiding Sheila since I'd broken up with her. I knew how vicious she could be. I did not want to go to Alaska with a face scarred by lye. At Mojo's, on North Capitol just up from New York Avenue, Mojo's wife, Harriet, told me he was away. I had a few sips of beer at the bar, and when Mary Saunders and Blondelle Steadman came in, I followed them to a booth. They had been in my brother's class at Dunbar High School. I once thought I loved Mary.

"What you out and about for on a nice Saturday, soldier man?" Mary said. She had come from Jamaica when she was about twelve and Jamaica was still there when she talked. "Hear Alaska was calling you. You done had all our women and now you want theirs." They were sharing a cherry Coke.

"Still going, but I have to do a few things fore I leave. Yall member Ike?" Blondelle nodded, and Mary drank some Coke. "Miss Agatha want me to find out who did it."

They laughed. It went on for a good minute. They had been together for many years, so that now one woman sounded like the other. Blondelle called to Harriet behind the bar. "Heard the latest? Soldier man's now a detective man. Like in the picture show." Harriet held a glass up to the light to see how clean she had gotten it. "Next he'll be a rocket-ship man, heh?" There were four women drinking milk shakes at the bar.

"The problem you have is everybody in the world hated Ike," Mary said. "Except his mother and his wife. They had to like him, had to love him." When I was a sophomore at Dunbar, and Mary was a senior, my brother told me I had nothing to lose by asking her out. "But after them two," she said, "what you should do is close your eyes and put your finger on a list of names. Whichever one you pick, thas who did it." I followed Mary from school one day in April. She was walking with Blondelle, who wouldn't peel off so I could be alone with Mary and ask her out. In the end, I just went up to Mary and asked to speak to her private-like. When I was done, she went over to Blondelle and said, "Would you mind if he and I went out?" "I would indeed," said Blondelle, who didn't seem mad, didn't sound upset. My brother kept a lot about the world from me. "If I had told you," he said to me later, "it wouldn't be the same as finding out yourself."

"Miss Agatha's in pain," I said.

"We love Miss Aggie," Blondelle said. "So we wish we could help, but we have nothin." She wore glasses, and it struck me for the first time ever that she was pretty. How had I missed that? The April day that Mary told me no, she took my hand and held it long enough for me to know that there should be no hard feelings. Blondelle walked away. Mary kissed my mouth. There was a pleasant smell I came to associate with all colored women. If a man is to be rejected by a woman, he should be rejected by a woman like Mary, for then he might not be bitter about women. Blondelle was saying, "You know what a devil Ike could be. You could accuse anybody in Washington." She sighed. "You have a high mountain to climb. And even if you do find the person, you gotta go back down that mountain and tell it to Miss Aggie." She drank. "You been to where they killed him?"

"What?"

"Where he was killed? He lived downstairs from Miss Aggie. The second-floor place."

"I ain't been there."

"They didn't teach you that in detective school?" Mary said. Blondelle killed the Coke. "They never taught you to visit the scene of the crime? You should use some a that mother wit you was born with."

Blondelle said to Mary, "Oh, you know the private-dick people don't like using mother wit. That would be too much like right."

I blinked and then blinked again. The white woman, lying across the streetcar tracks in the middle of New Jersey Avenue, was the first woman I had ever seen die. I never saw one woman die in Korea. Not one. *Zetcha kender lock gadank za tira vos ear lair rent doe.*

It was near on seven o'clock when I got to Mr. and Mrs. Fleming's house on 6th Street, where I was renting a room. It was late September, and though there was some sun left, I didn't want to visit a dead man's place with night coming on. In Korea I had got used to dead men everywhere, but that was different from one dead man on a street where I had grown up. I had played with that dead man when he wasn't either of those things. I had been a happy boy on M Street.

I took a nap, and as soon as I stepped through the dream door the dead white woman was waiting for me. She was alive again. She had a child on either side of her, and I kept thinking that those children would help me to save her, help me to keep her always alive.

I called Freddy on the Flemings' telephone when I woke, but he hadn't returned.

On Sunday, I cleaned my room and went to Ike's apartment, at 423 M Street. First I visited Miss Agatha on the third floor. She was glad to see me and I was glad for that. When I told her what I wanted to do, she gave me the key to her son's place below her. She herself hadn't seen the apartment since the night she and Alona, his wife, five months pregnant then, had found Ike. The landlord had had trouble renting the place even after it was cleaned up, Miss Agatha said, and no one had lived there since; colored people believed dead people should stay dead, but they also knew that dead people tended to follow their own minds.

Clinging to Miss Agatha's dress was her granddaughter, not quite two years old. "Hi," the kid kept saying to me. "Hi hi." I nodded to her and went downstairs.

I turned the key every which way, but the door refused to give, and I finally had to push my way in with such force that the place shook. I flicked on the light, though the sun coming through the bare windows should have been all a man needed. I looked at my watch and sighed. There was furniture, but I figured it was show furniture the landlord had put there to entice a possible tenant.

A cheap snapshot of Ike and Alona was taped to the icebox. In the picture, sepia, torn at one corner, Alona was smiling, but Ike, wherever they were, looked somber. Alona had a determined look. Perhaps she had been trying to get Ike to smile.

For some reason, there was only one chair at the table. At first, I thought this chair facing the window was the one Ike had been sitting in when the guy shot him in the back of the head. But with all the blood and stuff there must have been, this couldn't be the death chair.

In the bedroom there was a stripped-down double bed. At the head of the bed, on the left side, where a pillow would have been, I saw the faint brown ghost of blood. I knew that Ike wouldn't have moved from that kitchen table once he was hit, so it was blood from another event. In the bathroom there was a rather large bottle of Mercurochrome and three bottles of iodine in the medicine cabinet and, under the sink, a pasteboard box with bandages. There was also half a box of Kotex. I sighed again. I shook the pasteboard box and clumps of hair appeared from under the bandages. What could the landlord have been thinking, leaving all that shit there?

I returned to the kitchen. Whoever had cleaned it had done a good job. The apartment could have been rented if someone saw that room and didn't know its history. I stood in the middle of the kitchen and turned around and around, looking at everything as critically as I could for long seconds. I had no goddam idea what the hell I was doing.

Miss Agatha gave me sweet potato pie when I went back up. Alona was also at the table, holding the child. "Hi hi," the kid kept saying to me. The pie was good, but it wasn't reward enough for having to put up with that child.

"They say you're going to Alaska," Alona said once I was midway through the pie. I nodded. She had been one of the smartest students Dunbar had ever known, destined for things that I, with my average brain, could never imagine. "Hi hi," the child said. In her junior year Alona had fallen in, as my mother would have said, with Ike, and after that she was walking around on the plain old earth just like me and everybody else the Dunbar teachers never cooed over. Alona said, "I once read a *Life* magazine article about a man in Alaska who was seeking solitude. He made a place for himself that was eighty miles in any direction from other people. He lived there for twenty years."

"That ain't for me," I said. "I need bodies around." "Hi hi," the girl said. I waved to her. I was nearing the end of the pie. I wanted another piece and wondered if it would be worth it to put up with her.

Alona grinned. "You might try something like that when you get there. If the gold doesn't pan out, try it and write to me." There was something positive in the way she was talking, as if she had been to Alaska, looked around, and knew things would go good for me there.

"Alona's decided to go on to Howard, go to college," Miss Agatha said.

"Mama's always bragging on whatever I do."

"You deserve braggin on, child," Miss Agatha said. "You know how much I believe in you, honey." She said to me, "Alona's my future."

"Whatcha gonna be takin up?" I said, the way my mother would.

"I haven't decided," she said, and she looked a bit dreamy-like, like a man thinking about all the gold in his pockets. "I'll decide down the road. Won't I, sweetums? Won't I, sweetums?" She stood the child up on her lap and kissed her face until she collapsed in laughter. After a bit, the child got down from Alona's lap and scurried off to the living room. Alona stood up. "Have some more pie," she said. "It was as good as usual, Mama," and she put her arms around Miss Agatha and kissed her cheek and left.

"I don't know what I would do without her," Miss Agatha said. "Son, you find somethin down there?" She pointed her index finger down.

"I can't say, ma'am, cause I'm just startin out. But I plan to keep on it. Don't worry bout that."

"He was into some things I would never appreciate, I have to tell you." I nodded. "But towards the end I think he was tryin to get hisself together. Tryin to make things right with Alona, with the baby comin and all, you know. I'm sure it woulda been a new day for him." She swept a few crumbs from the table into her hand and then brushed them with the other hand into her empty coffee cup. Watching the crumbs fall, I wanted to do the very best I could for her. "You might hear some bad things bout Ike. I can't testify to that. People tend not to lie bout a dead man, so I can't testify to anything they say. All I can say is that even if he was the Devil hisself, he was still mine. I gave him life."

"Yes, ma'am." I got up and took my plate and fork to the sink, the way I had been taught. I ran hot water onto the plate. "I'd best get on, Miss Agatha, but I'll be back workin on things tomorrow."

"Maybe you shouldna been workin today, on the Lord's day. God might not appreciate it."

I went home to clean up before going to my mother's for Sunday supper. Every Sunday since I had finished high school and gone out on my own, my mother had made a big fried-chicken supper for herself, my brother, and me, usually with string beans, potatoes boiled with a bit of fatback, and corn bread with crackling. An apple or peach cobbler. Every other Sunday I got to choose the Kool-Aid, and I almost always picked grape. Freddy was a lime man. After Freddy married, his wife came, too, of course, so I got to enjoy my grape Kool-Aid only every third week.

Joanne was into orange Kool-Aid, which I hated. A punk flavor. God only knew what shit their twin girls would choose, but I had no plans to be around when those two started showing up and spoiling everything and putting my choice of Kool-Aid off to the fifth or sixth week. Gold could buy grape Kool-Aid every day of a man's life. My mother had never commanded that we be there each Sunday at six. It was simply in her sons' blood to know to show up. I suspect that if the Korean War had been fought as close as Maryland or Pennsylvania, my blood would have sent me to her every Sunday.

Afraid I would see Sheila Larkin, I took the long way—down 4th Street, then along New York Avenue to 6th Street. Afraid of lye in my face. I felt bad about her, but she wasn't in my future.

I sat on my bed in the upstairs back room and drank the last of some whiskey a friend had given me, listening to WOOK all the while. On Sundays WOOK was full of religious shit, and it always depressed the hell out of me. But I didn't change the station. *A moll is gav vain ah rav und ah rabbit sin.* I put some water in the empty bottle to get the last of the juice out of it. Then I took out the booklet on Alaska and turned to page six, the one with "little known facts about our northern neighbor." Alaska was not even a state. *Zetcha kender lock, gadank za tira vos ear lair rent doe.*

About a week before Sam Jaffe went to Israel, I was on the street-car headed down New Jersey Avenue to see a friend in Northeast when I decided to get off and visit Aunt Penny and her husband, on 3rd Street. My car was acting hincty, so I had put it in the Ridge Street garage. Three women preceded me off the streetcar at L Street. One of them was a white woman. The first two women went on across the street to the sidewalk, but just as I was about to step down from the streetcar the white woman turned and held her arm out to me. I thought she wanted to get back on the car. I stepped down and to the side to make way. She was less than three feet from me. She took two steps toward me and began to collapse, her arm still out to me.

I heard her say, *"A moll is gav vain ah rev und ah rabbit sin."*

I got to her before her head hit the ground.

She said, *"Zetcha kender lock, gadank za tira vos ear lair rent doe."*

Her head was covered with a gray woollen scarf, which was much too heavy for a warm day. I could see that beneath the scarf there was a wig. I thought, If we can keep her wig in place, just the way it was when she walked out her front door, everything will be fine. Her dark blue dress came down to her ankles. She was far too young for the old-lady black shoes she had on. I lowered her head to the ground, and just as I did, she closed her eyes. I looked around for someone to help, but no one came. I kept thinking, Where in the world is that streetcar conductor? Where the hell is that man? Isn't this his job? And then, seeing the stopped streetcar gleaming in the sun, I thought, Green and off-white are perfect colors for a streetcar. The woman struggled with each breath. I could see several colored women looking out the streetcar windows at me and the white woman.

I tilted her head back and tried to give her breath, the way the army had taught me. My mother had always told my brother and me that if she ever caught us kissing a white woman she would cut off our lips. "You ever try coolin soup with no lips? Try it and see. It won't work. That soup will never cool and you'll starve to death."

For a long time, I tried to help the woman, but I began to see that only the breath of God could help her. Would that white streetcar conductor show up and think that I was trying something untoward? Would he try to kill me for doing the right thing? *Try coolin that tomato soup yall love with no lips. Try it and see what it gets you boys.* Three of the colored women on the streetcar came to us and knelt down. One caressed the white woman's cheek. "It's all right, son," the colored woman said. I saw then that the white woman was dead. "You done your best. At least you walked with her all the rest a the way." In the end, I laid the white woman's head down on the ground, but a human head on metal tracks and concrete in the middle of a city street seemed so out of place that I put my hand under her head again. By and by, the dead woman let go of my other hand and one of the colored women soon put her own hand under her head where mine had been.

Another of the women took a new sweater with the tag still on it out of a Hecht's bag and put it under the white woman's head. I stood up. Traffic up and down New Jersey Avenue had stopped, and on any other day that would have been something to see. I went to the sidewalk and then I turned and went down L Street toward Northeast, which wasn't the way to my aunt's. Eventually, after a long time, I found my way to my mother's house. She fixed me something to eat, and though I didn't tell her about the white woman she saw how the hot food just went cold lying on the plate and said I should sleep at her place that night. I said I would go on home, but my mother said I would do no such thing.

I woke up Monday morning with the dead white woman speaking in my head. *A moll and a rabbit* . . . As I looked at my face in the mirror while I shaved, it came to me that I might not ever be able to get the voice out of my head. When my great-grandfather was a slave, a patroller who owned no slaves and little more than what he was wearing killed a slave who was coming back from seeing his wife on another plantation. The dead man had been my ancestor's best friend. My great-grandfather called himself by the dead man's name forever after that, and no one, not even his wife and seven children, could move him from it. I have that dead man's name. Way down in Choctaw, Alabama, there are two names on my great-grandfather's tombstone. Two dates of birth and two dates of death.

I didn't do much about finding Ike's murderer until the next Sunday. I spent some of that week getting stuff together at Sam's office. The rest of the time I just hung out at Mojo's. I didn't take Miss Agatha's advice about resting on the Lord's day and went out that Sunday morning after breakfast to do what I could. My Ford was acting up again, so I left it in front of the house. I went up 6th Street. There was a big crowd around Daddy Grace's church, but I didn't see anyone I knew. I turned onto M. Sheila Larkin slept very late on Sunday, so I wasn't afraid of meeting her.

I knocked at the front first-floor apartment in Miss Agatha's building. A woman opened the door, and as soon as she did a mynah bird in a giant cage behind her gave a wolf whistle, quite distinct and quite loud. It was about twelve o'clock; Sheila was stretching in her bed, wondering if today was the day she would get me. After I told the woman who I was and what I wanted, she opened the door wider to let me in. She was wearing a housecoat. She could have been thirty or forty. I was getting better at determining a woman's age, but I wasn't yet good enough to tell about her. She was good-looking, and she would be that way for a long while.

"Oh, yes! Oh, yes! Just like that!" the bird said.

The woman pointed to an easy chair for me to sit in, and sat across from me on a couch with cushions that had deep impressions. Somebody had sat on those things and the cushions had never got over it. She said her name was Minnie Parsons.

"I ain't sure what I can tell you," Miss Minnie said, crossing her legs. "I talked to some colored cop a day or so after it happened. He asked me questions, but he seemed more interested in Billie, there. 'How you make it talk?' he kept sayin. 'How you get him to say all that?' He didn't seem to care much about poor Ike."

"I'm only flesh and blood!" Billie said.

She said she knew Ike "only in passin," and as she crossed and re-crossed her legs, something told me that it wasn't true. "I knew Alona better. And Miss Agatha's like my own mother." Her apartment was well kept, pictures of children on the walls, pictures of adults in Sunday clothes on the mantelpiece. On the wall behind the couch there was just a cross, with Jesus' head hanging down, because he had given up the ghost. The obligatory cloth covered his privates. The nails through his hands and feet were painted red. No blood. "You at Number 2?" Miss Minnie said.

"No, ma'am." I told her I wasn't a detective and had just been in the military police in Korea.

"Don't treat me like I'm that old," she said. "Don't go yes-ma'aming me. I ain't old. You want somethin to drink?" I said no. "My husband was in the army," she said after a bit. "He was a cook. Still a good cook. Can't you tell?" She leaned to the side and slapped her thigh.

"Like that?" the bird asked.

I asked her if she had been home the night Ike was killed. She said that she had but that she heard nothing. She knew Miss Agatha had been out, maybe at church. She didn't know where Alona was. "Ain't no book that girl ain't read. . . . I heard Miss Agatha come in and go upstairs. It wasn't long before I heard both of them screamin. The whole buildin shook with them screamin."

"That a girl bird or a boy bird?" I asked.

She considered Billie for a while as it hopped down to the floor of the cage, stuck its head through the bars of the cage door, and looked to the left. *"I'm only flesh and blood! I'm only flesh and blood!"*

"I don't really know," Miss Minnie said. "Could be either. A woman once told me she could come and turn Billie upside down and inspect Billie's natural parts and then say one way or another, but I never sent for her. I suspect Billie's a girl."

"Oh."

"A woman knows when another woman's in her nest."

"There's more to come, somebitch!" Billie said.

Miss Minnie didn't react at all to the bad word, and I remembered my mother once saying that a woman comfortable around curse words would be comfortable around the Devil. I was ready to go. Miss Minnie said, as I stood up, "I will say that in my dealins with Ike he treated me with the utmost respect. Now, my husband . . . Hal didn't care for Ike too much. Billie liked him, though, cause she doesn't discriminate." She crossed her legs the other way again. "Would you like somethin to eat? Wouldn't be no trouble to heat up a little somethin."

"No, ma'am."

"Oh, yes! Oh, yes! Just like that!"

"What I done told you bout that ma'am stuff?"

"Your husband comin back soon?"

"Oh?" she said. "Whatcha mean by 'soon'?" She laughed. "He just went to the store for somethin for breakfast. But he always stays long enough to be out to butcher the pig and collect the eggs. He'll be gone a long time. He slow that way."

I left, went down to the corner of M and 4th, and stood there so I could see into Leon's store. The only man in it came out with a medium-sized paper bag and was walking on crutches. One of his legs had been cut off below the knee, while the other had been cut off above the knee. I watched him cross the street to my side and move past me so silently that if I hadn't seen him with my own eyes, I wouldn't have known he was there. No huffing and puffing, no rattling from the paper bag, no sound from the crutches hitting the sidewalk. Just a nothing spiriting on down the street. He looked mean and tough, but maybe that was just me trying to compensate for a fellow veteran who had lost so much. He said something to a little girl coming the other way and went into Miss Minnie's building. I got to the building and asked the little girl, who was holding an even smaller girl by the hand, if she knew the man.

"Everybody know Mr. Hal," the girl said.

I went through the files in my memory trying to recall if that was what Miss Minnie had called her husband. I couldn't remember at all. Billie, I knew, was the bird's name, because she had mentioned the thing many times. "Mr. Hal married to Miss Minnie, right?" I said to the girl.

The girls looked at each other and laughed. "Evbody know that," the smaller girl said. "How come you don't know that?"

"Forget him," the older girl said, and before the girls went off she twirled her index finger around and around an inch from her ear. "Yeah,"

she said. "Just forget him if he don't know that. I bet he don't even know
Mr. Hal ain't got no legs." "Forget him anyway," the smaller girl said.

I stood outside the building, trying to decide if I should give Hal a
pass on murdering Ike based on the crutches. I didn't have anybody else
to suspect right then, so I kept him in my mental suspect files. Miss
Agatha had let me keep the key to her son's place, but I decided against
going back up there, lest she hear me and I have to tell her I'd found out
nothing yet.

I felt as helpless as the day I first inspected Ike's apartment. Sheila
Larkin had her cup of coffee in her hand by now, was probably looking
out her N Street window, thinking about me. I left off detective work
and took the long way home.

Mojo's was closed on Sunday. It was just as well. My mother always knew if I'd had even a drop of something before showing
at her place for supper. Sometimes I gave a shit and sometimes I didn't
and would drink before going to her. "You been drinkin," she had stated
that last Sunday even before opening the door. That was all she talked
about the rest of the evening. Then she dredged up ancient history: A
month after I came back from Korea, I was still celebrating. One Tuesday I drank heavily at a friend's place, in the Augusta apartments at New
York and New Jersey Avenues, only two blocks up from where the white
woman would die. I made a mistake and told my buddy I could walk
home all right. I got out to the corner at about three in the morning and
dropped down on the sidewalk. Actually, I dropped more in the street
than on the sidewalk. In those days, most of D.C. was asleep at that time
of the night, so there wasn't any traffic to run over me. The street was
warm, and all that warmth told me to take a nap. *Man, just nap.*

Where the old lady came from at that time of the morning I'll never
know. But after she roused me I could see through all the alcohol that she was
dressed like she was going to church. At three in the morning on a weekday.

"Ain't you Bertha's baby boy? Ain't you Penny's nephew?" she asked after I managed to raise my head. *Nap on, boy, just nap on.* "You Bertha's boy?" Even in the feeble streetlights, I could see, up and through that glorious haze, that I had never seen that woman before in my life. "Ain't you Bertha's boy? Got a brother name Freddy that married Dolley and Pritchard's girl? You Bertha's boy what went to Korea? Ain't yall's pastor Reverend Dr. Miller over at Shiloh Baptist?"

Hearing the lady talking, my buddy came down and they got me back up to his place. The old lady disappeared, and I never saw her again. My mother bided her time. One Sunday, three months later, after I said something "mannish" at supper, she brought up the drunk scene for the first time, told me what I was wearing down to the color of my socks, told me about the "ratty furniture" in every room of my friend's apartment, told me how many empty bottles were on the kitchen table, about the half-naked woman on the couch. The drunken dog staggering from room to room. "Your life won't be nothin but a long Tuesday night of devilment—Tuesday night and all day Wednesday . . . Kissin Miss Hattie's hand with them drunken lips." She went on for some thirty minutes, her voice never rising above a conversational tone. When she was finished, she pointed at my brother and then at the potatoes, which meant he was to pass them over to me. It was an orange-Kool-Aid Sunday. Joanne never said a mumbling word.

When I showed at my mother's place on L Street at about four, Joanne and her big belly full of twins were there, my brother having dropped her off and gone to pick up something at the law library. We sat in the living room. I must say this: my mother never treated her living rooms like she was saving them for Jesus Christ to visit. No plastic slipcoverings and shit. "The key word in livin room is livin," she used to say, so wherever we were the living room was as comfortable for Freddy and me as our own room.

"Mama, is there anything you can tell me bout this Ike thing? Somethin Miss Agatha didn't tell me?" We were drinking grape Kool-Aid.

"I don't think I can, son. He was troubled. I was there when he was born, and Ike came into the world full of trouble, God rest his soul." Joanne was beside her on the couch, looking real satisfied with herself. "Son, you know all I know. You know he was into that . . . that mess." She pointed at the crook in her arm and made a needle with her finger. "I lived fifty years before I knew a colored person doin that. And it was somebody like a son to me." I perked up. My mother said, "What is the world coming to, Joanne? But he always yes-ma'amed and no-ma'amed me, I will give him that. And he wasn't no parrot, either, so he meant it when he said it. He was brought up right. His mama and daddy saw to that. But boys have a way of turnin into men, and then they sell their mother wit for thirty pieces of silver."

"Mama, you never told me Ike was doin that. Miss Agatha never told me, either."

"Son, how easy you think it is to tell anybody that your child has fallen far from the height you worked to put him on? How many people would I want to blab to bout your drinkin and foolishness? Not that people don't know already."

"But I'm tryin to find out who did that to her son and she didn't give me all the facts."

"Well, you got all the facts."

I went for more Kool-Aid and drank it at the kitchen window. She had raised my brother and me in Northwest, mainly around M Street, where Miss Agatha lived. Her new apartment was half a block past North Capitol Street, her first venture into Northeast. Slowly, place by place, my mother was trying to put herself midway between where I lived, on 6th Street, and where my brother and Joanne lived, in Anacostia. My brother saw Anacostia one day when he was nine—the hills, the Anacostia River, the indescribable pleasantness, the way the wind came up over the river as if straight from the cooling mouth of God—and he vowed then that he would live there when he became a man. I, too, saw the place that day, but all I remembered was the chickens running around. And the little white pig lounging under the shade tree.

I filled my glass again. Women. The evening of the day the white man attacked Miss Agatha, it was my mother who suggested that she, nearing eight, and my aunt, well past nine, and Miss Agatha, fourteen, go far away before the law came to get them. My grandfather and my grandmother, still in the doorway, thought it was the worst thing they had ever heard. But as the evening darkness came in and they lit the lamps and the candles and as the white man lay in the woods, they all knew the law would descend upon them. The law might even raise their dead and make them pay as well.

Along about midnight, after everyone had embraced them, the girls set out in two wagons, with my grandfather and his brother and Miss Agatha's father and his brothers. The men were armed. By late morning, the girls were near the Georgia border. By the morning of the next day, driven by other male relatives and friends, they were well through Georgia. It took a week for them to get into North Carolina, carried by new wagons and horses driven by other relatives and friends. The girls' belongings, what few there were, were always in the first wagon, and the girls, huddled together, were always in the second. All along the way, Miss Agatha cried to her companions that she was sorry for doing this to them. "Forgive me," she said. "It ain't nothin but a little bitty old thing," my mother kept saying. Within two weeks, after wearing out four pairs of wagons and three teams of horses, they were in Washington, at the home of my grandfather's cousin. He and his family were waiting. A week before, he had received a telegram: "Package arriving."

When I returned to the living room, my mother was saying, "Now, he"—and she pointed at me—"wasn't too much trouble comin out, but, oh, your husband was too much, Joanne. Two days. Two long days. I'm bound for Heaven cause I've had my hell right here in Washington, D.C. But I will say"—and she pointed to me again—"that he made up for that easy birth by havin his share a colic. And, when he slept, he slept kinda like this," and my mother leaned her head to the side with one eye open and one eye shut.

"I had to keep one eye on you," I said.

She didn't miss a beat: "I hope you still sleep that way, cause I ain't finished with you yet, boy. Just wait. Just you wait." Then to Joanne: "You see what war does? It makes a man lose all natural fear of his mother. Be thankful you havin girls."

I sat back in the chair with my Kool-Aid. They went on talking like that, my mother and my sister-in-law and her twin girls just dying to come out. There is a moment that a man hungers for when he's boozing—the conductor has already escorted him to the best seat on the train. This happens somewhere, depending on the alcohol, along about the fifth sip. The view from that window is extraordinary; God knew his business that day. A woman sits across from him and only when he looks out the window does she look away. Otherwise, her eyes are always on him. Her blouse is tight, and she shows just enough cleavage not to make herself out to be a tramp. He takes another sip, and emphatic waves of warmth come over him. The woman crosses her legs. She is not wearing old-lady stockings. Hers are sheer nylon, so the man can bear witness to the miracle of her legs. He raises his glass and tries to decide whether to look again at her legs or out the window at what God made just for him.

I went in to the office on Monday morning to continue clearing up. I was missing Sam, who had soothing words for every bad occasion. I worked away and all the while recited aloud the dead white woman's words.

A moll is gav vain ah rav und ah rab-bit sin.

Zetcha kender lock gadank za tire vos ear lair rent doe.

I was nearing completion of the "S" files when I felt someone watching me. I turned around. Sam's wife, Dvera, was standing in the doorway. She was crying. I stood and asked if it was bad news about Sam.

She took a while, but she eventually shook her head and covered her mouth with both hands. She continued to cry. I stayed near the window. This was all I needed before Alaska: a white woman crying and no witnesses to my innocence.

After several minutes, she pulled out a handkerchief that was tucked into her sleeve, and she stopped crying. "I'm sorry," she said. "It's been a long time since I heard those words." I didn't understand. I looked at the floor, but felt safe enough to put down the papers I was holding. "They were my father's words, his way of beginning stories to me. All his stories started that way. He used to tell me stories when the world got too much. Comforting, you know. Keeping the world away."

I nodded. This was more than she had ever said to me in all the time I had been working there. Sometimes one moment sweeps aside everything you ever thought about a person.

"Where did you hear those words?" she asked. I told her about the white woman. "I remember hearing about her, but I didn't know you were there." She looked long at me and said, "Let me see something." She turned with her fat ankles and went upstairs.

I wanted to leave now. Files or no files. The dead woman's words were loud in my head. Dvera Jaffe came back after about an hour. "Miriam Sobel," she said. "She was in my brother's congregation. For a week they didn't know what had happened to her. Young as she was, her mind had been going for a long time. She would disappear at times, trying to get back to Russia, back home."

Now that I had a name to go with my memory, her dying words were louder than ever. In my head, the woman Miriam Sobel rose up and stood in the streetcar tracks, just as she had before she began to fall, and set her wig in place.

The end of it all came rather quickly after that.

On Thursday, I went to Mojo's. I asked Mojo's wife who might have supplied Ike's stuff. Harriet had a quick answer—a man named Fish Eyes. "But he died two months ago. If you thinkin what I think you're thinkin, you could be right," she said. "Fish Eyes would kill God if He owed him money. He went back to Georgia, where he had people. God's cancer took a long time killin him."

By then I had talked to about fifteen people and I was tired of Ike and his murder. I wanted Alaska. I took a beer and sat in a booth and mumbled Miriam Sobel's last words. Not the mixed-up English ones I thought she had said but the Yiddish. *"Amohl iz gevayn a rov und a rebbetzin."* The English had died the moment Dvera told me the Yiddish. *"Zet zhe, kinderlach, gedenk-zhe, teireh, vos ir lert' doh."* After a second beer, I began fashioning a story that would let me go off to Alaska with as clear a conscience as a man like me could expect. I figured it wouldn't hurt anyone if I told Miss Agatha that it had probably been Fish Eyes who killed Ike. One bad man had killed another. That sounded good, and the first sip of the third beer confirmed it.

After four beers, I left Mojo's happy and headed down New York Avenue. I crossed 1st Street, passing Dunbar's field. I was nearing Kirby Street when Sheila Larkin and one of her many sisters came out of Kirby, heading toward me. They were only yards away. There was too much daylight for me to turn around and dash across New York Avenue. Damn! Damn! I kept thinking. The women walked on toward me, their arms linked, talking to each other as if their conversation were all that mattered. Well, I thought, we might as well get this shit over with right here and now. I hurried to compose what I would say: "I just felt like gettin on with somethin else in my life, Sheila. It ain't really about you. I just gotta disentangle before Alaska." If she tried to hit me, I decided, I would let her get in one lick, but no more than that. My time with her was worth one lick, I figured. Any more than one and it was going to be war. They were about five feet away, and Sheila still hadn't noticed me. We all kept on. Then, in a moment, she and her sister were past me. And it wasn't as if they had unlocked arms and walked around me, or stayed arm in arm and walked together around me to the left or the right. It was simply as if they had walked through me, still talking, still arm in arm. It was like a blow to the chest. It took my breath away, and I leaned over to pull myself together. That didn't help, and I stood up straight and found myself stumbling, struggling. I kept thinking it might help to know what their conversation was about.

I went on a few feet more, and at last I sat on the curb at Kirby. The world took its sweet time righting itself, and I began to wish that I was on my train and the conductor was asking me, "Sir, may I fill your glass again?" Forget all of them, I thought, forget Miss Agatha and Sheila and her billions of sisters and forget my mother and Joanne with her belly full of girls. Forget every bitch that ever lived. Forget em! Just go to Alaska, where a man could be a real man without any bullshit. I looked at my watch, at the second hand going round and round. I pulled out the crown a tad and the second hand stopped, just waited for me to start things up again. I told the conductor, "No." I saw Miss Agatha at her kitchen table brushing crumbs into her hand, and she said she was sorry. I told her it ain't nothin but a little bitty old thing.

I stood outside Miss Agatha's apartment door, resolved to tell her that it had been Fish Eyes. He was in Hell, anyway, so he wouldn't care—what's another twenty years in an eternity of fire? My mother would have had something to say about that, about lying on someone sitting in Hell on a two–legged stool with his ankles crossed, but I didn't care. I was about to knock when I decided to go back down to Ike's place. I planned to tell Miss Agatha that I had gone over the place four times, and two real visits would make it easier to lie.

This time the door opened without any trouble. I gave a perfunctory look to every room, then went to the kitchen. How far, I wondered with a little curiosity, had Ike's brain matter traveled after he was shot? I took a good look at the room's new paint and realized now what a shoddy job it was. I pulled out my pocketknife and scraped off paint around the kitchen window and began to see that someone had merely painted over the blood and everything else that had come out of Ike's head. I stepped back and then back some more. Fuck! Who would do such a shitty job of making over the place? No wonder Miss Agatha couldn't sleep at night— her son was still up and about just below her head. I opened the window and saw browned blood out on the edge of the sill. Why here, when the window should have been closed on the January night he was killed? And what power was in that blood for it to hang on for nearly two years?

I went out onto the fire escape and climbed up to Miss Agatha's place. Even after all the snow and sun and rain and time, there were faint bits of brown midway up the window frame, as if someone with bloody hands, just last night, had held on to it to steady himself before entering the apartment. Blood spilled with violence never goes away, I remembered my mother teaching Freddy and me, and you can see it if you have a mind to. I raised the window. Immediately, Alona's kid came up to the window. "Hi hi," she said, raising her hand to me. I looked at the other side of the frame and saw more bits of brown, and there, at the frame, it all stopped. "Hi hi." I adjusted my eyes and looked into the kitchen and saw Alona watching me. Her arms were folded across her breasts, her legs slightly apart. I looked at both sides of the frame again. Seeing Alona standing there, impervious for all eternity, I was suddenly chilled in every part of my body. "Hi hi," the kid said. "Hi hi." Mountains did not stand the way Alona stood. Dear God, I thought, dear God. Of all Ike's crimes against her, what had been the final one? I became aware that in only a few steps Alona could be at the window and one powerful push could send me toppling over the fire escape. I became afraid. "Hi hi." The kid kept holding her hand up to me, so I took her hand and I let her help me into the room. The child was named for Miss Agatha. "Hi hi," she said. "Hi," I said.

The white man who tried to drag Miss Agatha off into the woods when she was a child was never the same again, not in mind, not in body.

He awoke in the woods three days later, caked with blood from head to toe, and picked himself up from what all the Negroes had believed was his deathbed. He spent his life saying he had been attacked by "somethin from God, somethin big, big like this." God called him into preaching, but each sentence he spoke for the rest of his life had no relation to the one before it or to the one after it. He found a home at a very tiny church with a blue door, with people who believed his speech made no sense because that was how God wanted it. Never to be translated into understandable human talk. The law stayed satisfied that it was a drifter from beyond Choctaw who had attacked him. A stranger from faraway over yonder. The law let it be, and the world the white people had made for themselves was set right again.

I t came to me over the next few days that I would never find gold in Alaska, not even if my life depended on it. My mother was at first silent when I told her about the blood I'd found, when I told her who had killed Ike. She set a Tuesday-night plate of food before me as I sat at her kitchen table and bade me eat. Then she sat across from me with her cup, two-thirds milk and one-third coffee. She held the cup with both hands and sipped and fought back the tears. I rose to go to her, but she held me back. "You decide what you must tell Aggie and then leave her in peace after that," my mother commanded. "She knows what she knows. Maybe she needed someone like you in the world to know it, too. Tell her you know, if you got a mind to, and then leave us be. The only harm we ever done you was for your own good, and you must not forget that."

I found a note on my desk from Dvera, Sam's wife, when I returned two days later to the office I shared with him. The note, written in beautiful script, had a translation of Miriam Sobel's last words: *Once upon a time there was a rabbi and his wife. . . . Listen, children, remember, precious ones, what you're learning here. . . .* Funny, I said to myself. I would never have thought the words meant that just from what I heard. A moll, a rabbit, and his sin . . .

I went upstairs, where I had never been, to Dvera's back office. The door was open. From the hallway, it seemed a very small room. But, once I was inside, it felt very large indeed, with everything a woman might need to be comfortable when she's by herself. The doilies on the couch reminded me of my mother's living room. Just inside the door was a samovar with a brilliant shine. Dvera was on the telephone, and, as it happened, it was Sam, still in Israel. I stepped all the way into the room. Above the light switch was a calendar with the time of the sunset noted at every Friday. She waved me over and handed me the telephone. Sam said he would be sad to see me go. I did not tell him that I would see Alaska only in some third life. After I'd said a few words to him, the line began to crackle and I felt it best to tell him good-bye. I gave the telephone back to Dvera. She began closing the conversation and pointed at a photograph sticking out of a large brown envelope on her desk. Then she giggled at something Sam said and blushed. "Don't say that over the telephone," she said.

The photograph was of Miriam Sobel, younger than the dead woman by nine and two-thirds years, give or take a day or two. Two identical boys with forelocks had hold of her hands. I took the picture to the window, where the light was better. What part would the rabbi's wife play in the story? And, in the end, was the story really about her and not at all about the rabbi? I raised my eyes from the photograph of Miriam and saw a group of six little colored girls going down 8th Street toward E, all of them in bright colors. My eyes settled on a girl in a yellow dress. She was in the middle of the group and she alone twirled as they walked, her arms out, her head held back, so that the sun was full upon her face. Her long plaits swung with her in an almost miraculous way. It was good to watch her, because I had never seen anything like that in Washington in my whole life. I followed her until she disappeared. It would have been nice to know what was on her mind.

A POOR GUATEMALAN DREAMS
OF A DOWNTOWN IN PERU

For more than forty-seven years, there had been miracle after miracle, each one reaching down and snatching her back from death while forsaking all the souls—loved and unloved by her, known and unknown to her—who happened to be in her little sphere of life at that moment. Leaving one of the University of Maryland's libraries once, after failing to find an obscure book on the cohesion of solids, she had wandered over to the reference desk, curious at the last minute about a possible book on the meaning of names. The volume the librarian gave her was thin, lacking, and the best it could do for "Arlene" was to first offer a way to pronounce it, a way she wouldn't have understood if she didn't already know how to speak her own name. The "A" was upside down, and the "r" and the second "e" were facing the wrong direction. Then the book said of her name: "uncert. orig. and meaning." She had been young enough that day at twenty-eight—her hair the longest it would ever be in the ponytail, she leaned against a wall in a corner where the sun was uncomfortably generous in that part of the library—to have hoped for what the book bluntly gave the name "Milagro," which it assumed its readers already knew how to pronounce: Miracle.

Just about everything before that day at the creek was like something from a dream, a dream of some eight years. It had been a happy life, those years before the creek—an industrious father who, with his long workday over, liked to take Arlene's cheek between his lips and hum until she wiggled away from him; a mother under whose long dress she hid from creatures they pretended were at the door; a loving brother older by five years who preened for girls much too old for him. And a farm that took care of most of their needs, an apple when the heart craved an apple, some cured meat in the middle of the worst of winter evenings, a farm that looked out onto an horizon that made her mother sigh with thanks in spring and summer as she sat on the porch with her sweetened well water. Her grandfather, healthy then, was in her life as well, but he was off to the side, waiting for God to bring him front and center.

At the lovely creek that day, they met her father's brother and his pregnant wife. The wife had a baby finger with a long nail, and she had been wondering if she should cut the nail before her baby arrived, lest she accidentally mar the child with scratches or poke its eye out. It was Sunday morning, and what family deserved a day of rest more than theirs? Arlene's uncle had brought half a pig for barbecuing and they all paused but a moment or so in their joking and joy before going down to the bank to cross to where the best picnicking spots were. There was sun everywhere—a little wink-wink from God. With one hand holding the smaller picnic basket, her mother took hold of Arlene's hand and swung it back and forth as if her child were an old, old girlfriend. The two set off first. It had rained the night before, but it had rained a million nights leading up to that day and no harm had ever come to a single crossing soul. The wooden bridge to the other side was very new, and if a body interested in the chemistry and biology of life had bent down close to any part of it, she could have smelled what the woodsman smelled that moment after he made the first wounds into the trees that would create the bridge.

When they were all still on the bridge and many feet from the other shore, the creek water seemed to rise up and grow violent, with no reason at all except that it wanted to. The water chewed the bridge to splinters and razored the thick rope holding the wood together, and all the people tumbled into the creek, now nearly three times as high as it had been five minutes before. Her aunt went floating away first, the baby inside her only one and a third months old, the two pulled from the group with the ease of a twig and dispatched swiftly down the creek, which wasn't anyone's lovely sight anymore. Her father and uncle went next, partly in an effort to retrieve her aunt. They were all silent, amazed, and overwhelmed. The pig carcass slowly sank to the bottom of the creek, as if to hide from it all, while the other picnic fixings—the homemade barbecue sauce, the sodas, the two cakes, the potato salad, the pepper shaker on its side and the top of its head nudging the upright salt shaker—drifted away nonchalantly. Her brother followed her father and uncle, knocked down until he was flat on his back, kicking all the while, trying to swim or to right himself, his hair even now still as perfect as the jar of My Knight pomade had promised on the label, hair still looking like all of the forty-five youthful minutes he had spent on it that morning. Her mother was next, and maybe she knew that she was about to be parted from her child until that day somewhere in eternity when God decided otherwise, for she tried pushing Arlene away, toward the shore. Then she too was forced down and away, still silent, still moving her arms to try to give her child one more push into life.

The Israelites who found safe passage through the parted Red Sea could testify as to what it was like next. A shallow path of easy water presented itself and Arlene was pushed quite peacefully to the other side, her stomach heavy with a quart or more of creek water. She was exhausted once she hit the shore and did not move once there, her body expelling the water a spoonful at a time. She was eight years and two weeks, and this was the first miracle.

Even silent death can have a loudness that calls out for witnesses, and so a white man, arm in arm with his sweetheart, a short, plump Cherokee woman, happened upon them. He pulled Arlene completely out of the water in time to see everyone but her mother disappear around the bend folks called No Name Preacher. The white man, seeing Arlene's mother reach out and grab a hickory branch standing straight up like a flagpole in the rushing water, began to jump up and down, as if to cheer her on. Arlene's mother held on to the branch with both hands, and such a hopeful sight compelled the man, bony with almost transparent skin, to take off the new shoes his sweetheart had bought him.

He jumped in. He was only a few feet from the mother when the branch wobbled, uprooted itself and pulled her away. The water took the man as well, like some kind of punishment for interfering. His sweetheart, bending down over Arlene, now stood and called out to him. "Mitchell . . . Mitchell." It was at first a soft call, as if she wanted her lover merely to come away from doing some boyish mischief. "I say, Mitchell . . ." Arlene stood as well and began calling out to her mother. She and the woman were holding hands. "Mama!" Arlene was shivering with the emotion of it all. The woman was now screaming the man's name, even as the water began to calm and went back to what it had been all the days before that one. The Indian woman felt the shaking of the child and knelt down and pulled Arlene to her and began calling for her own mother, who had not been alive for thirty-five years, since before the Indian woman had turned three years old. She did not call the dead woman "Mother," but shouted to the water using her first and middle names, the ones her mother had been christened with.

Arlene Baxter went to live with her paternal grandparents. Her grandfather had lost his only children in the creek, along with a grandson named for him, two daughters-in-law he cherished, and an unborn grandchild whose future in his pained imagination became limitlessly bright, if only because now there was no future. The loss became his life, and no matter what grand things he might manage to think God still had in store for him, what small pleasures he had once enjoyed and might again savor—combing the rain from his wife's hair, the taste of the first peach of the season—he could, in one horribly short moment, be back at the first crushing second he had learned of the loss. He had been a man of few words, and now there were fewer still. Arlene suffered the same feelings, compounded by the fact that she had been a witness. She was too young to feel the guilt of a survivor, but not too young to see that the wondrous and bountiful forest that had been her good life had, in less than ten minutes, been cleared down to nearly nothing.

Her grandmother had endured the same loss, but she had God and He told her He had a plan. God held her hand every step of the way.

Then her grandmother died, a woman who had tried to keep everything going for the three of them, the curtains cleaned and ironed, the cow milked and happily sassy, the neighbors over for supper at least once a week to let Arlene and her grandfather know that they were still in life and life was still in them. With her death, that all went away. The cow mooed all day waiting to be milked and would sashay on up to the house in the early evening and poke her head in the side window; and when neighbors, country people all, came to offer a hand to do anything, the grandfather said they needed nothing and asked that they go away. He woke early one morning before dawn, three months after his wife's death, his beard filthy and stiffly matted and falling almost a foot down his chin until it turned and formed an "L" with the base pointing to his heart. He found Arlene at the kitchen table in half-darkness eating a breakfast of food burned black. With a doting mother and grandmother who nevertheless should have known better, a spoiled farm girl can be left to concentrate on things other than how long to fry an egg. The child was close to nine years old. "That food ain't good for you, sweetie," her grandfather managed to say. "I's so hungry, Paw Paw," Arlene said.

He understood enough about himself and the wreckage that was his life to know that wherever he was headed, this one innocent thing he was charged with caring for should not have to suffer the same road. He did a rough shave late that morning, got the beard down to a short "I," and became enough of himself to telegraph a distant cousin of Arlene's mother who ran a preparatory school for well-off Negro girls some forty-nine miles away in Nashville. The headmistress did not remember Arlene's mother, but she did remember quite well the mother's aunt, and that was sufficient for her to connect a line from her blood to Arlene's blood. "Will be there with next train," the headmistress, an economist and mathematician, telegraphed back.

The headmistress and the grandfather at first considered that Arlene go with her back to the preparatory school, but he was well enough to know that that would crush him once and for all. Instead, the headmistress wrote to a teacher, one of her former students, who lived and taught in a nearby place called Alamo. The headmistress asked that she come out regularly and tutor Arlene "before she descends into savagery." The teacher, Miss Waterford, had found several gems among her colored students in Alamo, and she was confident that she might find another in Arlene. She arrived with her fiancé in his car, a day after the headmistress returned to Nashville, and her spirits sank in those first minutes with Arlene: English so bad it sounded like a foreign language. And the child knew the sum of one and one only because she used her fingers. Miss Waterford returned to Alamo and immediately wrote to the headmistress, "Why have you asked still another burden of me, Dr. Hines? Am I always to be tethered?" Two and a half decades after that letter, Miss Waterford, then the Reverend Mrs. Campbell, would be rewarded, once again, when Arlene dedicated her second book, *The Relationship of Solids to Ethereal Matter,* to "Miss Waterford, Who Called Me Back from the Wilderness." After she received the letter following Miss Waterford's initial meeting with Arlene, the Nashville headmistress promptly wrote back to her former student, "Would I place this burden on your shoulders if I did not know that my blood, the blood of your teacher, flows through Arlene's veins?"

Arlene's grandfather sold the farms of his two sons and banked the money for Arlene's future, with the headmistress being given fiduciary responsibility. He then sold off parts of his own farm and used the proceeds to better his and Arlene's lives, including paying for Miss Waterford's teaching and for neighbors to come in to clean and cook. He kept enough land to make a buffer, so that he would not have to see from his window or his porch other men, strangers or friends, toiling land that had tried to break him and his father and his father's father.

The grandfather's mind slowly returned to that of a man who had no more than an hour before lost so many loved ones to the creek. There were some days with Arlene when he would manage to raise his head above the pain to enjoy a meal with her or a wagon ride into town for her favorite ice cream. Horseshoes out in the backyard. But more and more of the time with him were silent hours they spent sitting side by side on the porch. The sun came up to the right. He would sometimes try to step through the silence and take her hand in his and offer some memory of one of the dead, but before he could finish, he would turn quiet and take his hand from hers and place it back in what passed for his lap. The sun went down to the left, and throughout the day it dangled out there before them, not offering much that was good, and not offering much that was the other way either. When she knew he was not coming back with the rest of any memory, she would take from the crowded porch table beside her one of the many books Miss Waterford had purchased for her. The moon was out there, too, but when it was at its brightest, at its strangest, the grandfather was usually asleep, and Arlene was reading in her bed.

Miss Waterford, afraid that a child with Arlene's mind would pass too quickly into adulthood, had made playing with the neighbor children a part of Arlene's everyday regime when she was not there. But Arlene, who began to live only to read, was forever neglecting to go down the hill to the right to the Mason children or up the hill to the left to the Daileys, and so when her teacher returned and questioned her about playing, she would lie, and not very well, "another sign," Miss

Waterford wrote Dr. Hines, the Nashville headmistress, that "she may be becoming old before her time." And so despite all Miss Waterford's efforts, she became a child who could "live peacefully unto myself." That was what she wrote in her essay when she applied to the College of the Holy Cross at sixteen. An aging Jesuit—who had discovered too late in his life that while God walked with him, he did not enjoy walking with God—read the essay. He was a chemistry and biology professor at Holy Cross who had volunteered to read the essays of the college's science applicants as one small way to ease his growing despair. He loved the phrase "live peacefully unto myself," and he knew even before he had finished her essay that the school on the hill might not be such a bad place if it gave a home to a young woman who knew at least that one thing about herself.

But before Holy Cross, and before she went off to the headmistress's preparatory school in Nashville, there were three more miracles. The first and second saw the deaths of four human beings and two cows and three chickens; that second miracle, which took the lives of two humans and two chickens, occurred on a weekend trip with Miss Waterford to Alamo. ("When the roll of the dead is called," Arlene at eighteen wrote whimsically in her diary while at Holy Cross, "why should dead cows and dogs and chickens be excluded?") After those two miracles, a sad, tiny lot of the Tennessee dispossessed began calling Arlene "the blessed one." And some of them, from all around the state, traveled to the farm and knocked gently on the door and asked before it was opened if they might have a word with the good Miss Arlene: Parents with children crippled from birth with gnarled limbs. Men who had gambled away their pittances and vanished while their families were reduced to begging. Women going into madness because one of the first lessons they had learned in life was to bed down with any man who told them sweet but empty words. Arlene, who never came out to them, was never afraid, just curious as she watched from the parlor windows as neighbors shooed them away. ("Why did not anyone," she wrote in her diary at thirty in

Washington, D.C., "seek to burn me at the stake?") In the end, after a week of people coming by, the headmistress and the teacher, backed by the grandfather in an especially lucid moment, had to hire three armed men—one Negro on a horse, one Negro on a twenty-five-year-old motorcycle, and one white man in his father's noisy pickup truck—to keep people from coming onto the property. A few souls still came to stand across the road in the pasture a half a mile from the house. They sat and stood in all kinds of weather, and they, never more than ten at a time, were out there for nearly seven months, thinking only one thing—"If I have already been through a part of the doom, maybe this child can deliver me and mine."

It was only after the third miracle before going to Nashville that she began to see herself as special, but it gave her no optimism about her place in the world. ("If," she wrote in the diary her second week at Holy Cross, "you live your life and all about you they are dying, what kind of life can you ever have?") After the dispossessed stopped coming and watching from across the road, Miss Waterford told Arlene to go out and play again with the neighbor children. The teacher, having seen through her earlier lies about playtime, began requiring Arlene to write compositions of at least five hundred words about playtime episodes. And so not five weeks before going to the Nashville Beginning School for Negro Women, not two months after turning twelve, Arlene was playing school with the Dailey children who lived midway up the hill to the left. It was her turn to be in the role of teacher as the brand-new green Chevrolet with its brand-new driver topped the hill at a selfish speed and came down the road going past the Dailey property. Her hands behind her back, Arlene had shifted the pebble from her right to her left hand and presented her closed fists to the youngest Dailey girl, seven-year-old Petunia, who was on the bottom step there at the edge of the Dailey home. Picking the hand with the pebble would have sent Petunia from the kindergarten to the first grade, the second step. Her siblings had all passed and were on various steps and Petunia alone was on the kindergarten step, mumbling that she was being left behind and that it was not fair. The child, her knees almost up to her chin, raised one end of the Band-Aid on her right knee, peeked at her new cut, blew it a kiss, and then tapped the end of the bandage back down. As that hand prepared to touch Arlene's left hand, the car, which had swiftly left the road with its horn honking all the way, came speeding into the clean, flowered yard, into the children on the porch in their many grades. Arlene's closed hands, palms down, were still outstretched, and when she looked up from them as the wind and violence of it all blew her plaits and her dress, she could see the empty space the car had made, could see through the fence a half a mile away, all the way over to the mountains. It was, to be sure, a new view, and her mind took longer than it should have, given her history, to tell her why.

She was still in bed when Miss Waterford arrived late the next morning, Sunday. It was the morning after the night Miss Waterford had decided that marriage was not what she needed at that time in her life. The books were all closed when she opened the door to Arlene's bedroom. The grandfather was in a bright corner of the room in a chair with a cup of cold coffee in both his hands. He had been there all night, and he, like the teacher, had already decided about his life.

"I can't write a composition, Miss Waterford," Arlene said as the teacher took off her hat and stuck the hatpin down through the top of it. The man Miss Waterford would have married had a heart not of this world, and he had lent her his car to come to Arlene even though she had told him she would not marry him.

"I know," Miss Waterford said, "I know." She acknowledged the grandfather and then sat on the side of the child's bed. "Perhaps I have long asked too much of my students." She placed her hat at the foot of the bed. She took Arlene's hand. The journey to Arlene should have taken her by the Dailey place, but Miss Waterford had chosen the long way around. "Perhaps the sun and the moon are too much to ask of my students. Perhaps the moon is enough." It was something the headmistress, Dr. Hines, would have said. And Miss Waterford thought, I have become what I said I would not become.

A neighbor stayed with Arlene while the grandfather and Miss Waterford attended the funerals of the five Dailey children. The three surviving Dailey children had been away in town the day their siblings were killed, at the funeral of an aunt who died giving birth to triplets. The brand-new driver of the green Chevrolet had died as well, but his funeral was held on another day, just before dawn in a part of Tennessee he and his people had never seen.

As the grandfather had suggested, Miss Waterford took Arlene with her to Alamo. When they returned more than two weeks later, again in her former fiancé's car, the grandfather was nowhere about, and no one could tell them what had happened to him. Miss Waterford stayed with Arlene for almost a week as the authorities made a show of trying to find the man, but the grandfather was never seen again. "She is an orphan again," Miss Waterford, who would follow Arlene to the Nashville school, said to the headmistress on the telephone. "I'm an orphan again," Arlene said, thinking of the children in the work of Charles Dickens as she and Miss Waterford packed her things. "But you know more than you did before," her teacher said. "I don't think so," Arlene said.

The headmistress, Dr. Hines, had been taught home economics and not a great deal more as a girl and young woman at Mrs. Wilbur Ross's Finishing School for the Colored Elite. Years before Dr. Hines decided to establish her own Nashville Beginning School for Negro Women, her first husband, a teacher of English, a writer of many novels about "the highest and brightest" class of Negroes, had left her, her finishing school education, and their two children. She was certainly the best wifely material the finishing school ever turned out. In the home of that marriage, the collars of all her husband's shirts had been starched to cardboard stiffness, and there were homemade sachets tucked discreetly into the back corners of drawers. But one day, a child on either side of her, the woman who was to become the headmistress Dr. Hines opened the tastefully yellow door to that home and found that what her husband wanted was not in her repertoire. And with that inadequate repertoire after the writer-teacher left her, she, a child on either side of her, had had to go back out into the world and strengthen her credentials, becoming along the way an economist and a mathematician. "Numbers do not lie," Dr. Hines told Arlene and her entering class their first day of orientation. "If they do, the fault lies with you."

The Nashville school, with grades six through twelve, usually had about a hundred colored girls of all shades, mostly the daughters of a few enlightened, well-to-do Negroes from throughout the country who had looked at the world and discovered, as Dr. Hines had, that Negro girls, their daughters, should be fortified with as much education as possible. Those hundred students included fifteen or so poor girls, whose educations were paid for by scholarships primarily financed by the wealthier families. "Each One Help One" was the school's motto. Indeed, the headmistress, still overseeing Arlene's money, took from Arlene's bank account money that helped pay for room and board for an Alabama sharecropper's daughter.

The years there were over before Arlene knew it; in four years she absorbed what it took most girls six years. She had few friends, and Dr. Hines and the other teachers did not push her to go out and make any more than those three or four with whom she was comfortable. They were mostly satisfied that she had found comfort and success in the solidity and certainty of science, primarily biology and chemistry. If, Arlene had discovered happily, you did everything you were supposed to do—from the correct calculations to the right amount of flame under the Bunsen burner—it all came out right in the end. She found comfort in the caves of science where good and innocent people did not die for no other reason than that they were near her.

At twenty-two, she would write in her diary that "the world escaped fairly unscathed" from her time at Nashville and at Holy Cross. She could write that by not counting, for one thing, the fire at the tiny hotel in West Virginia that occurred in her last year at Dr. Hines's establishment. She had feigned an illness so as not to have to go to West Virginia, but Miss Waterford knew her well by then and made her go anyway. Her class went for a long weekend to a small and beautiful town where John Brown and his men were said to have spent their last night before the Harper's Ferry raid. One of the owners of the hotel, the husband, was nearly deaf and misheard on the telephone how many were in Arlene's class, and so one student was required to stay in an alcovelike attachment connected to the main building by a short walkway. Arlene volunteered and spent two and a half nights in a pleasant room big enough for only one. Next to her room was a larger one with a Washington, D.C., family of five. In the diary entry, she would also feel safe in not counting the alcove fire because it was started by the youngest child of the D.C. family and because one human being survived. The fire child died, and so did her mother and two siblings. The father escaped because that night he had gone into the woods where John Brown and his people had slept to be with the other owner of the hotel, the wife. That wife did not believe her husband was almost deaf and went to the woods so he would not hear her making love among the animals and the wind-touched trees and a brook that gurgled loudly even though it was nearly dry. The fire child had awakened in the night, afraid, and once again had found her father, a smoker, gone.

And in the diary Arlene did not count the disastrous boat trip while at Holy Cross, primarily because there were two survivors, one being a young man from Wesleyan University. The boat trip was their second date. Those dates were the first of her life. She was a senior, and he, Scott Catrell, was a junior at Wesleyan. Up from Connecticut to visit friends, he had seen her walking in downtown Worcester. Had followed her that day the two miles or more all the way back up the hill to Holy Cross. After three months of telephone calls and letters she had said yes to a date in late January of her last year, for no other reason than that her mentor, the priest of failing faith, had died a week before. "Scott is awkward in his own body," she wrote weeks after the boat trip to Miss Waterford, who had become the Reverend Mrs. Campbell, "as if he had been put together by a dozen Dr. Frankensteins. But that is not why I know I could never love him." She had come to believe that death, with all her miracles, had merely overlooked her somehow, and that to make up for such a stupendous mistake on its part, death was planning something quite spectacular.

After Holy Cross, there was Georgetown and then the University of Maryland as she worked for two doctorates. While earning the second degree, she secured a research position at the National Institutes of Health and was given a nice corner space to work in, alone. Not too much sun and not too much moon; and intercoms and telephones—and later computers—to connect her with two assistants down the hall and around the corner from her space. She could count her friends on her two hands, including those she had in Tennessee. And though she begged him not to, Scott Catrell followed her after Wesleyan to the area and entered Howard University's medical school. They never lived together, but dated and saw each other sporadically for nearly two decades and a half. He married three times—always to women who first asked him to marry them—and he was divorced three times. No children. Over all those years, he was comforted only by the fact that there were no other men in Arlene's life beyond those, living and dead, who had cleared paths and brought light to the mysteries of biology and chemistry.

When she was forty-three, and had not seen or talked to Scott for two years, they noticed each other at the 12th Street entrance to Hecht's—she was coming out, empty-handed, and he was going in. It was a very cold day, cold enough to snap the bones of steel-driving men, a day when five homeless people would die in their sleep. "How am I doing at not ever contacting you?" Scott asked, smiling. Four months later, Arlene became pregnant with his child. "How," she wrote the Reverend Mrs. Campbell, "could two intelligent people of science be so stupid as to become pregnant?" "People of science?" the Reverend Mrs. Campbell wrote back. "Despite all that has happened to you, you are, in the end, no better than all the rest of us, science or no science, who must fight to stay afloat. We want, we rage, we desire, we fail, we succeed. We stand in that long, long line. Where were you when they taught us that?"

Arlene had been in the family way for a little more than a month when she began weighing the pros and cons of an abortion. "I am trying to think of it as I have been trained to do," she wrote the headmistress Dr. Hines. "The word 'zygote' keeps playing in my head over and over. But lately I have been giving the zygote names. It looks into my eyes sometimes and dares me to blink first. It swims and I call it by name back from the edge of the pool because it has swum too far. Beyond the edge, there are dragons and monsters because that world is not round but flat."

One thing happened that caused her to have the child. And that same thing told her to give the child to Scott to raise. On the better days at the National Institutes of Health, she took her lunch on the grounds under an oak tree as far from people as she could manage. On a day in April, three months pregnant, she smelled the storm before there was a cloud in the sky. She continued eating and did not stop until the rain came, not a bad rain, just one that told her it was best to stand rather than to sit. There was no one about. After she stood, the thunder and lightning followed, which surprised her because the rain had not signaled that kind of storm. She decided to stay under the tree. Then, in seconds, as the storm grew fiercer, she heard two people laughing and talking on the other side of the oak.

She at first thought to walk away, but chose not to. After all, they were the invaders. And so, with the world quaking with the storm, she went around to confront the two. "Leave!" she shouted to them. "Leave this place!" They were a black girl and a white boy, not yet out of high school. It was evident that the boy was losing the war against his pimples. He did not seem to understand what Arlene was saying, but the girl said, "What is your problem, madam?" The newspaper article would come out with the girl's photograph—a face much lovelier than Arlene would remember, and that was because the black girl was defiant the day of the storm, and that defiance was not lovely. "What is the matter with you, madam?" The white boy said, "Let's just go, *ma chérie*," which was what his grandfather called his grandmother. The article would not have his photograph because he was not killed.

"Let's just go, *ma chérie*," the boy said again, and he began walking away in the storm as an example to the girl, a scholarship student at an awfully expensive prep school not far from NIH. The boy had gone but three yards when Arlene decided simply to go back to her side of the tree. "Suit yourself," she said before leaving. "Suit yourself," the girl mocked. The boy was five yards away when the earth quivered and the wind swept through and then the lightning came, down into the tree and down into the girl. After the sound of the lightning hitting them, there was nothing except a slight *yelp* from the girl and an ancient complaint from the tree and a cry from the boy as he ran toward her. The tree, wounded, began tumbling toward the boy, and whatever sounds he made after that were swallowed up by all the young spring leaves.

Arlene sank to her knees in a fit of crying, shivering as the heat from the lightning began to dissipate. Even after years of it, the incredible wonder of it still had the power to pull her down. She heard people on the other side of the tree rushing toward the couple. Her child came into the world in October, a late baby. A boy she and Scott agreed to call Antonio. Arlene tucked her purse under her arm and stood, now afraid that others would be hurt because the storm had not let up, and she stumbled down along the iron fence of the NIH grounds and eventually found a gate that took her out to Wisconsin Avenue. The baby was born bald, and then, in his ninth month of life, when Arlene gave him to Scott to raise, Antonio's hair came out, nearly an inch in one week.

She caught a cab some five blocks from NIH, hoping as she got in that the driver would complain about her wet clothes so she could tear him apart. The man said nothing. The picture of the dead girl in the newspaper would be a recent one, and as Arlene read about her, about what a grand future people had predicted for her, Arlene thought what a poorer world it would be without Antoinette Champion. The cabdriver, black and old, delivered her to the front door of her condominium, and he must have known something was the matter because after he helped her out of the taxi, he stood at the door as she tried first one key and then another to open the door.

On the Fourth of July some eleven years after the birth of Arlene's son, Avis M. Watkins, nine years old, spent most of the morning on the floor of her room in a three-bedroom house on Minnesota Avenue, N.E., sulking and telling all her troubles to three stuffed animals. The girl was the youngest child of Marvella Simms, who, three years after her divorce, had returned to her maiden name. The child was upset that morning because Marvella had told her, for the fifth time, that there would be no fireworks at home, that they were going down to the Washington Monument to watch the display with Francisco Padmore, her mother's fiancé. Avis liked Francisco, she confessed to the animals that morning, but the girl liked fireworks even more. "We all need some fireworks," Avis told the black bear as she took the back of its head and shook it twice. They, she and the animals, were under one of the windows, and the sun came down through that window and caught the bear's blue eye and made it twinkle as he nodded.

"Wouldn't you like to hold one of them sparklers insteada watchin stuff shootin up in the air?" she asked the bear, who nodded yes. The child, her parents had decided, was recovering quite well from what Avis's therapist had called "that unfortunate episode," which had occurred nearly a year ago. "Me too," she said to the bear. "You and me both." The night of the "episode," she had stayed at the Harvard Street, N.W., home of her best friend, and during an hour long before dawn, the friend's father, estranged from the mother, had broken into the home while everyone was sleeping. "When I get grown I'ma do all I wanna do and nobody will say no." The father shot to death the mother, his mother-in-law, his wife's boyfriend, and his own five children. Avis survived with no wounds, covered in her friend's blood, enough blood for the father to think in the near-darkness that she had been shot. This was her first miracle. "Make me go down to some stupid fireworks show." The father had only one daughter, Avis's friend, but for those moments after he shot into the bed with his daughter and Avis, he looked at Avis, who kept her eyes closed and breathed shallowly through it all, and the man, insane because his wife's love for him had shriveled down to nothing, thought he had two girls and said to himself that two dead daughters were better than one because it would hurt his father-in-law even more.

In the late afternoon of the Fourth of July, they—Avis, her mother, and her two brothers, Marvin and Marcus—drove to Francisco's house in Anacostia, a house his grandfather had built. They had a late lunch. Francisco was also divorced, a man who worked three floors up from Marvella at the telephone company, and though she had seen him about for three or so years, she had not noticed him until he sang "Ave Maria" at the company Christmas party. ("That dude got pipes!" Marcus said at the party.) He had no children. They drove to the Stadium-Armory Metro station in Francisco's Cadillac. ("Man," Marcus said during the ride, "I could live in this thing if it had a bathroom and a TV.") Of Marvella's children, Avis was Francisco's favorite because she was the first to like him, had silently taken his hand three months after she first met him as the five of them strolled out of a movie theater.

After the fireworks show on the Mall, they went back to the subway at the Federal Triangle stop, hoping to avoid the hordes at both Smithsonian stations. Arlene Baxter and Scott Catrell were there as well; their son, Antonio, was staying the summer with Scott's people in Philadelphia. "Go out with Daddy," her son had told Arlene before he left. "Hundreds die after fireworks explode prematurely," she read in her mind as he spoke. She and Scott had sat across Constitution Avenue from the crowds, practically alone on the lawn of the Commerce Department. She enjoyed the time with Scott and was not thinking as they arrived at the Federal Triangle subway platform a minute or so before Marvin, Marcus and Avis Watkins. The children had pushed ahead of Marvella and Francisco. He told them to wait, but the children were quickly separated from the adults, mainly by a large family from Seat Pleasant. The platform lights began to blink, announcing the approaching train, and one of the Seat Pleasant boys bumped into Marcus because someone was bumping into him. Marcus turned and pushed the boy back. "Yall tryin to squeeze me to death in this damn place!" Marcus shouted to no one in particular.

When he turned back, Arlene and Avis had tumbled over the platform. Scott reached for them but was too late. The people who saw them down, down on the tracks were stunned for a long moment, stunned to see human beings in the no-man's-land of the subway system where riders had never seen humans before, not even workmen. The blinking went on, and the entire platform cooled with wind pushed ahead by the coming train. People began reaching for the woman and the girl, but the confusion of arms and hands and the pushing and shouting only made things worse, and a man warned everyone that more would be falling to their deaths, and for several crucial seconds the bodies at the platform's edge leaned as one away from death. Arlene, realizing even in her panic that she herself would be saved, sought to lift the girl, but her arms, bruised and weakened from the fall, failed her. She heard the roar and thought the train was only feet away but when she looked to face it, there was nothing but forever blackness through the tunnel. Blackness and then, suddenly, the lights of the train bearing down like the eyes of a creature not to be denied. The train shook the ground and it shook all the hearts of those who knew the woman and the girl were done for. Seeing that the girl could not get back up to the platform in time, Arlene knelt and grabbed the waist of the girl and Avis, knowing the woman could not get to safety, turned and grabbed Arlene back and they fell down and Arlene rolled with her into the recess under the platform. She pushed Avis as close as she could to the wall and covered the girl with her body. Up on the platform, the blinking went on. Scott bowed his head. Three men six feet from the edge of the platform fainted, but the crowd was so thick they had nowhere to fall. Marvella and Francisco leaned forward but could not get close to the children. Marcus moaned to see his sister disappear, then he cursed, and so did his brother as he gripped Marcus protectively by the shirt collar. The face of the first car emerged from the tunnel and the woman running the train saw the chaos and the people only inches from the edge of the platform and she sounded her horn. The brakes, a screeching mess, were of no use, but still the subway woman tried. As the train came on, Avis, having survived a night that saw the murders of eight human beings, knew somehow that she would not die, and so there arose a need to protect the stranger holding her and she put one arm around Arlene's shoulder and one hand behind the woman's head and pulled it into the crook of her own neck. Dust and dirt stirred up by the oncoming train coated them, pushed into their nostrils and their ears. And with wind and noise and debris, the train arrived.

Arlene's telephone number was unlisted, but Avis begged her mother to help her to reach her and Marvella, the telephone company worker, got it. For some three weeks, the child left the same message: "Lady, would you please call me? I'm the girl at the subway." They had last seen each other that night at George Washington University Hospital. Avis did not know what she would say if Arlene ever called back; she only knew she wanted to hear the woman's voice again. After word spread about what had happened, with reporters setting up camp outside her home, wanting to talk to "the Miracle Woman," Arlene had left her home a day after the incident and had gone to stay with Scott. The reporters spoke to Avis, but two days after seeing his child on television and in the newspapers, Avis's father called Marvella and told her no more of that. He had despaired to see his daughter in one television interview, tiny and in a pretty blue dress, sitting on her couch between her mother and her brothers. Her responses reduced mostly to the shaking of the head and Yeses and Nos. "This is one reason why I divorced that woman," the father said to the television screen. "Lady, would you please call me? I was at the subway with you."

The newspapers said Arlene had saved the child, because that is what Avis told them, but as Arlene sat day after day in the dark at Scott's place, she became less certain of what she had done. By the second week, she started thinking that the child had actually saved her, which was not how the world worked. She began to long for the girl, for her presence, and had she known the girl had been calling, she would have called her back. Perhaps they had saved each other, she thought.

Near the end of the second week, Scott went to Arlene's home to collect her mail. He called her and told her the telephone message machine was full. She called her number and retrieved the messages. To hear the child broke her heart. She had heard the voice before, but she had heard it years and years before, and it had belonged to someone who was not alive anymore. Arlene was in her sixth decade of miracles.

They—Marvella and her children—came to Scott's apartment that first Saturday in August when Scott had gone to Philadelphia to get Antonio. Avis stared at the woman and held back and leaned against the door once Arlene shut it. Marvella said, "You been dyin to see her all this time and now the cat got your tongue."

Arlene seated them on the couch facing the long window in the living room, but Marcus soon got up to look out the window onto Massachusetts Avenue and down 13th Street. "You live pretty high up," he said of the tenth-floor apartment, "but my uncle lives even higher in Maryland." Arlene sat in the love seat catty-corner the couch. She and Avis did not take their eyes off each other. "Oh," Arlene said to Marcus, who returned to the couch. "He live out in Maryland and they not afraid to put up high places. But in D.C., they pretty scared of bein high." He looked up at his brother, but Marvin, sitting between his siblings, said nothing.

"Would everyone like something to drink?" Arlene said after several minutes, and when she stood, there was a sharp intake of breath from the girl.

"A nice cold Coke," Marcus said. "No," Marvella said, "orange juice for everyone." "Juice for sissies," Marcus said.

Avis continued to look at Arlene, who said, "Why not come with me?" But the girl seemed unable to move. "I'll help you," Marvin said at last, looking down at his sister. "She shy that way."

She's never gonna be the same again, is she?" the boy said, watching Arlene as she looked in the icebox.

"No, son, she won't be." Avis's father had called Arlene the night before to tell her about the eight murders. She remembered the crime but did not recall that a child had survived. "But in her way, she'll still be Avis. Her family will see to that." She turned from the open icebox. She had not expected such a boy. "We will all survive this, son." She had not felt such confidence until she saw Avis walk into the apartment and cling to her with her eyes. Marvin looked to a series of ten photographs to the left of the refrigerator, five in color on the top row and five in black-and-white on the bottom. "The top one to the far left," she said, pointing, "that is my son at one year old. Next to it is my son at two years old, and there he is at three years old. . . ." Each photograph was of the child at each of his birthday parties, and he was happy in all of them. "That is my son at six years old. That is my son at seven. . . ."

Marvin wanted to know why there were color pictures only on the top row.

"Those were taken by my son's father," Arlene said. "I was not there. I was away. The bottom photographs are mine."

"Color is better, I think," Marvin said. He avoided her eyes, afraid that he had offended her.

"That is what they are telling me, but I am too old to change that way."

Over the next months, there arose between the girl and the woman what Arlene described in her diary as "a love I cannot live without." She often felt a greater pull toward Avis than toward her own son. The girl and the woman talked every evening on the telephone, and the child spent at least one weekend a month with Arlene. Avis's father, seeing what Marvella was slow to see, would now and again give up one of his weekends with Avis so the girl could be with Arlene. Then, toward the end of January, Marvella began to see as well, and she allowed Avis to stay some weekday evenings with Arlene. They wrote to each other daily, as if there were ten thousand miles separating them. "One day you will see that Tennessee creek again for the first time," Arlene wrote her in March. The girl had never been near Tennessee. "And I will see the house again for the first time." She was speaking of the Harvard Street house of the eight murders, a house she had never seen. A year after the people had been killed there, two wealthy white lawyers bought it, not caring about its history. Indeed, they decorated the front hall with copies of the newspaper articles about the crime, about the girl who had survived but had lost her best friend.

❧

In April Scott asked Arlene to marry him, but she gave him no answer. He asked three days before he mailed a flyer about the Guatemalan woman. The creator of the flyer seemed to expect its readers to know who the woman was, and it gave little information about her, just where she would be speaking in Washington in May. At first Arlene could not understand why Scott thought she would be interested, but an article in the newspaper five days after she got the flyer told her more. There was a color photograph of the woman, Eulogia Rios, spread over a fourth of the top page of the style section. Eulogia, eighteen years old, was standing on a Washington street in simple brown shoes and a dress of brown and red and blue stripes. She was looking so deeply into the eye of the camera that Arlene felt as if she herself had taken the picture. In two separate photographs on either side of Eulogia were her paintings. The headline above her head read, "The Miracle from Guatemala." One painting was of Arlene's pregnant aunt, the one who had been pulled away and killed by the angry creek in Tennessee.

Avis's parents permitted Arlene to take the child to hear Eulogia speak, and the two got seats in the fourth row in an auditorium at the New York Avenue Presbyterian Church. Twelve framed paintings in the same style as those in the newspaper photographs were displayed along the stage. Not long after they sat down, Avis pointed to three of the paintings and whispered to Arlene, "I know those people." At seven thirty precisely, a nun walked onto the stage from the left, followed by Eulogia in a light blue dress and simple black shoes. There was applause, but after the nun, still walking, raised her hand, people stopped. The nun introduced her and Eulogia stepped to the podium, and in the English she had learned over nine years in the United States, she began speaking.

She talked without tears, in an even voice that a practiced traveler might use to share the stories of her travels. She had been eight years old, she said, sitting in the third row of a classroom of a school that the villagers had just begun building the week before. There were no walls and the children could see out all over the land as their family members and neighbors farmed and worked. "The wind was a good one that day, coming down the mountains and over the valley," Eulogia said, patting her hand gently to the side of her face. Their teacher, Eulogia said, was a young woman who had been born in the village and had returned to live there, bringing her husband, a doctor born in Peru. If she had told her story before, it was not obvious.

They were newlyweds, the teacher and the doctor, and the schoolchildren, that morning, had managed to get her to talk about their honeymoon in Peru. The soldiers, all of them in civilian clothing, were already in their trucks and jeeps on the outskirts of the village when the teacher, Mrs. Parados, began talking about the smoking and coughing bus that took her and Dr. Parados down a mountain toward the biggest town in the region. Eulogia said Mrs. Parados made every sound the bus made, and she imitated the other bus riders, including the man who held the rooster on his lap and made the bird dance by blowing on the back of its head. The teacher's story of the bus, which had about seventeen other passengers in addition to the newlyweds, had reached the point where the vehicle had gotten to the bottom of the mountain and was heading toward what passed for a downtown when the soldiers streamed into Eulogia's village and began killing the people farthest from the school. The village was not a big one and so it did not take them long to reach the school with Mrs. Parados and her twenty-three pupils. "The village was all killed, even down to the littlest chicken," Eulogia said, "all of them except me. One hundred and fifty-nine people, which does not count the unborn children still in their mothers' bellies." She stopped, as if remembering something. "I never heard the end of her honeymoon story," she said at last. "Mrs. Parados and Dr. Parados have yet to reach that downtown in Peru."

The paintings along the stage were of some of the dead in the village. Eulogia explained that because she had been alive only eight years at the time, she did not know all of the hearts of all of the people. But she had seen them all at one time or another as she lived her little girl's life. A painting of someone she knew, Eulogia continued, took some two months to complete, while one of someone whose heart she did not know sometimes took as long as nine months. At that time in her life, the evening at the church, she had completed nineteen paintings. She went to the left of the stage and picked up a painting of a very old man in a straw hat. His bony legs were crossed and he was looking straight at the young woman who painted him. "Señor Efrain Hernandez," Eulogia shouted. "Seventy-seven. All I know about him is what I learned as I painted him. Though he took eight months, the longest so far, he will not be the hardest to paint. The hard ones are yet to come." After several minutes, she put down the old man and raised up a boy, barely in his teens. "Fidel Rios," she shouted, "my brother who sat two rows behind me in class. Two and a half months to paint. He had wanted to be in the fields with my father that day, but my father had made him go to school." It was Fidel Rios, but it was also the oldest brother of Avis's best friend.

The painting of Arlene's aunt was not on the stage, but long before Eulogia reached the final painting on the stage, Arlene remembered that her aunt had looked at her long fingernail that beautiful morning and after several moments she had stared without words at Arlene. "The fingernail will have to go," that look told Arlene now, more than forty-five years after the aunt's demise. The long fingernail, the look said, was of a time when her man had been courting her and she did not know if she could give herself over to him to the exclusion of all other men. That was a different life, that courting life, and it would not do if something from that life left even the tiniest of scratches on her baby's cheek. Such is life, the look said to Arlene now. And then the aunt, arm in arm with her husband, had taken her place behind Arlene and her mother as they stepped onto the wooden bridge that was new and that was doomed.

❧

When the evening was done, the people in the auditorium rose as they applauded. Eulogia remained on the stage, looking out over the audience, her hands clasped before her. Arlene took Avis's hand and they went toward the front. Eulogia saw them and did not take her eyes from them as she came hurriedly to the end of the stage and down the stairs. There was a pool of many people in the aisle, and it took Eulogia some time to reach the woman and the child. Arlene picked up Avis. It was nearly two minutes before anyone spoke. "I have been looking for you from the beginning," Eulogia said to them both. "I know," Arlene said, though she had not known that before yesterday morning. "I know," Avis said, though she would not know the truth of what she was saying for three years, after her third miracle. "I looked," Eulogia said, "but I could only feel that you were somewhere out in the world looking for me as I was looking." "I know," Arlene said. Eulogia took Avis from Arlene and kissed the girl's cheek and Avis kissed her back. "I will see you all of the day tomorrow," Eulogia whispered to them and handed Avis back to her. She stepped to leave, then she turned back. "How will they be, if we who were present do not blow life into them and create them?" she asked Arlene. In all the belongings was there even one picture of her aunt? Eulogia said to Arlene, "You must tell me again tomorrow that it is this or it is being in the dark." "I will," Arlene said. "I will," Avis said. The nun came behind Eulogia and said her name, and Eulogia looked at the nun as if she had never seen her before. Eulogia disappeared through a side door, and the nun stayed with Arlene and Avis. Two men were on the stage, and first one and then the other told people that they were more than sorry but that none of the paintings were for sale.

The bus that took the newlyweds Arlene and Scott successfully through the forest one hundred thirty-seven miles southeast of Lima nearly went over a mountain three times, a mountain that their useless guidebook said "had grown up to keep the forest company." Arlene could see on her husband's face that he longed for the comparably easy roads of an Aruba or a Jamaica. She squeezed his thigh after the bus escaped going over the third time. The bus had done time on the streets of London for eighteen years and had then been imported to Peru seven years before. It was still red, but not a red any Londoner would know. Scott scooted closer to Arlene and put her hand in both of his. He was not afraid, but he knew her history by then and felt that if he were to be lost to her, he wanted her eyes and body to be the last things he saw and touched. Beyond the mountain, after four more tortuous miles, the bus and its people witnessed the road even out and they were fine for most of the miles into the town of Buena Serra—"Sweet Good-byes" was the translation of their guidebook, which not only offered poor translations but gave some Peruvian towns Italian names. Just outside of Buena Serra a field of purple cacti—all twelve feet or so high and none standing perfectly upright—rose up to greet them, and before long the bus coughed twice and gave out. Everyone had to get off, though the bus driver in his tuxedo promised that it would be repaired in no time, and he clapped his hands twice to the two Americans in case they did not know how quick Peruvian time could be. Arlene had, that morning before leaving their hotel, written her third postcard to her son and the fourth to Avis since arriving in Peru. Their luggage was two towns away, waiting at another hotel, and so it was not a difficult walk into the downtown of the very small Buena Serra. Arlene and Scott were thirsty and hungry and knew that if they were to enjoy more of what was ahead, they would need to fortify themselves. At the corner of a tiny one-story building that Arlene guessed was the town hall, a woman sat before a table with a pitcher of blue liquid and large paper cups. There was a sign in Spanish, but they did not know anything on it except for the word *aqua*. Scott, fingering his fanny pack, was skeptical, telling Arlene again that he wanted to drink nothing but Cokes and bottled water in foreign lands. *I hope that you, my love, might decide to see this place again for the first time when you are old enough,* she had written Avis two weeks before on that third Guatemalan postcard. *After Tennessee again for the first time, perhaps?* Arlene walked up to the woman, who stood and, without a word between them, poured some of the liquid into a paper cup. She handed the cup to Arlene and smiled and did not seem to mind that Scott held back. Arlene looked at her husband and at the woman, who was still smiling, and then, after she drank deeply, she handed the cup to her husband. "Drink," she said. "It will not kill us. I promise." "I miss Wesleyan," Scott said, which was what he often said when he was not quite certain of anything. "I miss Holy Cross," she said, which was her way of trying to ease his mind. "I miss Holy Cross." He did as she said, and as he drank, she stepped forward and looked at the road they were on. The road seemed to be shimmering and shuddering as it turned into a huddle of trees only a child's shout away. There the road quickly left her sight, so abruptly that it gave a small pain to her heart. She looked down at her dusty sandals, at her dusty feet, and then, a few seconds later, she took two steps forward and stopped. She was not a woman to carry a pocketbook everywhere, and so both of her hands were free that day. She made fists of them and rested the knuckles on her hips. She seemed to recognize what she was seeing now. A barely noticeable smile came to the edges of her mouth. The bright road eventually came back again and went on a bit until it dipped swiftly and disappeared once more. Momentarily. She waited and she could see, with some relief, where many people were walking and riding all along it once it reappeared, sloping gently down as it wound a crooked way to what her guidebook had told her was "the Valley of Enormous Science Mysteries and Smallest Happenings." She could see the eternal road emerge almost miraculously from the valley, still crooked, still shimmering, still full of humanity, and she turned to her new husband to tell him what the path ahead would be like.

ROOT WORKER

The witches began riding Dr. Glynnis Holloway's mother again almost as soon as the older woman returned that third and final time from St. Elizabeths Hospital. As before, the medicine—this time, a new brew of three different pills and a mauve liquid—that the St. Elizabeths people gave her did very little for the mother, Alberta Holloway; it served mostly to prevent her from knowing her own name for a few hours during the day. Dr. Glynnis Holloway and her father brought Alberta back to the doctor's $650,000 renovated home on S Street, N.W. In that house with three stories and a large basement where she practiced, the unmarried doctor had been living with her parents before the hospitalization. The witches had been riding Alberta off and on since her daughter had turned eleven, more than two decades before. Family love was a good thing, but it seemed that there was not enough love—from husband or from daughter—to stop the witches when they wanted to ride Alberta.

The subject of a voodoo practitioner, a root worker, entered Dr. Glynnis Holloway's home with Madeleine "Maddie" Williams, who had been hired to be Alberta's day companion after that last hospitalization. Maddie, a few years younger than Alberta, had a brother who had murdered his wife in cold blood while their two children slept, and the killing had taught her something about herself. During the interview for the companion job, Alberta's husband discovered that Maddie had come from the same spot in Person County, North Carolina, where he and Alberta had been born. Morton Holloway had not seen any of his family in North Carolina for almost as many years as his daughter Glynnis had been alive. But Maddie brought up name after name of the dead or the vanished, and each name relit a flame in Morton's heart so that before the end of the interview, he wanted no one else to companion his wife. Glynnis the doctor was less impressed but said nothing to her father, a chauffeur and a good man.

"Mr. Morton," Maddie said not a month after becoming companion to Alberta, "can I speak some words to you?" The murder of her best friend by Maddie's brother had awakened Maddie to the fact that she had been rather blind to the pain of others, even those close to her. "Just a few words, Mr. Morton," Maddie said. She spoke not long after lunch one day in late May, a rare mild day in a month that had seen more violently hot weather than even Washington was used to. Alberta was napping comfortably after her meal and after a long walk with Morton. And after the blue pill. Dr. Glynnis Holloway, a general practitioner, was in her basement office, seeing the nineteenth patient of the day. "Can I ask a few words about my patient, Mr. Morton?" "Patient" was how Maddie referred to all those she was companion to, although the firm she worked for referred to them as "clients" or "customers."

"I told you bout that 'Mr.' stuff," Morton said. It was a day off for the chauffeur, and while he had wanted to be with Alberta alone, Maddie had insisted on coming in, promising to stay out of the way. It had rained in the morning, but then the day turned kind. "I never know when my patient might need me," Maddie had said that morning, taking off her rain-soaked hat and coat in the front hall. The niece and nephew orphaned when her brother killed their mother were grown now, and her brother had long ago come out of Lorton Prison to face a world crippled by what he had done.

Morton said to Maddie, "Leave that 'Mr.' stuff for white folks. They got a need greater than mine." He was drinking his post-lunch coffee as he stood looking out the back window, at the miniature apple tree, at the garden in its first days of life, at the lovely winding brick path. The witches could come to ride anyone any time of the day, but they preferred a home when relatives or friends of victims were not up and about, so Alberta was sleeping peacefully.

Maddie asked how long Alberta had been suffering with "the head plague." He had not heard that phrase for some time, and he tried not to remember if it had last been in reference to his wife. In any case, the chauffeur was not offended. He set his cup and saucer on the table and lifted with one hand a chair up and away from the table and sat down. The maid/cook was quietly cleaning in the living room. Maddie sat as well, something she felt she could do, since they were of the same race. Two minutes later, she mentioned "head plague" again, and five minutes after that she began talking about witches, and Morton remembered that it had been some fifteen years since he had heard talk of witches. And it had not been in reference to his Alberta.

It would be days and days before Morton acquired heart enough to mention the conversation to his daughter Glynnis, and by then he had already decided he and Alberta would visit the root worker in North Carolina. He had long had faith in St. Elizabeths and their medicine, but now that faith was dying. They would have to go to North Carolina because the only competent root worker Maddie knew in D.C. had died the year before during her very first ride on the Metro. Cars and aboveground trains and buses and trucks were one thing, but a train snaking through the darkness of the Earth had done not very kind things to the root worker's heart.

After that final hospitalization at St. Elizabeths, Alberta would get sleepy in the evening far earlier than her husband and daughter, since the yellow pill was more effective at its job than the blue and magenta pills. Around nine o'clock, but never later than ten. And then about one in the morning, after a few hours of fitful sleep, Alberta, who slept alone after hospitalization and almost always slept on her back with a small Bible under her pillow, would usually become paralyzed after the first witch stepped boldly into the locked bedroom and took up her place across Alberta's legs. The second witch was a middle-body person, and she entered the room sitting on the whitest cloud through the window, open or closed, curtained or uncurtained. She sat on her haunches over Alberta's chest, her hands spread across the poor woman's breasts. Along about here Alberta, her heart and all the rest of her insides struggling to rise out of paralysis, began to sense some danger out there in the dark for her daughter and her husband. But never a thought for herself. *We'll kill em both. . . .*

Physician-to-be, never heal thyself. Not one soul in this room will ever, no matter what skills you acquire and master here, be able to cure fully the mechanisms of your own machine.

Glynnis Holloway's practice could have afforded her and her parents the kind of material life that they had not dared dream of as Glynnis was growing up in Washington, as Morton made a living for them as a chauffeur for the big boys with their big cigars at the Department of Labor. But, owing to Alberta's illness, so much was forbidden, like trips across the seas, or many consecutive nights of peaceful sleep, which even some of the poor in D.C. could afford. Glynnis could have paid for any psychiatric facility in the country, places the world had euphemisms for because fashion models and politicians and movie stars and the very wealthy went to them, people who—given their stations in life far above the nobodies who worshipped them—should have known better than to do such a common thing as lose their minds. But Morton had forever believed in St. Elizabeths. One day in 1963, not long after

Alberta's troubles began, he had taken his wife to D.C. General with the hope that they could help Alberta, who had, among other things, begun to neglect eleven-year-old Glynnis and her own appearance and so much else that had once come easily to her. Morton had met a psychiatrist at D.C. General, a woman who was losing her sight, and she had told Morton that first day, "We together will find a way to get your wife back to you." He had not wanted to believe anything as much as he wanted to believe that doctor's words. And even after the doctor, still wearing that tiny cross around her neck, had moved to St. Elizabeths and gone completely blind, he had clung to her words and would not take his wife anywhere but across the river to that place in Anacostia where they carted mad housewives, oppressed by a normal sunny day, and mad would-be assassins, launched by a kind of love, and even madder poets, crushed between the well-measured lines. And they carted in a few children who never knew that they had, in their own innocent ways, wandered off the civilized path. Alberta limped along, with good years and bad years.

H oney, you ever hear tell about root work?" Morton asked Glynnis as they sat side by side at the kitchen table two weeks after Maddie had spoken to him. Supper was over and the maid was gone and Alberta and the night companion, a young woman who did not yet believe in her own abilities, were in the living room, laughing at something on the big television. The witches had not come for two nights, and they would not arrive again for another night. Whenever Alberta screamed in the night, it was always Glynnis who reached her first, entering Alberta's second-floor bedroom with the key she kept around her neck. Alberta had insisted on the room being locked. The night companion, who slept on the third floor, did not have a key.

In the quiet of the kitchen, Morton and Glynnis were holding hands, two-thirds of an army that had fought battle after battle. She looked at the side of her father's face, at the well-trimmed hair and mustache. At a gray hair or two or three that were not easy to spot. Earlier that week, she had come upon her father looking for a long time at the labels on his wife's medicine. Glynnis had recently turned thirty-six, and it was only a year before that that she had started learning to measure men by a father who had read no more than ten books in his lifetime. Had started learning after Dr. John. After Dr. Theodore. In bed—with sex and the sweat and spit and other fluids the human body loved to produce—that was how she liked to call out to her lovers. After Dr. Frank. But she had never wanted them to call her Dr. Glynnis.

"You mean voodoo?" Glynnis said.

"Some's call it that. But when I was comin up in North Carolina, they was roots, done by a root worker." He knew well he was speaking to a woman who put her faith in science. *I know, I know,* she had thought as she watched him read the medicine labels, *I know science has failed us.* Morton now stood and placed both dessert dishes and forks into the sink and began washing them. He and the dishwashing machine did not get along. He knew well to whom he was speaking about root workers because that was how he had steered her life. Education. *Once they turn the lights on in your head, they can't turn em off.*

Glynnis laughed, and again the chauffeur was not offended. "Since when have you started to believe in that stuff, Daddy?" She could tell by the thoroughness with which he washed the dishes that his mind was made up about something. Already he had put a deposit on the chartered bus and already he had spoken four times to the root worker in North Carolina, a woman who sounded as if she had not had many conversations on the telephone. Each time they talked it seemed to take her nearly a minute to figure out which part of the telephone to speak into.

"I don't believe," Morton said, drying the second fork. "I can't says I ever will, but the world don't tell time by my watch. If the world say it's ten after seven"—he pointed to the clock on the wall—"and my faithful watch say it ain't even six o'clock, I got next to no choice but to change my watch around if I want to get there on time." Some ten years before, behind his daughter's back, he had put a little faith in a televangelist. Five hundred dollars of "love offerings." Seven prayer cloths. Eight little gold-plated crosses. A visit with Alberta to the D.C. Armory where the televangelist showed up drunk, though most of the four hundred desperate people there didn't notice because they thought the man was just broadcasting God's words on one of the man's weaker channels.

"What about the vacation, what about Massachusetts?" Glynnis said after Morton finally said he was planning a trip down to the root worker. Alberta did not enjoy going away from Washington, but she had found some peace in Massachusetts, in an enclave where many well-off blacks vacationed.

"Later in the summer, maybe," Morton said.

"I won't be going with you, Daddy," Glynnis said. She told herself she would not cry. He had always said no to one psychiatric facility after another, the ones with the wonderful brochures and the ones that had no brochures, just word of mouth among the wealthy who had fallen down and needed to be taught how to get up. "I am going to Massachusetts, just as I planned," Glynnis said. Morton went to her and held her. "I am going to Massachusetts to walk along the beach and read books that I should be ashamed to read."

"She wants me to bring the whole family," Morton said into his daughter's ear, speaking of the root worker.

"She wants the wrong thing," Glynnis said. She had considered becoming a psychiatrist, but in her second year in medical school, under the sway of the first woman to chair the neurology department, she had begun thinking that the entire human body was the larger territory she wanted to conquer. There were even things in the body that, if cured, could heal a sick mind.

St. Elizabeths Hospital across the Anacostia River was a very big place of land and many buildings and a few devoted workers. And some housewives and poets and a few children, the most innocent, had managed to find their lost minds there, only to lose them again. Morton Holloway, the father of the future doctor, would say to Glynnis, newly twelve, that day on K Street, N.E., "Child, whas done got into you? You lost your ever lovin mind?"

With the second witch now on her haunches across Alberta's chest, the doctor's mother sometimes got a feeling in her soul that there was a gas leak from the stove in the new kitchen on the first floor of Glynnis's home, a kitchen that should not have had any problems, since it cost more than some homes in the Washington area. *I must rise and warn them!* Alberta's mind told her. *Please, Lord, let me get up so my family won't die with all that gas!* (There was not always a threat to her family, but there was always paralysis.) Other times—and this was most common for Alberta, even with the increased police presence in the still-black neighborhood to protect the few white "pioneers" in their own renovated houses—the paralyzed Alberta became aware of robbers down at the back door. She could hear the thieves whispering, planning how to dismantle the alarm system and enter the house and kill her Morton and Glynnis and then steal, first, before anything, the drugs from her daughter's gleaming and glassy cabinets in the basement office. Comfortably perched on Alberta's chest, her hands over the mother's breasts, the second witch always twisted her upper body to acknowledge her sister, the first witch, with the slightest nod. Nothing more, for while they were family, they were not that kind of family. The greeting and the response—a deeper nod and two hissing bursts of breath into the second witch's face—were always the same. Downstairs, at the back door, one robber said to another, *I'll take the husband and you help me, cause he got them muscles.* And a third robber, coming leisurely up the lovely, winding brick path from the back gate to the steps, said, *I'll kill the daughter. I'll kill the doctor myself. We'll kill em both. . . .*

Physician-to-be, there are patients, and not very rare ones, who will come your way and tell you what is wrong with them and demand you follow along with a treatment they believe is best. First, physician-to-be, you must cure them of this barbarism that you are not the one who knows best, best about knowing what is wrong and best about knowing how to cure the machine and set it upright.

Her left hand holding a walking stick far older and far taller than she was, Imogene Satterfield was standing on her porch when the group from Washington rode up and parked across the two-lane road from her cottage of a house in the empty lot of Standing Rock Baptist Church. The driver of the chartered bus stuck her head out of the window and looked about, and when she noticed Imogene across the way, she shouted Hi and then she pulled her head in and stuck a hand out the window and waved to her. Imogene raised high the walking stick in greeting, the friendly though noncommittal one she reserved for people she could not remember if she had met before. She lowered the stick inch by slow inch, and when it touched the floor of the porch, the rubber tip said nothing. Snakes, each swallowing the tail of the one before it, were wrapped around the walking stick, and at the top there was a final snake with two heads, one looking up and the other looking down. Imogene was all dressed up, the way she would have been had she been going across the road to services at Standing Rock. It was late Thursday afternoon, and they were all about a mile outside of Roxboro, North Carolina.

While the bus driver remained behind to nap, Maddie, Alberta, Morton, and Glynnis crossed the road to Imogene's yard. The house, Glynnis could see while still in the road, was not large or small, and she decided as they came through the gate that it was just right for an old woman. A little less or a little more and it would not do. Imogene came down the stairs and put her arms about Maddie. The walking stick never left her hand. Maddie introduced her to the other three. "You's prettier than you was the last time," Imogene said to Maddie. "Them Washington waters got powers, I see." "I'm nearin fifty-five," Maddie said, blushing. "I know," Imogene said. "I was there at the birth fence." Glynnis saw that the old woman was cross-eyed, with thick eyeglasses. There was a medical term for cross-eyes, even though nothing could be done about it. *Two weeks from now I will beach myself in Massachusetts like a lost whale.* Imogene shook their hands and touched Alberta's cheek and then turned and led them into the house and set the walking stick down into a velvet-lined container just inside the door.

She settled them in the parlor and offered them something to eat and drink, "fresh mints" was how she put it. Maddie told Imogene to sit still, that she would bring in everything since she knew the kitchen. After Maddie left, Imogene devoted almost all her attention to Alberta, speaking comfortably to her, as if they had shared a womb together and had never lived apart aside from the last few weeks. And now they needed to catch up. While she had recalled many of Morton's people after Maddie's fourth telephone call to her from D.C., Imogene did not remember any of Alberta's people, and most of her gentle questions were about her family. Who was her mama? Who was her daddy? Imogene sat in an armchair at the edge of the couch where Alberta was sitting, and with just about every question, Imogene would lean forward and place her hand over Alberta's. Glynnis sat next to her mother, and Morton was across the room in a wooden chair next to a sealed box with a new television. Any sisters and brother around? Who was her grandparents on both sides of "the birth fence"?

Almost invariably, Glynnis would answer for her mother. It was a habit that had started in the early days of her mother's illness, one of many efforts to stand between her increasingly defenseless mother and a Washington world that mostly thought no one was safe when crazy people were roaming around among the sane. Roaming, like Alberta sometimes did, in her slip and no shoes and hair full of feathers because everything in the K Street, N.E., apartment, including the pillows, seemed to be coming apart. Glynnis, once one of the most popular girls on K Street where the witches began their campaign, had had her first fight at eleven with a girl who said she could get twenty-five dollars if she called St. Elizabeths. That had long been the rumor in Washington— St. Elizabeths gave twenty-five dollars in brand-new bills for every insane person that was turned in.

For a few questions, Imogene allowed Glynnis to speak for her mother, but then, just as Maddie was entering the room with a tray of drinks, Imogene excused herself to Alberta and reached across her and tapped Glynnis's knee with her crooked index finger. "Dr. Holloway, your mama deaf and dumb?" She was too old now for many of the courtesies once practiced. Time was no longer on her side. But she was not old enough to forget how she had been raised, and so the question came out in the sweetest of old-lady ways.

Glynnis was quite surprised at what she thought to be a derogatory term. She first looked at her mother and then over to her father, who had the look of a man very interested in what her answer might be. And as she looked down at the glass of orange juice Maddie placed on the coffee table, Glynnis realized that "dumb" for the old woman was not an ill-considered word for "mute."

"Please let her tell me, Dr. Holloway, with her own mouth words." Glynnis had been holding Alberta's hand, and now, embarrassed, she reluctantly let the hand go. "Please, Dr. Holloway," Imogene said, watching the hands come apart, "try some orange juice. It ain't fresh squeezed like Washington people might like it, but it be fresh and cold anough." Glynnis had been fortunate to find a doctor to replace her for what she told friends was a vacation that had to start earlier than planned. She had promised her father two weeks in North Carolina. But she was to be there seven weeks and would have to make a dozen calls before she could find two more doctors able to make way in their schedules for her additional time in a place not known for burning witches at the stake.

The questions from Imogene were ones that Alberta had not had to think about for a long time ("What crops your daddy grow?" "You look like a fresh butter woman, like me. You ever get that butter straight from them clappers?"), and she did not find it easy to root about the locked attic and come up with the answers. But as the afternoon wore on, she seemed to enjoy answering them, as if they were part of a difficult puzzle she was proud of finally coming to master.

Long before Alberta reached that point, Glynnis excused herself, rose, and left the room. She stood on the porch. The windows of the house were up and she could hear all of them, especially her mother, conversing. Maybe it was a North Carolina thing she, a D.C. baby, couldn't be party to. Maybe it was something put in the orange juice before their arrival. Her mother had said little all the way down from Washington. On the couch, with Imogene dominating her mother's attention, Glynnis had begun feeling something akin to what she felt way past the midpoint of so many relationships with men she had come to care about, something akin to what she felt when a professor in medical school praised a fellow student only minutes after the praise had come just as enthusiastically her own way.

She went down the three steps. There was a kind of garden on both sides of the pathway to the gate, a small garden, small enough, Glynnis decided with a smile, for a cross-eyed old woman given to dabbling in the black arts. There were no pretty flowers in the garden, nothing to please, nothing to say, "Come hither and feast of me with thy eye and thy nose." All of the garden, on both sides, was harsh-looking and forbidding, and of only a few colors, but particularly a kind of green, a green, one of Imogene's neighbors had once commented, that must have been painted by a tired God way late on the sixth day of Creation. No plant rose more than a foot above the ground. Glynnis smelled nothing but the warm earth. No problems with aphids or bunnies in this jungle, she thought. She did not know the names of anything in the garden and she shivered as she realized this, as she looked down and saw that her feet were but inches from whatever plant might assume a different life and slither from the garden.

She came to the gate and looked about at what was beyond the fence. North Carolina was nobody's Massachusetts. The name for what she felt as she listened to Imogene and her mother talking was coming to her, but it was not coming fast enough for the scientist in her. Across the road the bus driver was talking to a fellow with long dreadlocks. A black car was across the parking lot from the bus. It had been her father's idea for the bus, something, he said, with a comfortable cot or two and a place to prepare food and many cozy places to sit as they traveled from Washington to North Carolina. Like them big-time singers use when they go on the road, he said. The bus driver, Sandra, was the daughter of her father's friend, the woman who owned the chartered bus company. Sandra had shown up at the S Street house early that morning in the short skirt she was wearing now. Hoop earrings. Glynnis had been surprised at how well she drove.

Sandra now pointed across the road and waved at Glynnis, who nodded. Then the bus driver spoke to the dreadlock man, who looked at Glynnis only a moment, as if unimpressed. He finally shook the driver's hand and turned to the black car. His tied locks came down more than six inches below his neck and their tips flopped against his back as he moved. His hair reminded Glynnis of a mythological creature whose name escaped her as well. He drove to the edge of the lot and paused before going to Glynnis's right. He did not look her way again.

Sandra returned to the bus, and Glynnis went back to the steps. She reached the top of the steps, one hand on the post, and as her mother's laughter came to her through the light blue curtains that were blowing out the windows, through the tall lattice of the backs of the unmoving rocking chairs, the word also came to her. "I'll hold you tight, Mama, and nothin will get you tonight, you'll see." Many, many nights, after her mother began losing her mind, she had slept with her mother in her parents' bed. To make ends meet, her father, after chauffeuring all day, had begun taking odd jobs from seven in the evening until about two in the morning. Cleaning the floors of the bakery where they made Wonder bread. Holding the lamps for the skilled men who went down into manholes at night to fix leaking pipes or to turn the electricity back on. *Shine her a little brighter there, Morty. Just shine her that much brighter. . . .* "I'll hold you real tight, Mama. Don't worry." After Alberta told Glynnis about the riding witches, about how they came to her and threatened her family, the woman and the girl—slowly becoming mother to the mother—would plan how to fight the witches. She never told her husband. The fight amounted to no more than a Bible under Alberta's pillow and a butcher's knife under Glynnis's pillow. Weapons from an old wives' tale Alberta remembered from childhood. But they came anyway, after the two, exhausted, had fallen asleep. And in the day, from time to time, saying nothing to a sleeping Alberta, Glynnis would set out after the meanest girl in that K Street neighborhood, the meanest and the baddest among those who might have said something about her crazy-ass mama who shoulda had her flicted butt locked up in St. Elizabeths. Rocks, soda bottles, tree limbs, any weapon would do. Her fists still up, the toughest girl crying on the ground at her feet, Glynnis would sneer and threaten to beat them all up. The boys, liking her spunk, stayed out of it.

Imogene Satterfield was to say not a word about the fighting, but she would say, in six weeks, "They spit on the Bible, Dr. Holloway. Thas why it never helped. It ain't but a bunch of pages anyway. If every single Bible just up and disappeared from the Earth, Dr. Holloway, just about every last one a us would drop off to the fires cause all we ever had was pages to walk on." Imogene, that day, would test the moving water with the tip of the walking stick and then, in seconds it seemed to Glynnis, be on the other side. "And a witch ain't got blood to spill so a butcher knife is nothin but paper to them."

Glynnis now turned and looked about from the top of the porch. Jealousy was the word. Through all that time it had been her and her father who fought against the world. And when her father was away, she alone had barred the doors and dared the world and the witches to come in and touch one hair on her mother's head. "I'll hold you tight, Mama." And then, just that quick, she would wake to her mother crying or screaming beside her. No one knew what she and her father had gone through. No one knew her mother's pain. Not all the people at St. Elizabeths. She looked at Imogene's garden and heard music from the bus. She closed her eyes. Certainly not a cross-eyed woman.

Maddie came out to the porch. She said, "Dr. Holloway, you feelin all right?"

"Yes. Yes, I am." She opened her eyes. "I wanted to thank you for coming down with us."

"I must go with my patient," Maddie said. "I know you'd rather be someplace else on a vacation, Dr. Holloway, but sometimes black people from the South need to go back home. I'm sure your parents done said that." They had not. She herself had never seen North Carolina before that day, and she could not remember if her parents had ever seen the state again after her birth. "We leave, we run away and don't realize how much we'll need to go back home one day. The South is like that. It's the worst mama in the world and it's the best mama in the world." Maddie sighed and stepped closer. "Dr. Holloway, I needs to prepare you: she'll bring up the subject of you and Miss Alberta stayin here with her tonight. I just want to let you know."

"We have hotel rooms reserved, Maddie. For all of us, for you and Sandra, too." The plan had been for Sandra to leave the next day with the bus and return for them in two weeks. But the plan Imogene had, as Maddie had guessed, was for Glynnis and Alberta to stay with Imogene. Morton could stay in the bus parked in a larger lot on the other side of the church. Close but not too close.

"I know bout them reservations, Dr. Holloway, but thas why they invented the phone, for times like these. To say, 'I done changed my mind.' I've called my cousin and he'll take me and Sandra to his place."

Maddie touched Glynnis's arm so that the younger woman was forced to turn and face her. "Dr. Holloway, your mama is fine and maybe we should let that go on right now." They heard Imogene say something and then Alberta nearly shouted, "Yes, thas right. I almost forgot that, but that is right."

G lynnis woke about nine in the morning in a tiny back room of Imogene's house. She came from a dream in which several giggling girls were clustered in a corner talking about her mother. She, though a woman in the dream, was about to go to them and break it up. She had just raised her dukes when she told herself she was too old for such things and woke up. Glynnis sat on the side of the bed for several minutes and then went to the window and pulled aside the curtains and looked down at her mother and Imogene strolling through a garden far larger than the one at the front of the house. They were arm in arm and they were giggling and laughing. She did not feel the jealousy of the day before, and she wondered what could have gotten into her.

After she had showered and dressed in the bathroom adjoining the room where her mother had slept, she went downstairs. She was hungry but wary of eating anything in a voodoo woman's house. She went through the cabinets and the icebox and saw nothing appetizing. As she looked, she was trying to remember more of the evening before. After the entire group had eaten in the kitchen, Maddie and Sandra had been picked up, and her father had gone across the road to the bus. The last thing she fully remembered was sitting with her mother on the couch as Imogene poured tea from a cracked pot. Imogene then sat in her easy chair and took from a sweater pocket a small jar. After the teaspoon of sugar, after the wedge of lemon, she sprinkled dull green crushed leaves from the jar into her own cup. "A little for me," she said. "And a little less for you, sweet Alberta." And then, as her hand hovered over Glynnis's cup, she said, "And even less for the doctor from the state of Washington, D.C., where the president hangs his derby and picks his nose." Alberta laughed and picked up her cup. "Pinky out now, honey, like them white folks do," Imogene said. Alberta laughed again and Glynnis, before the leaves could fall, said she would pass on the tea.

The kitchen door had a window, and Glynnis could see her mother and Imogene, still arm in arm, come to the end of the garden. If the witches came during the night, she had not heard her mother scream. Beyond the garden, there was a wide field of green grass sprinkled with a few yellow and white flowers. Imogene raised her walking stick and pointed first right and then left. Alberta separated from Imogene and walked a few feet, pointed to the left and then turned and waved Imogene to her. The two entwined their arms again and stepped off to the left where, when the field ended, Glynnis could see the beginning of a kind of forest.

I will have to trust that she will be fine, Glynnis thought as she turned and surveyed the kitchen, which in the end was nothing special. Two plates with half-eaten toast on them testified to the fact that her mother had at least gone out with something in her stomach. Whether she had taken her medicine was another matter. To the right was an open door she had not seen when she came into the kitchen. She entered the small room, which she noticed had been built onto the original structure, and immediately became breathless at a grand and colorful array of thirty-five small jars on the five shelves facing her. Part of the grandness came from the simple uniformity of the lines of jars, all the size of the one Imogene had taken from her sweater the evening before. And the color was the ultimate result of the sun flowing into a window on the same side of the little room as the shelves. It poured in, rich and thick with yellow, and hit a series of framed photographs on the opposite wall, bounced and was transformed prismlike as it went back across the room to paint the jars in dozens of colors. And with those colors, the jars twinkled and shone and winked at Glynnis. She stepped closer and saw that none of the jars had labels, but it was obvious from the texture and gradations of limited colors that the contents were all different. The contrast between the world outside and inside the jars was great; everything inside them was dull, uninspiring, and so disappointing that she had to pull back her head and take in all the different lights again.

She picked up a few jars. So this is it, she thought, this is all the mumbo-jumbo shit, the workings of a cross-eyed root worker. She was tempted to open each one she held, but feared some pernicious odor would escape and overwhelm her. *D.C. Physician, a Credit to Her Race, Dies in Mishap at Crone's House.*

Once back in the kitchen, she was even hungrier. She found a box of crackers and stood at the entrance of the little room and ate them. She stepped in to see the photographs across from the jars. There were fifty or so, and they were all of babies and children, mostly black, but a good many were white and Indian. Some pictures, it seemed, had been taken ages ago. It was only now, her fingers finally touching the bottom of the box, that she wondered why she had not asked Miss Imogene what she had put into the tea.

"I have noticed," the dreadlock man with the black car was to say to Glynnis in two weeks, "that you have been calling her 'Miss Imogene.' I know it's routine to say it that way, but my grandmother has been conjuring for nearly seventy years, and no one around here, even white people, calls her anything but 'Dr. Imogene.'"

"I meant no disrespect," Glynnis was to say.

"I know you didn't, Dr. Holloway," the dreadlock man said, and when he lowered his eyes and then raised them again, she could see clearly that his blood and the old woman's blood were indeed the same. "And my grandmother would never say a word. Probably doesn't even notice that's what you are saying. But if people start hearing you call her like that, they will think less of you, Dr. Holloway. They will think you have no home training."

After the first two witches had taken their places on Alberta's body, she was never certain how the third witch entered the room. (Imogene Satterfield was to say offhandedly one day that while a human being might live in a one-room house with one door and one window, the Devil had a habit of making four more doors and four more windows just for his own convenience.) Alberta simply became aware that the third witch's upper body was suddenly across her face and neck, and her breathing became an awful struggle so that it was all she could do to suck in sufficient air that somehow found its way around the witch and through her clothes and into Alberta's mouth. *I'll kill the daughter. I'll kill the doctor myself.* Time was out of sorts. Once, only days after coming out of the hospital, she had managed to turn to look at the illuminated clock hands on the bedside table. Just before the paralysis—the riding—started, the clock had said 1:13, and when it ended, the clock told her 1:49. And another time, five days later, the elapsed time was but seven minutes. *We'll kill em both. . . .*

Maddie and Sandra left North Carolina, promising to return when they got the call. Glynnis's father spent his nights with Maddie's cousin, less than two miles down the road, and in the morning he walked back up that road to have breakfast with his family and Imogene. The old woman never called him anything but brother, and at first he, like his daughter, thought she did not even know his name.

For many nights, Glynnis, ever the good sentinel, stayed awake until well after one, waiting to hear her mother's screams, or some whimper of incapacitation. But her mother always slept through the night, and at first Glynnis was disappointed because the hum of nocturnal nothing, accompanied by a chorus of crickets and bullfrogs, would not get her to a shore in Massachusetts. Disappointed, too, that decades of science, hers and the world's, had not done the trick. Then, as they neared the end of the second week in North Carolina, as she started to simply give herself over to a full night's sleep, she saw how bad a daughter she was in being, at last, such a jealous soul. She did not know if her mother was still taking the medicine from St. Elizabeths.

It was in the third week that she began to suspect that they had fully turned a corner and that they might not have to go back to the old ways. That Monday Glynnis awakened in the late morning and looked down to Dr. Imogene attending to the garden in the back. The old woman was doing nothing special, simply going to various plants, bending down and touching them momentarily with her fingers. Caressing a few with the back of her hand. Her other hand held a watering jug, and to some plants she gave water, and to those she did not, she merely shook her head, not to them, but to herself. Since the last day of the second week, when Glynnis decided to stay even longer, she had been searching her memory. How long a period over the years had her mother gone without the witches riding, how long a time had she gone without doing something no sane person would do? She did not believe it had ever been more than a week. And now they were quickly approaching a month. Dr. Imogene stepped out to the path that divided the sections of her garden and took off her hat and fanned herself. She was mumbling. Dr. Imogene stepped into the other section of the garden, and Glynnis, still not fully awake, thought she saw the plants part to make way. A generous breeze came through and it moved the plants and it moved Dr. Imogene's red dress and it moved the curtain at Glynnis's window and it moved the babyish hairs on her arms. Glynnis raised her hands to her face and cried.

After showering and dressing, she came down and stood looking out the parlor window. There was not much in her view beyond the empty church across the road. Two mornings before she had stood at the window and saw her parents across that road in the church parking lot. Her father sat on the hood of the car he had rented for them. His back was to Glynnis and her mother stood just a tad to the side in front of him and her daughter could see her whole face. Alberta was talking and Morton did nothing but nod all the while. Alberta raised her arm and seemed to indicate with the movement of her hand something far off in the distance. Then Morton, as if he could no longer contain himself, pulled Alberta closer and kissed her for a long time. If they had ever kissed that way in Glynnis's lifetime, she could not remember. It would be another week before Dr. Imogene could disabuse her of the notion that there was anything magical in any of it. Her parents spent that night in a bed-and-breakfast in Roxboro, and they were there now. "Is it magic what sugar do to tea and cornflakes and cake batter, Dr. Holloway?"

Glynnis went out to the porch. She wanted to take a walk, she wanted lots of greasy food, she wanted a man to pull her close and put his hands over her behind and talk nasty to her, she wanted to get loud after two and a half beers in a bar surrounded by her girlfriends, she wanted to raise her eyes from a book and look briefly at the sea and think Lord what a dirty read. She went down the steps and stopped at the edge of one part of the garden. She knelt and took first one plant and then another in her fingers. There, close to them, she could see how different in color and texture was each section of plants on that side. But that was all she could see, and she sighed. "Is it magic what a little mint do to stinky breath? Is it magic that water be wet?"

Back in the house she found Dr. Imogene in her armchair holding the television remote control and pointing it at the television with channel after channel going by. Until the evening before, the machine had been in the box, and then, after Glynnis had gone to bed, Dr. Imogene's grandson, the dreadlock man, had taken it out and set it up. The old woman now punched button after button, trying to lower the volume. "May I?" Glynnis said and took the remote control, looked at it and cut the sound in half.

"Oh, dear," Dr. Imogene said. "Oh, dear dear dear. I never once wanted somebody's television box. I done had radios all my life and they done right by me, so what good would a TV do me? Till this one, I don't think I ever been in the same room with one for more than an hour or so."

"Then why one now, Dr. Imogene?" Glynnis asked. After five days of it, she had gotten used to calling her "doctor." She handed the control back to the old woman. On the television, a white man, his face red and very mean, was shouting at a woman, who was doing nothing in response but looking down at her feet.

"Jesse got it for me for my birthday. But I told him to keep it in the box till I got used to havin it. Last night he said it was time." She leaned her head to the side and looked puzzled. "Hmm . . . What done happened to those ladies talkin bout that princess lady? Where they done got to? Hmm . . ." Glynnis sat on the couch, her eyes fully on Dr. Imogene, who touched a button and watched as the channels sailed by again, her face growing ever puzzled. "Oh, dear. Where could they be?"

"Who?"

"The ladies on the TV talkin bout that po princess. I got sleepy last night and turned it off just when it was gettin interestin. I figured I'd get back to them ladies this mornin, but they gone. Where they could be?"

Glynnis began to realize what the root worker was thinking. "Doctor?" The old woman looked at her. "It does not stop, the things on the television. It all goes on, just as if you were still watching it. It isn't like a film you can stop." Dr. Imogene, reluctant to accept what she was hearing, pressed the button again, and the channels went on by. At last the old woman's shoulders drooped and she let out a breath. She gave the control to Glynnis as if to apologize for not believing at first. "I'll find out what happened to the princess and let you know. Every detail. I promise."

Glynnis would note the beginning of everlasting affection for the old woman from that moment. She had seen her do something extraordinary for Alberta, and the small jars and the pictures of the children on the tiny room's wall hinted at what she had done for others, but she did not know what a simple television could and could not do.

"Maybe we should turn it off for now," Dr. Imogene said and Glynnis did so. "We might as well go get some breakfast."

Physician-to-be, when it is all said and done, and the patient has recovered or is well on the way to recovery, you must not hesitate to say good-bye. By this point, you should have given only the prescribed amount of comfort and understanding. There should have been no love, because love, especially in its rawest form, risks wrecking the machine again and doing more harm to the mechanisms than what brought the machine to you in the first place.

As for the absence of recovery, as for death, there are machines that were not meant for the road.

They sat for a long time at the breakfast table, and somewhere toward the end of the meal of toast and one shared egg, Glynnis felt comfortable enough to ask about what had helped her mother, about the jars and the plants. The old woman pushed her glasses back on her nose and hunched her shoulders, as if all of it was no big deal, a mere stroll out to the end of the garden and back again.

She led Glynnis into the small room next to the kitchen and said, "Jesse once tried to put labels on them with some cellophane tape, but I always knew what I put in em, so them labels never done me no good. They got to fallin off them jars after a time, I guess cause they knew I didn't no more care bout em than the man in the moon."

"Which one sent the witches away from my mother? Which one gave her peace?"

Dr. Imogene reached up to the second shelf and took down a jar third from the end of the row. She handed it to Glynnis, who saw that while the dominant color was a muddy green, there were purple flecks along the edges of the leaves. "I was taught the names for all them things," Dr. Imogene said, "but then the root worker—bless her heart—who taught me died when I was young. I still didn't have a fixed mind, and it whatn't long fore I forgot the names of most things. My mind ain't never worked that way, even when sweet Evelyn was alive. This one"—she tapped the top of the jar in Glynnis's hand—"I just call Purple Mess. A body gets tired of callin em green this and green that. When Jesse was still in college, he brought by this book and showed me Purple Mess and a lotta other ones that was in it. Pictures pretty anough to frame, but none of that helped me member what the book was callin em."

"A rose by any—" Glynnis stopped as the old woman turned and considered the photographs of the children on the other wall.

"These many of the chirren I help bring into the world," Dr. Imogene said. "These was all trouble births. A root worker gotta know to fix them hands on a woman's stomach somewhere after the fourth month and know if the baby wants to come out easy anough or take the road harder than ordinary. Then you gotta know what to do to help em both." She turned back to the jars and the first fullness of the sun came through the window, hit the photographs and rested upon the women's backs. What was left of the sun went around them and over them and between them to hit the jars. "I failed many a one, but what root worker puts that up on the wall. You can see that clearer than a picture every minute of God's day you look inside."

Glynnis returned Purple Mess to the shelf, and it was then that the old woman told her there was no magic in any of it, for she had begun to feel that the younger woman was headed that way. She led Glynnis out to the garden in the back. She pointed to a patch of less than one square foot and told Glynnis that was Purple Mess. "It grows wild down at the creek. It's a nice spot and a body can sit there all day on it and watch the water flow on by." In the garden, Purple Mess was the smallest patch of all. "Not many people suffer with witches ridin em, but you can't stop growin it cause who knows what God'll put in front a you." Glynnis stood at the edge of the garden. "Go over to it, Dr. Holloway. Go on in there and see that Purple Mess ain't nothin special."

Talk of the jars and the photographs and the garden seemed to have opened a sad room in Dr. Imogene's heart, and she was mostly quiet throughout the last of the morning and into the first touches of the afternoon. She busied herself with minor chores—from washing the breakfast dishes to fluffing the couch pillows—and Glynnis followed her about, helping where she could, waiting in case the root worker needed to share something. Now and again Dr. Imogene would stop in the midst of some job and stare into the eyes of the younger woman, as if the latter could read her mind and aid by putting into words what the root worker could not say. In her beginning days as a doctor, Glynnis had had a patient who, a month or so into her treatment for hyperthyroidism, would stand silent for several minutes after her session. Glynnis, uncomfortable, new to it all, used the time at first to make notes as the patient stood with her back to the door, her eyes to the floor. Then, toward the end of a year of treating her, Glynnis learned to rid herself of the woman by asking before even a minute of silence had gone by, before she had started to wash her hands, "Will that be all, Mrs. Evans?" Hyperthyroidism became hypothyroidism, and the treatment and the seconds of silence at the door went on, until one day in their third year together Mrs. Evans failed to show up for an appointment, and her file was returned that very morning to the cabinet where it was even now.

Just before two Glynnis suggested that she fix lunch, and Dr. Imogene said that was the best idea of the day. As Glynnis stood at the kitchen counter, preparing the sandwiches, the root worker came up beside her and touched the young woman's shoulder and Glynnis decided right then to cut the sandwiches into fours rather than halves. "You know, Dr. Holloway, I must say the truth of it, but you would make somebody a good mama." Glynnis was both puzzled and moved by the statement. It was as if someone, seeing her step deftly over a small puddle, had told her she would make a good trapeze artist. "I'm not sure that's on the horizon for me." "It all be on the horizon, Doctor, until the horizon goes away and never comes back."

With each bite, the root worker returned to her old self, and before she had eaten half of her sandwich, she said out of the blue, "You know, I knew bout a root worker not far from here when I was just a little old girl who took to sittin under people's windows at night. I woke up with her on my mind this mornin for some reason."

"A Peepin Tom, huh?"

"Oh, no, Dr. Holloway, I don't think she was impish bad that way." The old woman leaned her head back and closed her eyes. "She just listened to what folks was sayin inside. She thought it was a way of gettin the rest of the story when folks came for help. A body comes to you for help, say like the witches with our Alberta. Maybe she thought it helped to know that her neighbor wanted her outa the way for somethin. Had it in bad for her."

Glynnis said, "There was no one like that around us."

"No, no, Doctor, I'm usin that as a xample of what that long-gone root worker was up to." She sensed that Glynnis had misunderstood and she endeavored to choose the right words. "She figured if she could know what folks did when the day was bein put to bed, then she could know more about treatin em. Or say you got a woman heartsick ova some no-good man and wants to keep him close. Maybe that worker thought it good to know what went on at night, and for every bad thing a woman would say about that, there'd be five good ones, and not very good ones. 'But he bathes every day . . . But he always says he sorry . . .' Why help a woman keep that kinda man? When a man's heart is rotten, no amount of bathin gonna help."

Glynnis nodded. "I can't see you listening outside someone's window."

"Oh, I neva thought of goin that route, Dr. Holloway. One little 'Boo' and I'm outa my skin." She smiled. "And cause I knew I ain't nobody's nightwalker, I knew I had to try to read folks as best I could, and thas somethin I ain't neva done well. Maybe it was better if I was one for the night. Woulda made things easier. You try not to do the wrong thing, but sometimes, many's the time, you fall down short." She drank from the coffee cup and set the empty cup in the middle of the plate. "I wish I could know what it was that happened to our sweet Alberta. . . . I knew of a situation where this woman carried this hatred for her friend—her best friend, mind you, Dr. Holloway—for years, clean outa the time they was chirren and into them bein grown women. Grown and owin to not one soul, but that hatred wouldn't ever go away. She carried it like we carry babies, only this neva got old anough to come out. So we gets round to one evenin. Maybe they was drinkin. Celebratin, maybe. And this pain, it just took a hold on the hurtin woman and she stole somethin from the friend's place. Only she took a thing that belonged to the woman the friend was stayin with. A handkerchief, a brush fulla hair. And the hurtin woman couldn't see cause the hurtin wouldn't let her. She just took it to a root worker, and that friend's friend neva walked again."

A few ticks beyond four o'clock, Jesse came. Glynnis and Dr. Imogene, who was holding the walking stick with the snakes, were standing on the porch. "I have a body comin," the root worker had said before rising from the lunch table. "We can talk some more later." Jesse parked in the church lot, got out, opened the door for a woman who was almost as old as Dr. Imogene, and helped her out, aided by someone Dr. Imogene said was her daughter. That woman was about Glynnis's age. The root worker went down the steps to the path leading to the gate, and Glynnis thought that that was how she was the day they all arrived from Washington, a long, long time ago. She watched the group cross the road, and before they had reached the gate, Dr. Imogene raised the empty hand Hello and the old woman coming her way raised her hand as well. Once they were inside the gate, the old women kissed, lips to lips, and the younger woman kissed the root worker on the cheek. And after the mother and daughter and the root worker went inside, Jesse asked Glynnis how the vacation was going.

"It's getting to be more and more like a busman's holiday," she said. Then she nodded toward the house and asked, "What's wrong with her, if I can ask?"

"Who?"

"The mother."

"It isn't the mother, Dr. Holloway. It's the daughter." The week before, Jesse had told her about not calling his grandmother "Miss Imogene." He was nearest the gate, and now he went past Glynnis toward the house, and as he went along the path, he seemed to scrutinize the plants on either side, as a gardener might look over the work to be done. He walked to the side of the house and down along the narrow passage that led to the back. "They're the richest people about," he said quietly, and she followed. In the back, he knelt and leaned forward and smelled several of the plants on either side. "Black or white. They are undertakers, but she and my grandmother grew up like sisters, with practically nothing." He stood up and went to the gate, and she continued to follow.

"She looks so healthy, the daughter. Extraordinarily beautiful and healthy."

"You should know better, Dr. Holloway. You of all people." He opened the gate. "Why don't we walk along. I have to return in a bit and take them back. I've become a jack-of-all-trades for my grandmother." He closed the gate after her, and they crossed to the field. "My grandmother has a saying—'The wellest day you ever had, you sick anough to die.' That means a pack of stampeding elephants could come down this way and run over you, Dr. Holloway, and no matter how perfect and beautiful you are, that would be it. Or a plane could drop from the sky onto your pretty head. What could your healthy body do against that? Healthiness certainly didn't help my parents in that collision with that fuck of a drunken driver. Going to church, no less." She would remind him of his words four years later, some weeks after the funeral, where the two, in utter mourning and despair, sat side by side as the crowd flowed down and about and then out the cemetery, beyond the road and all over the land of the old white farmer and his wife, who had not suffered headaches many a day and who themselves were standing but three feet from the preacher as the man of God spoke about her, failing even with his hour of talking to do her justice.

The field ended and they stepped into the forest. "I got to know this place quite well as a boy, after I became an orphan." There was a band holding his dreadlocks together and he took it off and shook the locks and put the band around his wrist. "I got a sense that you want to learn what she has. You should tell her. You should tell her you wouldn't mind being her student. After my mother died, I think she felt no one would ever come along. Then you show up, a little uppity, but still teachable. God knows I could never do it. Men don't make the best conjurers."

"Why?"

"I suppose we can be slow learners, Dr. Holloway. And by the time we get it, it's time to die." He laughed. The forest smelled as it might after a heavy rain, though it had not rained in several days. "I read this article once about the discovery of aspirin. Maybe the writer made the whole thing up. The aspirin plant, the guy said, was found near some riverbank. A woman with a bad headache wandered in pain and just started eating the plant, that's how crazy the headache had made her. She didn't know it would do anything. She was just crazy with pain. But it did the trick. Only steps from her front door. I told that to my grandmother and she said maybe that was a lesson for all those people who go around the world to India and Tibet and places, trying to find a cure for what ails them. They come back chanting and all, but that cure never lasts." They went deeper into the forest, and soon Glynnis heard the creek several yards ahead, a soothing sound that she thought must have been the same decades before when he was a boy. "The undertaker family has traveled everywhere trying to help the daughter, and now they are with my grandmother just up the road from that mansion." She asked if the undertaker's daughter was among the children on Dr. Imogene's wall. "No," he said, "but that would not have saved her. My father is on that wall. That did not save him. . . ." He came to a tree and touched the trunk. "I could have sworn I put initials here." He walked around the tree. "They aren't here now. . . . God how I loved that girl when we were young." Glynnis looked at him and he looked away from her because that was not a thought he had ever put into words. "We best be getting back, Dr. Holloway."

Her parents came early that evening to take her and the root worker to dinner, and during the trip to and from the restaurant, she watched from the back as Alberta would now and again reach over and pat Morton's thigh. Jesse had said he would join them, but he never showed. After Alberta had a glass of wine, she decided it was the perfect time to talk about the first time she and Morton met. It was on a narrow street in Durham and it was morning and there was fog, which lasted the whole day.

With the third witch covering Alberta's face and neck, the first robber opened the glass storm door at the back of Glynnis's house on S Street and turned the knob of the mahogany door that weighed almost as much as a small man, and despite the expensive lock and the expensive alarm, the door came open, as if someone on the inside had simply unlocked it. The robbers entered one by one, an orderly, unhurried line. *We'll kill em both. . . .* It was about here that Alberta's struggle for release from the witches began with a greater effort, and it always began with moving her left big toe. The first witch did her best, but Alberta's legs were a lot of territory to be covered. The toe was a summons, and its moving would lead to the slightest twitching of a muscle in the lower leg and gradually, as her body came back to life with movement—from legs to stomach to the twisting of her head—escape would arrive some time after a final heaving of her chest, and Alberta would sit up, clutching her throat and listening to the quiet of a house well made all over again. No sounds from departing witches or robbers, but somehow the quiet was even more frightening, and Alberta, a kind and generous woman created to one day accompany God sometimes as he strolled and pondered in the gardens of heaven, would find enough air to scream, the same kind of scream she had been uttering for more than two decades, whether her husband or Glynnis or the Bible was sleeping with her.

The night of the dinner with her parents, with the image of Alberta at the restaurant table stuck in her mind's eye, Glynnis asked Dr. Imogene about learning some things from her, that there were more than a few souls in Washington, D.C., who might be helped. The root worker nodded several times, but she said nothing, simply leaned forward and sprinkled into Glynnis's tea a third of the many crushed leaves she put into her own cup.

It hurt more than she had realized that Dr. Imogene had not responded, and Glynnis awoke the next morning knowing that despite the things of North Carolina, her place as a physician was in Washington where in twenty or thirty years few would know that there had ever been root workers. She showered, and as she dressed in her tiny room, she saw the old woman and Jesse in the back garden. The root worker's head was down, and she seemed to be shaking. Let North Carolina stay where it was. She could rent a car and be in Washington before nightfall. Jesse now put his arms around Dr. Imogene, whose back was to Glynnis.

She went downstairs and out to the porch. Her parents planned to travel to Florida. If the witches never returned, then the trip would have been worth it. She did not know what had become of the St. Elizabeths medicine. As she thought of the days in North Carolina, she began to think so much of it was like a spell, and to ask about the medicine might cause everything to fall apart. So let the death of the witches be the best thing that happened. She had always done well by her patients, and that would continue to be the case. What shit in a little jar could cure a broken leg?

A silver Cadillac came into the church lot and parked next to Jesse's car. A man in an off-white suit got out of the Cadillac and stepped away from the car and looked at it for a long time. If his face showed nothing else, it showed how proud he was of the automobile. The man came across and with every step he would look back at the car. As he opened and closed the gate, he was taking off his hat and smiling at Glynnis, looking up and down her body.

"And a good mornin to you, beautiful lady," he said, coming up the path and never taking his eyes from her body.

"Good morning."

Dr. Imogene and Jesse came out onto the porch, and the man said good morning to them. "Dr. Imogene, had I'da known you had such awful good-lookin company, I'da come along sooner." He put his hat on.

Dr. Imogene introduced Glynnis as "a professor doctor from the state of Washington, D.C." She added that Glynnis was a friend of long standing and, pointing to the man, told Glynnis that George was a patient of many years. He took off his hat again and kissed Glynnis's hand, which he had to pull from her side. "Dr. Imogene brought me into this world," George said. He went on to say that he had come with a problem of "the utmost urgency."

"Then les you and me go into the kitchen, George."

"And les bring along your mighty good-lookin company since she is a professor doctor. I love the ladies, Dr. Imogene. I have no secrets from those I love, and there is nothin I love more than the ladies. I love them in the mornin, in the afternoon, in the evenin, in the night. Ladies all the time."

He went on until the root worker opened the screen door and said, "If Holloway wants to come along, she is more than welcome." Glynnis followed George and looked a moment at Jesse, who smiled at her and went down to the path and out the gate.

In the kitchen, George continued about how much he loved women and everything that had anything to do with them. Dr. Imogene seemed to have nothing better to do than listen to him. Where, Glynnis wondered with amusement, was all that patience when she was answering for her mother that first day? In the end George turned in his chair at the table and winked at Glynnis, who was sitting off to the side. His two front teeth were gold, and even in the poor light of the kitchen, they shone. "But I must say that lately my potency has been sufferin and thas why I'm here." He looked back at the root worker, who was across the table from him. "What is any man to do in such situations who cherishes and treasures the ladies? I ask you, what is any man to do?"

D r. Holloway, when you hear a man going on and on about his love for women, he is talking pussy," Jesse said. They were in the front yard and George was gone and Dr. Imogene had gone into the backyard. "It's a sad truth, but a truth nevertheless." He would say a long time from that day that he sensed her drifting away from what he was saying and that the only way to bring her back was to use a crude word.

"You sound like you know all about it," Glynnis said.

"Only a sinner can tell you about sin, Dr. Holloway. And when the pussy is done, such a man would want the woman to turn into a pool table with one good opponent waiting at the other end. Or a lake full of the biggest fish around."

"What will she do for him?" George had left with only the promise by Dr. Imogene "to study on the matter."

"I don't know, but it won't be anything he's thinking. It might just be something to give him aura so that even the dumbest woman will know what she's in for. Unless she likes being a fish or an eight ball." He opened the gate and stepped to the other side and closed the gate. "If you're wondering why she hasn't spoken about telling you about that root work stuff, I think she was overwhelmed, rather amazed that someone like you would care enough to know what is in her head."

"I do care. I did not think I would, but I do. I was beginning to think I wasn't worthy of all those jars with the green stuff."

"Take her by the hand and walk out to the forest this evening after supper. You'll find that she is terrified of death. Not so much the dying part, but of dying with all that stuff in her head." He turned and looked up and down the road before crossing. "I was such a disappointment to her." He went to the other side of the road.

I had a little talk with Dr. Imogene day fore yesterday," Maddie said to Glynnis. They were alone in Dr. Holloway's kitchen. "She said give you all the love she has in her." It was Sunday morning in October, and Maddie had come at Glynnis's invitation to talk about what Maddie could do now that Alberta might not need the same kind of care. Glynnis's parents were at church, and they would be there most of the day. The doctor had been thinking that Maddie might assist in the basement office, especially with patients who would, with word spreading, come in search of help that came out of small mason jars, help from plants that were now growing in the backyard on either side of the lovely, winding path. She had spoken with Jesse only a few days before, because, strangely, the plants that received the most light were not doing as well as those with less light.

"How is she?" Glynnis asked. "I'll be calling her tonight. If I don't speak to her at least twice a week, I feel out of touch." Jesse had promised to come up that coming week. The problem, he had said of the plants, might be a fixable case of "a failure to thrive" under the Washington sun.

"She's well," Maddie said. "We didn't talk about you necessarily, Dr. Holloway, but somethin just stepped into my head no sooner I hung up that telephone. Somethin about Alberta."

"Oh?" Glynnis said. They were drinking tea. Half a pinch of Imogene's leaves in Maddie's. Two full pinches in Dr. Holloway's. It looks nice, Jesse was to say of her hair on Wednesday, as he stood less than a foot behind her. And she would say as she turned to face him, They treat you well at Cleopatra's Hair Emporium. It would not be Dr. Jesse.

"Yes. It occurred to me to wonder, Dr. Holloway, if you knew just how all the witches and everything started with your mother. Was there such a such somethin that happened on such a such a day that you can remember? Did Alberta bother such a such somebody without even knowin it?"

"No. I can't think of Mama hurting a living soul. You know her."

"I do. I do. I know her heart. I know my patient well," Maddie said and took her saltless cracker and dipped it into her cup and put the cracker into her mouth.

Glynnis told Maddie she knew where it had started, but very little beyond that, and Maddie dipped another saltless cracker into the cup. This one dissolved immediately and she had to spoon it out bit by bit and ate. She looked up at Glynnis with the last bit and said in a most offhanded way, as if the idea had only that second come to her, "Maybe if we went there, somethin might come back to you. That is, if you have a little time." The doctor knew enough by then to take seriously any suggestion from this woman. "It ain't a bad day out there."

L̲ong before they reached 1st Street, N.E., Glynnis found that so much had changed, disappeared, but everything that was important to white people remained. Gonzaga High School. The railroad. After 1st Street, she saw that many of the places she had known as a girl were still standing, and that gave her heart some relief. She turned off K onto 6th and found a parking space and then she and Maddie walked down to K and turned east, toward the house at 727 where she as a girl had lived on the second floor. She recalled some houses from childhood as they went along, though many had been renovated and repainted. She had expected more white faces, but there were not very many. At the corner of 7th and K, Glynnis looked back and then forward again and wondered if the world seemed smaller because she was bigger or because she knew more about that world. "It might be," Maddie had said just before they crossed from Northwest into Northeast, "that our sweet Alberta was conjured and thas why the witches was ridin. Who can know the truth, Dr. Holloway?"

Glynnis, with Maddie only two feet behind her, stepped onto 7th Street and immediately a car horn honked. She looked to the left, saw a car heading toward her and was confused about what it meant until the car braked only a few feet from her. She jumped back and Maddie took her by the arm. The car rolled forward and the driver leaned across the seat and said, "Sister, me and you both glad it wasn't your day." Glynnis, still somewhat confused, said quietly, "I'm on K Street. I'm walking on K Street, mister." The man blinked, looked at Maddie, sat up straight and went on.

The doctor crossed 7th Street and Maddie followed. A woman was coming toward them. Beside her was a boy on a small bicycle. On the woman's black sweatshirt were the red and green words IT'S A BLACK THING. . . . The boy, unlike any of the children when she was growing up, was wearing a helmet. Jack fell down and didn't break his crown. . . . The woman with the boy said Good afternoon and Maddie nodded and Glynnis only partly understood the words and could manage nothing more than a smile. A smile because though she didn't know all of what the woman was saying, she still didn't want the woman to think her parents had not given her the proper home training. The woman and the boy passed and Glynnis turned and looked at them. The back of the woman's sweatshirt offered the red and green words . . . YOU WOULDN'T UNDERSTAND. At the 7th Street corner, the two stopped and the woman leaned to the side and cupped her hand over the boy's shoulder farthest from her.

When the doctor turned back, she found that she was in front of 727 and she looked up to the second floor to see her mother standing between the parted blue curtains, blowing a kiss at her. Alberta was healthy, and Glynnis knew that because when she looked down K she saw herself at ten walking hand in hand with her father toward 8th Street. All that week of being ten her father had promised her a Saturday of shopping and a movie at the Atlas theater and a half smoke from Mile Long as they went up and down the busy commercial H Street. Just him and her, and no going away to work for him. She looked up again at Alberta, who blew her another kiss. She looked back down K and saw Maddie several feet behind, her hands behind her back. There was no look on Maddie's face that Glynnis could decipher.

And when she turned around, she saw a woman come around the corner of 8th and K. Morton took off his hat as he did with all women and he and the woman began talking. Had Glynnis let go of her father's hand and gone to the corner, she might have been able to look down toward H and see all the excitement of a Saturday on H Street. The happy children. The Atlas announcing in big letters on its marquee what extraordinary movie awaited a child just steps beyond the ticket booth. And candy without end that might rot a girl's teeth on any other day of the week, but not on a special Saturday.

The woman Morton was talking to had five children and a husband dying of a disease that was squeezing his lungs into balls no bigger than a child's fists. In fifteen years they would have a cure for that. Alberta and Morton had given the family money and groceries because once upon a time the family had done well and Alberta and Morton knew that that could be their lot one day. "Go by and see Alberta," Morton said to the woman, "and set your troubles aside for a bit. A little coffee, a little pastry might be just the medicine for a nice Saturday mornin." The woman said that was where she was headed, to thank Alberta for the ham. "We'll eat for days." And down on H Street there was Morton's Department Store, which Glynnis and Morton always joked was owned by him, but it had to be kept secret or the world would come knocking at his door wanting free clothes. Glynnis the girl thought she could hear the H Street gaiety, could smell the half smokes and hot dogs, could see some undeserving girl getting some dress that would be perfect for her.

But Morton and the woman talked on, for hours and hours and hours, it seemed, and not a single word of it was as important as H Street, and all the people passed on either side of them, no doubt heading down beyond I Street to H where everything wonderful was happening. The sun grew higher and all the precious time in the world drifted on by the girl who was destined to become a doctor. In the end, Glynnis, squirming as the pleasures sailed out of reach, said to the woman, "You so black and fat and ugly, I don't know why my daddy even talkin to you," and she pulled impatiently at her father's hand. "I wish your black self was dead." The woman, injured deep, all the way into the bone, could manage only a nearly silent "What?" She fell back half a step. "I meant to do no harm," the woman said to Morton, as if he shared what his daughter, in her pretty dress and her pretty shoes, was thinking.

The woman went back the way she had come. "Millie, wait now," Morton said, but in a twinkle the woman was gone. Morton jerked on Glynnis's hand as people came and went on K Street. "Child," he said, "whas done got into you? You lost your ever lovin mind?" Had a root worker, on her way to get eggs and milk or meet up with her boyfriend or take coffee with a relative, heard Glynnis and decided to come to Millie's aid? Les teach that naughty child a lesson.

Glynnis watched as Morton and the child she had been came back to 727. He was shaking with each step and he was calling for Alberta, who was darker than Millie. And the day—and many days after—was dead for Glynnis. She had bragged all that week to friends about the day she would have with her father, about all the things she would get. Less than two months later, the witches began riding Alberta.

Dr. Holloway, with Maddie still several feet behind her, now walked to 8th and looked down toward H and saw and heard nothing special. Had Millie gone to some root worker and asked for help in getting rid of Alberta so Morton would be free to be with her? But that was not the Millie she remembered. No, perhaps it had begun with her, with the future physician who wished the poor woman dead. Glynnis's words heard by some mischievous or well-meaning root worker strolling by, a misguided woman from the same school of roots attended by the worker in North Carolina who listened outside windows at night. Maddie came up behind Glynnis and called her by her full name without the doctor title, and Glynnis heard her. Yes, perhaps a passing root worker who had heard Glynnis that Saturday morning and seen Millie's pain and was determined to set the world straight. A root doctor who did not know or care about the facts and history of the case, but had decided nevertheless to prescribe, to grant, unasked, the lonely woman abused by a child—however innocent, however good and obedient all the other days of the year—one wish for free. Granted the wish with a brew of mumbo-jumbo and an innocent mother's hair and fingernail clippings and God only knew what else scrounged from the trash in the witch deadness of night. Granted the wish and then never came back to review and perhaps undo what she had done.

COMMON LAW

Seven-year-old Amy Witherspoon, only child of Idabelle and Matthew Witherspoon, knew pretty Miss Georgia real well, pretty Miss Georgia with all her precious clothes and her precious shoes, but the girl didn't know very much about the man who knocked Miss Georgia down the stairs in July 1955. Amy had never paid much attention to the man before that Saturday afternoon she looked up from the stoop leading to the stairs to Georgia's place, up from being on her foursies while playing jacks with Ethel Brown, and saw the man at the top of Miss Georgia's stairs, his fists balled up and his face full of meanness.

As it happened, the man who knocked Miss Georgia down the stairs had been introduced to the pretty woman just two weeks before by Amy's own daddy at the What Ailing Ya beer garden at the southwest corner of 5th and M Streets, N.W. Georgia Evans was her parents' third child, and before she left home, she had never seen any sky but the sky over Scottsboro, Alabama. Georgia had been married three times, but her mama and daddy had never seen the third man in the flesh because he was killed not long after the honeymoon in 1953 by a blind man who claimed he was shooting at someone else. The parents had a picture of the third husband with his arm around Georgia, taken the day before he died; it was stuck in their mirror frame just above the one of their youngest child in his high school graduation cap and gown.

Georgia had always considered the corners of 5th and M as her lucky corners. One night in a rainstorm, she had found a diamond ring on the ground in front of the liquor store on the northeast corner, and on the southwest corner she had met her second husband as she came out of the Goldbergs' basement grocery store. "Ma'am, do you know which way is Ridge Street?" the man who would be her second husband asked, arrayed in a blue sharkskin suit. "I sure do. I live on Ridge Street. Just come this way." He was a good husband, brought his paycheck home to her for many years, but he was forever homesick for Mississippi, and that was what did in their love, or so the children—who got it secondhand by listening in on grown folks' conversations—on Ridge Street said.

"Georgia, this here my friend Kenyon," Amy Witherspoon's father Matthew said the night he introduced her to the man who would knock her down the stairs and dare her to get up and come up for some more. It was a Thursday and the What Ailing Ya wasn't very crowded. Georgia was one of three women in the beer garden, the only unattached one, and for more than a half an hour she had been drinking beer in a corner booth a few feet from the jukebox, thinking about what numbers she would play tomorrow. Her pet number, 459, had come out 549 that day, and she was upset because she hadn't played it in a combination and had lost $200. She had planned to go straight home from being a maid all day at the hotel at 14th and Pennsylvania Avenue, but something told her to take in a beer in the same spot where she had first met her last boyfriend, and then, two months later in the same booth, told him to kiss her ass before kissing the Devil's ass. She wasn't necessarily looking for a boyfriend that night she met Kenyon.

"Hi you do, Georgia? Thas a pretty name," Kenyon said. Then he told his first lie: "Georgia my favorite state." He actually hated the state of Georgia because it had executed his uncle, an armless man who was as innocent as Jesus Christ. Kenyon was kind of tall, depending upon how much leaning he did, and he was as light-skinned as Sweet Daddy Grace, whose church at 6th and M Georgia sometimes attended. She went to that church only because she admired Sweet Daddy's long fingernails. Kenyon was a chauffeur and he had on his dark gray chauffeur suit. "And another damn thing," Georgia would say after he had slapped her three times that Saturday afternoon and before he knocked her down the stairs, "why don't you get another suit? I'm sick and tired of seein you traipsin round here in that one."

"Thank you, Kenyon," Georgia said after he told her she had a pretty name. She took a big swig of her beer because she knew another would soon be on the way. "Thank you very much. It was my mama's mama's name. Kenyon is a nice name, too. And thas a nice suit you wearin there."

"Just my everyday-go-to-work clothes."

"Oh? What kinda work you do, Kenyon?"

"Well," Matthew said. "I see you in good hands, Georgia, so I'm gonna leave you two to get acquainted."

"Good hands?" Georgia said. She was at the top of her second beer, and that was always the point where everything in the world started looking like Christmas morning after the second of ten gifts had been opened. "A girl sometimes needs more than good hands. She needs them capable hands."

Kenyon laughed, and then Matthew trailed behind him seconds later with his own laughter. Matthew, father to the child Amy, had been three days sober, was trying to stay sober for his little girl. And when he was sober he processed everything a mite slower, or so all his friends said. Actually, it was simply that the world wasn't very funny when he wasn't drinking. Matthew was in that beer garden because he figured that if Jesus could resist temptation in the desert with the Devil dogging him, then he, lowly Matthew, could face temptation in a bar. But the Devil had gotten smarter in two thousand years, and now he had less to work with.

"I got the best hands. Capable hands," Kenyon said, and Matthew slapped him on the back and went back to his Pepsi-Cola at the bar. Matthew didn't drink anything stronger that night, but the Devil sat down next to him the next night. It took the gray-suited Devil only eight minutes, and it wasn't long before Amy's father was raising his glass of rum and soda and singing to an applauding bar:

> *Pepsi-Cola hits the spot*
> *12 ounces that's a lot*
> *Twice as much for a nickel, too,*
> *Pepsi-Cola is the drink for you.*

"Mind if I have a seat?" Kenyon said, already on the way to sitting down before she could answer.

"It's a free country," Georgia said.

"Everywhere but in your space. Can I buy you a beer?"

"Sure," Georgia said. "But why don't you wait till I'm finished this one."

He looked at how much was still in her glass and said, "Then you don't plan on kickin me away from your table any time soon."

"I don't know. It depends on how much you get on my nerves. I might kick you out, but your beer gonna stay." He laughed and she laughed. The last woman Kenyon Morrison was boyfriend to was even now in the house of her childhood on East Capitol Street, N.E., recovering from a broken jaw and a dislocated eye socket. The pain medicine the D.C. General people had prescribed gave her nightmares, and she would wake and scream that she had to hide from Jesus. After she had been beaten up the last time and her jaw made to wobble from side to side like a rickety streetcar and her eye threatening to become mush, she and her children had to move in with her parents because she could not care for them anymore. "I love you, Kenyon," she said to the ambulance attendant through a delirium of pain on the way to D.C. General. "I love you." The woman and her nightmares had set the house of her child-hood on edge, and her little girl and her little boy were failing life and her parents, who had never raised their hands to each other, thought that this would be their lot for the rest of their days—caring for a once-upon-a-time good and strong woman who had had so much promise but now was going insane in the light blue room she had been happy in as a girl.

"Oh, so thas how it gonna be, huh?" Kenyon said. "Love my beer but don't love me."

"I didn't say that," Georgia said and took a large sip of the beer that would be the last she would buy for herself that night. "I didn't say that atall. Don't you be puttin words in my mouth."

"I'm sorry. I wouldn't do that. It's just that the idea of you kickin me away made me kinda sad, thas all."

"Awww, sweetums. I apologize. Okay? Does that feel better? I'm sorry."

"I don't know if I'm ready to cept your pology yet. We'll see. We'll just have to see." He was a very handsome man and had teeth so beauti-ful that women often thought at first that they were false. But he would click them for a woman, and she knew right off that they were real. Georgia prided herself on not being one to go for looks in a man, but that was not true, and any of her friends—from Martha Smith to Frieda Carson to Cornelia Walsh—would have said so.

Kenyon moved into Georgia's place at 459 Ridge Street, N.W., eigh-teen days after they met. "I know it's sudden," Georgia told Cor-nelia Walsh. It was the Sunday before he moved in, and Cornelia and her daughter Lydia had come to visit. Lydia was in the big easy chair next to the window, playing with her Chatty Cathy doll, listening and not listen-ing to the grown folks. "My name is Lydia and I live in Washington," the girl sang, bouncing the doll on her knees. "Lydia is my name and Washington is my city."

"Well, just be careful," said Cornelia, a religious woman whose one dream was to see the Holy Land before she died. Her daughter had promised her that she would become a doctor and make enough money to take her there.

About then Kenyon knocked at the door and Georgia got up from the couch to let him in. Tomorrow, before twilight, he would have his own key. He came in and Georgia introduced him to Cornelia and her daughter Lydia and he shook Cornelia's hand and told her he had heard what a good and fine woman she was and then he pinched Lydia's cheek and told her she would be as pretty as her mother one day. Sooner, he added, if she drank her milk every day. "Whas that dolly's name?" he asked, still leaning toward the girl and her doll. He stood up straight before she could answer and told Georgia he didn't want to be late for that double feature at the Gem, that she'd better get herself ready and tell her company she'd see them another day. Georgia started to say something, but she didn't think it was worth the effort, and besides, he had dressed up nice to take her to the moving picture show.

Downstairs out on the street, the child Amy Witherspoon said Hi to Georgia and Cornelia and Lydia, and then everyone had to say Hi back to her and her two little friends, Carlos Newman and Ethel Brown. Georgia asked Ethel how her mother was because her mother had been doing poorly since she had her second child, and Ethel said she was doing better and that the baby was going to be christened Saturday, no maybe not Saturday but Sunday if her grandmother got down in time from Philadelphia, which was in Pennsylvania, Miss Georgia, you know. And Georgia said she was glad to hear that. Kenyon stood to the side of everyone, the sweetness was gone from his Juicy Fruit gum, and he wanted another stick real bad. Then the two women listened as the two girls talked about their dolls and Amy said she had left her doll at home to rest up from the big Princess ball that was held last night, and the two women looked at each other in a ain't-that-cute way and the boy Carlos popped three big bubbles with his Bazooka bubble gum, which still had plenty of sweetness left. The third pop made Kenyon grab Georgia's shoulder and tell her loudly that he didn't want to miss that gotdamn double feature at that gotdamn Gem Theater. And Ethel went Oohh oohh you said a bad word and Kenyon walked away toward 5th Street.

"I best get on," Georgia said to everyone, but especially to Cornelia, her friend of fifteen years.

"I talk to you later," Cornelia said and Georgia went off after Kenyon, who was only a few feet from 5th. The Gem was playing something with Robert Taylor and he liked Taylor, liked him even more than he liked John Garfield.

"I tell my mama you asked bout her," Ethel shouted to Georgia. "We still waitin on my grandma from Philadelphia, down in Pennsylvania. . . ." Ethel's mother had been a Crenshaw before marriage, and everyone in the neighborhood said that if you married a Crenshaw you had a good partner for life, that they were true and blue and everything one might want in a good wife or a good husband. You could take that to the bank and they wouldn't blink when they gave you a million dollars on it.

The four of them, the woman and the boy and the two girls, watched Georgia catch up with Kenyon and shift her pocketbook to her right hand and slip her left arm through his. He was walking a bit away from the curb, not giving her enough room to walk between him and the houses on the right, and so she had to bump bump bump him with her hip toward the curb because etiquette required that a woman walk on the inside and a man walk on the outside to protect her from whatever might come from the street and the gutter. Kenyon resisted because even as they walked, he could see Robert Taylor already up on the Gem's screen saying and doing things that made his heart flutter and his brain go Yeah, yeah, thas the way to do it, Bobby. You tell em.

Judy Hathaway came up from the other side of Ridge Street and said Good afternoon to Cornelia, mentioned what a nice Sunday it was. Judy was sixty-seven years old, and if anyone in the neighborhood had to play a number, they went to her. She was the mother to four children, but they had all perished in their thirties, a child each year for four years in a row—breast cancer, heart attack, a questionable accident while in the navy, a self-inflicted wound to the temple. Judy knew what it was like to lose a child, Amy's mother once said. "I couldn't find a better godmother to look after my child."

"Where you headed?" Cornelia asked Judy.

"Just round to the sto. Got a taste for some stew meat tonight."

"That sounds just right," Cornelia said. "I know where I'm eatin tonight." Most colored people on Ridge Street ate chicken on Sunday, but Judy wasn't most colored people.

"Can I come, too, Grandma?" the girl Ethel said. They were not blood kin, but nearly every child on Ridge Street who could speak called Judy Grandma. Carlos Newman was one of the few who didn't. The boy had two grandmothers already, and he knew and loved them very well. But more than that, he was very new to Ridge Street and was just feeling his way. He, like Amy and Ethel, was seven years old.

Judy laughed at Ethel and swept the girl to her. "Sho. I make anough for everybody," and she kissed the child not once, but three times about the cheek. At twenty-four Judy had killed her first husband way deep in the woods where they had lived and then she had run away from Arkansas, telling everyone she ever met that she was a child of Louisiana. The only witnesses to her murdering her husband were the animals they had around the place—the chickens the husband always threw his shoe at. The brown dog that whimpered to see his master dead in the kitchen; the same dog that always brought the shoe back. The white dog that followed Judy as she dragged the dead man out the back door and around the well and to the garden. She had fewer muscles than she would have when she arrived in Washington seventeen years later, so hauling her dead man around the garden would have taken her another half a day. Instead, to save time, she pulled her dead man through the garden, a ragged trail through that bed of perfect and ripe food, then out along the beaten path to the place behind the privy. The brown dog stayed home.

The white dog did not follow through the garden because his master had trained him with sticks and stones not to go near the garden, so he took the long way to the grave. They had no neighbors to speak of. When it was time to leave—after the grave had settled so that anyone seeing it might think a body was the very last thing buried there—the white dog followed her quite eagerly, but the brown one would not go, despite all her pleading. "There ain't nothin for you here anymore. Come with us." But the brown creature knew what the white dog was to learn beyond Arkansas—that leaving that place could break your heart, even while traveling with a loved one.

"Well," Cornelia said to Judy, "me and Lydia might as well come along to the sto since we goin that way anyway."

"Can I come, too, Grandma?" Amy said, and Judy said the same thing to her that she had said to Ethel.

"Yall go tell somebody where you at then." The two girls ran to their homes to tell somebody.

Carlos looked at Amy running away, then looked up at Judy, who said to him, "You can come, too, if you mama say so." She did not know him very well, but that would change.

Carlos nodded and set off for home, across Ridge Street. He didn't care about the store and Miss Judy and playing about on a bright Sunday, but he was in love with Amy Witherspoon and he could barely stand to be out of her presence. Amy knew he cared about her but always told people she was going to marry her daddy when she grew up. I just can't marry you, she would tell Carlos, less my daddy died and I was a poor widow woman. Daddy being Matthew Witherspoon, who had returned to drink after the Devil sat down next to him at What Ailing Ya. Carlos knew marriage to her father would never happen, and he believed that if he held on long enough she would be his to marry. In three months he would be eight years old. His heart would not beat for very long on Ridge Street, but as long as it did, it would beat for Amy.

"I wish I could find me some nice greens," Cornelia said. "I done had a taste for greens for the longest."

"You and me both," Judy said.

"I mean what I said bout comin over to supper," Judy said. "Vinnie eat like a bird and I end up havin all them leftovers. Leftovers leftovers. Sometimes I think I'm gonna die of leftovers."

Lydia, holding her doll up in front of her, skipped down past three houses over the brick sidewalk, turned and hopscotched back over an invisible board. She chanted:

Yo mama and my mama was out back, hangin up clothes
My mama socked yo mama in her big old fat nose.

Two weeks later, on a Saturday morning in early July, Carlos woke in his bed at 450 Ridge and raised his hand and traced the cracks in the ceiling with his index finger. It was going to be a long morning because Amy had told him she was sleeping over at her father's mother's house and wouldn't be back until about noon. He had made three good male friends on Ridge, but they sometimes said nasty things about girls, about pussy and stuff, and he was worried that any day now they would say something bad about Amy and then he'd have to fight them, use his fists just the way his father had taught him. But maybe not; after all, the three had sisters and they would have to put their own sisters in that nasty bag they put all the other girls in.

He cocked his finger and shot at the crack that was a robber man. "Badge 714 got you again," he said. He rolled over and thought of watching television. They had one, but his father didn't think much of it and had gotten one just to placate his wife and Carlos and Carlos's older brother. His father had bought the television set on time, though he could have afforded to pay for it outright.

Carlos sat on the side of the bed and picked at the scab on his knee, the result of a fall the day before. He pulled out his quarter from under his mattress and flipped it once, dropping it and watching it roll across the floor and fall next to one of his brother's socks. The television had a little metal box on the side, and whenever the Newman family wanted to watch it, they would insert a quarter in the box and the television would give them an hour's worth of viewing. Sometimes the box gave them a few minutes more of viewing, sometimes a few minutes less. Every Saturday afternoon a white man in a noisy little truck came and opened the box and gave the Newmans a receipt for whatever was in the box, as well as a receipt for any extra money they wanted to pay down on the television. "At this rate," Carol Newman once told her husband, "we'll be paying on this thing when we're too old to even see it." "Thas the whole idea," Brandon said and kissed his wife full on the lips. "But you'll still have this." "I might be too old to enjoy that, too," Carol said. "Oh no, my lovin never goes outa style." The worst thing for Carlos was to be watching wrestling on a Saturday night and have the set go dark just when the program got good and there weren't any quarters to be found in the whole house. Even Brandon Newman hated that.

Carlos got down to crawl to retrieve the quarter. For that moment he forgot the sore and the pain of hitting the floor jolted him. "Damn!" he said. He stopped and waited and listened. His door was closed, but his mother had a thousand ears and most of them were in the walls. For her, cursing was one of the biggest sins because, as she told her sons time and time again, it led to greater sins, like robbery and the end of the family and rape and the suffering of children in Africa and even murder. "Damn" in itself was not a very big word, only four letters, and yet it could lead to the end of the world. Carlos's brother believed her, but Carlos was a little slow in accepting.

He crawled the rest of the way to the quarter. He picked it up and read the words on it. Was an hour of television worth it right now? He stood and remembered all that he could buy with a quarter for Amy. Twenty-five Mary Janes. Twenty-five Squirrel Nuts. They could feast for days, while television was here and then gone. And who knew what was on right then? He put the quarter in his mouth and said, "Mother, may I?" and made two giant steps over to his side of the room. On the other side, he decided to save his money.

"Put your clothes on, boy. I want you ready to eat when your father gets back from the store." His mother was standing in the door. Her face said she hadn't heard the bad word. "Yes, ma'am. Mama, what time is it?" "Near about nine o'clock." She closed the door. Three hours until Amy. God was such a mean man. Why couldn't he put noon closer to nine? Nine, twelve, ten, eleven, one. . . .

He got outside about ten-thirty and saw Georgia's Kenyon moving slowly across the street. Kenyon stood outside 459 Ridge and called up to Georgia, who stuck her head out the window. Carlos couldn't hear what they were saying, but Georgia kept shaking her head to everything Kenyon said. Carlos lived next door to Judy Hathaway and her third husband, Vinnie, who had two cars. He was working on one of them, a Dodge he called Portia Did-Me-Wrong, and after a while he raised his head from under the hood to look at Kenyon. Finally, Kenyon said loud enough for Carlos and Vinnie to hear, "I don't give a sweet gotdamn bout that, Georgia!" Across and down the street, Ethel and Billie Montcrief heard him, too; nine-year-old Billie still had the cast on his arm from falling out of the tree a week before. "Just throw it down here, Georgia! Do I gotta do everything myself? Can't you listen to a damn thing I say. Lord have mercy!" Vinnie and Carlos looked at each other, and the man smiled and wiped his hands with a dirty cloth he pulled from his pocket and the boy shrugged. Kenyon had a suit on, but it wasn't his chauffeur suit.

Billie saw Carlos and shouted for him to come cross the street to play with him and Ethel and Tommy Carson, who was trying to skate toward them but was doing more falling than he was skating. Georgia threw something in a paper bag out of the window and after Kenyon inspected it, he said, "This ain't the shit I want, Georgia. You fuckin dumb bitch."

Vinnie kept on looking at Carlos. The night of the day Vinnie married Judy, she told him what she had done in Arkansas. She began to cry and he pulled her to him; it would be another two days before they would consummate their marriage. One-arm Billie shouted to Carlos, "My mama won't let me cross the street no more since my accident." Everyone knew that by now but Billie felt he had to repeat it as much as possible so no one would think he was being a sissy on his own. "I got this cast on and stuff . . ." In two giant steps, Kenyon was up the stoop and then through the door to the stairs leading up to Georgia's apartment. Carlos couldn't hear him bounding up the steps to the apartment, but Tommy could because he, sitting on the ground and tightening his skates, was the closest to Georgia's place. "Come on over, Carlos," Billie said. Standing between Vinnie's car and his father's car, Carlos looked right and left and then dashed across.

Amy came back early, about eleven, and Carlos was happier. A small group of children gravitated down the street to the shared stoop onto which Georgia and Tommy Carson's doors opened. Tommy and his family lived in the downstairs apartment. The skates were hand-me-downs from his brother, which was why he was having so much trouble with them. His mother had promised him a brand-new pair for Christmas, but this was July and if there was anything Tommy Carson could do right, it was count.

Kenyon had left the door open when he had gone upstairs, as well as the door to the apartment itself, but none of the children noticed as they sat and played around the stoop about one-thirty. One-arm Billie and Carlos were making copies of the funny papers from some Silly Putty Carlos had brought over, and Tommy was on the ground putting WD-40 into the wheels of the skates. He had surmised that that was the real problem with them—ball bearings thirsty for oil. "Now do that one," Billie said to Carlos, pointing to a fat man on the funny page with a green suit. Billie liked the way everything came out on the putty the reverse of whatever the funny page showed. "Then do his wife after that." "How you know thas his wife?" Carlos asked. "I can just tell thas his wife."

On the stoop with the boys were Amy and Ethel, playing jacks. Amy always had trouble after passing her foursies. She had just kissed the ball for good luck and started in on her threesies when everyone save Tommy, who was spinning the skate wheels to see if they sounded any different, heard the *thump* and then the *thumpety-thump* coming from up at Miss Georgia's place. Amy made her threesies and kissed the ball again and threw the jacks. She had just picked up her first four when there was another thump and Georgia came tumbling down the steps. Her body twisted about midway the descent as she tried to grip the banister, but Kenyon had hit her too hard for her to get a good grip, and after her body twisted she began to fall, about halfway, with her head first. She had on a housecoat, and the girls and the boys could see her shame with her red underwear as the housecoat came loose in the fall. She bumped her way down to the entrance, screaming and crying on every step. At the bottom, she lay silent for a minute or so, her eyes closed, and each boy and each girl thought she was dead. "Miss Georgia?" Amy said. Georgia was a good woman, Amy's mother had once said, but she wouldn't make the kind of godmother that Miss Judy would.

Georgia opened her eyes and looked at Amy from upside down. And then, like some kind of afterthought, a small jewel of blood appeared at the corner of her mouth. "Miss Georgia?" Georgia used what strength she had left to lift her arm from her chest, which was heaving, and raise her hand to the little girl. "Just leave her be," Kenyon said from the top of the stairs. He had on the same suit from that morning and his fists were on his hips. A lion tamer in a movie had stood like that, Carlos thought. Amy, sitting, scooted closer to Georgia, her hand out to the woman. "Miss Georgia?" "I said to leave her be!" Kenyon took his fists from his hips to emphasize what he was saying. "Miss Georgia, I'm here . . ." Kenyon was down the steps, straddling Georgia. He raised his foot to tap Amy's hand away. Georgia's hand was still reaching out to Amy. "Hey!" Carlos said, looking at Kenyon's foot. "Hey!" Kenyon pulled his foot back even though Amy had kept her hand out to Georgia. "You little shit," Kenyon said to Carlos. "Learn to respect your damn elders." "Ooh, ooh," Ethel said. "He said a bad word." Kenyon closed the door with his foot.

Amy fainted as soon as the lock on the door clicked in place. She would have hit her head on the concrete, but she fell toward Carlos and her head hit his chest, and, once again, the boy thought he was looking at a dead person. "Amy," he said, "please don't be dead." Tommy ran up the steps of the stoop and said he was going to get his father. One-arm Billie said he was going to get Amy's mother and he took off. Ethel stood watching Carlos hold Amy. He was a boy all skin and bones, but that wasn't why she hadn't liked him very much until that very moment. "She ain't dead, Carlos," Ethel said, "I can see her breathin and stuff." "You sure, Ethel. You sure . . . ?" The boy was crying. "I'm sure, Carlos. I can see her breathin right on like all the time before."

Tommy's father Moses came out and collected Amy in his arms. "What yall doin out here for her to get hurt?" "Nothin, Daddy," Tommy said, one skate in each hand. "It was Mr. Kenyon and Miss Georgia fightin." Moses Carson took Amy down the street to her house and the children trailed after him. "We didn't do nothin, Daddy," Tommy kept saying. Moses was not a father to be shy with the switch or the belt and Tommy needed to get his innocence on the record real quick. "We was just playin, havin fun. Thas all." Amy woke halfway there, and halfway to her house her mother and one-arm Billie met Moses. "I think she just fainted or somethin, Idabelle," Moses said. "She gon be all right." "It was them, Daddy," Tommy said. "We didn't do nothin." Moses said, "Les just get her in the house." Idabelle went to her house and opened the door and Moses stepped through the door and put Amy down gently on the couch. "You gon be fine," Moses said. "Daddy, we was just playin and—" "I heard you, Tommy. For goodness sakes!"

The children crowded around the couch. "Yall back off," Moses said, "and give her a little room." They stepped back, Carlos drying his tears on the bottom of his polo shirt and Ethel saying it was the bad man that hurt Amy and Idabelle putting a wet cloth to her child's forehead while asking Ethel what bad man, what bad man would hurt a child? Still holding his skates, Tommy, emboldened by the knowledge that he was free and clear, told Idabelle that nobody really hit Amy but Kenyon did hit Georgia. The adults looked at each other. "Ain't that right, Carlos?" Tommy asked. Amy moaned on the couch, her eyes closed.

The children in the living room were not among those in the neighborhood known to be liars—the-wolf-is-comin-so-you-better-get-your-gun type of liars. Twelve-year-old Larry Comstock down the street at 412 Ridge was that kind of liar; people said they couldn't be that big a liar if their middle names were Liar. He lied like a grown man, people said. He said he saw his grandmother's best friend burn his grandmother's hair in a brown-and-white cereal bowl and turn around three times while the hair burned green and then purple and while the friend shouted Jesus get way back and Devil come forward. By the time people realized he was lying about that and most everything else, the two women, who had come up together from South Carolina when neither had child nor chick, had fallen out with one another, and Larry was on his way to reform school for breaking into houses and drinking people's liquor and falling asleep drunk in their beds with his dirty tennis shoes on.

So when Moses looked at Idabelle and they both looked at the moaning Amy, they were thinking of Larry, and they knew that Tommy and Ethel and Carlos were not in Larry's league. But still, there was too much strange talk of a child and hitting and a man, and so they called the police. An hour later, the police came, the white one staying outside in the squad car reading the newspaper with a giant magnifying glass while the Negro went into Idabelle's. The policeman listened to the children, then went down the street to talk with Kenyon while the white man drove the car down the few doors. After the Negro policeman finished, he came back, walked into the wrong house, then found Idabelle's, and the white policeman reversed the car and came back to where he had been reading the newspaper with the magnifying glass.

Kenyon was innocent of hitting the child, the Negro policeman concluded and left the home and got into the passenger seat and they drove away.

Amy did not go back out to play that day. Despite the truth as determined by Idabelle and Moses and the police, the word went around that day among the children of Ridge Street who had not been witnesses that Kenyon had beaten up not only Georgia but Carlos and Tommy. He had half killed Amy, which was why she wasn't outside. He had broken Billie's other arm, which explained his absence, though in fact the boy had only gone to the movies with his father and two sisters and his aunt Lavenia Middleton, who was getting married in September for the first time at forty-nine. She was marrying a Jasper, one of the Northeast Jaspers. People said she was lucky not to get mixed up with one of the Southwest Jaspers.

Amy slept the rest of the day and all night, and in the morning she had her first dream that Georgia was coming to get her, and not her daddy or mama or Grandma Judy with her walking stick or anyone else could protect her. Her mother had to shake the screaming girl awake at about ten on Sunday morning. "Is she here?" Amy kept saying after she woke. "Is Miss Georgia here to get me?" "Nobody's here but me and Abe," Idabelle said. Abe Thatcher was the man who loved and wanted to marry Idabelle if she could straighten out where in her life Amy's father fit. Day by day she was coming to the conclusion that there was no future with her estranged husband Matthew.

Idabelle took Amy in her arms. The fan in the window blew on them and Idabelle wiped the sweat from her daughter's face and Abe Thatcher stood in the doorway with his hands in his pockets. Amy was the first child he had ever been close to as a man, and he didn't know what to do.

His parents, a Negro and a Jewish woman, had headed a socialist organization in New York City. He had wanted Amy to call him Abe but Idabelle, like most everyone else in D.C. who wasn't raised a New York socialist, didn't believe in children calling grown-ups by their first names. Amy usually called him Mr. Abe, though only yesterday she had taken the first step to him and called him "my Able Abe with the missin tooth." The fan was blowing too loud, and Abe wondered if it was the motor or the blades hitting the protective grill. "Miss Georgia's comin to get me, Mama," Amy said after she had calmed. "Georgia likes you, honey pie. She wouldn't hurt you for anything in the world." "She did in the dream, Mama. She really did. She had her hand out and she said, 'Ima get you, Amy. Ima really get you this time.'" "Well, we gon give you a bath and some of Abe's famous flapjacks and you gon feel right as rain. No more bad dreams after that." "What about my tattoo?" Amy said. She had a temporary tattoo of a butterfly that Carlos had applied on Saturday; Carlos had bought ten tattoos on a piece of paper for a nickel and Amy had licked a spot on her wrist and he tore off the corner with the butterfly and applied it to the spot. "We'll wash all around it. You just hold your arm up from the water and it'll stay on forever."

The dream came back that afternoon and the girl sat on the couch wrapped in a blanket for the rest of the day. She begged to sleep with her mother, and she managed to get a little sleep that Sunday night with her mother's arms around her.

Generally, she stayed with Judy during the summer days while her mother worked. That Monday she begged her mother to stay home, but Idabelle said she had to work for them to live right. Amy didn't cry and let her mother go off without a word. During her lunch break as a keypunch operator at the Federal Housing Administration, Idabelle called around and found Matthew and told him his daughter needed him. "I just saw her on Saturday morning," Matthew said, "and she was doin fine." He was confused and was thinking of a Saturday two weeks before. "You fool," Idabelle said, "that was then. This is Monday and she

needs you to go by to see how she's doin." "Why don't you get your Abe
to see how she's doin?" He knew he didn't love her anymore, but the
Devil in the gray suit made him say some awful things.

They were both quiet, for he knew Abe was a good man. Matthew
was many things, but he was not a blind fool. "I like him," Amy had said
to her father and his mother. The fault had long been Matthew's, the
drinking, this woman, that woman. Idabelle had been long-suffering; a
blues woman could sing a whole album about her, and she and Matthew
both knew that. So after the silence, he said he would go by to see Amy.
She hung up and stared at the telephone dial. For many years she had
remembered his telephone number from when they first met, afraid that
to forget meant he would disappear from her life. It was DECatur 7-4
something or other; nowadays, she had to consult her address book for
the numbers after the four. Abe had said he was ready to buy her a ring
when she was ready. He sometimes used big words when little ones
would suffice, but she liked the way she could put the very tip of her
tongue through that space in his teeth and make him tingle.

Amy Witherspoon did not fare well for much of the rest of the
summer. When not plagued with the dreams about Georgia,
the child suffered a lethargy that caused her to sleep most of the time
on her mother's couch during the evenings and weekends or on Judy's
couch during the days while her mother worked. Amy, "poor Idabelle's miracle after goin through so many miscarriages," was well
liked in the neighborhood, and everyone prayed that she would get
better, but in their beds at night, after the lights had been turned out,
adults feared that the girl was not long for this world. The doctors,
none of whom were native Washingtonians, knew nothing, blaming
everything on the D.C. heat. "Keep her cool," they said. Children
continued to play on Ridge Street that summer, but they tried to be
quiet when near Idabelle's or Judy's. "Shhh, stop bein so loud," they

told each other. That was also the way they were when near a house where there had been a recent death. "Shhh, Miss Rita just died in there. Les go someplace else."

Carlos and Ethel came each day to see her and Amy would rouse herself to play on the living room floor at her mother's or Judy's. Carlos, to be sure, was particularly affected by not having her play with him outside. He bought her Sno-Ball cupcakes and Nehi sodas and Kits by the handful, but the girl of early summer was not there. While she slept, he came to enjoy talking to Miss Judy, usually over sodas in her kitchen. She had pictures of a colored Jesus in every room in her house and Carlos asked her, during their first full conversation, if she had had some little boy put a brown face on Jesus with a crayon, for he had known only a white Jesus.

By mid-August, he felt comfortable enough with Judy to tell her that people said Amy was going to die and he had to beat one boy up for saying it. "I didn't wanna hurt him, Miss Judy, but I had to." It was a Friday. He, like Amy and several other children, usually stayed with Judy while their parents worked. "Thas two fights I been in this year," Carlos said. He showed her the sore on his knuckle and she put Mercurochrome on it and told him he should watch himself because he might get into a fix he couldn't get out of.

Then he told her that if Amy hadn't seen Kenyon do what he did to Georgia, everything would have been all right. "She saw him beat Georgia?" Judy said. They were talking in early August.

"Saw him knock her down the steps," Carlos said. "I did, too. We all did. He kinda went like this—POW!—and down she went. POW!"

"Oh, mercy!" Judy peered around the corner of the kitchen to make sure Amy was still sleeping on the couch. She knew the girl often dreamed of Georgia, but she hadn't known that she had seen the violence, and as she listened to Carlos, she wondered why Amy didn't dream of Kenyon.

"Miss Judy, she was bleedin, too."

"Who?" People had rarely come to visit her and her first husband in those woods in Arkansas. Not being a very strong woman, she had had to dig the grave over three days after she had killed him. And, too, one of her shoulders had been dislocated two weeks before by her husband; the broken finger from two months or so before had already healed. It would have been easy to leave him lying with his head split open on the kitchen floor, but their house had always been a neat one, and she thought all Aunt Hagar's children deserved a place in the ground. Dragging him out the back door, down the steps, through the garden bursting with beans and tomatoes and okra, along the path beside the new privy, past the old privy and then to a spot where the ground whispered that it would be amenable to receiving him—that dragging was almost as hard as the digging. "Who?" Judy said.

"Miss Georgia. She was bleedin right here."

There was a knock at the door and Tommy came in wearing a baseball glove and holding a tennis ball in his other hand.

"Didn't she, Tommy?" Carlos said.

"Didn't she what?" Tommy said, putting his glove on the table after tucking the tennis ball in the glove.

"Didn't Miss Georgia start bleedin after she got knocked down them stairs and everything?"

"Yes, ma'am," Tommy said. "She sure did. They be fightin upstairs all the time." He dashed around the table and started to playfully choke Carlos's neck. "Like this," and he gave Carlos a play-punch when he wasn't choking him. Tommy said, "Ima kill you, you no-good somebody. Take this! BAM!" Carlos flailed his arms and pretended to be the battered Georgia in her apartment. He moaned, "Don't you be killin me, Mr. Kenyon." "She don't say 'Mr. Kenyon,'" Tommy said. "That ain't what she say." "Okay. Don't you be killin me, Kenyon." "Yeah," Tommy said. "Thas it," and he pounded a laughing Carlos on the top of the head, saying, "You ain't no good! I don't know why I waste my p-precious time with somethin like you!"

"All right, yall," Judy said. "You gon wake Amy." The boys continued on, silently fighting and reacting, silently mouthing words.

"My mama told my daddy to go up there and make him stop," Tommy said.

"Oh, you storyin me," Carlos said.

"Uh-huh," Tommy said. "She really did. She said . . . she said like this, 'Moses, why you don't go up there and make that man stop hurtin her?' And my daddy said, my daddy he said, 'As long as he ain't hittin you, why you worried, Lois?' Thas my mama name," Tommy informed Carlos, though Carlos knew that already. "And my mama said like this, 'That ain't the point, Moses.' 'Well, what is the point, Lois? For goodness sakes!' And my mama said, 'What happens if he kills her, Moses? What happens if he kills that poor woman just above your own children's head? What happens then, huh, Moses?' 'She'll be dead and you and the kids won't be dead. Why you want me to get mixed up in another man's business? Why you wanna put me in the middle of that mess?' And my mama said, 'I don't know what I'm gonna do with you, Moses Carson.' My daddy just got up from the table."

"What he do then?" Carlos said. Judy was at the stove, tending to a pot of neck bones. Vinnie, even with his appetite like a bird's, liked all parts of the pig, from the ears to the tail, and she cooked it all for him. Her doctor had told her to stay away from pork because it raised her blood pressure. Vinnie enjoyed neck bones with Great Northern beans, but three stores had been out of them, so now the bones were simmering with Navy beans. The corn bread could be cooked at the last moment.

"He went into the living room and turned on the radio."

"Oh," Carlos said. He liked a good story and hated that this one ended with a man in a living room listening to the radio. "Thas all?"

"Thas all I heard, cause then I went outside to play. You member? I came to see you and you was eatin your dinner. Carlos, you member when we saw her shame?"

"What?" Judy said.

The boys eyed each other. Tommy realized he had said too much, but he wanted to say more to hold Carlos's attention.

"What you say?" Judy said.

"We saw her shame, Grandma," Carlos said. He had followed the other children into calling her "Grandma." He was rolling the tennis ball around the table and swinging his feet in the brand-new Keds just an inch above the rung of the chair and waiting for Judy to take the ball off the table because he didn't know where it had been.

"Yep," Tommy said. "She was showin her underwear."

Judy tasted from the pot of neck bones. She had seen Georgia the other day, limping. "Just woke up with a touch of rheumatism," Georgia said. How, Judy asked herself as they talked, had it all dissolved into plain open lies? How could it be that two women, one old enough to be mother to the other, could talk on such a nice summer day, and one lie with not a lot of blinking or looking away to hide the lie? And how could one accept the lie and carry it away like somebody's everyday truth? "I had the same thing," Judy told Georgia. "And what you do?" "I took a aspirin with a Stanback," Georgia said. "You mix them two?" "Yeah, it don't hurt me atall," Georgia said. "I think them two would give me a stomachache," Judy said.

"Grandma, can we go outside and play?" Carlos asked.

"All right," she said. "But stay where I can see you. Yall got away yesterday, and I don't like it."

She put the top back on the pot of neck bones and wondered if there was enough crackling to go in the corn bread. Crackling could make a good pan of corn bread even better. The boys went out quietly, and she followed to make sure they closed the door all the way. Hers was one of the few houses on Ridge Street with air-conditioning. Amy was still asleep on the couch, a new tattoo of five many-colored balloons on her arm. Judy stood over the girl, remembering her christening, remembering the baby peeing as the priest held her, remembering the priest asking her and Vinnie and everyone else gathered who would stand for the child, asked if they would renounce Satan and all his ways. The Catholics had such strange rituals, she had thought again that day. At least the Baptists waited until a child was big enough to stand and have some idea of all that mumbo-jumbo. She looked up and could see the tennis ball pass by the window, going from one boy to the other. Vinnie did not know her as a woman who made a bad pan of corn bread, so maybe it would not matter if there was no crackling in the cupboard. "Throw it a little harder," she heard Carlos say. She and Vinnie had said together, "We renounce Satan. . . ." Her first husband had died back in Arkansas before he had even finished his breakfast, some biscuits, some eggs, some bacon, some coffee. Maybe that was one of the punishments of hell—an eternal yearning for the unfinished meal. ". . . and all his ways."

She fed Amy and Vinnie an early supper. The girl was stronger, even playing with Ethel and Carlos before those two had to go home. Matthew came a little before six to take his daughter for the weekend to his mother's place. The day had cooled and Judy followed them out and left the door open. Matthew slowed his gait to match his daughter's and they went down the street and Kenyon came out of his door and called to Matthew, who then said something to Amy and set her little suitcase down beside her and went across Ridge to Kenyon. The two men were young enough to give each other boyish taps on the shoulders and then pretend to be boxing. Judy looked at Amy, who danced around the suitcase. The girl stopped and looked at her and waved, though they were less than twenty feet apart. Amy blew her a kiss and Judy blew her one back.

Judy saw Georgia on Sunday and told her straight out that she would be a better woman if she got rid of Kenyon. She was good looking, she had her own money, she could find another man, Judy said.

"I don't think it's any of your business what I do," Georgia said. Judy had seen Cornelia, Georgia's best friend, the day before and suggested that Cornelia put a word in Georgia's ear about how she was wasting her life away with a man like that. Georgia was to go by Cornelia's place that afternoon.

"You better than all this, Georgia, you really are." The limp was gone and so were all the lumps on her face. She just looked a little tired, but that could have come from a long night of drinking. Maybe, Judy thought, things have gotten better and I done made a fool of myself.

"I don't go to your house and tell you what to do," Georgia said. "I don't come to you and talk bad bout your husband." Georgia walked away.

When Cornelia came at her later, Georgia first told her friend of more than fifteen years that things were not as bad as the whole neighborhood was going around saying. Then, as Cornelia kept at her, Georgia said Cornelia was just jealous because she didn't have a man. She got up from Cornelia's couch without any more words and rushed out the door, out past Cornelia's daughter Lydia who was playing with friends. "Bye, Miss Georgia," Lydia said. "Say bye, Cathy. Say bye to Miss Georgia."

Amy's mother, Idabelle, confronted Matthew about being friends with a man who had no more respect for their daughter than to beat up a woman in front of her. They were two weeks from the divorce, both knowing that an important time in their lives was ending and there wasn't anything they could do about it anymore.

"Idabelle, I don't think he woulda done a thing if he knew Amy was my child. He didn't know."

"He probably knew and didn't give a damn," she said. "The fact is, he did it in front of children period." He had just returned Amy, who had gone upstairs to unpack her suitcase. Her parents were in the kitchen, far enough, they thought, from her bedroom. But the child came to the top of the stairs. She had never been one to entertain their getting back together. She liked them apart, and she didn't mind Abe at all.

"You know, I don't know what's become of you," Idabelle said.

"I could say the same bout you." He took a beer from the icebox, needing something to do with his hands because he knew his were the greater sins. "Where the can opener?"

"Where it's always been." He fished in the silverware drawer and found it. Idabelle said, "You used to be everything. You used to be everything in the world." He opened the can and dropped the opener back in the drawer and sat at the table, nearest the open back door.

"I'm not a bad man, Idabelle. I never hit you or anybody else like Kenyon."

She was leaning against the sink with her arms folded. Abe had gone up to New York City to visit his parents. "No, Matthew, you ain't a bad man, as men go. You was just never as good as you coulda been. And bein that good coulda been so easy for you, too." He drank half the beer in one gulp and then looked at the words on the can. Was it this week or last week that he had promised to drink no more? Go, my son, and drink no more. He knew he had better pace himself because Idabelle would not allow him a second one from her icebox. He studied each letter of the words on the can. Was Carling some guy's name? Was his whole name Carling Black Label?

"Leave me in peace, Idabelle."

"I will," she said. "I will. I can promise you that. I been thinkin bout all you promised me once. You even promised my daddy how you would take care of me forever. I can still see you, sittin at my daddy's table, soppin up my mama's gravy with my daddy's biscuits. Sittin there and promisin how good you would treat me forever."

He downed the rest of the beer and set the can gently on the table. "Forever ain't as long as it used to be." He walked away. "I be seein you."

It was Tommy Carson's father who told Kenyon it might be time for him to move on. A week before the school year started, he knocked on Georgia's door and Kenyon came down and Moses said how their arguing and fighting had kept his new baby up all the night before.

"We pay our rent, thas all I know," Kenyon said. The two men had rarely spoken before. It was early, and Kenyon had had only a little taste of something and was feeling not unhappy and he was rather disappointed that there had not been good news at the door, as the liquor had been promising him as he came singing down the stairs.

"It ain't got to do with payin rent, man," Moses said. Kenyon was standing in his doorway and Moses was standing one step down on the stoop. Lois was just inside her door, her baby in her arms and Tommy and his brother behind her. "It got to do with all this noise you and your woman makin practically every night." Georgia was standing at the top of the stairs. "Whas goin on, honey?" she asked Kenyon, who ignored her.

"I don't tell you how to act with your woman, and you don't tell me how to act with mine."

"Just watch the noise, is all," Moses said and turned away.

"I ain't finished talkin," Kenyon said and grabbed Moses's shoulder, turning him half around before punching him in the face. Lois screamed and her baby began crying to see her mother's distress. Moses blocked the second punch and hit Kenyon as hard as he could in the stomach, then managed a quick one to the jaw, and Kenyon fell back on the stairs. Georgia screamed, "Honey, be careful!" Lois handed the baby to Tommy and came out. Moses reached in to Kenyon's place and was set to give him a solid one to his nose, but Kenyon raised his arms to cover his face and his whole body shook. Kenyon said nothing, just crossed his arms at the wrists. He was a pretty man, Moses could see now that they were so close, and his face was everything. It was the pretty men, Moses thought, who made it such a bad world. The pretty men and their puppy-hearted women. Georgia screamed that he should let her man be. Kenyon kept his hands up before his face and Lois told her husband to step away. "Back off, Moses, I'm tellin you! Just back off!"

All through the Labor Day weekend, the children on Ridge Street talked about the fight that none of them had actually witnessed and only Tommy and his brother had heard. Tommy's father had won hands down, they all decided. The children of ten years and under reenacted the fight with wrestling, and no one wanted to be Kenyon because he was destined to lose. If a boy playing Kenyon happened to wrestle a victory, he was accused of not playing fair, because the rules of a reenactment dictated that Kenyon be the loser. "I don't wanna play with you no more," the losing Moses would say. "You ain't doin it right." "I gotta win sometime," the winning Kenyon would say. "You get to win all the time. I don't like that." "Tough titty."

Amy had been fine for more than two weeks, but the night before school started she dreamed again that Georgia was coming to get her. This time her father came up beside Georgia and together they took off after the girl. Abe heard her in the night and went and put her in the bed beside Idabelle and then went downstairs to sleep on the couch. Idabelle thought her daughter would not be able to go to school, but the next day Amy said she wanted to go.

She entered the third grade, and Carlos was disappointed that she was not in his class at Walker-Jones. It had been one of his greatest hopes during the summer. Please, please, he had prayed to God, put us in the same room. Pretty pretty please. He always thought of himself as a good boy, despite what his mother and father sometimes said. If he had something to trade to God, he thought his prayers would have been answered.

He was a curser and he promised God not to do it anymore, but God was not impressed.

The first Saturday after school started, he had just split an orange Popsicle with Tommy on Carlos's side of the street when they saw Kenyon chase Georgia out of their place and down Ridge Street toward 4th Street. Ethel saw them, and so did Amy and Billie and Larry Comstock's younger brother. The men working in the garage across from Georgia came out and watched. Amy backed away toward her door. Kenyon caught Georgia two doors from Amy, just about when Judy came across the street with her walking stick. Kenyon slapped Georgia twice before Judy knocked him once in the head with the stick. Georgia crawled away toward Amy and Amy opened her door and Georgia crawled inside. Idabelle came out and stood with Judy, and Moses, Tommy's father, came out, with Lois following with their baby, and he stood on the other side of Kenyon as the man raised his hands in a I-don't-want-no-trouble-with-yall fashion. Kenyon went back to his place. Georgia went back three hours later, and they were quiet for the rest of the weekend and for a few weeks after. They walked about arm in arm, as they had in the first days of their relationship. They had long ago become known as common-law wife Georgia and her common-law husband Kenyon, though a few people held back and said two years, not several months, was the mark of such a marriage.

They went out to the What Ailing Ya one evening in October, not long before the schoolchildren got Columbus Day off, and got to fighting outside the beer garden after Kenyon claimed he saw her winking at a man nicknamed Frisky Fred. This man went to Baltimore, sometimes even to Philadelphia, to have his hair processed so he could come back and tell people in D.C. that the process was his own natural good hair. The police were called on Kenyon and Georgia. It was the first time ever that anyone had called the law on them, and it would be the last. They took Georgia just a block up 5th Street to the Women's Bureau, and Kenyon just down 5th to the Number 2 Precinct. She got sick during the night, and though she called for one, said her head was killing her, no one brought her a Stanback. About six in the morning the woman with whom she was sharing the cell, a nightclub singer who had forged three Post Office money orders, got tired of Georgia calling for "my Kenyon" and made up a song on the spot that all the other women in their cells took up and sang until it was time for breakfast. When one part of the cell block would flag with the song, another would take it up and the song would continue again for some time.

Oh my Kenyon, where is my boy?
Oh my Kenyon, you done took my joy.
Oh, Kenny, my pretty face is all yours
Play with that face, Kenny, like you do all your toys.

By seven, before the sun came up, Georgia was cursing them all, and then, not long before eight, she was crying and asking of no one in particular why they wanted to hurt her damn feelings when they didn't even know her, didn't even know what her life was like.

She got back home about three in the afternoon, walked right across 5th and into Ridge Street. From the jail, she had managed to get ahold of Cornelia's neighbor just before noon, and the neighbor told Cornelia, who didn't have a telephone. Cornelia had come over and bailed her out. "This the first time I ever been in that place," Georgia said of the Women's Bureau. "The first time for me, too," said Cornelia, who had left Lydia with the neighbor because she didn't want her child getting too familiar with the law.

Kenyon did not come back. That morning he had returned from jail and gotten most of his clothes and disappeared. Georgia wondered why he left, and put the word out everywhere that she was looking for him, that they should talk things over. School and all else went on for the children, and Carlos's love for Amy did not falter. Her bad dreams were still there, but she was learning that when Georgia and her father came for her in them, she could hide behind a talking tree that lied and told them Amy had gone way over there. The big subject among the children as October came to an end was of the men who played the Lone Ranger and Tonto on the television coming to D.C. four days before Halloween. Their horses Silver and Scout would even be there, or so the rumor went. But when adults saw the children of Ridge Street getting excited about going to see them, they let them know that the theater where the Lone Ranger and Tonto would be appearing would not let colored children in. "What a gyp!" the kids responded. "Dag!"

Somehow the song composed that night by the nightclub singer made its way out of the Women's Bureau, across 5th and all along Ridge Street. Girls jumped rope to it. Georgia heard them, could not help but hear them as she went on with life in her apartment and the girls played outside her window, not really knowing what they were saying but happy with something that they could jump rope to. The song was fine for jumping single rope but with double Dutch the rhythm suffered except with the most expert of girls. Day by painful day Georgia would take something of his that was in her way and put it aside in a closet in the second bedroom.

Carlos and Amy and Billie and Tommy and Ethel and a few others were playing on Ridge near 4th that Saturday in November when Kenyon came up 4th and turned onto Ridge. He was in a suit few chauffeurs could afford, and he had not been drinking. Amy saw him first. The street was busy that day, women sweeping the sidewalk and cleaning their windows and men gossiping and washing their cars and just generally showing off. Amy stood up from her jacks game and watched him walking down the middle of the street, avoiding either sidewalk. Almost as soon as the other children saw what she was looking at, the girl fainted and Carlos and Billie, who was now free of his cast, caught her and lowered her bit by bit to the ground. Carlos was not afraid this time, because he knew fainting was a long way from dying. Ethel called Amy by name and sat down beside her, dropping the jacks ball, which rolled away into the gutter. Tommy ran to get Idabelle.

Carlos watched Kenyon come toward them, and then, not knowing what else to do, he came out to the street and got up onto William Mc-Gavin's new Chevrolet and put his hands to his mouth, megaphone-style. "Boo boo boo!" he shouted. He felt better with each second. Seeing him up there, the other children took up the cry, some of them not having even seen Kenyon and thinking it was all just another of Carlos's games, and some of them actually seeing Kenyon and just not liking the man who beat up Miss Georgia and then got beat up by Tommy's father.

"Boo boo boo!" the children shouted.

Kenyon came nearer to Carlos, came within a foot of him and raised his hand as if to swat him. Carlos fell back but went on shouting. "Boo boo boo!" Idabelle came running, followed by Matthew and Abe, and they found Amy waking up. Kenyon continued on down the middle of the street, and more children were shouting. Carlos saw Judy five or six doors down come out of her house and he called to her. She and other adults began to fill the street and Kenyon found himself having to maneuver through a growing crowd. Carlos and Judy looked at each other until she turned her head to see Georgia, four doors down and across Ridge, open her door and step out on the stoop to find out what all the commotion was about. The two women stared at each other and Judy began her own booing, a weak, self-conscious cry.

William McGavin came out of his house and saw Carlos on his new car. "Boy, your daddy ain't got anough to fix anything you might break! Get on down from there," and he raised his arms and Carlos sailed into them and took off up the street behind Kenyon and the crowd. "Boo boo boo!" He pushed his way through to get closer to Kenyon, who was slowing. Then about midway up the block, Kenyon could see Georgia, who had not gone beyond her stoop. She saw him but did not come down the stairs to the sidewalk. Some children near her were crying "Boo!" at whoever was near, and some of them directed "Boo!"s at her. Anyone who knew her could see the difference in her face, the way the nose was off to the side from where it had been all her life, the little bump at the edge of her lip, engorged with blood months ago and now full of something part blood, part pus, and part bile that had traveled to the lip from some distant place in her body. Kenyon looked at Georgia and Georgia looked at Kenyon. He noticed that she had cut her hair. She knew full well that he hated short hair.

The crowd became too thick for Kenyon to move, and he turned around to see Matthew carrying Amy back to the house. Abe was a step behind him, but Idabelle was standing on the sidewalk watching Kenyon, who started back toward 4th Street. The crowd made way. He got to 4th Street and turned the corner and the children and the grown-ups stopped following him but continued to shout "Boo"s and each one rained down upon him.

Once fully on 4th heading toward M, he was free of them. He stopped mid-block and remembered that he had been two months sober. He felt weak, and at 4th and M he went into Leon's to buy two bottles of Rock Creek cream soda. He opened both bottles on the opener attached to the cooler and kept one bottle in the bag and drank the other as he came out of the store. He looked down M Street to where New York Avenue ran right into New Jersey Avenue. On that corner where he stood, wobbly, 4th took a dip and continued to dip all the way to K Street. Farther up M was 5th Street and What Ailing Ya. He went down 4th, drinking the soda. He remembered that there was a store at 4th and L. The two sodas he had would last him until he could reach that store and fortify himself with two more. The problem would be if that store didn't have cream soda. What would he do after that? What would he do?

❈

The people on Ridge Street became afraid that Kenyon would come back and hurt Georgia, so they started looking out for her, driving her to and from work. Throughout the rest of 1955, the big liar Larry Comstock's twenty-three-year-old cousin, only one year out of Tennessee, got the job of taking her to work. He was Randy Comstock, and he had become engaged to a young woman whose family had lost their home in Georgetown when the city and federal government people forced all the colored people out of there and brought in the white people. Randy liked to talk and Georgia enjoyed listening to him.

One day near the end of December, he started in talking about the life he and his fiancée were planning in a house on South Dakota Avenue in upper Northeast. "It's a nice house, Miss Georgia . . . Real nice. You should see it sometime. I figure we can be happy there with one, maybe two kids, then after that, if we have any more, we can move up to somethin bigger. We got plans, Miss Georgia, we got real good plans, and I figure the sky's the limit." He was a cautious driver, both hands on the wheel where they should be, as Judy knew before she picked him to drive Georgia. "Now Irma, she want three kids, Miss Georgia. I say four. I want four cause thas a nice number. My mama and pappy had four children, and each of their mamas and pappies had four children, so I figure thas good anough for me. But Irma . . . Well, I don't know . . . I will have to defer to Irma on that score. A real man has to defer to his wife on such matters, thas what my pappy told me. But I think I can live with three kids. You think I can live with three kids, huh, Miss Georgia? You think three kids will suit me?"

Georgia was one and a half years from marrying Alvin Deloach. She was more than eight years from marrying Vaughn Anderson, who would worship the ground she walked on, but that was not the kind of love she was used to. "I think three children will do me quite well, Miss Georgia." She was nearly twenty years from going to Israel with Cornelia and Lydia, who would not be a doctor but who would make more money than all her ancestors put together, all of them, all the way back to Eve. "A real man can defer to his wife and still be a real man, is what I say, Miss Georgia." She was just about thirty years from seeing her first grandchild come into the world. "A little give and a little take make a good marriage, my mama always said." She was more than forty and a half years from death.

ADAM ROBINSON ACQUIRES
GRANDPARENTS AND A LITTLE SISTER

Tuesday

After the cab turned off East Capitol onto 8th Street, Noah Robinson saw further evidence that trees were disappearing from Washington. Where were all the oaks and maples and birches, even the odd pear, apple, or peach tree, that had been there in the time when he did not yet know himself and the city seemed always as green as his grandparents' idea of Heaven? Even when he had become responsible for a wife and children, the trees had still been there, reminding him year after hard year how far he had to go and how far he had come. Now the landscape of the city, high and low, seemed barren, no grand trees for children playing hide-and-go-seek, no spreading refuge for old people out in the fire of summer. Why had he not noticed the death of the trees before, at age forty, at fifty-five, at sixty? When he was seven, and his family first arrived in Washington, he'd had a teacher at Stevens Elementary School who taught her students about the trees of the city. Mrs. Waters hung her eyeglasses on a pink string around her neck and told them how lucky they were to have trees in Washington. The boy loved the teacher and he loved learning about trees, and he loved the way the trees told him through the teacher's words that he, pining for South Carolina, might yet be happy in this new world.

The cab now bumped its way over potholes up 8th Street. The tree devastation had extended even to the modest showy trees, the trees that the other Washington, known for facade and neglect, might have endeavored to save. That world liked to talk only about the biggest showoffs, the trees they gave all the care to—the cherry trees. "The blossoms are coming, the blossoms are coming!" went their hallelujah each spring. But the young man Noah, ever a student of Mrs. Waters's, had known the beauty of the black locust and the paulownia, flowering away their magnificent hearts in April, May, and June. And they did so without school bands and beauty queens and tourists, without the articles in the newspapers that year after silly year heralded the cherry trees. The apartment of the woman with whom he had committed adultery was in a building that had oaks in the backyard, and once, lying with her, he had heard acorns falling and mistaken them for footsteps. And he had stayed away from the woman for weeks. His son had appreciated the trees of Washington, but his girls had found more joy in rosebushes and Queen Anne's lace, and even goldenrod, perhaps because they didn't have to climb to admire the blossoms. His son loved to climb trees and call down to his father, "Watch me!" When people died, Noah Robinson's people dreamed of them, and so far there had been no dreams about his son, the baby of the family. His son might yet be alive.

The cab approached H Street, N.E. He could see that box after box meant for trees existed now only to support litter. Between the parked cars, Noah could see that the city government people had thrown up the occasional young tree, like the one in front of his apartment building. Most of those trees had few leaves—frail generic things propped up with wooden supports. They would not live out the year. "Root, little pig, or die," his father and grandfather liked to say.

The cab turned onto H Street. Noah forgave that street for being virtually treeless, for that had always been its way. He had courted Maggie up and down H Street, with all its stores and gritty life, one symbol of a people used to doing much with less. The darkness of the Atlas Theater on H had given him the courage to lean over and kiss Maggie's cheek that first time. She had not yet seen sixteen, and he still had the gentlemanly quality of the countrified South about him. Someone, some adult in a nearly empty theater, watching them the way adults once watched over all the children in Washington, saw the quick kiss and told Maggie's father, and he forbade her to see Noah for two months. Now, as the cab went along H Street, Maggie Robinson took her hand from Noah's knee and placed it over his open hand resting on his thigh. She sighed, frustrated, a woman who had had time for only half a cup of coffee that morning. "I am satisfied now. I am done with having your children, Noah," she had said to him the day after Caleb's birth. Caleb who might yet be alive.

"Remember," Noah said now, observing the stained and indecipherable zone map on the back of the cab's front seat, "when you couldn't walk down a D.C. street without trees jumpin in your way and makin a nuisance of themselves?" He had been a pallbearer at Mrs. Waters's funeral. Because she had been a great woman and teacher, the mayor had been there, with a mouthful of expensive teeth and a manufactured brand of camaraderie that the elite schools had taught the mayor's kind to pass off as charm among the common people. The mayor's limousine had got lost on the way to the funeral, because it wasn't used to going to Anacostia. In Noah's youth, most of the politicians had confined themselves to their pen on Capitol Hill.

"I remember," Maggie said.

"I'm sure you do." He looked at her and winked. One tree was as good as another to her, a woman with more than two hundred years of Washingtonians behind her. He squeezed her hand and raised it and kissed it once, then once again. He had waited forever for that woman with whom he committed adultery to show up on his doorstep and tell his wife, "I laid with the father of your children." He was still waiting.

He let go of Maggie's hand. They had been married forty-five years. Last year, to celebrate that anniversary, their friends had given them a king's catered dinner at the Elks Club and so many gifts that it took two cars to get the gifts home. A month later, their two-year-old grand-daughter—no mother, no Caleb for a father—had come to live with them. That first night, as their granddaughter, Elsa, slept in the bed beside Maggie, he had sat most of the night in the darkened living room, looking over at a Waterford vase, one of the gifts presented at the Elks dinner. It had cost more than his grandfather earned in two years of plowing behind a mule. With no light to bounce off it, the vase sat dull and uninspired on the table beside the couch. So many of the descen-dants of slaves had done well in Washington, for themselves and for the flesh of their flesh, but his own son had failed as a father, the first to do so in a long, long line of good and righteous fathers. "Yes, ma'am, I'm talkin bout your Noah, father to your children. I laid with him." Could a man, even one worshipped by his children, be considered a good fa-ther if he was an adulterer and had hurt the mother of his children? Had he in fact been the first in that line to fail and thus doomed his own son?

Months before their granddaughter came to them, they had gone to Kenya. Oh, but he had loved Kenya! What would seeing the rest of the world have done for him? After Maggie fell asleep that first night in Kenya, he had stood in his robe at the hotel window for a long time, but all the sounds and smells of Nairobi couldn't lull him to sleep. That was the way it was for most of their twelve nights there. But he had so adored Kenya. They had planned to see Africa and the world in their retire-ment. He knew now, though, that his two grandchildren, first Elsa and now Adam, would cost him the rest of Africa and the world.

The cab came to a stop at North Capitol Street. The traffic light was out again, and the city government people had sent a policeman to do the work of the light. Noah turned his head and saw a black man with banana-yellow hair standing in the small crowd waiting at the corner.

The man was bobbing his head to a tune that came through his head-phones. Noah and the yellow-haired black man looked at each other, and after a second or so the man raised his hand to greet Noah. Noah slowly raised his hand. "You know him?" Maggie said. "I think I did once," Noah said. "I don't remember. I do know it ain't long after ten o'clock in the morning and already he's made twenty white people happy."

He often felt a momentary dizziness with the high-blood-pressure pills he took after rising in the morning. Get the hard work done and over, like the extended exercises he had started with Elsa's coming. There had been no dizziness this morning. Perhaps his body knew it might have to clank off to battle and had no time to waste on dizziness. Where had he gone wrong with Caleb? Was the woman the beginning and end of it all? To have failed with one child, with a boy, even. It did not matter that he had succeeded with three girls. Caleb cried out in somebody's wilderness, and he was crying Noah's name. Perhaps that woman had knocked on the door of their lives and only God had heard her, and God from his Heaven had reached down and punished with the tip of one of his fingernails.

The taxi crossed into Northwest D.C. H Street seemed to have become blocked with potholes, and somehow, to avoid the potholes, the taxi ended up on Massachusetts Avenue, where the city government people never failed to battle the pothole problem because the senators and congressmen went back and forth on that street to Capitol Hill. At 7th Street they turned left. Farther down the street was Lansburgh, a once-upon-a-time department store that white people in the past few years had made into a building of expensive apartments. His father had bought him a fifteen-dollar blue suit at Lansburgh when he was thirteen. He was wearing a suit now, as was often the case with men of a certain age, from a certain age, black men who had grown up comfortable with such attire because their fathers and grandfathers had done it that way. They wore suits out into the world the way knights had worn armor; they wore suits even to baseball games and to shoeshine jobs.

Elsa, his granddaughter, had cried to see him leave that morning. She had a good vocabulary for a three-year-old who had been so long around the city government people and their foster families, but she could not say "Grandpa." "Grandma" was no trouble. She had begun to cry as soon as she saw him put on his tie, one that his own father had worn. He had picked her up and her teary face had fallen into the crook of his neck.

Before the cab turned back onto H Street, Noah asked his wife, "What do you think he eats?"

"Little-boy food," Maggie said, and tapped the knobby knee of a man who could do a hundred deep knee bends.

The city government people made a show of putting their offices all about the city. "We Are Where You Are," their signs proclaimed. The building in Chinatown at 622 H had only five stories, though a city government woman in another part of the city had told Noah on the telephone that they could find Adam on the eighth floor.

They found Adam on the fifth floor, where a man in front of the building smoking two cigarettes at once had told them "they keep all the boys." The piece of paper on the door said "824." The paper was flapping though there was no wind in the hall. The boy, their grandson, was sitting on an orange plastic chair beside a majestic desk, his back to them, his feet unmoving, a foot or so up from the floor. He was six years old, and they had last seen him when he was but seven days old, wrapped in one of the three blankets Maggie had bought for him at Hecht's. A hatted black policeman looking at a magazine with pictures of naked women sat at the big desk. He was facing them, and when he saw Maggie and Noah, he pointed at them and Adam looked around the side of the chair. The policeman and the boy were alone in the large room filled with nothing but telephones and chairs and huge desks. The policeman had on headphones under his hat and there was a radio playing on his desk. When Noah came closer and the policeman took off his hat and headphones, Noah could hear that the music on the radio was different from the music seeping out of the headphones.

Adam got down from the chair and stood very close to it, his arms at his sides. His hands were empty, wide open, one finger twitching. There was something coming, his body seemed to say, and he had best face it head-on. It was the middle of July, and the city government people had dressed him in corduroy pants and a long-sleeved black shirt, which reminded Noah of gangsters in the movies. He was the son of Maggie and Noah's only son, and Elsa's brother, and anyone in the world who knew their son Caleb could see that. Caleb—along with Adam's mother, Tamara—had disappeared out in that world and no one had seen them for hundreds upon hundreds of days. Maggie went to the boy and knelt, pulled him to her. There was a shopping bag near the boy, and someone had penciled his name on it and that someone had misspelled it. There was nothing else with him, and it was the nothing else that made Maggie pull him closer. At six, Caleb Robinson had had a trunk full of toys, a teacher mother, three sisters who treated him like a prince, a father who commanded a good wage because even blindfolded he could repair any car. Maggie continued to hold the boy and Adam's arms stayed at his sides.

"You know who I am?" she asked him, pulling back a bit and then kissing him.

"Yes," he said, but that was not true. A yes was always easier, safer, than a no. The no's were always trouble for some reason, and the boy was sick and tired of trouble.

"I'm your grandmother, and I'm taking you home for good."

Adam looked up at Noah, who smiled down and cupped the boy's chin. "That's your grandfather. Forever and ever," Maggie said. Adam said, "Yes."

The policeman put down his magazine open to the page he was studying and stood up. He reached out his hand to Noah, but Noah ignored him and took up the handles of the shopping bag. When they learned that Adam was not with his mother's people, they had paid five hundred dollars to a man who, though on the D.C. payroll, spent half his workdays as a private detective. "I'll find that boy," he had assured them, but he had never gone looking. Three months ago, the city government people called out of the blue to say they had their grandson, "one Andy Robinson of an unknown age." But when Maggie and Noah went to the Southeast address to pick him up, the city government people did not have him. They lined up five teenage boys for the couple, but none of the boys would answer to the name Adam, despite all the pleading from the city government woman. "That ain't me. How many times I gotta tell ya, lady? That just ain't me," the smallest of the five kept insisting. Adam had stayed lost until the city government people called again, two days ago, at four on a rainy Sunday morning. "Why you call so early?" Noah asked. "I got nothin better to do, mister."

They took the stairs, because the elevators refused to go down when there were people in them. Outside, Noah rolled up the boy's sleeves and pants legs and Maggie held tight to Adam's hand. He did not turn his head to look left or right but stared only at where he was going. It was a busy street, H, and yet he seemed to have willed himself not to be curious about what was going on.

"You hungry, Adam?" Noah said.

Adam said Yes. The people he had come upon in and out of the city government had taught him that they could not hear him shaking his head. Shaking or nodding the head was as bad as a no to them. And yes was preferred, not yeah. "Good black children never say 'Yeah.' You ain't back down on some slavery plantation, boy."

"You like Chinese food?" Noah said, looking up and down H at all the restaurants.

"Yes."

Noah and Maggie looked at each other. "Oh," Noah said. "You like their corned beef and cabbage, huh?"

"Yes."

"We'd better find a McDonald's or something," Maggie said. "I think he'd drink hemlock if we put it before him."

They went to the McDonald's on E Street across from the fortress that was the FBI headquarters. Maggie and Adam sat at a place near the window while Noah got the food. "I got five dollars," Adam said while they waited. Don't you know food cost money, boy? Don't you know that? Black children gotta learn the value of money.

"Oh?" Maggie said. "You're rich." He looked puzzled and said, "I got it from a lady who used to be my mother." Sometimes they liked the truth.

"Tamara? You got it from Tamara?" Wherever his mother was, she was not with Caleb. The grapevine had told Maggie that Tamara and Caleb had come to despise each other toward the end, not long before Elsa was born. Dope fiends, Noah began calling them. But worse than that, he continued, they were bad parents who had flung their flesh and blood to the winds. Root, little pig, or die. "You got the money from Tamara?"

"No," Adam said softly. "The other lady who was my mother. Miss Joyce. She wasn't even my mother no more, and she gave me five dollars. I had baths with millions of bubbles. She gave me five dollars when Miss Billie was my mother. Miss Billie hit this man in the head with a fryin pan and made blood pop out his head." Adam tapped the top of his head several times with his knuckles. "He fell down and went to sleep. She hit him again." He continued tapping, then rested the hand on the table, the edge of which came midway up his chest. "Miss Joyce had a big house. Bubble time."

Noah came with the food. He sat across from them, his back to the window. He spread out napkins for a place mat for Adam, unwrapped a hamburger for the boy, and popped a straw through the top of a chocolate-milk-shake container. Adam watched his grandfather's hands. Noah tore open the cardboard box with the French fries sticking out and squirted little packets of ketchup over them. It was nearing noon and the sun was high and they were shaded where they sat.

Adam put his hands in his lap. There had been one city government mother who made him and the rest of those at her table say a five-minute prayer to Jehovah Our Loving Master before and after meals. "Eat, boy, eat," Noah said. "There's plenty more where that come from." Adam ate. Each time someone came near them he leaned forward, hunched over his food, and when the person had passed he sat up straight again.

Noah ate little chunks of chicken. "Why'd you get that?" Maggie said. "The fish would have been better for you."

"I read in the paper where the fish was worse. Somethin bout how they make it up, what they put in it. And all that sauce. With chicken I kinda know what I'm gettin. You have to do a lot to a chicken after you wring his neck before you turn it into a mystery meat." He looked at Adam. "Right?"

"Yes."

"He's rich," Maggie said. "He's got five whole dollars. His mother gave it to him." She looked hard at Noah to make certain he got what she meant. "Not Tamara. Miss Joyce."

"I got it in my shoe."

"Don't tell people where you got your valuables, baby," Noah said. "It's okay with us. But don't tell other people, baby."

Maggie put down her hamburger. "You do know," she said to Adam, "that you are coming home with us?"

"Home to Mama Wilson?" He stopped eating. "Goin home?"

"No, to our place," Noah said. "You live with us now. We're your people, we're your family." Noah pointed at Maggie and then at his own chest. Just a week before, a retired friend of Noah's had got on his boat and sailed off with his fourth wife around the world. A black man and woman on the wide blue sea.

Adam resumed eating, but they could tell that whatever joy he had found in the food was now gone. "Yes," he said after a bit. "Yes, ma'am" or "Yes, sir" was disallowed more times than allowed. People sometimes thought a "ma'am" or a "sir" made them seem old. "Dontcha put me in my grave before I'm ready," one city government man had warned him. "I just won't have livin in my grave before the good Lord calls me."

Their granddaughter, Elsa, stood tiny and eager when Maggie opened the door. She ran and grabbed Maggie's leg, then she put her arms around Adam and reached up and kissed his cheek, though she had never laid eyes on him a day in her life. Adam, having known some good children in his life, giggled. Finally, Elsa went to Noah and he picked her up with an arm that could do seventy-five push-ups, dropping Adam's shopping bag just inside the door. Elsa kissed his mouth.

"I thought she'd have a conniption fit waitin for yall," said Mrs. Battle, a neighbor from downstairs. "It was 'Grandma' this and 'Grandma' that. She kept pointin at that picture of yall on the side table. But she settled down after a while. If you start tellin a child how to pick cotton, they go quiet. How you go up this row and down that row, pickin them little bugs outa your cup of water. Talkin bout pickin cotton is like a mother's lullaby. A child will calm down and drift along."

Noah said nothing. Maggie introduced her to Adam. "A full house now, huh?" Mrs. Battle said. "My, my." She had nine grandchildren and three great-grands, but they all went home in the evening after visiting. And if she allowed one to stay the night—for she loved all of them more than she let on—the child's parents had to come get him or her before noon or she would put the child in a cab bound for home. Before the taxi arrived for the pickup, she would pin an enveloped note to the child's blouse or shirt: "I raised one set and I don't plan on raising another."

Adam watched Mrs. Battle leave and then stood beside his shopping bag. It was all wrong because it was all so perfect. The way the carpet soothed his feet even with his tennis shoes on. The table of many flowers in front of the window, a clean window with the ever so blue curtains fluttering in the wind from the machine that cooled everything. The thousand photographs of grown-ups and children who had more right to stand where he was standing, because they were family. The girl's doll sleeping on the floor against the couch, waiting for another go-round. He had known perfect before, but there had always been a tilt, and that tilt told him that this was home, however temporary: Music all the time, even in the middle of the night. A big dog gnawing at a chair leg and turning its head to eye him. Whatcha lookin at, boy? A finger in his face to emphasize a thousand rules. Mustard-and-ketchup sandwiches. Cigarette smoke curling around his nose before it dashed in. Even in Miss Joyce's big house there had been unlit corners that whispered, Stay away. The basement.

Whatever this was, it was not home in the way he had been taught. He put his fingers around the shopping bag's handles. "When I'm goin home?" he said at last in as submissive a tone as he could muster.

"What?" Noah said. He put Elsa down. Maggie was adjusting the thermostat. "You are home," Noah said. Adam blinked but didn't release the handles. Noah reached out his hand to the boy and Adam took it, dragging the bag along. Noah led him into the first bedroom of the apartment. "That's gonna be your bed." The man pointed to one of the twin beds on either side of a window adorned with a green curtain. The bedspread was beige and covered with cartoon people Adam remembered from a television in a city government home in Northeast. "And that's your teddy bear there, waitin for you to give him a name." Adam had once seen a dog named Cecil tear open the stomach of a teddy bear. The brown bear on this bed sat propped against two pillows, one on top of the other, and the bear's arms were wide open.

Elsa was now standing in the doorway.

"And here," Noah said, leading him across the room to a chest of drawers. "These two drawers up here belong to you." He pulled out the drawers and picked Adam up to show him the shirts and pajamas and underwear in both drawers, the result of Maggie's quick trip downtown the day before. "And this here middle one you can share with Elsa for socks and whatnot. Okay?" He pulled the drawer out and pointed to the boy's socks on the left side. "See?"

Adam said, "Yes."

"You do know that Elsa is your sister, don't you?"

"Yes."

Noah noticed that the yeses were piling up and weren't amounting to even a speck of caring or understanding. He put the bag on the floor beside the bed and sat on the bed, taking Adam between his legs. "I know how bad this might be right now, but you'll see. It'll work out." Noah did not believe that. The second bank had yet to call back about cashing in one of his retirement funds, money that would have paid for a trip to China when they were seventy. "Can you trust me? Can you trust your grandma and me to do the right thing by you?" Noah opened his hands, made a bowl of them, and offered it to the boy. Adam put one of his hands into the bowl. Elsa came up to them, standing very close to Adam. She said nothing, but watched the man and the boy. Adam looked at her and she put her face hard against his arm. He remembered her from somewhere, and as he kept his hand in his grandfather's, he thought that if he could remember her he would be home again, at Mama Wilson's, and everything would be jim-dandy.

Thursday

For five weeks, Noah had been tending a new, frail tree in front of their two-story apartment building. He took the children out that evening with his can of water. The tree box was now eight straight days without debris, a record. There was an oak about midway down the street, the 1500 block of Independence Avenue in Southeast. It was sturdy, maybe owing to the prayers of the three older women who lived in the house facing it. Across the street, down near 16th, were the remnants of a catalpa that refused to die.

Noah handed the can to Adam. "Give it some," he told the boy, and Adam watered the tree. "Now let her." Adam gave the can to Elsa, who had trouble with it and got most of the water on the sidewalk and in the gutter. Adam looked at Noah and Noah winked knowingly at him. Girls, Noah mouthed, and rolled his eyes.

His car, a year-old Toyota, was parked a few yards beyond the building. Noah opened the front passenger door and let Adam crawl into the driver's seat. He sat in the passenger seat with Elsa on his lap. He waited for the boy to pretend to drive, the way all boys did, the way Caleb did, but Adam just looked out the window. "Go on, take us somewhere," Noah said. Adam said, "Where?" "Anywhere you want," his grandfather said and took Adam's hands and placed them on the steering wheel. "Why don't you take us home?" "Home," Elsa said. Without a word, Adam moved his hands slowly about the wheel. Noah said, "That's what I'm talkin about." "Talkin bout," Elsa said.

"You been in a airplane?" Adam said, not looking at his grandfather and still moving his hands on the wheel.

"Yeah," Noah said. "A whole lotta times. You been in one?"

Adam did not answer.

"We'll take you up in one. We'll go see your aunt Charlene, in Chicago. Surprise her before she comes to see us. We'll drive to Baltimore to see your aunt Laverne and your uncle and your cousins. And we'll go across the river to see your aunt Imogene."

The boy put his hands in his lap and looked out the window. Jesus Christ, Noah thought. Now what did I say? What had done it, he wondered, talking about the airplane, Aunt Charlene, Chicago? "You ain't thinkin bout goin home again, are you?" Adam said nothing. Noah took one of the boy's hands and placed it back on the wheel. "Drive us some more, Adam," he said. "Take us somewhere."

Saturday

While Noah did the dinner dishes, Maggie bathed the children. There were two quite noticeable scars on the boy's back, a superficial one of some two inches at his left shoulder and a more profound one of less than an inch down near the base of his spine. She did not yet have the courage to ask about them. "We have to fatten you up," she said, squeezing warm water from the washcloth over his back. "Make you as fat as a little piggy." He told her he knew a bath song, and he started singing a bunch of nonsense words. Elsa, her back to the spigot, joined in. Her back was unblemished.

Later, after the children had watched one of two dozen videos their youngest daughter, in Virginia, had sent, Noah sat between them on the couch and read from a fairy-tale book. He had not been a good reader until he met Maggie. After Mrs. Waters, he and school had not got along, he once told her. Not three weeks after Elsa came to them, he had sat her on his lap for a simple bedtime story. She pointed to magazines on the coffee table, and he had to suffer through three copies of *Ebony* as she asked about every picture in them. Hundreds of pages and thousands of pictures. "What this?" she asked as she pointed to each picture. "Thas a doggy." She certainly knew a man and a dog and a woman when she saw them in her everyday life, but for some reason she needed him to make the connection between what was in her mind and the colorful pictures in the magazines. "What this?" "A truck." And she needed him to connect them over and over. He started cheating with the third magazine, turning five and ten pages at a time. "What this? What this?"

Adam fell asleep before the fairy tale had ended, leaned over against Noah's arm, his open mouth forming a very small O. His grandfather carried him to the bed where the teddy bear was waiting. "He sleepin," Elsa said as Noah went out of the room. "Now you," Maggie said, picking the girl up.

On the couch, Noah put his arm around Maggie. "I don't want no more hanky-panky with my daughter," her father had said to Noah after he had been exiled because of the Atlas Theater kiss. Her father had guided fifteen-year-old Noah by the neck around to the side of the house. An ancient elm straddled the properties of Maggie's family and the people next door. "I can't help that Maggie wants to see you, boy, but I can help how many of your teeth I knock outa your head." The elms had not fared well in other cities, Noah had heard, but all the ones he had seen in Washington had been thriving. "Open your mouth, boy. Open it wide. Thas one I'll get. And them two teeth over there, I'll knock them out, too." He had eulogized his father-in-law, named his son after him. "This is the saddest day of my life, cause I come here to bury one a my fathers," Noah had said in that church, with a thousand people looking on.

"You want some more cake?" Maggie said.

"Naw, I'm done for the night." He squeezed her shoulder. "Want some TV?" He had struggled on through his last year of high school, hoping that that would impress her father.

"What's on?" Maggie asked. She had a Ph.D. His three daughters had four Ph.D.s and an M.D. among them. He and Caleb had only high-school diplomas. "What am I gonna do with you, Noah?" her father had said the day Noah asked to marry Maggie. Falling acorns had a way of sounding to an adulterer like the footsteps of a father-in-law.

"Let me turn it back on and see." He reached for the remote control, but she pulled his arm back.

"Let it come on by magic," she said. "Let's see it come on by magic." In Rome they had turned on the television, but none of it made sense because they did not know the language. It rained a lot in Paris their first days there, and they would sleep until eleven or so in the morning. "I will see you again, Kenya," he had said, buckling his airplane seat belt. "I'll see you before the by-and-by."

Monday

In the newspaper's obituaries, he saw, for the hundredth time, a name that he thought could be that of the woman, but he could not be certain, because he had long ago forgotten her name. They, he and the woman, had started what they had nearly a year before Maggie became pregnant with Caleb. "What's the use a eatin your lunch in this dirty old garage?" the woman said to him the day she brought her broken-down Chevy in and saw him sitting on a stool eating a tuna-salad sandwich that Maggie had made. Maggie's coffee still hot in the thermos. "I got a nice table and chair just waitin to be used." Maggie had asked him once what he thought of having just one woman for the rest of his life, and he had innocently thrown it back at her and asked what she thought of having but one man for the rest of hers. She said she was fine with that. Just fine, thank you very much. That was when they had had only one child, and it was nighttime when she asked and right then that one baby girl started crying for more of everything and he never got to answer her and she never asked the question again. One baby, two babies, three babies . . . He waited two days after the woman's offer of the chair and table and got her address from the work order, told his fellow workers, Big Tiny and the rest, he was taking lunch in the park. Big Tiny said, "Dontcha get into any fights with them sassy trees in that park, y'hear?" "I knowed it was you even before I opened the door," the woman said after his two knocks—knocks so soft they wouldn't have awoken a sleeping baby. It was a few days after Palm Sunday and she had palms sticking out between her bedroom mirror and the wall. The wind came through the window and disturbed the palms, and when the wind stopped, the palms on the bottom were the first to come to rest. The top ones took a while, as they held on to the memory of wind for a longer time. "I'm Catholic," the woman said when Maggie was five months pregnant with Caleb. "Catholic on my mother's side. Pure dee Catholic. On my father's, I'm straight up and down Baptist."

At home, his daughters continued to worship him, and his wife grew big with Caleb. When Caleb was two weeks old, Noah told the woman he would not ever come back. The woman shrugged. "Easy come, easy go. A tree has more leaves than I can count. Why cry bout just one leaf fallin away?" He came back before Caleb was two years old and would always believe that it was the return that had doomed him and his boy. God told the Israelites that he would punish men who stole grapes by setting their children's teeth on edge. Oh, that God. God and his long, punishing fingernails . . . Before Caleb was two and a half, Noah said good-bye to the woman again. Caleb took sick the night of that good-bye. In the ambulance, he held Caleb as the boy shivered and shook, and all the way to the hospital Noah thought his boy would be fine if only the siren would hush and give them some peace. "Can't you stop that noise?" he said to the driver. "That noise tells folks your son is somebody important, mister," the woman said.

Wednesday

For many nights after Adam's arrival, Noah had managed to get some three hours of sleep. But Tuesday night he slept for no more than two hours. After lying with his eyes open for an hour and trying to will himself back to sleep, he got up at about two and went quietly out of the room. Maggie had always been able to fall asleep within five minutes of putting her head on the pillow. A woman who had never committed adultery. He stood in the little hallway until his eyes adjusted to the dark.

At the door of the children's room he heard nothing, but he felt that Adam was awake.

He took one step into the room and said, "Adam?"

"Yes?"

"You should be sleepin." Adam was sitting up in the bed. "You need a lotta sleep."

"Yes."

"Then why don't you try to get some?" Adam lay down. The man stood for more than fifteen minutes, but the boy did not go to sleep. The air-conditioning began to chill Noah and he finally went to the couch and sat and covered himself with a throw his daughter Laverne had given him for his sixty-fifth birthday. Maggie had been taking Elsa to church each Sunday, and she was planning to take Adam again that Sunday. "It won't hurt them," she had told her husband. Noah had not been to church in three years. Would a grandfather going to church give a grandson just a little peace at night? Would God let him live until the children were grown? Could God forgive the adultery? Could God manage that?

About three he put his feet up on the couch. At four he went to the refrigerator and got a slice of cheese, the throw around his shoulders. At four-thirty he went in and saw that Adam was asleep. At five he went back for two more slices of cheese and folded them and dipped them into the mayonnaise jar. At a quarter to six the deliveryman dropped the newspaper at his door and Noah opened the door and stood at the threshold with the newspaper in his hand and looked at the metal stairs that led up to the roof. Noah had a lodge brother who seemed to sin every day of his life and nothing bad had ever happened to him. He had died at eighty-five in his sleep beside his seventh wife, in a big house, with his thirteenth child, an infant, sleeping nearby. Noah had been a pallbearer at his funeral. He read the headlines on the front page and heard someone downstairs drop a pan. It was hard thinking about God playing favorites all the time. At the threshold he read the obituaries.

Tuesday

Noah rose about six-thirty and yawned as he took in the *Washington Post*. He had been retired three years, as had Maggie. Coffee with the newspaper alone in the morning kitchen was one thing he looked forward to.

He wasn't much for sports, just liked to read the front and Metro sections to see what bad things the world had done to people. The door to the children's room was cracked, and as soon as he opened it all the way he saw Adam standing before him, holding the shopping bag. The boy was a heartbreaking sight. He still had on the pajama top, but he was wearing the corduroy pants and tennis shoes of that first day. Noah could see that the shoelaces weren't properly tied. Adam had an odd alertness about him, as if he had been standing there all night, just waiting for someone to push open the door. "When I'm goin home?" the boy said. He put a little more pep in the words than he had the day before.

"You tryin to rile me this early in the mornin, boy? I told you yesterday that you were already home. Thas your room, thas your ceiling, thas your closet, thas your sister, thas your floor. This your grandfather. All yours."

Adam looked about, convinced of nothing. Elsa was sleeping.

"Put down that bag." Noah wanted to shout, thinking that loud words might sink in better than soft ones. "Put it down right now. Put down that bag, I say, and come get some breakfast."

Adam let go of the bag's handles.

"Where your slippers at?" Noah said. Adam looked over to the bed. The slippers were resting neatly together on the floor at the side of the bed. There had been a little boy's attempt to make the bed and the thing was all lumpy. "Put on them slippers. A man can't enjoy breakfast in his street shoes." Adam changed and came back to stand before his grandfather. "Come on and les wash up." Elsa slept on.

He buttered a piece of toast for Adam and set a bowl of Cheerios before him. "Your daddy liked Wheaties," Noah said, sitting across from Adam and spooning sugar into his coffee. "We bought you some Wheaties just in case."

"The yellow box is nice," Adam said, pointing to the Cheerios box.

"Well, don't pick a cereal cause of the box. A pretty box could be holdin poison. Get a cereal you like. You like Cheerios?"

"Yes."

"Tell me somethin—where is this home you keep talkin about? Whose house is this thas so good you don't want to be here?"

The boy looked at the space next to the plate with his half-eaten toast. "Mama Wilson," he said. "But I guess she already got some other boy for my bed." He put down the spoon.

"Sooner or later you're gonna have to learn to trust me and your grandmother. We won't take away your bed."

"I had a nice bed over her house," Adam said, finally looking at his grandfather. "She a good mama."

Noah said nothing. Was it too late to find Tamara's people and give him to them? Why couldn't Adam be more like Elsa and go along with the program? He had read in the newspaper where all kinds of orphans never got over what had happened to them. Once adopted, they threatened their new siblings and their new parents with death by stabbing. Death in the night. Adoptive parents put locks on their bedroom doors, they took turns staying awake and guarding the door. The children became teenage criminals, even murderers, and drifted off into their own kind of night, never to return to that good new home. In the newspaper, the parents said they still loved the children, but there was relief between the words. "Good riddance to bad rubbish," an old white woman Noah knew in South Carolina liked to say about bad people way over there in another county.

"It sleeps good," Adam said of the bed. "She givin it to some other boy right now." In the end, Noah said, "Eat," and pointed to the toast and the cereal. Adam followed his grandfather's hand as the finger pointed and as it retreated and picked up the coffee cup. When the hand was resting in his grandfather's lap, the boy picked up the toast.

Friday

The man awoke after a half hour of sleep and sat up in bed, orienting himself. In two months he would be sixty-eight. He got to his exercises, managing seventy-seven push-ups but only thirty sit-ups before something told him to stop. As his sweat dried, he pruned the bonsai tree he kept in a special compartment in one of the bedroom windows. The compartment allowed the tree to be in the room and then, with just a turn of its wooden platform, to be outside. And with the press of a button a transparent covering emerged from the side of the compartment to cover the tree outside. The bonsai was a gift from his youngest daughter, who lived in the suburbs of Virginia, where trees with all the life of plastic had been put up to decorate the new developments. Someone had warned him that bonsai trees in people's homes did not live very long, but his had gone on for more than six years, and it had given him unimaginable pleasure. The tree was so small that he could cover it with both hands. A booklet that came with the tree said it had been "trained" for thirty-five years. He had waited the first two years for the tree to wither and die, but it went on and on. Now he believed that it could live forever. In the National Arboretum he and Maggie had seen bonsai trees that had been living—"trained"—for three hundred, four hundred, five hundred years. If them, why not his own?

After washing up, he changed from his pajama top to a T-shirt. He peered long into the bathroom mirror, at his father's and his grandfather's face. His father had died at seventy-five, and his grandfather had made it only to sixty-six. He turned his face this way and that to see if he wanted to shave right then. Last week Elsa had fallen in the playground and cried as if her world were falling apart. He decided to shave because his granddaughter liked smooth cheeks. He left the bathroom and stood just outside the children's room and listened to them playing. Adam was pretending to be a dog for Elsa. "If you give me a biscuit, I'll jump over here," he said. He barked. If only he could be like that all the time.

He found Maggie at the stove, singing. The coffee was waiting. He stood watching her. The newspaper was on the edge of the table. A man on the radio was telling him the news. The window was open and he could hear a man and a woman talking.

"Why you always so cheerful with all this?" he asked and fanned his hand to indicate all that was wrong, including Adam.

She placed bacon on a plate covered with paper towels and put another towel over it. Then she danced over to him and did three slow twirls. "Because I have you," she said and twirled back over to the stove. "Don't you see, Noah, how easy it would be if you were married to you? Your days would be good. See me? Watch me. I'm standing on your shoulders." She raised herself up on the tips of her toes and looked over as if from the edge of a mountain. She called down into the valley from the mountain, "Nooooaah, thank you." She settled back on her feet, swaying her hips. "Two eggs or three?" She took an egg in each hand and danced over to him, with her hips still swaying. She kissed him. He put his arms around her and kissed her with such passion that one egg cracked in her hand and she had to place the other one on the newspaper before it, too, cracked.

They did not move. She rested her cheek against his chest. He had got lost on his way to the woman's place that first time. "I'll have to give you a map for the next time," she said.

"Two eggs, then," Maggie said. She leaned to the side and found the children watching them. "Hey," Elsa said. Noah did not move. Adam was holding Elsa's hand. "Hey yourself," Maggie said. Elsa pointed to the egg Maggie had crushed against the back of Noah's robe. "He's pretty messy that way," Maggie said to Elsa. Boys, her grandmother mouthed.

Sunday

In the newspaper he read about a mother across the Anacostia River whose eight-year-old son had disappeared. The police told her to go home, that the boy would find his way back. "He's not a runaway and he stays close to home," the mother told them. "He's a good son. He's a good student. Something must have happened to him." When the police refused to help, she and her neighbors looked for the boy but could not find him. Finally, with night coming on, a group of former convicts at the neighborhood halfway house—the Light at the End of the Tunnel— gathered to search for the boy. The men found the boy in a little piece of woods with a man who was holding him under a blanket. "I ain't doin nothin," the man was reported to have said as one former convict pulled the boy free and another punched the man in the mouth, knocking his jaw far off track. "This is all some big misunderstandin," the man said through a broken jaw before he was kicked once in the head and twice in the chest. "I can clear this whole mess up." That was Washington now, Noah thought, that was the world now—people forced to get criminals to do police work.

In the evening, the reverend, Colbert Prentiss, called to say he had missed Noah that morning at church. "Saw Maggie and the children," he began, "but I didn't see you." Noah and Colbert had grown up to- gether, had first met at Stevens Elementary. Colbert had also been a pallbearer at Mrs. Waters's funeral.

"I'll try to make it next time, Colbert."

"You better. I don't wanna have to stand up in the pulpit and talk about you."

Tuesday

"Listen," Noah said, sitting on the floor, "why don't we get rid of this old shoppin bag?" Adam had just asked about going home and had a grip on the edge of the shopping bag. Noah gently shook the bag loose. It was already coming apart and wouldn't have survived a trip beyond the apartment. Noah tore the bag down to the bottom, right through Adam's name that someone had misspelled. And at the base of the bag he tore some more. Adam sat down, apprehensive. "I'll tell you what," Noah said. "You can have one of my suitcases if it makes things easier. If you need something for your things, I'll give you one a mine. I got one I took to Africa. Your bag only been to D.C. My suitcase been cross the sea and back again over and over."

There were still two shirts in the bag, both shirts at least two sizes too big for the boy. "Mama Wilson gave me this one," Adam said, picking up the blue shirt.

"Well," Noah said, taking the shirt and tossing it over his shoulder toward the door, "we don't need somebody else's shirt, do we?" Adam looked at the shirt. He wanted to go to it, pick it up.

"No," Adam said. He got out the white shirt. "They had this in the home. Another boy got it outa a big box. He got one and he gave me one. It's a church shirt." He reached into the muddle of things in the bag and pulled out a clip-on tie. He placed the tie over the front of the shirt lest Noah not know what he meant.

"I like the tie, so we'll keep that. But the shirt . . . the shirt."

"It's a church shirt," Adam said.

"All right, we'll keep it for like two years from now when you've grown into it." Noah threw it on top of the blue shirt. Adam said nothing. He was thinking of the phrase "two years from now." Noah tossed the tie up onto the chest of drawers.

Adam went into the bag. "I got this truck at Mama Joyce's," he said, and ran a green Matchbox truck back and forth a few inches over the floor. He shook the bag, spreading the things about. He was looking for something, but he couldn't find it. "She gave me three of em," he said. "I had two, but this big boy took one, said it was his. But I guess I lost the other one. They ran real good. See?" He gave the green truck to Noah and bade him move it about. Noah did. "Yeah," the man said. "It runs real good."

Adam pulled a tiny wooden box from the bag. He began tapping on its sides. "It's a secret box, and it won't open if you don't do the secret." After the tapping, he raised the lid slowly, and inside was a desiccated june bug. "We caught this and Bobby put this lady's thread on his leg and we flew him. *Whoosh-whoosh!*" He picked the bug up. He offered it to Noah, but Noah shook his head. "It won't hurt you," Adam said, putting the bug back in the box. "It won't hurt. It's dead."

For the next half hour or so, the boy went through all the things he had acquired, and for each one he had a story. A broken yo-yo that had belonged to a big-toothed boy with broken eyeglasses. A snapshot of him in a group of children; he pointed to each child and gave their full names. None had a parent. A tiny book with just the New Testament. He opened it to where someone had written his name and the day he was given the book. There was even the time of day—11:05 A.M. He flipped a few pages. "I can read these words right there," he said, and moved his finger along the lines. "The book of the Jesus Christ, the son of David, the son of Moses, the son of Abraham, the son of God." He stopped. "Thas all the far we got." He set the book aside. He picked up two gray stones, hefting them in his right hand. "You can hurt somebody with these. You can make em leave you alone. Here," and he gave them to Noah, and Noah hefted them and dropped them into his shirt pocket.

Adam went on and on, and in the end his grandfather said he would build him a shelf for all he had acquired.

"You got a picture of your mama and daddy?"

"I think I did," Adam said, and he looked out the window, trying to remember a woman he had last seen walking away from him. He had no memory of Caleb, but in the boy's mind his father was always smiling, because that was what fathers did. "But I think somebody took it. Maybe Oscar Tremont. He already had a mama and a daddy picture, but he wanted another one." Noah came to him and put the boy in his lap and they looked out the window together. Adam said, "I ain't never goin home, huh?" Noah was silent.

Friday

Noah did eighty-four sit-ups and a hundred and five push-ups, then lay down where he was beside the bed, his arms folded under his head.

Maggie came into the room and saw him, waited a long time for him to move. He was still. The life insurance was paid up, but she could not remember if the policies were in the apartment or if they had returned them to the bank's safe-deposit box. She began to count the seconds, and still he did not move. If she could survive picking out his casket, then maybe she could make it until after the funeral. There would be no end to the men who would be proud to be his pallbearers, to carry him home. He had been that kind of man. A good father, a good husband, a good grandfather, a good friend. Rest in peace, my love.

She went closer, and Noah stirred. She had trouble catching her breath. He turned and saw something on her face. He asked, "What's the matter, honey?"

"Nothing." She herself had been looking forward to seeing India. She knew widowed grandmothers who had been forced to raise grand-children alone, but she had never thought she could.

Noah sat up. "Well, somethin is the matter, cause I can see it on your face."

"Stop doing all those damn exercises, Noah." She sat at the foot of the bed.

"I'm addicted, honey." He leaned back on his elbows.

"Addicted, schmaddicted. Why don't you stop?"

"Look." He rolled up his pajama sleeve and flexed the muscle. "If I stopped, who would save you from the bad guys? Answer me that. Who would save you?" He scooted closer and offered the muscle to her and she felt it, tried unsuccessfully to press down on it. Noah looked at his arm, at the scars up and down it, and he looked up to see her watching him and rolled his sleeve down. He knew how each scar came to be, could describe the day it all happened and how long the pain had been with him. She got down from the bed onto her knees and he pulled her to him and sat her sideways in the valley that his thighs made with his chest. He kissed her hard, and when they opened their eyes and looked around, Elsa was staring at them, one of her dolls in her hand. The child was blinking but was not impressed one way or the other with what she was seeing.

Monday

At dawn he rose after only fifteen minutes of sleep, with the conversation he had had the evening before with Colbert Prentiss, the preacher, playing over and over in his head. "You ain't gonna give up on me, are you?" Noah joked. "It ain't in my nature to give up," Colbert said. "Give some thought to coming for next Sunday's grandparents' day." Noah did not have it in him to tell his friend that he did not think he would ever return to church. Noah asked before they hung up, "Didn't God have some responsibility to make nice so people would want to go on worshipping Him? Why should it be so one-sided just because He happened to be God?"

He left Maggie still asleep and went to the children's room. Adam was standing in the middle of the floor, waiting, his tennis shoes on but still in his pajamas. Noah dreaded the question, so he jumped in: "Tell me about this home you so anxious to get back to." Elsa had just awoken and lay in bed with her eyes half open. Noah stood in front of Adam. "Tell me about it. I might wanna go live there myself."

Adam began describing the front yard, a grassless place, as it turned out, "except way over there in the corner." Elsa got out of bed and began singing and running around her grandfather and her brother. Adam then began talking about Mama Wilson's downstairs, but as he went on he had to correct himself many times, because he was confusing that woman's place with many others. "No," he said, "that big TV wasn't at Mama Wilson. She had a tiny one. No flowers, neither." He looked up at Noah, as if hoping the corrections hadn't done damage to the overall truth of what he was saying. Noah sat on the floor, and Elsa immediately began climbing about him. Adam sat. In his last weeks at

Mama Wilson's, he managed to say, he had had to share that bed with a boy who screamed in his sleep. Adam waited for his grandfather to say he had never mentioned having to share the bed. Elsa left off her grandfather and began climbing about Adam. "He wasn't such a bad little boy," Adam said, "once he stopped all that screamin." He hesitated, avoided his grandfather's eyes. "Really. He wasn't a bad little boy. Really and true." Noah did not speak. "Honest. He wasn't a bad boy after the screamin."

Thursday

A little before two that night Noah awoke after a few minutes of sleep and heard tiny voices.

At the children's bedroom door he saw Adam standing at Elsa's bed, telling her to go back to sleep, that he would keep her safe. "I tell you a story if you go back to sleep," Adam said. "All little chirren gotta be asleep." And Elsa said Yes, yes, she would sleep for a story, but not no scary story. She lay down and Adam stayed at the side of the bed, pulling the covers up to her shoulders and placing a doll on either side of her. He began telling her about a little girl and a little boy who were driving alone to the beach in a car with bird wings. Noah went into the living room, the boy's voice still all around him. He did not know which way to turn, but after a long while the voice of Adam led him to the couch. The voice bade him to lie down. Noah covered himself with the throws and listened to the story of the little boy and the little girl going to the beach. It seemed to be a trip that had no end, and Noah kept waiting for them to arrive at the beach. The boy and the girl shared the driving. Sometimes they lost their way and squirrels with cowboy hats and boots had to drop from trees onto the hood of the car and tell them which way to go. There were mothers and fathers standing in Easter baskets along the road to the beach, and other children who were going places in their own cars—

to the circus, to the movies. But no one except the boy and the girl were going to the beach. "Can they come, too?" Elsa asked. "Tomorrow," Adam said, "but not right now."

Noah began to fall asleep at the point where the girl was behind the ice-cream steering wheel and it began dripping on her new tennis shoes. "I can't drive with them dirty tennis shoes," the girl told the boy. "I can't, I can't, I can't." In a dream Noah applied cold hands to the ice-cream wheel and it froze over again. The boy thanked him and the girl thanked him, but when Noah asked about a short ride on up the road, the little girl said no. "First you," the girl said, biting into the chocolate wheel, "then all them other people will wanna ride, too. We gotta put a stop to this thing right here and now." As they drove off, the boy stuck his head out the window and said to Noah, "I come back for you way before the by-and-by. Okay?"

Noah had watched his father putting on his tie not two days after they had arrived in Washington. His father's first job was as a dishwasher at the Willard Hotel. His mother had straightened his father's tie seconds before he walked out the door. "A man," his father said as he sat his new hat atop his head, "must do what a man must do."

When Noah woke again, it was nearly three o'clock and Adam was still talking. The boy in the story was driving up a mountain. "Don't go too fast," the girl told the boy. "We gotta save on the gas. Gas expensive. Five dollars." Noah turned on his side, and in no time at all he was asleep again. He was never to know when Adam went back to bed. In the dream, Noah began begging for a ride as the car came to a stop. The girl was a lost cause, he could tell that just by the confident way she had gripped the ice-cream wheel, but Noah, turning his pockets inside out to show how empty they were, began to plead his case before the boy. "Just a short ride on up the road," Noah told the boy. "We'll come back for you," the boy said, starting up the motor, "and when we do you must be ready."

Sunday

That last Sunday in August was grandparents' day at church and Noah, at the final moment, decided to go with them. "You sure you know the way?" Maggie said before they set off. Something compelled Colbert Prentiss to depart from his text near the end of his sermon that morning. It might have been all the grandparents he saw before him, all the people who had struggled into old age only to find themselves parents once again. Clement Carson. Mr. and Mrs. Harrelson. The widow Anderson. Colbert's own sister and brother-in-law. Mr. and Mrs. Apacka. Maggie and Noah Robinson. All of them the kind of people the preacher had built his rock on. The world was turned upside down when the mature ones were forced to do what the younger ones should be doing. Indeed, it was August, so why not have it snow outside, Colbert said to the hundreds. Why not lift our eyes to the sky and see all the pigs flying with their cherub wings?

He had the grandparents and their grandchildren stand and apologized to any who might have a touch of the shyness fever. He told his congregation that the people standing would lead them all out into a better day. The people sitting applauded.

Maggie helped Elsa stand up on the seat. Noah looked at those standing. Clement's three grandsons were not wearing suits, just white shirts and ties and dark pants. They were all taller than their grandfather. He found Mrs. Anderson's granddaughter across the aisle looking at him and he smiled at her, but she did not smile back. She blinked once and looked ahead. Noah's son Caleb had had a hard time sitting still in church, was forever turning and staring at what was about him. Noah looked down at the top of Adam's head. The crown had the same tuft of hair his son's had had. The barber always had a tough time mowing it down. "Should charge you extra for that bit a hair, Noah, but maybe I'll let it slide," the barber always said. And Noah would say,

"You charge me the regular for the regular hair. Any damage after that and Caleb gonna pay."

The congregation began singing "The Blind Man Stood in the Road and Cried." The spiritual ended and everyone sat down and Adam looked up at Noah, sensing his grandfather's eyes on him. Elsa curled up in Maggie's lap and soon went to sleep, one arm stretched out to the wooden pocket on the back of the pew in front of them. The congregation sang "I Done Done What Ya Told Me to Do." Without even thinking about it, Noah pulled Adam close to him and they looked at the words in the book and Adam began to cry. The boy put one hand behind his grandfather's back and grabbed hold of his suit coat as best he could. Still crying, he went over the words in the book with his finger. It was an old trick of an old boy: if you pretended to read, maybe they wouldn't notice that you really couldn't. Adam held on to Noah's coat, for he knew it was possible for people to rise up and disappear out of his life. He could not then know that Noah had already told God that he planned to live forever. Why should eternal life be only for bonsai trees? Why should men, the greatest glory of God, come second to trees? Noah placed his hand over Adam's as it went over the words in the book. Adam grabbed more of the coat and it was then that Noah, feeling himself go light as a blossom in the wind, leaned down and anchored his lips to that difficult tuft of the boy's hair.

THE DEVIL SWIMS ACROSS
THE ANACOSTIA RIVER

Some fourteen years after her grandmother walked out into the Atlantic Ocean on her way to heaven, Laverne Shepherd went into the Safeway on Good Hope Road, S.E., and for the first time came face-to-face with the Devil. That morning in the store, she had, like so many times before, taken a shopping cart from just inside the door and maneuvered it to the aisle farthest to the left. She neared a face-high display of canned pinto beans and glanced at a short shopping list after she took it from her sweater pocket, and when she looked up from the list of four or so items, the Devil was before her. She stopped, not out of fear, but because to go any farther would have meant running into him with the cart. "Himself been studyin you," the Devil said. Laverne looked down at her wedding ring on the hand resting on the cart's handle, and when she raised her eyes, the Devil was taking off his hat, in that dramatic way men did in old movies to impress women who needed very little impressing.

The Devil was dressed in a splendid gray gabardine suit, and down through the metal rods of the empty cart Laverne could see that on feet small enough to belong to a little girl, he wore two-tone, black-and-white shoes. The knot of his purple tie was situated just so to the left of his Adam's apple, as if he had dressed himself without the benefit of a mirror. There was an almost boyish quality to the off-center knot, and

for a moment Laverne thought it would have been the most natural
thing in the world for a woman, any woman, to reach over and center the
knot and end the whole gesture with a final tap of the finger on the knot.
There . . . That'll do you for a while . . . The tie was held in place against
his white shirt with a ruby tie clip, about the size of a candy fireball.

Himself been studyin you," the Devil said again, now smiling. All
the teeth in his head were perfect, exquisite white marvels that
were an artwork all their own. A woman could spend all day and part of
the next just laying about looking at them. *Turn a little bit and lemme see
how the light shine on em that way . . .* Both her grandmothers had come
to know the Devil so well that he, in all his guises, called them always by
their childhood nicknames. At various times in her life, Laverne's grandmothers had tried to tell her how she would know the Devil that first
time. It will be, they had explained as best they could, the way you know
that you are hungry or that you are thirsty: the body will say it and you
will take it as gospel. But they had not told her what to say, what to do,
whether to run or go forward and attack him with the fury of an angel
doing God's work.

Once more the Devil said, "Himself been studyin you." He came
toward her and as he did he lowered the arm with the hat down to his
side. The fedora was the same pleasing gray as his gabardine suit. The
Devil himself was the color of an everyday brown paper bag. He rested
a hand on the side of the cart, less than a foot from where her wedding
ring hand was resting, and turned down his smile a few degrees, turned
it down in disappointment, as if he had come upon a long-lost friend
and the friend had denied knowing him.

"What?" Laverne said. "What?" She was nine weeks pregnant with
her second child, happy in all things, happy in her twenty-fifth year of
life.

The Devil said, "Himself come all this way, come all the way cross the river, swim all the way cross that Anacostia. Himself swim all that way to say 'Good mornin' and say 'Hi you do?'"

She was still not afraid but looked about, mostly with a strange wonder that they were at last together, and together in such an odd and bright place of food and people and things to clean the kitchen floor with. *Only here only at Safeway can you get the best bargain for your dollars . . .* The sign on the display of canned pinto beans said eight for a dollar. It occurred to Laverne that that might be a particularly good price, but she could not remember if her husband or son liked pinto beans. It was when she looked back at the Devil that the smell of him came drifting her way, a nonthreatening fragrance that didn't mind taking all the time it needed to get to her. It was a wonderful though subtle cologne that for Laverne simply said everything good about men. No doubt, the man in the apartment downstairs from hers had a similar smell, though when that man washed his car in his T-shirt and shorts there was just the sweat, or so she thought as she looked down at him from behind her curtain. *Look up this way. Don't look up here . . .* She had not yet gotten close to the man downstairs and so could only imagine how he smelled as he stepped out of his apartment dressed to kill and went to his car with yet another new woman on his arm and opened his car door for the woman and watched her take her sophisticated time settling down on his bucket seat. A final look up at the man before he shut the door. Her husband believed that a man did not have to perfume himself as long as he bathed every day. It would be her luck, she thought, if there were no specials on Dial soap that day. "Himself been studyin you," the Devil said, quietly now, as if he were sharing the great secret of her life.

Laverne stepped away from the Devil and the cart and walked uneasily out of the Safeway.

On dishrag legs, she made her way a block and a half up Good Hope Road, and on a bench in front of Cleopatra's Hair Emporium, she sat, the crumpled shopping list in her left hand resting on the green bench. She was back in the world, back in life, and was so glad that she felt like reaching out and touching a body or two passing by the Emporium. Two women went into Cleopatra's, and one of the women was saying she really wanted some bangs, but her companion told her bangs would make her face look fat. "But I really want them bangs," the first woman insisted before they closed the door to the Emporium. Laverne crossed her legs and with the tips of her fingers rearranged her skirt down over her legs. *Himself been studyin you* . . . For the third time that morning she wished she had not stopped smoking. It was near about twelve o'clock.

She considered calling her mother, or her mother's wealthy mother, who had known the Devil mostly in his guise of an old woman for nearly sixty years. She turned her head and looked into the window of the beauty parlor. The woman who wanted the bangs was being seated in a chair two seats from the window. In the chair at the window was an old woman who was getting her black hair unfurled from light blue curlers; standing beside the woman was a little girl who could have been the woman's granddaughter. The girl's hair was done up quite nicely and she seemed to be watching the old woman and her hair as if to make certain that the same care was given to her grandmother. The woman who wanted the bangs was talking, talking a mile a minute to Cleopatra, who waded through the woman's hair with her fingers in preparation for the job ahead. Laverne's mother would be back from confession and mass by now. She went to church every day. Laverne could see herself getting up, putting the dime into the pay phone next to the beauty shop, could see herself dialing her mother's number and hearing the promising ring, but she could not see beyond that.

She had, after the birth of her son, tried to do good to put off as long as possible this day, the day of meeting the Devil. Sending money to the Salvation Army. Going to church every week until all that singing and preaching began to depress her. Trying to banish impure thoughts. And in the last place they had lived, on Maple View, she had befriended a dying man, Mansfield Harper, had even held his hand in those moments before he died the evening Mansfield's woman had stepped away on an errand. His fingers had wiggled there at the end and, because she had not known Mansfield's sins, Laverne had thought the wiggling meant he was on his way to heaven. But all that good had not put off this day.

She had paid little attention to the story that the Devil had a special thing for the women on both sides of her family, a thing born with Eve. It was said that all the women in her family had the answer to a riddle that would make the Devil the King of Heaven. All he had to do was pose the riddle in the right way to the right woman, alive or dead, and the answer would send God tumbling from his throne and down to the narrow perch the Devil had been consigned to for all history. And so the Devil had sought out all the women in her family, sought out millennia of women who had known the big and small of life before Laverne but who had failed to tell the Devil the answer of the ages. Laverne's great-aunt's grandmother had said that if the Devil could get the right woman in hell, he would have an eternity, small time for him, to get what he wanted. Morning after morning, that grandmother had said, he could wake the right woman on her bed of fire and ask about the answer.

Now the Devil had knocked at her door.

Laverne looked at the shopping list and then put it back in her sweater pocket and patted the pocket. She lived to dance, lived to party, even though her mother liked to remind her that she was now married with a child and another waiting in the wings. A friend across the Anacostia River in Northwest was giving a party that Saturday night and it was all Laverne had been able to think about for days. She tried not to place herself in the middle of the party, abandoning herself the way she was known to do, sweating gloriously from all the dancing with black men made to make her knees buckle. Her husband was a dancer, too, had met her on a dance floor in someone's apartment, but he had long since stopped trying to keep up with Laverne. He sent her off and told her go and be happy. She labored now to put herself on the floor of the party to come that night, but once more she could not place herself where she wanted.

❖

A car going up Good Hope Road tooted its horn at her, but she did not hear it. Her mother said all Anacostia seemed to know her. After several minutes she closed her eyes and took herself down Good Hope, across the bridge and out through Washington, through Maryland until she was on the August beach fourteen years ago, the Atlantic Ocean only a few yards away and the heat waves shimmering all along the dull blue horizon, one seagull conversing with another. She was wearing her cousin's bathing suit and sitting on the beach with her feet dug into the sand, snuggled close to her paternal grandmother, who was in her after-church, all-day Sunday dress. And on the other side of the grandmother were Laverne's brothers, boys of eight and five years. Laverne's father and mother had gone to a refreshment stand near the parking lot to buy snacks. The beach was full of colored people.

What her grandmother had heard before she was compelled to stand up, Laverne never knew, but once her grandmother did stand up, the voice was clear for all the Negroes along the beach to hear. Only her grandmother, after putting on her shoes, moved toward the water and the voice. And, as if there were a silent command, those Negroes who had been swimming came out of the water and looked at the horizon, from where the voice was coming. There was a kind of roar that seemed to ascend from the ocean, and another roar that seemed to descend from the sky, and there at eye level, the roars became words. The voice, emphatically clear and distinct, was not female and it was not male.

Laverne's grandmother hesitated, stopping a yard or more from the water, and the voice, without rebuke, asked the grandmother, "Did you come all this way to lose your faith, to drop down into the bottom of the sea? Ahead of you is this water and behind you he's coming? Did you lose your faith?"

"No," her grandmother said. "No. I stand on my two feet." Before she set off again, she turned around and from her pocketbook pulled out three ten-dollar bills. She gave one to each of her grandchildren, which was unusual for a woman who had never given them more than fifty cents at any one time, lest they be corrupted. Laverne's youngest brother, a boy of easy giggles, looked suspiciously at the ten-dollar bill; he was still at an age where he did not trust paper money. It could tear; it could burn; it could fly away with the wind. But he folded the bill as small as he could and tucked it into the pocket of his swimming trunks. Laverne's grandmother set off again and the youngest brother said, "Granny, you gon ruin your pretty shoes in all that water."

Their grandmother looked down, somewhat worried, as if deciding between her $12.95 Hahn's shoes and the command of the voice of the universe. "We have waited since the first day," the voice said with the greatest patience. "Have you not waited since the first day?" the voice said with the greatest patience. "Have you not waited with us?" Their grandmother turned and looked at the boy, dark-skinned, bony, painfully perfect. He waved though they were but a few yards apart. After several moments, she took a step and was standing where water met dry sand. She stopped, her brown patent leather pocketbook hanging from her left arm. Then, in a few more steps, she was standing a foot above the bottom of the sea. She continued walking, one uncertain step after another. All the Negroes along the beach were quiet, so that the loudest sound when the voice was silent was the ocean hitting the beach and then retreating.

By now, Laverne's mother and father were back, followed by a lifeguard who was looking about as if there was something that would make more sense than an old woman walking on water. Laverne's father watched until his mother was about five yards out on the water, and then he said, "Mama."

Haltingly, Laverne's grandmother turned around for the first and only time. "Ain't I always told you it might come to this?" she told her son. "I've done nothin that I couldn't clean up by the next day. And it was hard, but now I wanna go and complain to somebody about it. Then shut up for good." Then she said to Laverne's mother, "Cheryl, you try to splain it to him. Just to let him know. I got somethin I have to do right now." Laverne's father moved toward the ocean. He was crying but did not speak. He was joined by his wife and she was followed by the lifeguard. The children had not moved since their grandmother handed them the money.

The grandmother set off again. With each step, all the Negroes on the beach could see that she was gaining confidence. Still, the lifeguard, when the grandmother was more than twenty yards out into the sea, shouted to her with complete sincerity, "Ma'am, you all right out there? You need some help?" He was eighteen.

Not stopping, the grandmother raised her right arm and wiggled her fingers that she was fine. For all the purpose and certainty of her step, she could have been walking down 7th Street on her way to St. Aloysius Catholic Church. There was nothing on the ocean and the horizon except the old woman, not a boat, not a buoy, and even the seagulls had disappeared from the air. When the grandmother was but a foot tall on the sea, her son sat down on the beach and refused to look anymore. When the grandmother was an inch or so, Laverne walked to the ocean's edge and raised a hand to shade her eyes, and her youngest brother came up beside her and put his hand in hers. The other brother took a place beside his father. Then, in the time it took to sigh, the grandmother was gone completely.

There was no more of that day for anyone, even though the sun was way up in the sky, and little by little the Negroes collected what they had brought to the beach and went back to their cars and buses. Now and again a stranger would come up to Laverne or a member of her family. The strangers did not speak but simply touched a shoulder or hand in sympathy, in understanding. Laverne felt no sadness and she slowly began to fear that she had not loved her grandmother as much as the old woman had always said she loved her. The family's eyes stayed focused on the horizon where the grandmother had disappeared, and Laverne and her family remained on the beach until well after the sun was down, accompanied only by the lifeguard, who had caught a chill but who felt it was his duty to stay with them.

She opened her eyes and looked about at the world of Anacostia. A woman and man holding hands walked by her. "I told you not to buy that kind," the woman said to the man. "I told you you'd be sorry." "I don't know what I was thinkin," the man said. "I musta been crazy." Laverne had been born and raised in Anacostia. After Anacostia High, after her first job at Woodward & Lothrop, she had wanted to move across the river where she believed the real Washington had been waiting all those years for her to grow up and come over and be a woman people could not stop talking about. They would say wonderful things about her, about how a party wasn't a party until she arrived. They would say she was loyal to her friends. That was about the extent of all the wonderful things she imagined people saying about her, something one man pointed out to her. She fell in love with him. He said he had gone to high school with her but she did not remember him. That man, Mason, did not want to move across the river, and six years ago when they married she said that was fine. Washington across the river had not stopped telling her that she was missing so much by living in that Anacostia place where people had molasses in their blood. People were still waiting to say glorious things about her, the city said.

She took out the shopping list. Some cookies for her son, shaving cream for her husband, just enough to carry up the hill and not tire herself. Some time away from them on a busy Saturday. A car's horn tooted, and a woman shouted out the window, "Vernie, Vernie. See you tonight." The car was gone before she could say Yes, yes, they would see her. Her family would be waiting at Sears, Roebuck and Co. on Alabama

Avenue—still another pair of pants for the boy, a tie for her husband and his assistant manager job at Murphy's Five and Dime Store. She looked down at her body. In a few months she would start to show. Should she buy new maternity clothes or settle for what was left over from her first pregnancy? "Styles don't matter when you're pregnant," her mother had once said. The dancing would have to stop for a while. That would be difficult. The best time she ever had at a party she had when she was three months pregnant with her son. An all-night thing where she had sweated through her clothes and every man she danced with told her the sweat just added to the beat. "Gimme, gimme," said one man, who was drunk but didn't show it, and she had shaken her head and watched him close his eyes and open his mouth to receive a few drops of sweat. "Mother's milk," the man said. Her husband had slow danced with her but mostly he stood on the party-giver's balcony looking down toward the Monument and talking to a woman whose mouth was wired shut because of an accident. Laverne had thought her son would inherit her love of dancing from her, but he was as clumsy as her husband. Her husband had been born with three webbed toes on his left foot. The boy was free of that.

She stood up from the bench, more annoyed than anything else that the Devil stood between her and a fairly perfect day of shopping and partying. The mind had to be uncluttered to enjoy a party. Why had he waited until she was twenty-five to come to see her? The paternal grandmother who had walked into the Atlantic Ocean had first met the Devil when she was five years old; a schoolbook under her arm, she had turned onto a red country road in Georgia and there he was, ugly as homemade soap with next to no teeth, just done with doing it to her grandmother's cousin and both of them covered with the dust of the road. "I just got tired of his beggin all the time," the cousin would say later. And he had come to her maternal grandmother when she was thirteen, wrapped in a long yellow shawl that dragged along in the upstate New York snow. As far as Laverne knew, he had never come to her mother, but she could not be certain because the Devil was not something her mother talked about to any of the women in her family. He was forever on the women's minds, but Laverne had tried to live in a different world. Now, riding her annoyance, she wished she had picked up a trick or two for dispelling him, for getting on with the rest of her life.

Back in the Safeway, he was standing just as she had left him and he waved her over as soon as she was in the store. "Himself been waitin," he said. "Himself swim all the way over that Anacostia River."

"I know. You told me once. I'm not deaf." Laverne got the cart. The grandmother and the girl from the beauty parlor came behind her and the woman told the girl to get a cart. "Make sure it's a good one," the woman said. "You didn't get a good one the last time." They moved off to the right.

"No, no. Himself would never cuse you of that. To be deaf, to be blind," he said, setting his hat back on his head, "would not be how himself wants things for you." She noticed that one of his incisors was the brightest gold. As a girl, she had believed that men with gold teeth had gotten them by drinking too much beer. No one in her neighborhood had nice things to say about such men.

"I don't want none a what you sellin today," she said.

"Himself ain't sellin," he said, stepping to the front of the cart to get her attention. "Himself ain't buyin or sellin right now. Thas all a long way from himself's mind. You can believe that."

He did have a pleasantness about him. She took the cart to the left, toward the fruits and vegetables, and the Devil followed, in step beside her. The colorful array of the produce seemed especially dazzling today. When he was younger, she liked to have her son name the colors as the two of them shopped; he was more inclined to eat squash after he had stood in the Safeway aisle and held it by the green stem and called it a yellow fellow over and over again. She could see her son now, standing with the towel about him, just after his bath, soft and brown and waiting for his kisses. She turned to look over her shoulder, as if the boy, holding his father's hand, might be just outside the window. She looked into the Devil's face and he said, "When bout is your baby due?" His fragrance swirled about her and she thought that maybe he wasn't who her mind told her he was, but was only some man with tiny feet out to romance her.

"What?" she said. Some men liked pregnant women, could sense their condition even when, like her, they were not showing.

"When your baby due?"

"What's it to you? It ain't your baby."

"Just passin the time with a beautiful woman, is all. Can't himself do that?"

"Himself can do whatever he pleases." She reached the end of the aisle and turned the cart to the right, stopping at the head of the aisle with sodas. Was there some small store between here and where her husband and son were waiting? Nothing really had to begin and end with the Safeway. Could she leave and end this? But she said, "In seven months. My baby's due in about seven months."

"See? That whatn't so hard," the Devil said. "That mean a October baby. Nothin pleases himself more than October babies. They so . . ." and he stopped, and because she wanted to know what he had to say, she stopped after a couple of feet as well. "They so accommodatin, them October babies. Himself ain't never met a October baby yet that didn't like him. October is one big accommodatin month, all thirty-one days."

"My baby won't be accommodating to anything," Laverne said, moving on.

"He has to be, Miss Laverne. If he born in October, he has to be accommodatin to himself."

"I don't care what you say." She knew there was something in that aisle she needed but couldn't remember what it was. She stood before two shelves of canned and bottled Pepsi-Cola. Why wasn't the Dial soap here like it was supposed to be, so she could use it to dial her mother and ask if her husband and son liked pinto beans? Who would know better than her own mother about Safeway specials? "You say that like bein born in October is some kinda bad thing."

"Himself didn't say that. Himself didn't say anything bad about October."

"My child will have October to be happy and not be accommodating to you or anyone else." She picked up a large bottle of soda. The price said thirty-five cents. Should I buy it? What was it last week?

"Himself knows that. Please. Please, Miss Laverne. Himself wants all October babies to be happy. Himself told you—Octobers like himself. They don't cuss himself; they don't tell himself to get thee back, get way back in the line like some do. Like them April babies."

"Why are you doin this to me?"

"Aprils are so disrespectful. April got thirty days too many. April would be a perfect month if it had only one day. And October should have thirty-one more days. Give October all April's days and see what a good world we would have then, Miss Laverne." Laverne put the soda back. "Why, ain't it that your grandmother was born in October?"

She looked at him. He was talking about her mother's mother, the one in her giant house on the Gold Coast on Crittenden Street, a place she hated for people to call a mansion. Her grandmother had torn down the two large houses originally on two plots of land and built herself the biggest in that area, to the ire of the wealthy blacks around her who usually had nothing bad to say about the ostentatious. She had four fireplaces in that house and they all burned every day of the year.

"All himself is sayin is that October has good things to recommend it. And soon it'll have Laverne's new baby to recommend. Thas all himself is sayin." He touched his hand to his heart. "Please, Miss Laverne, les not dirty the sweet month of October here in the Safeway. Please, Miss Laverne."

"My grandmother has nothin to do with any of this." She went on and turned onto an aisle with canned goods. "I'm not my grandmother."

"If Miss Laverne says so, then himself says so, too." He came up close beside her again. "Which one, Miss Laverne?"

She ignored him. She remembered the eight cans of pinto beans for one dollar. Could she carry all eight cans up the hill? It would be just like her husband to get tired of them after only the second can. Heading out with her son one trash day morning, she had seen the trash can of the man downstairs on the sidewalk, the top leaning against the side of the can. On top of the pile was an empty tray that had held some red meat, perhaps hamburger. Was he a good cook? she had wondered. What did he specialize in? Did he do lasagna? There was an empty package of Oreos, a few black crumbs huddled in one corner. The top of a liquor bottle was poking up as well, and had she not been trying to get her son to school, she would have picked it up to see what brand he drank.

"Himself asks, which one?"

"I only want to be left alone," she said and began to walk quickly. But a man, reading a label on a can, was before her with his cart and she had to slow to make her way around him. The man had the can very close to his face, and as she approached he looked at her and back at the can and then back to her. He seemed to want to ask her for help but he put the can to his face again and finally settled for tossing the can into his empty cart. Once they were around the man the Devil was at her side again. He began to hum, and with each note she calmed so that by the time they reached the end of the aisle, she wanted to know what he was humming. The fireplace on the second floor of her grandmother's house, the one nearest 16th Street, was the most inviting, created just for cold rainy days and hot chocolate and stories about people who had met death up in a snowstorm and survived. Her mother had never seen the house on Crittenden Street, had never seen her portrait hanging over the first-floor fireplace.

They turned onto another aisle, this one with more canned goods, including canned juices. "Which one?" the Devil asked. She feared that pulling out the shopping list would make her seem weak. "Himself asks, which one?"

"What do you want?"

"Just to know which one?"

"Which one?" Laverne said.

"Which grandmother ain't you like? The one with all the money and the fine house and the fine clothes or that one that pulled that trick on the beach that day? The one livin high on the hog or the one call herself walkin on water?"

"It whatn't no trick," Laverne said. She remembered now that her son wanted cookies. But which kind? He could be as fussy about things as his father. She herself liked vanilla creams, but last time the Safeway was out of them. "We'll be sure to have them for you the next time, ma'am," some assistant manager had told her.

"But it was a trick, Miss Laverne. You know. Himself knows. And that granny of yours know it, lyin down on the sea bottom like she is."

She stopped. "You shut the hell up. It wasn't a trick. I was there. I know."

"Himself was there, too, Miss Laverne. Himself always there." He stepped so she could see him fully in the face. The tie was still off-center, and she still wanted to center it. Would he take her hand and kiss it if she did? Would he take her hand and ask her how he could become King of Heaven?

"You weren't nowhere."

The Devil turned and picked up a can of Hi-C orange drink from the middle shelf across from them. "He has ruled all of them with all them tricks a his. Don't let him do that to you, Miss Laverne." A man in a Safeway smock was walking toward them. The Devil held the can in his left hand, and looking at her, he raised his right hand three inches or so above the can and brought his index finger down to the top of the can. "Tricks, tricks, tricks. Mornin, noon, and night. Himself gets so tired of all them tricks. Himself thought you was better than to believe in tricks, Miss Laverne." The Safeway man stopped a few feet before them. The Devil wiggled his finger twice and then, ever so slowly, the finger went down through the top of the can. Laverne and the Safeway man did not move. "Tricks. Even a new October baby can do a trick." He pulled his finger out and licked the juice from it, then plunged it down so that there was another hole next to the first. "Nature abhors a vacuum." He pulled it out again and wiped it on the man's smock, just to the side of his name tag. The Devil upended the can and poured juice on the floor and handed the can to the Safeway man. "Watch himself walk on water fortified with vitamin C." He walked back and forth over the juice on the floor. "Now," he said to Laverne, "you can call himself god. Watch himself a few aisles over from here when himself multiply all them fishes and all them loaves. Watch himself, Miss Laverne, and then bow down and worship himself, Miss Laverne, if all it takes is tricks."

"She did no tricks," Laverne said. Gingerly, she moved over the juice. "She was good and that is how she did it."

"Young fellow," the Devil said to the Safeway man, "himself is from headquarters. All the way from headquarters in Oakland, California. What they learn you bout liquids on a Safeway floor?" The man nodded and went around Laverne and out to the side door.

At the end of the aisle Laverne turned onto the one with the cookies and other sweets. Her grandmother had loved her, had said so each time they were together, at the beginning of a meeting and at the end. She tried to remember her grandmother's voice now, the confidence in the voice as she walked out into the sea. Had she told Laverne she loved her that Sunday? Had she gone out into the water before telling her, "I love you, child, and don't you ever forget it"? No, she hadn't said it. Had she stopped loving her before she set off? Had her grandmother set off for heaven and not blessed Laverne with her love?

She remembered now that her son liked Nilla Wafers. Were those wafers so far from the vanilla creams she liked? Why did her son adore those wafers, but turn his nose up at the creams? Were they not of the same family? I love you, Grandma. She moved down the aisle and just before the midway point she felt the Devil behind her. She stopped at the Oreos. She had guessed that the man downstairs was a man for Oreos. The darkness of Oreos had a mystery, too. She had awakened one night not long ago and heard a woman being pleasured and she knew right away that the man downstairs was responsible. She picked up a package of Oreos and could hear the woman moaning. She had lain quiet beside her husband, afraid that he could hear her heart beating, afraid that the moaning woman would wake him and he would turn to Laverne and know her heart at that moment.

"He dreams of you," the Devil said. "He lay down every night with a different woman, but in his secret dreams, you walk up to him on some beach downstairs and he renounces everyone but you. Did you know he dreams of you? He downstairs and he can hear you walkin around upstairs, livin your life, and he thinks and thinks and then when he sleeps, there you be."

"I don't care," Laverne said and returned the package to the shelf. "I don't care nothin bout that."

"Then how come it is that last night when you come, you come with him in mind? How come that be, Miss Laverne?"

"You don't know me." She reached for the Nilla Wafers. She picked up a box, but decided that an identical one next to it would be best. She studied the corner of the box. Nabisco made these. Nabisco knows I love my husband. Nabisco knows my grandmother loves me and it is not a trick. A little bit of magic here and there. Before you know it you done walked all the way to heaven. My my my, child.

She dropped the box of cookies into the cart. She said, "Is that a trick, pretendin you can read my mind when I'm with my husband?"

"There be tricks and there be truth. Himself opens your head up and just stands there reading all your pages. D double dare me, Miss Laverne."

She found that they did have vanilla creams and thought at first that it might be best to get some because the next time could be too late. But her cookies were not on the list. What else was there on the list? The Devil wet his thumb and turned an imaginary page in an imaginary book. "Page 138," he said. She picked up the creams and set them down beside the wafers.

"If you so wonderful," she said, "why you let my grandmother's brother die in that place?"

"Himself lets no one die. Himself doesn't have the power of life and death. You die cause you wanna die. You live cause you wanna live." The Devil closed the imaginary book.

Himself is a big fat liar." She tried to recall the name of her great-uncle, a man dead in upstate New York before she was even born, tried thinking back to those Sunday visits with women relatives when all that yak-yak about the Devil had just washed over her and out the nearest window. It wasn't talk about boys or new clothes after all, so why give a real listen? *I kissed a boss boy named Freddy . . . Oh, willya, oh, willya, be my steady?* And a young woman whose name was known by fine men on both sides of the Anacostia River, a woman who would dance all night for the asking, that woman could take care of herself. Laverne came to the end of the sweets aisle and turned onto the one with coffee and tea. What was that dead man's name? Uncle, uncle, tell me your name.

The Devil had slowed behind her and she hoped that he was afraid she would remember her great-uncle's name and fling it at him the way people in the movies threw holy water on vampires. The name would *poof* him into nothing. She stood before the coffee. Was Maxwell House, her husband's favorite, on the list? It was coffee good to the last drop, and to convince a shopper, the blue can had a final drop of coffee right at the lip of an empty cup tipped on its side. The Devil said in her ear, "How could himself let him die when himself ain't never laid eyes on that boy?" There was a coffee she had been meaning to try, the one the television woman sang was a heavenly coffee, "a better coffee money couldn't buy."

"My grandmother," Laverne said, "wouldn't lie to me." This was the grandmother with the house on the Gold Coast, the one fearful to live without fire, the one who had turned away from meat. The brother, eight years old, had wasted away in that upstate New York farmhouse as he and his older sister had waited for their parents to return from a trip to Albany, a trip begun before one flake of snow had fallen. It had been snowing for fourteen days straight when the Devil as an old woman, trailing that long yellow shawl, had come up over the mountains of snow with the ease of a woman strolling on the beach. Laverne, on all those Sundays, had listened to what the women had to say about the dying boy, how gnawing on a table leg had not been enough to save him until the sixteenth day when his parents returned, arms full of food. "She wouldn't lie to me."

"Then," the Devil said, "you best tell your sweet lil grandmother to get the story straight and stop puttin the lie to himself. Himself wouldn't lie on her, so she shouldn't lie on himself." He sauntered away two feet or so and turned to face her. He put on his hat.

The Devil was telling the truth, and she knew this, though just an hour ago it would not have mattered one way or another. She pushed the cart past the Devil. No coffee. No tea. No me. "Don't hurry now," the Devil said. "There's a big money-off offer comin your way."

She came to the personal items. She remembered the few things on the list, cookies for her boy, shaving cream for her husband. The can of Burma Shave was before her eyes. She opened the top, hoping the smell would remind her enough of her husband. There was nothing and she pushed the button and released a dab of the cream onto the top of her finger. There he was, webbed feet and all. Why hadn't she remembered the uncle's name? Was it less of a sin because she had never known him? Laverne put the cream closer to her nose and inhaled as deeply as she could. Was it less of a sin? The grandmother had gone out to hunt for more dead leaves, more roots, even though she had found nothing for three days. Her brother lay in the living room, already nearer death than he was to life.

Laverne rubbed the cream between her fingers and smeared it across the top of her lip, continuing to inhale as much as she could. And over the mountains of snow the old woman had come, greeting her grandmother. "Well, fancy meetin you out here," the Devil said to her. "Fancy fancy fancy." The snow was so thick that even two feet apart each was sometimes obscured from the other. "We hungry," the grandmother said. And from somewhere within her shawl the old woman had pulled out a fried chicken leg, golden and plump, still giving off warmth as she unwrapped it from the wax paper. Laverne put two cans of shaving cream into the cart. "Lemme take it back and share it with my brother," her grandmother said. "Please, ma'am." The Devil did not say no to this. The Devil said, "Oh, there's more, honey. There's plenty more where that come from. You just eat this here. Go on now. There's plenty more." And the grandmother ate as the snow peppered and salted the chicken. The old woman disappeared back over the mountains of snow, and as the snow covered and absorbed the chicken bones, the grandmother waited, first in the snow and then in the house. The boy died way late in the night, well after the chicken had become a part of her body.

Laverne came to the last aisle, the one with the fresh meat. She turned the corner just in time to see the old woman from the beauty parlor lean over the section of the meat case with the hamburger. The woman picked up a package and as she moved to put it in her cart, a man bumped into her. "You piece of shit," the old woman said to the man, "why don'tcha watch where you puttin down them clodhoppers of yours?"

"Ain't no call to be like that, lady," the man said. "I'm sorry. It was just an accident." The Devil was again beside Laverne. His hands were clasped behind his back and he watched the man and the old woman.

"Ain't that much fuckin accident in the whole goddamn world, you piece of shit!"

"Grandma, please," the little girl said as she took the meat from the old woman and placed it in the cart. "Please, Grandma, les just go."

"I'm sorry," the man said. "I'm really sorry."

"You're a fuckin animal, you hear me?" the old woman said. "You and that mule-fuckin mother a yours!" The little girl began to cry but the Devil did not look at her.

"Leave them alone," Laverne said to the Devil.

"I have no power," the Devil said. "Ask em."

"If they'd shot that goddamn mule fore your mama got to it, I wouldn't have this goddamn problem right now."

"Please, Grandma, les go."

The girl grabbed her grandmother by the waist, pressing her face and her new hair into the woman's side. The old woman pushed her away.

"She's just a child," Laverne said.

The Devil said, "A child, a chick, a big fat dick. What's it to you, Miss Laverne? What's it to me?"

Laverne went to the girl and knelt and pulled her close. Laverne told the girl that it would be all right and in a few moments the girl stopped shivering and crying. The girl continued to cling to her and Laverne told her she would never leave her.

"They should lock you up for this," the man said to the old woman, who called him more names as he walked away.

Laverne stood and looked at the old woman. The woman blinked and bowed her head, staring into the cart, then she looked at the girl, who drifted to her side. "The nerve of some people," she said, still not looking at Laverne, each of her words getting softer and softer. "Come on, sweetie," she said and placed one of the little girl's hands on the edge of the cart and moved away.

Laverne turned around. The Devil's suit and hat and tie and two-tone shoes were gone. He had on a baseball cap and green T-shirt and shorts and tennis shoes. "Tell your mother," he said, "that I will see her next Friday, just after she's eaten all that good Catholic fish."

"Leave her be," Laverne said. "She's sickly, and gettin older."

"Sick and old," he said, "but not yet dead." He straightened the cap with the Washington Senators logo. "You and I are not yet finished. There's more to talk about, starting with what does your husband think of that boy not being his. Have you and him had that conversation, Laverne?" He tucked the T-shirt into the shorts. He raised his arms and twisted his torso from side to side, then he twisted his neck. "Oh, the men out there in the world who just love to follow in Joseph's footsteps. Is your husband named Joseph, Laverne? Can I call you Mary, Laverne?" He leaned over and touched his toes three times. "You and I will talk later, but right now your grandmother is waiting for me with a nice glass of brandy in that mansion on the hill that cost an arm and a leg. And one soul."

He stepped around her and was gone.

Laverne looked at her cart, at the few items in it. She made her way around the shoppers to the door of the Safeway. The uncle had had a name but the more she tried to think of it, the more it fluttered out of reach. Uncle Somebody, please tell me your name. Outside, the sun was even higher and Good Hope Road was even more crowded. She looked to the left, toward the 11th Street Bridge. Why had all the men in her family escaped days like this? Why had the key to heaven been left with the women? Down where Good Hope met the bridge would be a good place for him to jump into the Anacostia River and swim over to the rest of Washington. She went to the right. There had never been a Saturday when she had thought that her son and her husband were not waiting for her on up the road. Now, something told her with utter finality that they were not there, that the boy was not standing and holding his father's hand, his little heart beating just to see her again. Something kept telling her she was alone. Laverne waded into the crowd, and the current of the colored people was so strong that it simply carried her on up the road.

BLINDSIDED

After the white woman Roxanne Stapleton worked for in Silver Spring gave her a ride across the northern border into Washington, Roxanne, without much waiting, was able to catch the D.C. Transit bus heading down 14th Street, N.W. The bus going down 11th Street would have put her closer to her room on 10th, but it was still early Friday evening and the show at the Howard Theater wasn't until eight-thirty, and the white woman would be far away in another world until Monday. And, too, going down 14th had always been good luck: long ago she had met Cedric on a 14th Street bus. Dark Cedric with green eyes. Cedric of the two and a half years. She had once found a twenty-dollar bill on a 14th Street bus. So because there was time to spare, she took the 14th Street bus.

The bus was half full and Roxanne managed to get the first seat after the side door, her favorite spot. "Now you be sure to have a good weekend, Roxanne," the white woman she worked for had said, the same thing she had been saying for four years. Her white woman was to tut-tut over the telephone on Monday morning and ask, "Did you injure yourself inadvertently over the weekend, Roxanne? Maybe at one of your Negro functions?" The white woman had her ideas about what black people did with their lives, especially on weekends, and just about everything they did in her mind could lead to blindness.

By the time the bus reached Rittenhouse Street, a woman had sat down beside Roxanne and the haze was already over her eyes. Roxanne blinked once, and her eyes started to clear, and then she blinked twice more and all was as before. Between Randolph Street and Park Road the haze returned and refused to go away with more blinking. It was October, the days growing shorter as they rushed toward the end, and she, ever a poor daughter of the universe, attributed the haze to the world's gradual loss of daylight. And she was exhausted. Oh, but the things the body did when it was tired. Gonna make you a little blind, Roxanne, so you can't see that stage at the Howard Theater tonight. What will Sam Cooke sound like when you blind, child? The universe told her to smile. But after they crossed Harvard Street and before they could reach Girard Street, with the bus now offering standing room only, she became worried because the haze remained steadfast. She considered herself a woman of some refinement and would not talk to just anyone on a bus, but she was so worried that she turned to the woman beside her and asked, "Miss, you see somethin on my eyes?" Leaning toward the woman, Roxanne opened her eyes as wide as she could.

"Lemme see," the woman said and took Roxanne's chin in her hand and pulled it to her. Some people thought nothing of taking large liberties when a small one was all that was needed. "No, they just look like regular eyes to me. You got somethin in your eyes?"

"There's somethin growin over my eyes, thas all. It's like cheese-cloth."

"Cheesecloth?" the woman said. She had a southern accent so thick it insulted Roxanne's ears. She was much older than Roxanne was when she came to Washington with her own accent, so the woman would probably never speak any other way, as Roxanne had succeeded in doing. "Whas cheesecloth?" And she was louder than she needed to be in public.

"I just can't see the way I usually see, thas what I'm sayin." Roxanne closed her eyes and used her index fingers to massage her temples. Just relax, she told herself. Her Catholic friend, Agnes Simmons, had prayers to some saint for every ailment. Who was the saint for blind people and had he himself been struck blind?

At Clifton Street, the bus stopped for some time after a man got on and dropped the twenty-five pennies he had for his fare. Not one fell into the fare box. People laughed as the bus driver said to no one in particular that they should outlaw paying with pennies. "I pay your salary with these pennies," the man said at one point, down on his hands and knees. Each time he found a penny he would stand up and drop it in the box. "You don't pay my salary with nothin," said the driver, who refused to move until the man had paid his full fare. "Oh, yes, I do, too. Here. Here's a little bit of it now," and he stood and put in a penny. "All right, yall," a man seated behind the driver said. He had roses in one arm, cradled there like a small child. "I'll pay his G-D fare and you just get this bus goin." People applauded. He leaned over the penny man on the floor and put a quarter in the box, the roses still nestled in his arm, and the driver pulled back into traffic. The man with the pennies stayed on the floor and the bus driver said he would have to move behind the white line, as required by the laws and regulations of Washington, D.C. "On that floor is my tip for you," the man said and stood up.

Roxanne, trying to remember if she had seen any white people on the bus, did not laugh with everyone else. She had kept her eyes closed once the woman next to her had looked into them, but before the intersection at Florida Avenue, she opened them and there was nothing but darkness. Her heart sank and she gave up a tiny yelp. "Lady," she said to the woman beside her, "I think I'm blind. I don't know what I'm gonna do."

"You a blind lady?" Yes, Roxanne decided, the accent was eternal. "How long you been blind, honey?"

"Just now. It just happened. You have to tell the bus driver because I don't know what I'm goin to do."

"You blind? You do good to be blind. I wouldn't go about if I was blind, I can tell you that."

"Please, just tell the driver. I got here seein and now I can't see. Tell him that. Please."

"Oh, you just *got* blind? Thas what you sayin?"

"Yes, just now. I could see all day, but now I can't."

"Dear Jesus sittin on the throne!" The woman stood up. "Driver, we have a poor blind woman here. You hear me!"

The word was taken forward. "We got a blind woman that want off this bus, driver," people from Roxanne up to the front began saying. "Driver, ain't you listenin?" the penny man said. "Thas just like D.C. Transit to hold a blind woman up."

The driver stopped between Swann and S Streets. "What is this commotion?" he said after he stood up and looked back. His view was not good because of the standing people. "Somebody hurt?"

"There a blind woman that wants off," said the penny man, who was standing midway between the driver and Roxanne. What he said was repeated until it reached Roxanne, who said as loud as her dignity would permit, "No, please. I was just now struck blind. I could see when I got on, and now I can't. I was just struck blind."

"She was struck blind on your rickety-ass bus," a woman across from Roxanne said. "I hope she sue D.C. Transit for everything yall got."

"You workin for that blind lady now, bigshot," the penny man said to the driver, who was making his slow way back to Roxanne. "Try bein nasty to your new boss lady and see how long you keep your job. Fire him right now, lady. He made you blind."

The driver reached Roxanne. "Lady, why ain't you tell me you was blind when you got on? I coulda put you by me and it woulda made things easier."

Roxanne thought she remembered his face, the bill of the hat cocked a bit more up than it should be, and a face too womanish to suit her. "Is your fellow a handsome colored man, Roxanne?" her white woman had once asked. "Thas just it," Roxanne said to the driver. "I wasn't blind when I got on." And the driver was also short. Cedric and Ray and Casey and all the rest had been tall men of long shadows. Her new man, Melvin, was a good foot taller than she was. "Can't you understand? I was just now struck blind." But was this driver really short, or had that been the one yesterday? Last week? How can a blind woman trust her memory?

"Right now? Right here? On my bus?"

"Yes. I could see when I paid my fare." She sighed because at last her words and his words made it all real, for herself, for the entire bus: Roxanne Stapleton was blind. "I could see," she said, and the words were only a few degrees above a whisper, which was how she liked to speak in public. People said she got loud when she drank, but she didn't believe them. I ain't just like every colored person from every corner of the world. "I just can't see now." Would the show at Howard Theater ever come back? Was Sam Cooke the kind of man to wait for a blind woman?

"You wanna go to the hospital?" the driver said.

"I don't know. There's no pain. I do know I wanna get home now."

"Where you live?"

"Seventeen-oh-eight 10th Street."

"I know where that is," the penny man said. He had followed the driver through the standing crowd. "Round the corner from the fire station on R Street. Right?"

"Yes," Roxanne said. Please, Lord, give me help from anybody but this jackass.

"You mind takin her home?" the driver said.

The man leaned over and looked out a window, up and down 14th Street. When he rose up again, pennies in his pockets jangled. "This way before my stop," the man said, "but I could see her home."

"You want this man to see you home, lady?"

She would have preferred anyone but the absurd man with his pennies, but in the end Roxanne nodded her head. "I'd appreciate it."

The driver led her to the front and wrote down her name and address and her friend Agnes's telephone number because Roxanne used her money for clothes rather than a telephone. "I'm sorry bout all this," the driver said and placed in her hand a slip of paper with the names of the D.C. Transit people she should contact. Then he opened the door and people started saying, "Good luck to you, lady. Good luck to you, blind lady." The man went down the steps first, his pennies jangling with each movement, and then he reached up and took her hand and guided her down. The door of the bus closed and it went on, and the sound of it leaving was the saddest sound she had heard in a long time.

At the corner of S and 14th Streets she asked the man where they were. She was surprised when he told her because she had thought they were still on the other side of Florida Avenue. She knew the area well, the liquor store at the corner, the office of her notorious landlord, Roscoe L. Jones, behind her at the corner of Swann, and across 14th on S was a little restaurant Melvin had taken her to on their first date. But maybe this wasn't the place. Maybe this was Southeast and everyone was out to get her.

"If you get a good night's sleep, your sight might come back," the man said, placing her right hand around his left upper arm. "Whas your name again, lady?"

She told him.

"I'm Lowell and I'll see you home safe." He did not sound like a man so down in the world that he had only pennies for money.

"I really appreciate this, Lowell." Two weeks ago a woman on New Jersey Avenue returning home from work had been robbed and hit twice in the head with a gun, the worst crime many had heard about in some time. Roxanne was realizing that Washington was getting less and less safe for people like her. The good and the decent. Men with little in their pockets had done the city in. "I've told Mr. Shepherd we just cannot chance coming into the city after dark, Roxanne," her white woman in Silver Spring had said once. "It is not a city for the good and the decent anymore the way it was when Mr. Truman and General Eisenhower were here. There are new elements there."

Lowell said, "No big deal. I knowed a blind woman when I was a boy in Anacostia. She raised five children by herself after her husband died walkin to work. That lady could fill your cup up to the top and not spill a drop while she was doin it."

They turned and went up 10th and within a few steps they could smell what was left of the storefront church that had burned down just the Sunday before. "I hope nobody was hurt," Lowell said, looking through the skeletal thing all the way into the back. It was a frightening mess, and the man was tempted to tell her that she was lucky she could not see it. The church's reverend was to knock at Roxanne's door within the week, having heard about what had happened to her. She would talk to him only at the door, would not allow him in, thinking that he was looking for a donation to help rebuild the church. He would see that in her face. "I only came," Reverend Saunders said, putting a basket of fruit in her hands, "because God would not allow me to do otherwise."

At her building, a lime-green two-story brick structure, she wanted to know if there was a light on in the basement, and when he said there was, she asked that he go down and knock at the door. Mary Benoit and her two children lived there. Mary wasn't a drinker, a partyer, but she and Roxanne, ever a woman in search of a good time, were friendly enough. She wanted now to be with people she knew, hear voices she recognized. Mary's nine-year-old daughter, Adele, came out. "Hi you, Miss Roxanne?"

"I'm blind, honey. It just happened."

"Blind? Oh, no, Miss Roxanne. You want me to help you?"

"Your mother home yet?" Lowell had placed Roxanne's hand on the railing before knocking, and now he took that hand and put it in the girl's hand.

"My mama not home yet," Adele said, "but Taylor, he home." The girl began rubbing the hand Lowell had given her, rubbing it in both of hers, the way she had seen people in the movies do with someone's cold hands.

"I best get on," Lowell said. "Less you need me for somethin else."

"Oh, no," Roxanne said. "You been so good to me. Lemme give you a little somethin for all your trouble. I know you went out your way." She began to open her pocketbook, but he put his hand over hers. "I don't need your money, lady. Just try to get better, thas all." He stepped away.

"Adele, baby, would you see me to my place?" Her room was on the first floor, a few feet beyond the front door, a large room with a sink and an icebox and a stove, along with a bed and dresser and everything else she needed to make a good life. She had been there six years. Adele unlocked the door and Roxanne switched on the light just inside the door and stepped inside. The room smelled the same—Spic and Span mingling with the perfume she had put on that morning before going out to clean her white woman's house and cook her food. Suddenly, taking small steps into the room, both hands out before her, she could see herself the day she picked up the box of Spic and Span at the Safeway on 7th Street, had taken it from a shelf two up from the bottom and looked at the price to compare it with the larger size one shelf up. No, she had told herself, the small size will do for now; the price had been in blue numbers on a tiny white sticker. She could also see herself the Sunday she got the perfume at Peoples Drug at 7th and M. She had gone in with Melvin; he bought prophylactics in a red box, and she wandered over to the perfume kiosk. "Pick one, and I'll buy it for you," he had said and kissed her shoulder from behind. But, no, had that been Melvin, or Cedric of a long time ago, Cedric of two and a half years?

Roxanne sat on the bed. Adele helped her take off her sweater.

"Miss Roxanne, you really blind?"

"Why would I lie bout somethin like that, girl?" There was an edge in her voice, and Adele, not used to it, closed down. "Why would a body lie bout bein less than what they was?" Roxanne had a daughter, way back

in Louisiana, nine ugly miles outside of Baton Rouge. But she had not
raised the daughter, and she had not seen her in two years, the last time
Roxanne had visited Antibes Nouveau. Had left that place, without planning to, for good at twenty-six years of age in the middle of the night
with two men friends as the daughter, then three years, slept at the home
of Roxanne's parents. Sipping rum and Coke, Roxanne and the two men
had only planned to visit four juke joints before morning. I be back fore
breakfast, she had said to her parents when she left the girl at nine
o'clock that night. But she did not see Louisiana or the daughter again
for a year. Long before they hit the second juke joint, one of the men,
the driver, had suggested that they drive all the way to Washington,
where folks partied seven days a week. Of the three, only Roxanne knew
geography and distance, but the rum said she did not know what she
thought she did. On the third day, more than halfway to Washington,
somewhat sober and committed now to nothing else but salvaging a bad
idea, the man spoke not about parties but about his third cousin who knew
how to get well-paying jobs in the federal government. After finding a
pathetic government job in Washington, Roxanne telegraphed her parents eight days later, after they had already begun rehearsing how to tell
their granddaughter her mother was dead. *Will send for Carolyn soon.*
Give me a few months to save for her ticket. She was hungover when she
telegraphed, and she would be hungover the times over the years when
she started her visits home from Union Station. But every year as she set
out for Antibes Nouveau, Washington was ever in her heart and mind a
new city, still a place with men who did not yet know about "the Jewel of
Louisiana," still a place where she needed to be.

There was a picture of her daughter in a gold-looking metal frame
on the tiny table beside the bed in her room; the girl was five years old
in the picture, but that had been six years ago. Roxanne turned now to
Adele and said, trying to put a little warmth in her voice, "Baby girl,
would you mind hangin up my sweater?" The room had no closet, just a
long wooden rack that Roxanne hung all her clothes on. Her daughter

had never seen Washington. "I don't think I can reach up there, Miss Roxanne, less I get on the chair." "Well, just hang it on the back of the chair." During the visit to Antibes Nouveau two years before, her daughter had first avoided her, and then, on the eve of her return to Washington, the child had begged her not to go.

With Roxanne still on the bed, Adele remained near the chair, which was unlike her when around Roxanne. When grown-ups talked mean, the child liked to stay to herself.

"Adele?"

"Ma'am?" Next to the chair was a tiny table, a twin to the one at the bed, and on it was a record player. The records were on the one shelf below that.

"You lookin at me?"

"Yes, ma'am, but I whatn't starin hard or nothin." She was not a child of lies.

"Come over here. I'm still the same Miss Roxanne." She opened her arms, and the girl put her head into the woman's lap. Roxanne felt herself wanting to cry; maybe this wasn't just something to mess up her weekend. Maybe this was always and always. "You go on back downstairs and tell your mama to come up when she get here."

"I can stay if you want me to. I'll stay with you."

"No." Roxanne told her to take the lock off the door and pull it shut. Behind her room were stairs that went down to the basement and she could hear Adele going down. Long ago she had heard of a man in a foreign country, a man the doctors had made into a woman. If they could do that, then they could restore her sight. Those doctors had had a long way to go, for the man had never been a woman. They might not have to go as far with her, for she had known sight all her life.

She stood and put her arms out. This how blind people act, she thought. This how all them poor blind people act. At the mirror over the sink, she blinked and blinked, hoping. She put her face close to the mirror, so close that the breath came out of her and bounced against the glass and returned to warm her nose. "You look like a million dollars to a man that been poor all his life," a boyfriend had said not long after she arrived in Washington. Pulling her head back, she reached up and touched the mirror. She was beautiful, and the whole world had always told her so. That boyfriend was dead now. And being that he was dead, and being that she was blind, how true were the words? Fine, fine Roxanne, the best thing ever to come out of Louisiana. "You could be one of those colored models they say your people have," her white woman had said. What would happen to her beautiful face now? She tapped the mirror and then touched all the features of her face. What would happen? She had not learned very many big things about herself while living in Washington, but one big thing she had learned was that if she was not first beautiful in her own eyes, then she was beautiful in no one's eyes.

Agnes Simmons got off the D.C. Transit bus at R and 11th Streets, N.W., and stopped at Cohen's grocery store on the corner. She knew she needed something, but she couldn't remember what. Bread, yes. Eggs? Was it eggs? She bought bread and told herself she would just have to come back if she had no eggs. Her friend Roxanne was not a lender. *I work hard for what I got, Agnes . . .* She walked to 10th on the southern side of R to see if Tenth Street Baptist Church had changed the signboard in their yard. For nearly three years of living above Roxanne, she had enjoyed the little sayings they put there, though lately they had been rather tame. A year ago they had had the best yet: I COMPLAINED BECAUSE I HAD NO SHOES UNTIL I MET A MAN WHO HAD NO FEET. That had touched the Catholic soul in her, something she still thought about as she closed her eyes and opened her mouth and accepted the host. *This is my flesh . . .* She was twenty-eight and had never been married and had not had a steady boyfriend in four years, but she was not in pain. *This is my flesh . . .* No one had told her she was beautiful in a very long time, since before the last boyfriend who had wanted only one thing. Beware of boys who want only one thing, her Catholic mother had warned as they shopped for Agnes's first brassiere.

The church's signboard that night had nothing but the names of the church and the pastor and the times of services. *Eat . . .*

S he knocked at Roxanne's door and Roxanne said to come in.

"Where the hell you been, Agnes? I been waitin and waitin for you. Where the hell you been?"

"Why? What's wrong?"

"I been struck blind, thas what's wrong." Roxanne was in the easy chair in front of the large front window.

Agnes laughed. "Oh, just give me another one, because that one won't do it." She had been educated in Washington's Catholic schools and worked now across from the gas company in a shop on 11th Street that sold buttons and sewing supplies and cloth and all else that a woman needed to help make a good home. Becoming the manager after five years of service. Once, looking out the store's window, Agnes had seen passing two former teachers, nuns, from Holy Redeemer, and had gone out to them. But as she watched their sturdy backs, the ironed perfection of their long, black habits that seemed not to swish one bit from side to side like women's dresses, she had said nothing. Agnes's mother had always prayed that she would become a nun, but her mother was dead now, and so there was no one to want such a life for her anymore. Her father had converted to marry her mother. His good Catholic wife had suffered up to her last moment of life, and the kneeling convert had raised his bowed head at her funeral mass and never lowered it again. "Agnes," he told her whenever she asked if he had been to mass, "you can be Catholic for both of us now."

"I should slap your damn face!" Roxanne shouted.

"Why? What did I do, Roxanne?" Agnes came in and set down her grocery bag and purse next to the door, something she always did so as not to forget things on her way out.

"'What did I do, Roxanne? What did I do?'" Roxanne stood up and nearly fell, and when she took a step, she bumped into the small table beside the chair. "'What did I do, Roxanne?' You make me so sick! I tell you I went blind and all you can do is laugh."

Agnes went to her. "But I thought you were kidding, Roxanne. You know how you kid sometimes." Agnes touched her arm.

"Well, I'm not kiddin now, you dumb bitch." Roxanne pulled away. "I don't know why I bother with you. Why do I waste my damn time with someone like you?"

"I'm sorry, Roxanne. I really am. Here, why don't you sit down. Please tell me what happened? Dear Jesus." Agnes made the sign of the cross.

"'Dear Jesus. Dear Jesus.' For Chrissakes!" Roxanne sat again and misjudged where she was and so sat on the arm and tumbled onto the seat. "Get me a little vodka from the icebox, and mix some orange juice in it." Why had she lost her sight and Agnes hadn't? What did Agnes do with her sight all day anyway? Sell a few buttons here, a few needles there. Not even anough makeup on her face to cover a roach's back.

Agnes brought the glass with three-quarters vodka and one-fourth orange juice, the way Roxanne liked it. "Here it is." She waited until Roxanne had a firm grip on the glass and then released it. Roxanne drank nearly half of it in one gulp. They were both facing the large window onto 10th Street, and Agnes looked down to see two boys on the sidewalk counting money and Roxanne heard first a car honking its horn all the way up to R Street, followed by a pickup chugging along. Two cars with well-tuned engines came after the pickup. Roxanne was listening for Melvin's car. Three more cars went almost silently past her window. It was like Melvin to be late when he knew she needed him. Agnes remembered that soon everyone would have to turn their clocks back one hour. Fall back, spring forward, that was the rule from the nuns arrayed in their black. *Black is not my color, Mama.* "*Black's everyone's color, Agnes.*"

There were playful taps at the door and Roxanne called out, "Melvin? Melvin? That you?" Melvin Foster came in and started singing a medley of Sam Cooke songs. "If he can't make it," Melvin said, "I'm gonna go up on that stage and replace him." He was in a dark blue suit and a bright gray tie, Agnes saw, and he was wearing black Swiss Ballys, the kind with the graceful stitching at the toes. She had seen such in the window of Rich's on F Street, as she strolled about on her lunch hour.

"Oh, Melvin," Roxanne said, "where you been, honey?"

"I'm real early," he said, "so don't give me none a your stuff."

"She's blind, Melvin."

"She's blind, she's blind as a bat," Melvin sang. When neither woman responded, he stopped, took off his hat, and put it on a peg on the wooden rack. He was nothing if not a man who took the awful silence of women seriously. "Temporary, temporary," he said after Roxanne had explained as he sat on the arm of the easy chair, his arm around Roxanne as she drank a second vodka. "Fuckin temporary, baby." Agnes was now only a few feet beyond the door. He remembered how religious Agnes was and he looked at her and said, "Just temporary."

In the end, Melvin said they had best get to Freedmen's Hospital, and Agnes asked if she should accompany them.

"Of course, you should," Roxanne said. "What kinda stupid-ass question is that?"

"Let her alone, Roxanne. She ain't responsible for this," Melvin said.

It snowed that night in October, two inches, and people said that was one for the record books.

Through the months of the fall and the winter, Roxanne saw a series of ophthalmologists, neurosurgeons, and psychiatrists from Freedmen's to D.C. General, and none could tell her where her sight had gone. "It may well be, Miss Stapleton," a psychiatrist in a darkened, borrowed office at D.C. General said to Roxanne late one morning as Agnes sat in a chair beside the door, "that you could awaken tomorrow and your eyesight will be back." This woman, who had been imported from Georgetown University, was herself losing her sight, though none of her patients—many of whom were prisoners from the D.C. Jail next to the hospital—had been informed. She saw Roxanne alone that morning for some forty-five minutes and then brought in Agnes, who had been accompanying her friend to many of the doctors' visits. And when Agnes was not able to come, Melvin had been there. So many of the friends Roxanne lived to party with had drifted away. They might catch her blindness, and blind people couldn't dance very well, and they certainly weren't known as partyers. "Or it could be," the psychiatrist continued, "that when you are sixty or seventy or eighty, you will awaken and be able to see again." A social worker at Howard University had thought a psychiatrist going blind would know the proper things to say to a woman who was already there. "But then, too, you might die without ever seeing again." Some of the jail's prisoners, who knew what no one had told them, called her the Bat, and others called her the Mole behind her back. It was like God to do that shit to a colored woman, the prisoners said—make her a doctor with one hand and make her blind with the other.

That lousy bitch doctor!" Roxanne complained as Agnes led her out to the D.C. General entrance where Melvin, who had driven them there and was outside smoking, was to pick them up. "That lousy, no-good bitch!"

"There is hope there somewhere," Agnes said quietly.

"Let me fuckin go!" Roxanne pulled her arm away. "You worse than she is, you silly-ass thing. Take that hope shit and stick it up some priest's ass!" People stopped and stared at her, but Roxanne did not know.

Agnes stood with her arms at her sides, and when Roxanne heard nothing from her, she swung at the place where she had last heard Agnes speak. "You worse than nothin!" It had been more or less this way between them for some time, though that effort to strike Agnes was at the end of a very long road. Neither woman would know it for some time. Agnes leaned to the left and Roxanne hit nothing, then stumbled and caught herself before she fell.

"Hey! Hey!" Roxanne could hear Melvin coming closer. "What the hell you doin out here, Roxanne? Why you actin up?"

"Oh, Melvin baby, I'm tired of this stuff from her and everybody else." He took her gently by the arm and led her to the nearest wall.

"I know," he said. "I can only think I know." He held her shoulder for several moments, and then he turned and faced Agnes, who had a look he could not fathom. He reached across to Agnes and touched her cheek with his open hand. People watched the two. As far as either Melvin or Agnes could remember, this was the first time they had ever touched in such a way. Agnes closed her eyes and moved into his hand.

This was late April, and up until then spring had not been unkind to Washington. It stayed that way until mid-June when the humidity hit, thick and mean and unforgiving, and ordinary people with ordinary lives had to slog and claw their way into a more horrendous beast of an August where they lived each day thinking September would bring them relief. That was not to be so.

"I sometime think I'm gonna lose my mind," Roxanne said now, and Melvin returned to her.

"You made of better stuff than that," Melvin said. Agnes went toward the door; he could not make out anything bad in her walking, not hatred or bitterness or even resentment. There was merely—or so it seemed as he saw her step onto the rubber pad before the electric doors and watch them, first one and then the other, open to her—there was just a passable day out beyond the door that she wanted to enjoy before returning to many hours at the shop.

"I useta think I was, honey," Roxanne said. "I really useta think so."

❖

Weeks before this, in March, after the city government people had officially declared her "a blind entity with no feeble-mindedness," the social worker at Howard and some D.C. government people got Roxanne into a program aimed at teaching the handicapped, especially the blind, how to live like everyone else. Someone, for three days, came to the homes of the five blind students then in the program to show them how to maneuver around their "habitable space." Then Roxanne and the four other blind people began to learn the basics of accounting and how to operate tiny stores that were in various federal government office buildings around the city. The stores sold snacks and cigarettes and newspapers and small packets of Kleenex that could be tucked into a woman's pocketbook. The instructor, an accountant with a blind husband who ran his own little store at the Justice Department, told her students at the end of the first day that the federal government employed people who would be mostly honest customers but that there were some who did not have the fear of God. "They will give you a dollar and swear to their thieving and useless god it was five dollars," she said. "But our all-seeing God is a money God and knows money backwards and forwards. He will guide you."

The store they ultimately gave Roxanne was on the sixth floor of a ten-story building at Thomas Circle, with a large window that faced Vermont Avenue. On the building's seventh floor was an outpost of the Atomic Energy Commission with people who did nothing but read reports only from scientists based in Nevada and Utah and the southeastern portion of North Dakota. In time, as these people came to know her, they would come into the store and joke with Roxanne that if her doughnuts weren't fresh enough, they would "atomize" her and her stale doughnuts. On the fifth floor and on her own sixth floor there were outposts of the Internal Revenue Service and the Department of Commerce. These were primarily silent people, except for the Negroes who laughed with Roxanne as they complained that the federal government had outlawed soul food. A good part of the rest of the building were D.C. government employees, and though they came and went all day and were as friendly as any of the federal people, few of the federal people knew exactly what their jobs were.

It became not such a bad life, the life of a small store operator, and by the beginning of August Roxanne had assured herself that she could conquer "this blindness thing," or at least learn to live side by side with it. She had worried that she would become a next to nothing, floating out in the universe alone and penniless. She could see herself becoming like the blind man with his milky gray eyes she used to see sitting on a wooden folding chair on the corner of 9th and F Streets, N.W., his quart-sized mason jar of donated bills and coins on a green handkerchief on the ground in front of him. Blowing on a silver harmonica when he wasn't mumbling to himself. "Blind man here, blind man here, blind man here just tryin to get by," he sang to passersby.

On the Monday evening of that second week in August, the accountant instructor took Roxanne to dinner at Scholl's Cafeteria just down the street from her job on Vermont Avenue and then saw her home. "I'm so proud of you, Roxanne," the woman said. "You and me both," Roxanne said before she got out of the car and unfolded her white cane. Once in her room, after she had turned on the fan, she banged on the ceiling with a pole—a device to open high windows—for Agnes to come down to her. The pole had been given to her by Melvin, back when the blindness was such a new thing to them all. Roxanne hit the ceiling five times and waited, but Agnes did not come down. She waited several minutes more and hit the ceiling again. She thought she had heard footsteps above her, but she knew by now that blindness played tricks with the rest of her senses. She got a beer from the icebox and sat in her easy chair in shorts and an old Dr. Ben Casey shirt from

Melvin. The oscillating fan blew on her and then blew to the nothing on either side of her.

Upstairs, Agnes sat on her bed. She also had one room but, unlike Roxanne, there was a small kitchen attached to hers. After Agnes had heard the first banging, she had immediately stopped walking across the floor, and then, as quiet as an old thief, she had gone lightly to the bed and sat as she listened to the second round of banging. "I want you to write a letter to my parents when I get home tonight," Roxanne had told her that morning. Now, Agnes looked down at the red fingernail polish she had applied two evenings before. It had taken her more than an hour. She had long ago seen Roxanne paint her own nails in less than ten minutes. Agnes touched the nails, the redness, the smoothness. They were cut short to suit a functional life. "Is this not pride before a fall?" she said of the polish and waited for the pole to hit her floor again. She had tried putting on lipstick that morning, but the face she saw in the mirror with the lipstick was such an alien one that she was forced to wipe it off. The three of them, Agnes, Roxanne, and Melvin, had been sitting on the porch two evenings before, enjoying the sight and sound of children playing along 10th Street. Roxanne had gotten up and made her way upstairs to the building's only bathroom. Agnes and Melvin could, despite the sounds of the street, hear Roxanne's hands along the wall behind them as she made her way. No sooner was she on the stairs going to the second floor than Melvin looked at Agnes for a long time without words. She blushed and took her eyes to her lap. "I think I'll go for a walk. Please tell Roxanne," Melvin said as he stood. He went down two steps to the sidewalk and turned and looked up at her. Less than fifteen minutes before, Roxanne had said to Agnes, "Go get me another beer." "I'll get it," Melvin had said. "No, I told Agnes, honey." On the sidewalk, Melvin looked up the two steps at Agnes and said, "Why you scared to even put lipstick on?" He seemed more hurt than anything else. He left without an answer. And as she heard Roxanne making her way back down, Agnes picked up the beer that was still cold even with the crushing heat about them and asked herself who would know if she spit in the can. She had had confession that Saturday and had escaped from the confessional with a penance of only two Our Fathers and two Hail Marys. "Go in peace," the priest had told her. She put the can back down in the same place.

Agnes now got up from the bed and went into the kitchen, not caring what sounds she made along the floor. A third round of banging began, but she ignored it and prepared her dinner. Across the city, on North Capitol Street, Melvin sat in a booth in Mojo's and thought how nice it would be to have another beer. He had told Roxanne that he needed to visit a sick relative in Arlington for a few days, but she did not know that all his kin there had died out a long time ago. He took his time with two more beers, and then, a little before midnight, he got in his car and traveled to S Street, N.W., between 10th and 11th. He parked and the time went on and on until it was nearly one thirty in the morning. He had a job to go to in a few hours, but he was lovesick and no job in the universe could matter now. The beer had taken him there, but as he sat in the car and smoked cigarettes, the beer lost its hold and he gradually became just a man thinking about a skinny woman, not altogether attractive with her eyeglasses and her unpainted lips and the habit of crossing herself whenever a dead person's name was mentioned.

Melvin got out of the car and went around the corner and up 10th Street to where Roxanne and Agnes lived. He took the outside stairs slowly, one at a time, and walked by Roxanne's door. Agnes opened her door after the third knock and stood with her robe tightly around her nightgown, one hand holding the bunched cloth at the neck. It would be like you, Melvin thought, to have on a nightgown in this weather. She squinted without her eyeglasses. She had a life that burrowed through the world with few surprises, and there was no surprise on her face now. It was as if, every day over years and years, he had said to her, "On such and such a night, I will knock at your door and I want you to answer without giving it any thought."

"It's late," he said as she stood in the space the partly opened door made.

"I know," she said. They were not whispering and it was nearly two in the morning. Roxanne had stopped banging on the ceiling after about half an hour, and she had not sent anyone to get Agnes.

"You can shut that door in my face and I'll turn around and leave," he said.

"Leave? And go back downstairs?" she said. They had never spoken man-and-woman talk like that, but no one listening would have known this.

"I didn't come from downstairs."

Once he was inside, she put on her eyeglasses and fixed him a cup of coffee while he sat at the small table at the window, and again she moved about her place without thinking once of the woman below her. The world outside her window looked different to Melvin from one floor up.

"I've been thinking of moving from here," she said after placing the cup and saucer before him and taking the seat across from him.

He said, "I would miss you. It would be like all the pain in the world if I couldn't see you again."

The priest who would instruct him in the Catholic faith told him he would have to choose a middle name for himself. "Why?" Melvin would ask. "Because there was no Saint Melvin, and God wants you to have a saint's name." Agnes's father, a Catholic no more, unearthed a small book giving all the saints' names and why they had been canonized. "Pick one," his father-in-law-to-be said. "George. Sebastian. John. Pick one . . . But try to stay away from Xavier. I don't remember what he did, but that name ain't done all that right by me."

For weeks, Agnes and Melvin did no more than talk in the night when the human beings in that building were all away in sleep. And when the talking was done sometime near dawn, he would stand, stretch, drink the last of his coffee, and go off to work. Then, late one night in October, a year after she went blind, Roxanne got up from her bed to go upstairs to the bathroom. Melvin had told her he would be away again that day. Before she had even reached the top of the stairs, she heard a most unfamiliar sound from Agnes's place—the sound of a woman moaning in pleasure. She knew the sounds Melvin made when he made love, but she did not have to hear him to know he was with Agnes. All that her life was at that moment told her he was in there. And that life, such as it was, flowed out of her and she fell back and had to catch herself before falling down the stairs. She went down four steps and was in such pain that she had to sit. She wanted to cry out, but she prevented that by putting the sleeve of her nightgown in her mouth. I must get back to my place, she thought, even though she knew she lacked the strength. Melvin had always been such a good man, even as she had strayed a few times. What could have happened to him? And to be with such a wretch of a woman. Perhaps, just perhaps, she thought after some time, it was not herself who had been beautiful all those years, but maybe it had always been Agnes.

He came to her three days later, planning to tell her he was taking his life in a different direction and not knowing she had heard Agnes with him. He picked up the chair under the wooden rack and sat across from Roxanne as she sat in the easy chair. He said a great deal but none of it contained the right words, and in the end they heard Agnes moving about upstairs and Roxanne turned to accuse him and he looked away because her eyes were the same as always—not at all milky and full of nothing like those of other blind women. They were as full of life as ever and they told him she saw all as before. They were silent for a time. "You'd best go now," Roxanne said, "your whore be callin you." "You got no call." "I got every call in the world," and that was the last time for the couple.

The next month Agnes moved away. And a week later a woman, Mercy, came into Roxanne's store, a woman she had known from all her partying years, a woman she had not seen in a long time. "You still look as good as ever," the woman said. "Oh, go on away from here," Roxanne said. They were the best words she had heard since going up that night to the bathroom. "I mean it, girl. I still run across men who go on and on about you. 'Roxanne this, Roxanne that.'" She invited Roxanne to a party that Saturday night, and Roxanne said as she gave the woman change, "Why not? Why the hell not?" It was so good to talk to the woman Mercy that Roxanne told her to take whatever she wanted, and Mercy took three packs of cigarettes, a package of doughnuts, and two sodas, though she told Roxanne she was taking only one soda and no cigarettes.

She had a sweet old time at the party—her first since Melvin went out of her life. The music, the cigarette smoke, the voices, a woman shrieking with laughter across the room—it was all familiar, and it was all her. Being blind might not be so bad. That Monday a fellow she had met at the party called her job and asked her out to lunch, but she said no. His voice had not grabbed her, and he had held her as they slow-dragged in that way of desperate men—as if he wanted to melt his body into hers. Two days after his call she received a letter from her parents, who asked for the tenth time that year if she wanted them to come up to her. "Don't fight alone," they said. "That would be just like you." Her parents also wrote that Roxanne's daughter—who had only been told in October, the month before, what had happened to her mother—had been trying to think of what to write. "She needs the time to take it in," her parents said in a letter of one page. Roxanne had Adele's brother, Taylor, write a letter to them and get a money order for their train tickets to Washington for an extended Christmas visit. Had it not been for the party, for Mercy telling everyone at the party that the Jewel of Louisiana was back and better than ever, she might have had him write, "My boyfriend abandoned me and I am utterly alone." "Utterly" was one of the favorite words of an early boyfriend after she first arrived in Washington. *"I'm utterly ashamed, baby." "I'm utterly hungry." "He was utterly dead."*

When Taylor had finished the letter, he sat in the chair under the wooden rack and studied the stamp on the envelope to make certain all the edges adhered. And after he knew the stamp would stay in place all the way to Antibes Nouveau, he said, "It hurt to be blind, Miss Rox-anne?" She had become close to him and his sister and their mother, but the boy was nothing if not a barrel of questions. Maybe that came from having a mother who was a nondrinker. No parties. A life that seemed devoted only to her children. A boy with a mother like that could stop being afraid of asking grown people questions.

"Whatcha think, Taylor?" She was at the sink, putting a wet wash-cloth to her face.

"I say yes, but Mama said no. It hurt in other ways."

She touched the washcloth to her throat. The cloth was cool, but she knew that in moments her body would warm it. "Your mama right, Taylor." She faced the mirror and saw darkness and then turned and could make out the faintest of light in the rest of the room. Would her own daughter be like this boy? Questions, questions, always questions. Blind people, she remembered from the days when she could see, had that jumping thing with their eyes, and she wondered if she would get that, too. One more blow to a beautiful face. Adele had told her only two days ago that her eyes looked like regular eyes. But whatever could that mean? "I suppose blind people hurt in ways you don't understand now, Taylor." Maybe it was only people who had been blind for a very long time who got that jumping disease, people who had never learned to teach their eyes to pretend that they could see. She was coming to understand that it was not the questions, but the fear that she would not have the proper answers, answers that would not stand the test of time. If Taylor was this way, how much worse would it be with her own daughter? Who knew what kind of girl she had grown into? "Well, is it like pins in the arm or somethin?" the boy said. "Or gettin shot by a BB gun?"

In the end, she put him off by telling him to put on a record Taylor's mother had given her on Thanksgiving. It was a 45, and on it a Puerto Rican was singing about the Earth as an apple moving silently through space. "I love his voice," Mary had said, "and I thought you might, too." Roxanne had not learned until much later, from someone at work, that the singer was blind.

Mercy took her to three office parties that second week in December. The morning after the third, Roxanne, hungover, could barely pull herself out of bed to get ready for work. Mercy came by her job near the end of the day and laughed that Roxanne would be drummed out of the blind people's union because she was having more fun than blind people were allowed.

A Saturday party at a house before the Tuesday her people were to arrive was the best in years. She had been introduced early to a man Mercy said was her third cousin "once removed," but Roxanne tried to discourage him from monopolizing her time. Still, he had a wonderful way about him. The Kearney Street, N.E., event was cut short at about midnight because it began to snow, and while the house where the party was held was nice enough, it would not comfortably keep the fifty or so people throughout a snowbound weekend.

Roxanne and Mercy and her boyfriend and her third cousin returned to 10th Street just before twelve thirty. The cousin had a wreck of a stomach and was living on practically nothing but baby food, so he was the only one who had not been drinking. He had put his hand on Roxanne's knee during the ride from Kearney Street, but she had not minded that. Indeed, she found it rather pleasant.

The boyfriend parked only two doors from Roxanne's place, and they got out of the car, giggling and dancing through the snow, which was already coming to an end. Just inside the front door, in the hallway, the cousin began kissing Roxanne and then the boyfriend began kissing Mercy. "Oh, whas this," Roxanne laughed, "an early Christmas present?" "Thas what it feels like to me," Mercy said. "Well," Roxanne said, "the least you could do is find us some mistletoe."

"Just shut up and enjoy it," the cousin said and placed his open mouth violently over hers so that his expelling breath went rushing into her body. His tongue pushed in and down her throat. His mouth was at an angle to hers, as boys have been taught to do, but in its violence, the mouth covered one of her nostrils, and the free nostril was the only way she could breathe, but that one had a very hard time of it. She felt as if she were drowning. She struggled, for breath and for freedom from the prison of his body. Then he put his hand between her legs, and that seemed to pull her back from drowning. Finally she pulled her face away and managed an insignificant scream. "Stop! Stop!" She thought, *I done seen this before. I done been in this play before.*

"Oh, Roxanne," Mercy said, "just lay back and enjoy it. It's Christmas, for God's sake. It's Christmastime."

Roxanne began punching the cousin's back. The accumulation of hits must have said something to him, because he pulled back and said to her, "You blind bitch! You should be happy a man like me would even give somethin like you the time a day." He tapped her jaw with his open hand, the one that had been between her legs. She hit the back of his head, and again he placed his mouth over hers. *I have no memory of singin this song. Dancin this dance . . .* His hand returned to that place between her legs.

Roxanne heard two yips, and then a little voice called her name. "Agnes," Roxanne said, "is that you out there? Please, Agnes, is that you? Agnes?" Adele asked, "Miss Roxanne, you all right?" Roxanne could see herself through the child's eyes—a blind woman being assaulted in a hall. By a man she had been weak in the knees for only an hour earlier. Was the desperation plain as well? In a hall with two drunks doing what no child should see. *I done danced this dance and sung this song before . . . This is what happens to blind people in the end.* "You betta leave Miss Roxanne alone," Adele said. There was no other sound in the hall but the tiny voice of the child. The third cousin pulled back. In the dim light of the hall, Adele was standing in her nightgown holding the puppy her mother had given her children early for Christmas. "Call Mr. Young for me, baby," Roxanne said. "Call him. Call your mama."

The cousin stepped back. He turned to Mercy and her boyfriend, who had not stopped kissing, and said, "Les blow this scene, yall." Once they were gone, Roxanne turned to the wall and began crying. She could still see what Adele was seeing. She had never felt more vulnerable, and never so small. The child put down the puppy and stayed where she was and the dog went to the woman. "If," Adele's mother had explained to Roxanne a week before, "it was a doll or a bicycle, I could hold it back from em till Christmas. But it's a puppy. It's life, and I can't keep that from em." The puppy sniffed at Roxanne's heels, and then Adele came to her. "I was goin to the bathroom," the girl said. "Number two. I tried to make him stay downstairs, but he jus a baby and won't listen." Adele picked up the puppy. Roxanne turned around and reached for the child and the puppy licked her hand. "You want me to stay with you, Miss Roxanne? We all be missin Miss Agnes."

A t about six that morning, she got out of bed and stood there and felt the precious life that was the sleeping Adele. The puppy scrambled from its bed of blankets and came to her heels and sniffed. "We will have to do somethin for you, or you'll piss and shit up my house," she said to him. She went to the window. *I shoulda wrote you and told you what to expect when you get here. A daughter deserves that . . .* During the night the snow had returned briefly. It amounted to next to nothing, but after Roxanne raised the window a bit, she could smell that far, far more was on the way. She wondered what someone looking in the window would see—would they see a blind woman who was trying to get on with the rest of her life? She began humming the song by the blind Puerto Rican, about the Earth as an apple moving quietly through the universe. In her mind the world was moving through heavy snow. She boiled water and waited for the snow to come into their lives. When the coffee was ready, she took the cup with both hands and blew into it and sipped. Too much sugar, but the cream was just right. She sat in the easy chair. *I am your mother. That is first,* she should have had Taylor write. *Before there was anything else in the world for you, I was your mother . . .*

The snow came, and she felt it begin to cover and silence the world. She took another sip of the coffee, and as she did the snow grew heavier. Did her daughter like pancakes? She closed her eyes. Adele turned in her sleep. *In the beginning, before there was any breath in your body, you had your mother . . .* The puppy came up to her feet and turned around and around until it found a comfortable place beside her. She reached down and patted its back. *I am blind and that is all there is to it.* Eyes closed, she listened to the snow falling, each flake supplying a note in a long and wondrous song, and in moments, as the song played on, she was sitting on the giant apple that was the Earth and that was taking her through the snowy universe. They were moving away from the sun because she had all the heat she needed, so there was no reason to go that way. She leaned against the stem of the apple that was the Earth. As she and the apple neared Mars, she turned to the right and saw the puppy, but it was all grown up and was a dog that she had known back home when she was a girl no bigger than Adele, no bigger than her daughter in the picture on the table beside the bed. She pointed to Mars because she knew the dog, being as smart as he was, would appreciate the sight, and as she took her hand down, she saw Adele beside her on the left on the apple that was the Earth moving through the universe.

"You cold?" Roxanne asked the girl.

"No, ma'am," the child said. "The snow is warm, Miss Roxanne."

The woman and the girl and the dog looked at Mars, and after a long time, they were past it, and the girl sighed that Mars was now gone and Roxanne told her that they would see it again. The three were some ways from Jupiter when Roxanne began to worry that she would not remember the proper order of the planets. Could she be true to memory? She knew for sure that Jupiter was next, but was Uranus or Saturn after that? She knew all that once upon a time, could stand in front of that classroom nine ugly miles from the capital of Louisiana and recite their order and how far they were from the sun. What did she know now? On the apple, still traveling silently through the universe, she crossed her legs at the ankles and wiggled the toes of the foot on top. Then, as Jupiter showed itself hundreds and hundreds of thousands of miles away, she pulled the girl and the dog closer to her and the stem of the apple grew a covering as soft as that on her easy chair. It would be Uranus next if that was what she wanted it to be. She would put rings around it and give it a million moons, each a different color. Could she be true to memory? Maybe memory was what you made of it. She looked and the dog nodded Yes, ma'am, memory was what you made of it. Yes, then, rings around Uranus and Neptune. And she would put all the best singers and all the best dancing bands on Pluto, which was still a hundred million miles away, and on the outside of that planet, in blue and orange neon letters that even those blind from birth could read, she would put a sign that said Pluto was open all the time to all of God's children. Yes, open even to the least of them.

A RICH MAN

Horace and Loneese Perkins—one child, one grandchild—lived most unhappily together for more than twelve years in Apartment 230 at Claridge Towers, a building for senior citizens at 1221 M Street, N.W. They moved there in 1977, the year they celebrated forty years of marriage, the year they made love for the last time—Loneese kept a diary of sorts, and that fact was noted on one day of a week when she noted nothing else. "He touched me," she wrote, which had always been her diary euphemism for sex. That was also the year they retired, she as a pool secretary at the Commerce Department, where she had known one lover, and he as a civilian employee at the Pentagon, as the head of veteran records.

He had been an army sergeant for ten years before becoming head of records; the secretary of defense gave him a plaque as big as his chest on the day he retired, and he and the secretary of defense and Loneese had their picture taken, a picture that hung for all those twelve years in the living room of Apartment 230, on the wall just to the right of the heating-and-air-conditioning unit.

A month before they moved in, they drove in their burgundy-and-gold Cadillac from their small house on Chesapeake Street in Southeast to a Union Station restaurant and promised each other that Claridge

Towers would be a new beginning for them. Over blackened catfish and a peach cobbler that they both agreed could have been better, they vowed to devote themselves to each other and become even better grandparents. Horace had long known about the Commerce Department lover. Loneese had told him about the man two months after she had ended the relationship, in 1969. "He worked in the mail room," she told her husband over a spaghetti supper she had cooked in the Chesapeake Street home. "He touched me in the motel room," she wrote in her diary, "and after it was over he begged me to go away to Florida with him. All I could think about was that Florida was for old people."

At that spaghetti supper, Horace did not mention the dozens of lovers he had had in his time as her husband. She knew there had been many, knew it because they were written on his face in the early years of their marriage, and because he had never bothered to hide what he was doing in the later years. "I be back in a while. I got some business to do," he would say. He did not even mention the lover he had slept with just the day before the spaghetti supper, the one he bid good-bye to with a "Be good and be sweet" after telling her he planned to become a new man and respect his marriage vows. The woman, a thin school-bus driver with clanking bracelets up to her elbows on both arms, snorted a laugh, which made Horace want to slap her, because he was used to people taking him seriously. "Forget you, then," Horace said on the way out the door. "I was just tryin to let you down easy."

Over another spaghetti supper two weeks before moving, they reiterated what had been said at the blackened-catfish supper and did the dishes together and went to bed as man and wife, and over the next days sold almost all the Chesapeake Street furniture. What they kept belonged primarily to Horace, starting with a collection of six hundred and thirty-nine record albums, many of them his "sweet babies," the 78s. If a band worth anything had recorded between 1915 and 1950, he bragged, he had the record; after 1950, he said, the bands got sloppy and he had to back away. Horace also kept the Cadillac he had painted to honor a football team, paid to park the car in the underground garage. Claridge Towers had once been intended as a luxury place, but the builders, two friends of the city commissioners, ran out of money in the middle and the commissioners had the city government people buy it off them. The city government people completed Claridge, with its tiny rooms, and then, after one commissioner gave a speech in Southwest about looking out for old people, some city government people in Northeast came up with the idea that old people might like to live in Claridge, in Northwest.

Three weeks after Horace and Loneese moved in, Horace went down to the lobby one Saturday afternoon to get their mail and happened to see Clara Knightley getting her mail. She lived in Apartment 512. "You got this fixed up real nice," Horace said of Apartment 512 a little less than an hour after meeting her. "But I could see just in the way that you carry yourself that you got good taste. I could tell that about you right off." "You swellin my head with all that talk, Mr. Perkins," Clara said, offering him coffee, which he rejected, because such moments always called for something stronger. "Whas a woman's head for if a man can't swell it up from time to time. Huh? Answer me that, Clara. You just answer me that." Clara was fifty-five, a bit younger than most of the residents of Claridge, though she was much older than all Horace's other lovers. She did not fit the city government people's definition of a senior citizen, but she had a host of ailments, from high blood pressure to diabetes, and so the city people had let her in.

Despite the promises, the marriage, what little there had been of it, came to an end. "I will make myself happy," Loneese told the diary a month after he last touched her. Loneese and Horace had fixed up their apartment nicely, and neither of them wanted to give the place up to the other. She wanted to make a final stand with the man who had given her so much heartache, the man who had told her, six months after her confession, what a whore she had been to sleep with the Commerce Department mail-room man. Horace, at sixty, had never thought much of women over fifty, but Clara—and, after her, Willa, of Apartment 1001, and Miriam, of Apartment 109—had awakened something in him, and he began to think that women over fifty weren't such a bad deal after all. Claridge Towers had dozens of such women, many of them attractive widows, many of them eager for a kind word from a retired army sergeant who had so many medals and ribbons that his uniform could not carry them. As far as he could see, he was cock of the walk: many of the men in Claridge suffered from diseases that Horace had so far escaped, or they were not as good-looking or as thin, or they were encumbered by wives they loved. In Claridge he was a rich man. So why move and give that whore the satisfaction?

They lived separate lives in a space that was only a fourth as large as the Chesapeake Street house. The building came to know them as the man and wife in 230 who couldn't stand each other. People talked about the Perkinses more than they did about anyone else, which was particularly upsetting to Loneese, who had been raised to believe family business should stay in the family. "Oh, Lord, what them two been up to now?" "Fight like cats and dogs, they do." "Who he seein now?" They each bought their own food from the Richfood on 11th Street or from the little store on 13th Street, and they could be vile to each other if what one bought was disturbed or eaten by the other. Loneese stopped speaking to Horace for nine months in 1984 and 1985, when she saw that her pumpkin pie was a bit smaller than when she last cut a slice from it. "I ain't touch your damn pie, you crazy woman," he said when she accused him. "How long you been married to me? You know I've never been partial to pumpkin pie." "That's fine for you to say, Horace, but why is some missing? You might not be partial to it, but I know you. I know you'll eat anything in a pinch. That's just your dirty nature." "My nature ain't no more dirty than yours."

After that, she bought a small icebox for the bedroom where she slept, though she continued to keep the larger items in the kitchen refrigerator. He bought a separate telephone, because he complained that she wasn't giving him his messages from his "associates." "I have never been a secretary for whores," she said, watching him set up an answering machine next to the Hide-A-Bed couch where he slept. "Oh, don't get me started bout whores. I'd say you wrote the damn book." "It was dictated by you."

Their one child, Alonzo, lived with his wife and son in Baltimore. He had not been close to his parents for a long time, and he could not put the why of it into words for his wife. Their boy, Alonzo Jr., who was twelve when his grandparents moved into Claridge, loved to visit them. Horace would unplug and put away his telephone when the boy visited. And Loneese and Horace would sleep together in the bedroom. She'd put a pillow between them in the double bed to remind herself not to roll toward him.

Their grandson visited less and less as he moved into his teenage years, and then, after he went away to college in Ohio, he just called them every few weeks, on the phone they had had installed in the name of Horace and Loneese Perkins.

In 1987 Loneese's heart began the countdown to its last beat, and she started spending more time at George Washington University Hospital than she did in the apartment. Horace never visited her. She died two years later. She woke up that last night in the hospital and went out into the hall and then to the nurses' station but could not find a nurse anywhere to tell her where she was or why she was there. "Why do the patients have to run this place alone?" she said to the walls. She returned to her room and it came to her why she was there. It was nearing three in the morning, but she called her own telephone first, then she dialed Horace's. He answered, but she never said a word. "Who's this playin on my phone?" Horace kept asking. "Who's this? I don't allow no playin on my phone." She hung up and lay down and said her prayers. After moving into Claridge, she had taken one more lover, a man at Vermont Avenue Baptist Church, where she went from time to time. He was retired, too. She wrote in her diary that he was not a big eater and that "down there, his vitals were missing."

Loneese Perkins was buried in a plot at Harmony Cemetery that she and Horace had bought when they were younger. There was a spot for Horace and there was one for their son, but Alonzo had long since made plans to be buried in a cemetery just outside Baltimore.

Horace kept the apartment more or less the way it was on the last day she was there. His son and daughter-in-law and grandson took some of her clothes to the Goodwill and the rest they gave to other women in the building. There were souvenirs from countries that Loneese and Horace had visited as man and wife—a Ghanaian carving of men surrounding a leopard they had killed, a brass menorah from Israel, a snow globe of Mount Fuji with some of the snow stuck forever to the top of the globe. They were things that did not mean very much to Alonzo, but he knew his child, and he knew that one day Alonzo Jr. would cherish them.

Horace tried sleeping in the bed, but he had been not unhappy in his twelve years on the Hide-A-Bed. He got rid of the bed and moved the couch into the bedroom and kept it open all the time.

He realized two things after Loneese's death: His own "vitals" had rejuvenated. He had never had the problems other men had, though he had failed a few times along the way, but that was to be expected. Now, as he moved closer to his seventy-third birthday, he felt himself becoming ever stronger, ever more potent. God is a strange one, he thought, sipping Chivas Regal one night before he went out: he takes a man's wife and gives him a new penis in her place.

The other thing he realized was that he was more and more attracted to younger women. When Loneese died, he had been keeping company with a woman of sixty-one, Sandy Carlin, in Apartment 907. One day in February, nine months after Loneese's death, one of Sandy's daughters, Jill, came to visit, along with one of Jill's friends, Elaine Cunningham.

They were both twenty-five years old. From the moment they walked through Sandy's door, Horace began to compliment them—on their hair, the color of their fingernail polish, the sharp crease in Jill's pants ("You iron that yourself?"), even "that sophisticated way" Elaine crossed her legs. The young women giggled, which made him happy, pleased with himself, and Sandy sat in her place on the couch. As the ice in the Pepsi-Cola in her left hand melted, she realized all over again that God had never promised her a man until her dying day.

When the girls left, about three in the afternoon, Horace offered to accompany them downstairs, "to keep all them bad men away." In the lobby, as the security guard at her desk strained to hear, he made it known that he wouldn't mind if they came by to see him sometime. The women looked at each other and giggled some more. They had been planning to go to a club in Southwest that evening, but they were amused by the old man, by the way he had his rap together and put them on some sort of big pedestal and shit, as Jill would tell another friend weeks later. And when he saw how receptive they were he said why not come on up tonight, shucks, ain't no time like the present. Jill said he musta got that from a song, but he said no, he'd been sayin that since before they were born, and Elaine said thas the truth, and the women giggled again. He said I ain't gonna lie bout bein a seasoned man, and then he joined in the giggling. Jill looked at Elaine and said Want to? And Elaine said What about your mom? And Jill shrugged her shoulders and Elaine said Okay. She had just broken up with a man she had met at another club and needed something to make the pain go away until there was another man, maybe from a better club.

At about eleven thirty Jill wandered off into the night, her head liquored up, and Elaine stayed and got weepy—about the man from the not-so-good club, about the two abortions, about running away from home at seventeen after a fight with her father. "I just left him nappin on the couch," she said, stretched out on Horace's new living-room couch, her shoes off and one of Loneese's throws over her feet. Horace was in the chair across from her. "For all I know, he's still on that couch." Even before she got to her father, even before the abortions, he knew that he would sleep with her that night. He did not even need to fill her glass a third time. "He was a fat man," she said of her father. "And there ain't a whole lot more I remember."

"Listen," he said as she talked about her father, "everything's gonna work out right for you." He knew that, at such times in a seduction, the more positive a man was the better things went. It would not have done to tell her to forget her daddy, that she had done the right thing by running out on that fat so-and-so; it was best to focus on tomorrow and tell her that the world would be brighter in the morning. He came over to the couch, and before he sat down on the edge of the coffee table he hiked up his pants just a bit with his fingertips, and seeing him do that reminded her vaguely of something wonderful. The boys in the club sure didn't do it that way. He took her hand and kissed her palm. "Everything's gonna work out to the good," he said.

Elaine Cunningham woke in the morning with Horace sleeping quietly beside her. She did not rebuke herself and did not look over at him with horror at what she had done. She sighed and laid her head back on the pillow and thought how much she still loved the man from the club, but there was nothing more she could do: not even the five-hundred-dollar leather jacket she had purchased for the man had brought him around. Two years after running away, she had gone back to where she had lived with her parents, but they had moved and no one in the building knew where they had gone. But everyone remembered her. "You sure done growed up, Elaine," one old woman said. "I wouldna knowed if you hadn't told me who you was." "Fuck em," Elaine said to the friends who had given her a ride there. "Fuck em all to hell." Then, in the car, heading out to Capitol Heights, where she was staying, "Well, maybe not fuck my mother. She was good." "Just fuck your daddy then?" the girl in the backseat said. Elaine thought about it as they went down Rhode Island Avenue, and just before they turned onto New Jersey Avenue she said, "Yes, just fuck my daddy. The fat fuck."

She got out of Horace's bed and tried to wet the desert in her mouth as she looked in his closet for a bathrobe. She rejected the blue and the paisley ones for a dark green one that reminded her of something wonderful, just as Horace's hiking up his pants had. She smelled the sleeves once she had it on, but there was only the strong scent of detergent.

In the half room that passed for a kitchen, she stood and drank most of the orange juice in the gallon carton. "Now, that was stupid, girl," she said. "You know you shoulda drunk water. Better for the thirst." She returned the carton to the refrigerator and marveled at all the food. "Damn!" she said. With the refrigerator door still open, she stepped out into the living room and took note of all that Horace had, thinking, *A girl could live large here if she did things right.* She had been crashing at a friend's place in Northeast, and the friend's mother had begun to hint that it was time for her to move on. Even when she had a job, she rarely had a place of her own. "Hmm," she said, looking through the refrigerator for what she wanted to eat. "Boody for home and food. Food, home. Boody. You shoulda stayed in school, girl. They give courses on this. Food and Home the first semester. Boody Givin the second semester."

But, as she ate her eggs and bacon and Hungry Man biscuits, she knew that she did not want to sleep with Horace too many more times, even if he did have his little castle. He was too tall, and she had never been attracted to tall men, old or otherwise. "Damn! Why couldn't he be what I wanted and have a nice place, too?" Then, as she sopped up the last of the yolk with the last half of the last biscuit, she thought of her best friend, Catrina, the woman she was crashing with. Catrina Stockton was twenty-eight, and though she had once been a heroin addict, she was one year clean and had a face and a body that testified not to a woman who had lived a bad life on the streets but to a nice-looking Virginia woman who had married at seventeen, had had three children by a truck-driving husband, and had met a man in a Fredericksburg McDonald's who had said that women like her could be queens in D.C.

Yes, Elaine thought as she leaned over the couch and stared at the photograph of Horace and Loneese and the secretary of defense, Catrina was always saying how much she wanted love, how it didn't matter what a man looked like, as long as he was good to her and loved her morning, noon, and night. The secretary of defense was in the middle of the couple. She did not know who he was, just that she had seen him somewhere, maybe on the television. Horace was holding the plaque just to the left, away from the secretary. Elaine reached over and removed a spot of dust from the picture with her fingertip, and before she could flick it away, a woman said her name and she looked around, chilled.

She went into the bedroom to make sure that the voice had not been death telling her to check on Horace. She found him sitting up in the bed, yawning and stretching. "You sleep good, honey bunch?" he said. "I sure did, sweetie pie," she said and bounded across the room to hug him. A breakfast like the one she'd had would cost at least four dollars anywhere in D.C. or Maryland. "Oh, but Papa likes that," Horace said. And even the cheapest motels out on New York Avenue, the ones catering to the junkies and prostitutes, charged at least twenty-five dollars a night. What's a hug compared with that? And, besides, she liked him more than she had thought, and the issue of Catrina and her moving in had to be done delicately. "Well, just let me give you a little bit mo, then."

Young stuff is young stuff, Horace thought the first time Elaine brought Catrina by and Catrina gave him a peck on the cheek and said, "I feel like I know you from all that Elaine told me." That was in early March.

In early April, Elaine met another man at a new club on F Street, N.W., and fell in love, and so did Horace with Catrina, though Catrina, after several years on the street, knew what she was feeling might be in the neighborhood of love but it was nowhere near the right house. She and Elaine told Horace the saddest of stories about the man Elaine had met in the club, and before the end of April he was sleeping on Horace's living-room floor. It helped that the man, Darnell Mudd, knew the way to anyone's heart, man or woman, and that he claimed to have a father who had been a hero in the Korean War. He even knew the name of the secretary of defense in the photograph and how long he had served in the Cabinet.

By the middle of May, there were as many as five other people, friends of the three young people, hanging out at any one time in Horace's place. He was giddy with Catrina, with the blunts, with the other women who snuck out with him to a room at the motel on 13th Street. By early June, more than a hundred of his old records had been stolen and pawned. "Leave his stuff alone," Elaine said to Darnell and his friends as they were going out the door with ten records apiece. "Don't take his stuff. He loves that stuff." It was eleven in the morning, and everyone else in the apartment, including Horace, was asleep. "Shhh," Darnell said. "He got so many he won't notice." And that was true. Horace hadn't played records in many months. He had two swords that were originally on the wall opposite the heating-and-air-conditioning unit. Both had belonged to German officers killed in the Second World War. Horace, high on the blunts, liked to see the young men sword-fight with them. But the next day, sober, he would hide them in the bottom of the closet, only to pull them out again when the partying started, at about four in the afternoon.

His neighbors, especially the neighbors who considered that Loneese had been the long-suffering one in the marriage, complained to the management about the noise, but the city government people read in his rental record that he had lost his wife not long ago and told the neighbors that he was probably doing some kind of grieving. The city government people never went above the first floor in Claridge. "He's a veteran who just lost his wife," they would say to those who came to the glass office on the first floor. "Why don't you cut him some slack?" But Horace tried to get a grip on things after a maintenance man told him to be careful. That was about the time one of the swords was broken and he could not for the life of him remember how it had happened. He just found it one afternoon in two pieces in the refrigerator's vegetable bin.

Things toned down a little, but the young women continued to come by and Horace went on being happy with them and with Catrina, who called him Papa and pretended to be upset when she saw him kissing another girl. "Papa, what am I gonna do with you and all your hussies?" "Papa, promise you'll only love me." "Papa, I need a new outfit. Help me out, willya please?"

Elaine had become pregnant not long after meeting Darnell, who told her to have the baby, that he had always wanted a son to carry on his name. "We can call him Junior," he said. "Or Little Darnell," she said. As she began showing, Horace and Catrina became increasingly concerned about her. Horace remembered how solicitous he had been when Loneese had been pregnant. He had not taken the first lover yet, had not even thought about anyone else as she grew and grew. He told Elaine no drugs or alcohol until the baby was born, and he tried to get her to go to bed at a decent hour, but that was often difficult with a small crowd in the living room.

Horace's grandson called in December, wanting to come by to see him, but Horace told him it would be best to meet someplace downtown, because his place was a mess. He didn't do much cleaning since Loneese died. "I don't care about that," Alonzo Jr. said. "Well, I do," Horace said. "You know how I can be bout these things."

In late December, Elaine gave birth to a boy, several weeks early. They gave him the middle name Horace. "See," Darnell said one day, holding the baby on the couch. "Thas your grandpa. You don't mind me callin you his granddad, Mr. Perkins? You don't mind, do you?" The city government people in the rental office, led by someone new, someone who took the rules seriously, took note that the old man in Apartment 230 had a baby and his mama and daddy in the place and not a single one of them was even related to him, though if one had been it still would have been against the rules as laid down in the rule book of apartment living.

By late February, an undercover policeman had bought two packets of crack from someone in the apartment. It was a woman, he told his superiors at first, and that's what he wrote in his report, but in a subsequent report he wrote that he had bought the rocks from a man. "Start over," said one of his superiors, who supped monthly with the new mayor, who lived for numbers, and in March the undercover man went back to buy more.

It was late on a warm Saturday night in April when Elaine woke to the crackle of walkie-talkies outside the door. She had not seen Darnell in more than a month, and something told her that she should get out of there because there might not be any more good times. She thought of Horace and Catrina asleep in the bedroom. Two men and two women she did not know very well were asleep in various places around the living room, but she had dated the brother of one of the women some three years ago. One of the men claimed to be Darnell's cousin, and, to prove it to her, when he knocked at the door that night he showed her a Polaroid of him and Darnell at a club, their arms around each other and their eyes red, because the camera had been cheap and the picture cost only two dollars.

She got up from the couch and looked into the crib. In the darkness she could make out that her son was awake, his little legs kicking and no sound from him but a happy gurgle. The sound of the walkie-talkie outside the door came and went. She could see it all on the television news—"Drug-Dealing Mama in Jail. Baby Put in Foster Care." She stepped over the man who said he was Darnell's cousin and pushed the door to the bedroom all the way open. Catrina was getting out of bed. Horace was snoring. He had never snored before in his life, but the drugs and alcohol together had done bad things to his airway.

"You hear anything?" Elaine whispered as Catrina tiptoed to her.

"I sure did," Catrina said. Sleeping on the streets required keeping one eye and both ears open. "I don't wanna go back to jail."

"Shit. Me, neither," Elaine said. "What about the window?"

"Go out and down two floors? With a baby? Damn!"

"We can do it," Elaine said, looking over Catrina's shoulder to the dark lump that was Horace mumbling in his sleep. "What about him?"

Catrina turned her head. "He old. They ain't gonna do anything to him. I'm just worried bout makin it with that baby."

"Well, I sure as hell ain't gonna go without my child."

"I ain't said we was," Catrina hissed. "Down two floors just ain't gonna be easy, is all."

"We can do it," Elaine said.

"We can do it," Catrina said. She tiptoed to the chair at the foot of the bed and went through Horace's pants pockets. "Maybe fifty dollars here," she whispered after returning. "I already got about three hundred."

"You been stealin from him?" Elaine said. The lump in the bed turned over and moaned, then settled back to snoring.

"God helps them that helps themselves, Elaine. Les go." Catrina had her clothes in her hands and went on by Elaine, who watched as the lump in the bed turned again, snoring all the while. Bye, Horace. Bye. I be seein you.

The policeman in the unmarked car parked across 12th Street watched as Elaine stood on the edge of the balcony and jumped. She passed for a second in front of the feeble light over the entrance and landed on the sloping entrance of the underground parking garage. The policeman was five years from retirement, and he did not move, because he could see quite well from where he sat. His partner, only three years on the job, was asleep in the passenger seat. The veteran thought the woman jumping might have hurt herself, because he did not see her rise from the ground for several minutes. I wouldn't do it, the man thought, not for all a rich man's money. The woman did rise, but before she did he saw another woman lean over the balcony dangling a bundle. Drugs? he thought. Nah. Clothes? Yeah, clothes more like it. The bundle was on a long rope or string—it was too far for the man to make out. The woman on the balcony leaned over very far and the woman on the ground reached up as far as she could, but still the bundle was a good two feet from her hands.

Just let them clothes drop, the policeman thought. Then Catrina released the bundle and Elaine caught it. Good catch. I wonder what she looks like in the light. Catrina jumped, and the policeman watched her pass momentarily in front of the light, and then he looked over at his partner. He himself didn't mind filling out the forms so much, but his partner did, so he let him sleep on. I'll be on a lake fishin my behind off and you'll still be doin this. When he looked back, the first woman was coming up the slope of the entrance with the bundle in her arms and the second one was limping after her. I wonder what that one looks like in a good light. Once on the sidewalk, both women looked left, then right, and headed down 12th Street. The policeman yawned and watched through his sideview mirror as the women crossed M Street. He yawned again. Even at three o'clock in the morning people still jaywalked.

The man who was a cousin of Darnell's was on his way back from the bathroom when the police broke through the door. He frightened easily, and though he had just emptied his bladder, he peed again as the door came open and the light of the hallway and the loud men came spilling in on him and his sleeping companions.

Horace began asking about Catrina and Elaine and the baby as soon as they put him in a cell. It took him that long to clear his head and understand what was happening to him. He pressed his face against the bars, trying to get his bearings and ignoring everything behind him in the cell. He stuck his mouth as far out of the bars as he could and shouted for someone to tell him whether they knew if the young women and the baby were all right. "They just women, yall," he kept saying for some five minutes. "They wouldn't hurt a flea. Officers, please. Please, Officers. What's done happened to them? And that baby . . . That baby is so innocent." It was a little after six in the morning, and men up and down the line started hollering for him to shut up or they would stick the biggest dick he ever saw in his mouth. Stunned, he did quiet down, because, while he was used to street language coming from the young men who came and went in his apartment, no bad words had ever been directed at him. They talked trash with the filthiest language he had ever heard, but they always invited him to join in and "talk about how it really is," talk about his knowing the secretary of defense and the mayor. Usually, after the second blunt, he was floating along with them. Now someone had threatened to do to him what he and the young men said they would do to any woman that crossed them.

Then he turned from the bars and considered the three men he was sharing the two-man cell with. The city jail people liked to make as little work for themselves as possible, and filling cells beyond their capacity meant having to deal with fewer locks. One man was cocooned in blankets on the floor beside the tiered metal beds. The man sleeping on the top bunk had a leg over the side, and because he was a tall man the leg came down to within six inches of the face of the man lying on the bottom bunk. That man was awake and on his back and picking his nose and staring at Horace. His other hand was under his blanket, in the crotch of his pants. What the man got out of his nose he would flick up at the bottom of the bunk above him. Watching him, Horace remembered that a very long time ago, even before the Chesapeake Street house, Loneese would iron his handkerchiefs and fold them into four perfect squares.

"Daddy," the man said, "you got my smokes?"

"What?" Horace said. He recalled doing it to Catrina about two or three in the morning and then rolling over and going to sleep. He also remembered slapping flies away in his dreams, flies that were as big as the hands of policemen.

The man seemed to have an infinite supply of boogers, and the more he picked, the more Horace's stomach churned. He used to think it was such a shame to unfold the handkerchiefs, so wondrous were the squares. The man sighed at Horace's question and put something from his nose on the big toe of the sleeping man above him. "I said do you got my smokes?"

"I don't have my cigarettes with me," Horace said. He tried the best white man's English he knew, having been told by a friend who was serving with him in the army in Germany that it impressed not only white people but black people who weren't going anywhere in life. "I left my cigarettes at home." His legs were aching and he wanted to sit on the floor, but the only available space was in the general area of where he was standing, and something adhered to his shoes every time he lifted his feet. "I wish I did have my cigarettes to give you."

"I didn't ask you bout *your* cigarettes. I don't wanna smoke them. I ask you bout *my* cigarettes. I wanna know if you brought *my* cigarettes."

Someone four cells down screamed and called out in his sleep: "Irene, why did you do this to me? Irene, ain't love worth a damn anymore?" Someone else told him to shut up or he would get a king-size dick in his mouth.

"I told you I do not have any cigarettes," Horace said.

"You know, you ain't worth shit," the man said. "You take the cake and mess it all up. You really do. Now you know you was comin to jail, so why didn't you bring my goddam smokes? What kinda fuckin consideration is that?"

Horace decided to say nothing. He raised first one leg and then the other and shook them, hoping that would relieve the aches. Slowly, he turned around to face the bars. No one had told him what was going to happen to him. He knew a lawyer, but he did not know if he was still practicing. He had friends, but he did not want any of them to see him in jail. He hoped the man would go to sleep.

"Don't turn your fuckin back on me after all we meant to each other," the man said. "We have this long relationship and you do this to me. Whas wrong with you, Daddy?"

"Look," Horace said, turning back to the man. "I done told you I ain't got no smokes. I ain't got your smokes. I ain't got my smokes. I ain't got nobody's smokes. Why can't you understand that?" He was aware that he was veering away from the white man's English, but he knew that his friend from Germany was probably home asleep safely in his bed. "I can't give you what I don't have." Men were murdered in the D.C. Jail, or so the *Washington Post* told him. "Can't you understand what I'm sayin?" His back stayed as close to the bars as he could manage. Who was this Irene, he thought, and what had she done to steal into a man's dreams that way?

"So, Daddy, it's gonna be like that, huh?" the man said, raising his head and pushing the foot of the upper-bunk man out of the way so he could see Horace better. He took his hand out of his crotch and pointed at Horace. "You gon pull a Peter-and-Jesus thing on me and deny you ever knew me, huh? Thas your plan, Daddy?" He lowered his head back to the black-and-white-striped pillow. "I've seen some low-down dirty shit in my day, but you the lowest. After our long relationship and everything."

"I never met you in my life," Horace said, grabbing the bars behind him with both hands, hoping, again, for relief.

"I won't forget this, and you know how long my memory is. First, you don't bring me my smokes, like you know you should. Then you deny all that we had. Don't go to sleep in here, Daddy, thas all I gotta say."

He thought of Reilly Johnson, a man he had worked with in the Pentagon. Reilly considered himself something of a photographer. He had taken the picture of Horace with the secretary of defense. What would the bail be? Would Reilly be at home to receive his call on a Sunday morning? Would they give him bail? The policemen who pulled him from his bed had tsk-tsked in his face. "Sellin drugs and corruptin young people like that." "I didn't know nothin about that, Officer. Please." "Tsk-tsk. An old man like you."

"The world ain't big enough for you to hide from my righteous wrath, Daddy. And you know how righteous I can be when I get started. The world ain't big enough, so you know this jail ain't big enough."

Horace turned back to the bars. Was something in the back as painful as something in the stomach? He touched his face. Rarely, even in the lost months with Catrina, had he failed to shave each morning. A man's capable demeanor started with a shave each morning, his sergeant in boot camp had told him a thousand years ago.

The man down the way began calling for Irene again. Irene, Horace called in his mind. Irene, are you out there? No one told the man to be quiet. It was about seven and the whole building was waking up and the man calling Irene was not the loudest sound in the world anymore.

"Daddy, you got my smokes? Could use my smokes right about now."

Horace, unable to stand anymore, slowly sank to the floor. There he found some relief. The more he sat, the more he began to play over the arrest. He had had money in his pocket when he took off his pants the night before, but there was no money when they booked him. And where had Catrina and Elaine been when the police marched him out of the apartment and down to the paddy wagon, with the Claridge's female security guard standing behind her desk with an oh-yes-I-told-you-so look? Where had they been? He had not seen them. He stretched out his legs and they touched the feet of the sleeping man on the floor. The man roused. "Love don't mean shit anymore," the man on the lower bunk said. It was loud enough to wake the man on the floor all the way, and that man sat up and covered his chest with his blanket and looked at Horace, blinking and blinking and getting a clearer picture of Horace the more he blinked.

Reilly did not come for him until the middle of Monday afternoon. Somebody opened the cell door and at first Horace thought the policeman was coming to get one of his cellmates.

"Homer Parkins," the man with the keys said. The doors were supposed to open electronically, but that system had not worked in a long time.

"Thas me," Horace said and got to his feet. As he and the man with the keys walked past the other cells, someone said to Horace, "Hey, Pops, you ain't too old to learn to suck dick." "Keep moving," the man with the keys said. "Pops, I'll give you a lesson when you come back."

As they poured his things out of a large manila envelope, the two guards behind the desk whispered and laughed. "Everything there?" one of them asked Horace. "Yes." "Well, good," the guard said. "I guess we'll be seein you on your next trip here." "Oh, leave that old man alone. He's somebody's grandfather." "When they start that old," the first man said, "it gets in their system and they can't stop. Ain't that right, Pops?"

He and Reilly did not say very much after Reilly said he had been surprised to hear from Horace and that he had wondered what had happened to him since Loneese died. Horace said he was eternally grateful to Reilly for bailing him out and that it was all a mistake as well as a long story that he would soon share with him. At Claridge, Reilly offered to take him out for a meal, but Horace said he would have to take a rain check. "Rain check?" Reilly said, smiling. "I didn't think they said that anymore."

The key to the apartment worked the way it always had, but something was blocking the door, and he had to force it open. Inside, he found destruction everywhere. On top of the clothes and the mementos of his life, strewn across the table and the couch and the floor were hundreds and hundreds of broken records. He took three steps into the room and began to cry. He turned around and around, hoping for something that would tell him it was not as bad as his eyes first reported. But there was little hope—the salt and pepper shakers had not been touched, the curtains covering the glass door were intact. There was not much beyond that for him to cling to.

He thought immediately of Catrina and Elaine. What had he done to deserve this? Had he not always shown them a good and kind heart? He covered his eyes, but that seemed only to produce more tears, and when he lowered his hands, the room danced before him through the tears. To steady himself, he put both hands on the table, which was covered in instant coffee and sugar. He brushed broken glass off the chair nearest him and sat down. He had not got it all off, and he felt what was left through his pants and underwear.

He tried to look around but got no farther than the picture with the secretary of defense. It had two cracks in it, one running north to south and the other going northwest to southeast. The photograph was tilting, too, and something told him that if he could straighten the picture, it all might not be so bad. He reached out a hand, still crying, but he could not move from the chair.

He stayed as he was through the afternoon and late into the evening, not once moving from the chair, though the tears did stop around five o'clock. Night came, and he still did not move. My name is Horace Perkins, he thought just as the sun set. My name is Horace Perkins, and I worked many a year at the Pentagon. The apartment became dark, but he did not have it in him to turn on the lights.

The knocking had been going on for more than ten minutes when he finally heard it. He got up, stumbling over debris, and opened the door. Elaine stood there with Darnell Jr. in her arms.

"Horace, you okay? I been comin by. I been worried about you, Horace."

He said nothing but opened the door enough for her and the baby to enter.

"It's dark, Horace. What about some light?"

He righted the lamp on the table and turned it on.

"Jesus in heaven, Horace! What happened! My Lord Jesus! I can't believe this." The baby, startled by his mother's words, began to cry. "It's okay," she said to him, "it's okay," and gradually the baby calmed down. "Oh, Horace, I'm so sorry. I really am. This is the worst thing I've ever seen in my life." She touched his shoulder with her free hand, but he shrugged it off. "Oh, my dear God! Who could do this?"

She went to the couch and moved enough trash aside for the baby. She pulled a pacifier from her sweater pocket, put it momentarily in her mouth to remove the lint, then put it in the baby's mouth. He appeared satisfied and leaned back on the couch.

She went to Horace, and right away he grabbed her throat. "I'm gonna kill you tonight!" he shouted. "I just wish that bitch Catrina was here so I could kill her, too." Elaine struggled and sputtered out one "Please" before he gripped her tighter. She beat his arms, but that seemed to give him more strength. She began to cry. "I'm gonna kill you tonight, girl, if it's the last thing I do."

The baby began to cry, and she turned her head as much as she could to look at him. This made him slap her twice, and she started to fall, and he pulled her up and, as he did, went for a better grip, there was time enough for her to say, "Don't kill me in front of my son, Horace." He loosened his hands. "Don't kill me in front of my boy, Horace." Her tears ran down her face and over and into his hands. "He don't deserve to see me die. You know that, Horace."

"Where, then!"

"Anywhere but in front of him. He's innocent of everything."

He let her go and backed away.

"I did nothin, Horace," she whispered. "I give you my word, I did nothin." The baby screamed, and she went to him and took him in her arms.

Horace sat down in the same chair he had been in.

"I would not do this to you, Horace."

He looked at her and at the baby, who could not take his eyes off Horace, even through his tears.

One of the baby's cries seemed to get stuck in his throat, and to release it the baby raised a fist and punched the air, and finally the cry came free. How does a man start over with nothing? Horace thought. Elaine came near him, and the baby still watched him as his crying lessened. How does a man start from scratch?

He leaned down and picked up a few of the broken albums from the floor and read the labels. "I would not hurt you for anything in the world, Horace," Elaine said. Okeh Phonograph Corporation. Domino Record Co. RCA Victor. Darnell Jr.'s crying stopped, but he continued to look down at the top of Horace's head. Cameo Record Corporation, N.Y. "You been too good to me for me to hurt you like this, Horace." He dropped the records one at a time: "It Takes an Irishman to Make Love." "I'm Gonna Pin a Medal on the Girl I Left Behind." "Ragtime Soldier Man." "Whose Little Heart Are You Breaking Now." "The Syncopated Walk."

BAD NEIGHBORS

Even before the fracas with Terence Stagg, people all along both sides of the 1400 block of 8th Street, N.W., could see the Benningtons for what they really were. First, the family moved in not on Saturday or on a weekday, but on Sunday, which was still the Lord's Day even though church for many was now only a place to visit for a wedding, or a funeral. Perhaps Easter or Christmas. And those watching that Sunday, from behind discreetly parted, brocaded curtains and on porches rarely used except to go back and forth into homes, had to wonder why the Bennington family even bothered to bring along most of their furniture. They had a collection of junk that included a stained queen-size mattress, a dining room table with three legs, a mirror with a large missing piece in one corner, and a refrigerator dented on two sides. One neighbor, his second cup of morning coffee in hand, joked to his wife that the Bennington refrigerator probably wouldn't work without a big block of ice in it to cool things. During the move-in, the half-dressed little Benningtons occupied themselves running to and from the two medium-size moving trucks, taking in clothes that had busted out of the cardboard boxes during the trip from whatever countrified shack they had left. Over the next two weeks or so, it became clear that the house at 1406 8th, with its three bedrooms, would be containing at least twelve people, though that number was always fluid, so neighbors on both sides of the street would never get a proper accounting, and they would never know who was related to whom.

They came in the middle of October, the Benningtons, bringing children—a bunch of five or so, from a two-year-old to a girl on the verge of being a teenager. Children who sometimes played outside on Friday and Saturday nights until at least nine thirty. And they were loud children, loud in a neighborhood where most of the children were now in their teens and did no more harm than play their portable radios too loudly as they washed their parents' cars. And the Benningtons came with a few men who sat on the porch on a legless couch with a cheap bedspread, drinking from containers in paper bags. Grace Bennington appeared to be the matriarch; she could have been fifty, but with her broad weight and gray hair, it was difficult for anyone to be certain. On a good day, her 8th Street neighbors might have been able to say forty or forty-five, but on a bad day, and the Benningtons seemed to have not a few bad days, seventy-five would not have been an unfair number. Only one thing was certain—she, in face and body, had known hard work. She moved about on stubby legs, favoring the outsides of her feet as she walked, so that all her shoes had soles run down on those sides. The soles of her shoes on the inside were almost as new as the day she brought them out of the store. There was a man—always bringing groceries—far older than Grace, tallish, a less flashy dresser than most of the men in the rest of the family; he came and went, always in the uniform of a man who worked in the railroad yards. A woman who could have been a bit younger than Grace was rarely seen, and when she was, the children would be holding her hand as they took her for a walk. She wore coats and sweaters even on the warmest day, and that fall and winter saw many good days. She might have been beautiful, but no one could tell because she was always wearing sunglasses and a scarf pulled around to cover most of her face. Then there was Amanda, no more than seventeen, Amanda in her tight blue jeans. The oldest male the neighbors saw most often was Derek, a man in his early twenties, a well-built and too often shirtless loudmouth, who seemed to go off, maybe to some job, whenever he could get his nineteen-year-old Ford to run, the kind of car most of the men in the neighborhood had owned on their way up to where they were now. There were two or three men in that family, but they also came and went. Only Derek was constant.

It was the quietness of Neil Bennington that caused Sharon Palmer—who had noticed in his demeanor even across 8th Street in those first weeks after the clan moved in—to introduce herself to him at his locker in the hall at Cardozo High School. He was in the tenth grade, small for his age and somewhat awkward, unlike his brother Derek. Sharon Palmer, who lived at 1409 directly across 8th from the Benningtons, was to witness the fracas between Derek and Terence Stagg, and seeing the fight, which was actually far less than that, she would begin to think her father and most of their neighbors might not be so wrong about most of those Benningtons. By then she would have had her third date with Terence, and he would have kissed her five times, twice surprising her as he thrust his tongue into her mouth. She mistook what she felt at that moment for blossoming love.

A senior, Sharon had, in the eleventh grade, become aware of her effect on boys—almost all of them (Terence Stagg, whom she had long had eyes and heart for, was a week or so from paying her any attention). And Sharon, coming rather late to an awareness of her womanhood, had begun to take some delight in seeing boys wither as they stood close enough to smell the mystery that had nothing to do with perfume and look into her twinkling brown eyes she had inherited from a grandmother who had seen only the morning, afternoon, and evening of a cotton field.

Neil was bent over into his locker, and when she said Hello, he rose slowly as though he knew all too well the accidents that came with quick movements. He seemed more befuddled than taken with her femaleness after she told him who she was, and the innocence of him made her wish that just this once she could turn down all that mystery that transformed boys into fools. He squinted and blinked, and with each blink he appeared to get closer to knowing just who she was. And as the brief conversation went on, it occurred to her that he was very much like one of her younger brothers—Neil and the brother had the forever look of true believers who had to start every morning learning all over again that the Easter bunny and Santa Claus did not exist.

That day of the first conversation, she saw him walking alone down 11th Street after school and she separated from her friends to go with him the rest of the way home. She thought Neil, like her brother, was adorable, a word she had started using just after the New Year. Her father, Hamilton Palmer, saw them turn the corner from P and thought nothing about it. As the morning and afternoon supervisor at the main post office at North Capitol Street, he was home most days by three thirty. He was watering plants on his porch, and Neil said good-bye to his daughter and Hamilton opened the little gate on the porch that had been installed ages ago when his children and the puppy were too small to know all the ways the world beyond the gate could hurt them.

It was three weeks later, more than a month after the Benningtons moved in, that Sharon's father Hamilton began to think something might be amiss. Thanksgiving had come and gone, and people all over Washington were complaining that it just didn't feel like Christmas weather. Who could think of Christmas with people still in their fall sweaters and trees threatening to bud again? Neil and Sharon turned the corner again, this time accompanied by three other students who lived farther down 8th. Before the four left Sharon in front of her house, Hamilton's daughter touched Neil's shoulder, and the boy smiled. It was not the touch so much as the smile that bothered him. He had been thinking that his Sharon and Terence Stagg might be a good match some time down the line when they had finished their education. Hamilton noticed for the first time that Derek was watching everything from across the street. He could not tell for certain, but he thought he saw Derek Bennington smirking.

Two days later the Prevosts up the street at 1404 had their place burgled, with a television being the most expensive thing taken. No one said anything, but the neighbors knew it had to be Derek. The next week the Thorntons at 1414 had their car stolen. The car was only a Chevy. Five years old, but that was not the point, said Bill Forsythe at 1408 next door to the Benningtons. His wife, Prudence, had complained about what a noisy heap the Thornton car was and the neighborhood was well rid of it. A man's property is a man's property, Bill said, even if it's one skate with three wheels. After the car was taken, someone called the police and they came out and spoke for some fifteen minutes to the Benningtons in their house. No one knew what went down, as the police came out and left without talking to any of the neighbors. Derek walked out soon afterward and stood on his porch, smoking a cigarette. He was alone for a good while, and then his mother Grace came and said something that made him put out the cigarette in the ashtray. She continued talking to him, and for every second she was speaking, he was nodding his head slightly.

More than a month before the January fracas between Derek and Terence Stagg, Sharon Palmer returned to Neil a book she had borrowed from him. It was a Saturday afternoon, and she went up the steps to the Bennington home at 1406 and saw that the screen door was shut but that the main door was open. There was no one she could see from the threshold and she called "Hello" and "Neil," and then, with no answer after moments, she knocked on the wood of the screen door. The radio and the television were playing. She did not want to think it, but she felt it said something about them, maybe not Neil but all the rest of them. She waited about two minutes and after she again called for Neil, she opened the screen and stepped into the house, saying "Hello, hello, hello" all the way. On the couch the woman in the sunglasses was watching her, and when Sharon asked for Neil, the woman said nothing. There were two small children on either side of her and they were watching a black-and-white television. Sharon immediately thought about the

Prevosts' television, but she did not know if it had been color or black-and-white.

"I knocked, but I got no answer," Sharon said. "Is Neil here? I brought his book back." The woman tilted her head to the side as though to better consider what she had heard. "Is he here?" The children were silent and their eyes were big as though Sharon was a creature they had not seen before. Sharon told the woman again that she was looking for Neil. It would be better, Sharon thought, if I could see her eyes. Finally, the woman moved her face toward the next room. "Thank you."

The dining room was crowded with boxes, the state it must have been in since the first day they moved in. The dining table's missing leg had been replaced with one that had yet to be painted the color of the rest of the table.

"Hello, Neil? Neil?" She stepped into the kitchen, and she was not prepared for what she saw. It was immaculate, the kind of room her mother would be happy with. "Hello?" The floor was clean, the counters were clean, the stove was clean, the tiny table and its three chairs were clean. "Hello?" She turned and looked about the room with great curiosity. When she turned back, Derek was standing at the open screen door to the backyard, watching her.

"You lost?"

"No, I'm sorry. I knocked but no one answered."

"The May maid swayed away to pray in the day's hay," Derek said, not smiling. "Thas why you got no answer."

"I just came to return Neil's book. Is he here?"

Derek shouted twice for Neil. "Well, you can just leave it on the table, lady from across the street."

"He said I could borrow another. A book of Irish stories the library doesn't seem to have."

He shouted for Neil again, and as she listened to his voice thunder through the house, she noticed the small bookcase beside the refrigerator.

Four shelves, each a little more than two feet across. He saw her looking at it. "Just leave it on the table. That readin fool'll get it."

"I can come back for it another time." She set the book on the table.

"Which one was it?" He was wearing an undershirt, and it hung on him in a way that did not threaten the way those shirts seemed to on other men. The bare muscular arms were simply bare muscular arms, not possible weapons. It was a small moment in the kitchen, but she was to think of those arms years later as she stood naked and looked down at the bare arms of her husband as the red light of the expensive German clock shone down on him. A night-light.

"A book of stories—Mary Lavin's *Tales from Bective Bridge*. My teacher shared two with me and I'm hooked."

"Hooked is good cept with junk, ask any junkie," Derek said, and he looked across at the bookcase. "The almighty reader might have it up-stairs or in some box somewhere. His shit is all over the fuckin place." Shit, fuckin, she thought. Shit, fuckin. In a few quiet, swift steps, he was at the table. He took up the book and looked at the spine and wrin-kled his face. "Hooked, hooked," he said. The same kind of steps took him to the bookcase. He knelt, peered for a moment, and put the book between two green books on the second shelf up from the bottom. "L is for Lavin," Derek said and found the book. "M is for Mary." He looked at it front and back. "I know one thing for sure: He loves this woman's work so you bet not lose it. I think the almighty reader is part Irish and don't know it yet." In two more steps he was before her, and she took the book and promised to return it just as it was. There was nothing untow-ard in his face, the lust, the hunger, the way it was in all the boys except Neil, boys with pimples, and boys without. There was no smile from him and he did not look into her eyes, the twinkling and the brown. He turned and went to the refrigerator and opened it. "You know," he said, his back to her, his head bent to look in, and the light of the refrigerator pouring out over him, "you shouldn't be afraid of wearin blue." He took out a beer and closed the icebox with great care. "Forget the red. You wear too much red." He did not turn around but found on the counter beside the icebox an opener for the beer.

"What?"

Neil came in, and Derek pointed to him. "Where you been, boy?" Derek said. "Your girlfriend been waitin. You the worse fuckin boyfriend in the world."

"She ain't my girlfriend," Neil said and raised his hand Hello to Sharon.

"I gave your girlfriend one of Lavin's books, man."

"I told you she's not my girlfriend, Dee."

"Whatever, man." He still had not turned around and he drank from the beer as he walked to the back door. "You should tell your girlfriend that red doesn't suit her. She ain't believe me so maybe if it comes from her boyfriend." He went out the screen door, and Neil walked her back to the front of the house.

Three neighbors saw Sharon Palmer leave the Bennington house that day—her father Hamilton from his upstairs bedroom, Terence Stagg next door to the home of Sharon and Hamilton Palmer, and Prudence Forsythe next to the Benningtons. This was a little more than a month before that January thing between Terence and Derek. Terence was standing at his living room window and watched Sharon walk down the Bennington steps with a book in her hand. Neil Bennington was a wisp of a boy, not worth noticing to a young man like Terence. But Terence had seen Derek about, and like most of the men on 8th Street he didn't think much of him; men like Derek had never seen the inside of Howard University, where Terence was in his second year, and they never would. As Sharon waited for the few passing cars going up and down 8th, she lowered her head in a most engaging way, lowered it only for a second, as if to consider something, and Terence could see how Sharon had filled out. Filled out in her pink sweater and her blue jeans not trampy tight, but tight enough to let a man know if he should bother or not. She had filled out since the last time he had really taken a look at her, and that was a time he could not remember.

Terence was at her door that evening, asking a beaming Hamilton Palmer, who had also gone to Howard, how he was doing these warm days and then asking the father if he might talk a bit with his daughter this evening. He and Sharon stepped out onto the porch and Terence invited her to a movie and a meal on Friday night. She had had two dates before—and one of those had been with a young man who was brother to her cousin's husband. Sharon was not one to keep a diary, but if she had been, the meeting of a few minutes with Terence would have taken up at least two pages.

Terence stepped back into her house and called good-bye to Hamilton Palmer, who came out of the kitchen with Sharon's mother. The parents said they hadn't seen much of him lately and then wanted to know how his studies were going and Terence told them they were going very well and that he was hitting his stride. He was, in fact, going with a fellow Howard student, but Howard students not D.C. natives were taught from day one never to venture into Washington neighborhoods except where they could find a better class of people, meaning white people for the most part, and so that Newark girl would never know about 8th Street. That girl at Howard was so clingy, with her Terence this and her Terence that. And as he had watched Sharon earlier come across 8th, he remembered something his father Lane had recently told him: You are young and the world is your oyster. You shuck it, don't let it shuck you. What oyster would Derek ever shuck? Well, fine, Hamilton said about Terence hitting his stride, and Hamilton came across the living room with his hand extended. And he added that Terence was way ahead of the game, because Lord knows he didn't hit his own stride until he was a junior at least, isn't that right, honey? And his wife just smiled.

Sharon, ecstatic, did not get to Mary Lavin's *Tales from Bective Bridge* that evening as she had planned. She could think of nothing else but an evening with Terence. She tried sleeping, but found it was no use and so got up from bed and sat in the dark at her window, which, like the one in her parents' bedroom, faced 8th Street. She would be at the window three nights before Christmas, near about midnight, when she saw Neil Bennington, carrying a small package that was bright even in the dark, dash across the street to her house, take the steps two at a time, and then dash back across the street to his place, his hands now apparently empty. It would be a rare cold night for that December, and she was tempted not to go downstairs. But she did. She opened the main door to find a small gift-wrapped package on the threshold between the door and the storm door. It had her name on it. With anxious fingers, just inside the living room, she tore open the shiny wrapping and found in a velvet-covered box a figure of brown wood, nearly perfectly carved, a figure of a little girl no more than an inch and a half, in a dress that came down to her feet. She had on a bonnet. When Sharon held the figure to the light of the lamp on a table in the living room, the girl's nose told her unmistakably that the figure was of a black girl. The child seemed somehow recognizable, but for years she was never able to recall where she had seen it. One of the girl's arms was extended somewhat, and there was a bracelet on it. Through the bracelet ran a gold-like chain; that the chain was shining told it might be gold, that it was from a boy of no means from across the street told her that it might not be.

She was disappointed because she did not want Neil to think that there could ever be anything between them, and such a thing, with such intricacy, with a compellingly quiet beauty, told her that was what he was thinking. But she did not want to hurt his feelings by returning the gift. Adorable people should not be hurt. She thought for a day and decided to give him a book, and she chose a small paperback edition of Ann Petry's *The Street*. She came up to him as he stood at his locker at school, his head cocked to the side as if he was trying to decide what was needed for the final period of the day. Terence was picking her up after school. Neil Bennington seemed genuinely surprised. "I didn't get you anything," he said, blushing and blinking. "This is straight-up embarrassin."

"That doesn't matter," Sharon said. "It's the season for giving. What are neighbors for?"

"I'll get you somethin, I promise," he said, biting his lip.

"If you do, I'll think you'll be trying to reciprocate, and you'll hurt my feelings."

"All right," Neil said. "All right, but I won't forget this. Ever."

In more than three years after that day, on her way to becoming a nurse, she would attend a party at the home of one of her Georgetown University professors. Her husband would not be able to be with her that night, but that was the way it had become. She would spend a good part of the evening near a corner with a glass of ginger ale; none of the food would appeal to her. Just as she was about to excuse herself and leave, a white woman of some seventy years would come up to her.

"I have been admiring that wondrous thing you're wearing," the white woman said. "Even from across the room, you can see how unique it is." She looked closer. "The carver must have used up all his eyesight making it. You have exquisite taste." The woman smiled, not at Sharon but at the Christmas gift that she would only recently have unearthed from a trunk in her parents' basement.

"It's not much. Someone gave it to me. It isn't very much."

"It is much in that other way," the woman said. "I know a place down on F Street that would give you five hundred dollars for it. . . . Please. May I?" and the woman raised a tentative hand, and Sharon nodded and the woman took up the little girl in the bonnet and rested it between her fingers and then looked fully into Sharon's eyes. "If the carver lost his sight, he may well have thought it was well worth it." That evening, for the first time, Sharon would notice the initials down in one of the folds of the girl's dress. No, she said to herself, I would not sell it. I don't even know if the carver is living anymore.

It was actually Amanda Bennington who first got into it with Terence Stagg, which led to something that ultimately allowed the whole neighborhood to see the Benningtons for what they were. She and her brother Derek had come from the Safeway late on a Saturday morning in mid-January. They parked in front of the Staggs' house, across the street at 1407. Derek took bags of groceries into their house while Amanda looked to be tidying up the car.

Sharon Palmer was watching from her bedroom next door to the Staggs'. Nothing had really been spoken, but it might as well have been said that she and Terence Stagg were a couple. Neighbors all said what a nice couple they made; she and Terence had driven up in his father's Cadillac one evening the week before and she saw Neil watching from his porch. She waved and he waved back. They were not walking home as much as they had been, but they still shared books. Derek came out and stood beside Neil as Terence walked Sharon into her house.

Terence, that Saturday morning, was heading out his door when he saw Amanda fussing around in the trunk of Derek's Ford, which was parked in the same spot his father, Lane Stagg, had been parking his Cadillacs in since even before Terence knew what good things life had in store for him. It may as well be said that his father owned that dot of public real estate. Before his family had awakened, Lane had gone out on an errand that morning, purring quietly away about seven thirty in that new tan Cadillac that had less than three thousand miles on it.

"Hey, you," Terence said to Amanda and came down the steps to the sidewalk, too upset to even take full notice of her behind as she bent over and puttered in the trunk. He was to excel in anatomy and dermatology when he got to Howard's medical school, but genetics and neurology would nearly cost him his future. Amanda took her head out of the trunk, holding jumper cables, and looked Terence up and down. "Hey! You know you parked in my father's space?" Then, watching Amanda toss the cables back in the trunk and try to clean the dirt from her hands with a Kleenex she pulled from her back pocket, he pointed to the space her car was in and said: "Hey, do you know that you are parked in my father's space?" Since the first month at Howard as a freshman, he had stopped referring to Lane as "my daddy" when talking to a third party.

"Hay for horses, not for people. Go down Hecht's and get em cheaper," Amanda said. Words of a child of eight or nine, and they upset Terence even more. "It's a free country, man," Amanda said. "We all got a right to park where we wanna park." She pulled another bunched-up Kleenex from the back pocket of her jeans and tried to wipe her hands with it. She was dark and pretty, and in another universe Terence would have been able to appreciate that. "And besides"—she turned and pointed with the hand with the Kleenex across the street—"somebody's got my brother's regular spot." The Forsythes at 1408 next door to the Benningtons were already fed up with them and showed it by parking in front of their house as often as they could, though the Benningtons had never complained. That Saturday, the Forsythes had company from out of town and the visitors' Trans Am was where Derek's Ford would have gone, on a spot covered in oil that was forever leaking from his car. "We had stuff to take and it whatn't no use parkin way down at the corner. Maybe that Trans Am'll move before your daddy gets back."

"I don't care about that," Terence said. "You're just going to have to move that thing somewhere else."

Her mother Grace had been trying to teach her to control her temper, but Amanda knew there were days and then there were days. "First off," Amanda said, "I ain't movin shit. Second off, it ain't no thing. It's a classic. Third off, you better get out my damn face. This a free country, man. You ain't no fuckin parkin police." She closed the trunk with both hands to make the loudest sound she could manage.

"I would expect something like this from trash like you."

She flicked the Kleenex at him and he dodged it. "Since it's that way, you the biggest trash around here." She had seen him about many times, and in another universe before that moment she would have liked him to come across the street and knock at her door and invite her to the Broadway on 7th Street for a movie and a hamburger and soda afterward. She had also seen Terence's well-dressed mother, Helen Stagg, quite often as well, had studied the woman as she came out of her house and looked up and down 8th Street as if waiting for the world to tell her that it was once again worthy of having her. She loved her own mother, in all her dowdiness, more than any human being, but she knew Grace would never be Helen Stagg. "If I'm trash, you trash."

"Typical," Terence said. "Real damn typical."

"Whas up here?" Derek came across the street, his keys in his hand.

"Derek, this guy say we gotta move the car cause his father's got the spot."

"Ain't nobody own no parkin spot, neighbor. This a free country, neighbor," Derek said, the keys jingling with his arm at his side.

"I'm not your neighbor."

"Oh, oh, it's like that, huh?" Derek said, turning around twice and raising his arms in faux surrender. "You one of those, huh? All right." Amanda had stayed in the street behind the car but Derek had continued on up to the sidewalk. "All right, big shot. Les just clear the way, cause I don't want no trouble. Nobody want any trouble." He stepped back into the gutter. "All I can say is we got a right to be there, as much right as your daddy and that Cadillac of his with that punk-ass color." He looked at Amanda. "You done?"

"Yeah, I'm cool."

"Well, les go," and they waited to cross as two cars passed going up 8th Street.

"I told you to move that damn thing," Terence said. His knuckles tapped the top of the trunk. "You people should learn to wash your ears out." Terence spat on the car.

Derek turned. "Just leave that somebitch alone, Derek," Amanda said. "He ain't worth it."

Grace Bennington came out of her house and yelled at Derek to come on in. Neil stood beside her and he held the hand of a girl of seven or eight. "Wipe that shit off," Derek said of the spit, a slow-moving blob on the black paint heading down toward the fender. The car didn't always run, but he kept it clean.

Derek counted all the way to ten and Terence said, "Tell your funky mother to wipe it off."

"Even you, even poor you," Derek said calmly, "should know the law against sayin somethin like that. Man oh man oh man . . ."

It took but one hit to the lower part of the jaw to send Terence to the ground. He had seen the fist coming, but because he had not been in very many fights in his life, it took him far too long to realize the fist was coming for him. Grace and Amanda screamed. The Bryants at 1401 and the Prevosts at 1404 came out, as did the Forsythes and their company who had the Trans Am, all of them still digesting their breakfast. Sharon Palmer had watched with growing concern from her bedroom window. She had not been able to hear all that was said by the three, but, on the path to love, she had admired the way Terence seemed to be standing up to Derek. By the time she got downstairs and out to the sidewalk, Amanda and Grace were comforting Terence, and only seconds after he awoke and saw the women, he told them to get the fuck away from him. Neil was holding his little sister by the hand to keep her from going into the street to be with their mother, and Derek was already back across the street and on the legless couch, watching the group around Terence and smoking a cigarette and waiting for the police to show up.

Lane Stagg was more disturbed about what had happened to his son than if it had been a mere fight between young men of equal age and status, and his Terence had simply lost after doing his best. No doubt, Lane Stagg knew, men like Derek Bennington had never learned to fight fair. Terence, after the trip from the hospital, was out of it for a day and a half, but his father did not need to hear from his son that he had been jumped before he could properly defend himself. Terence suffered no permanent damage, and he would recover and become the first person anyone in the neighborhood knew to become a doctor. "Let them crackers," Lane Stagg said at the graduation dinner after his second drink, "write that up in their immigration brochures about how descendants of slaves aren't any good and so all you hardworking immigrants just come on over."

The police came out that Saturday, but because they didn't like doing paperwork and because no white person had been hurt, Derek was not arrested. That would not be the case with the white man in Arlington who owned the Bennington home.

That Saturday evening, after the hospital visit, Lane, working on his second drink, broached the idea again of buying the house the Benningtons were renting from the white man. He sat in his living room with his wife perched on the arm of his easy chair, and across from him, on the couch, were Hamilton Palmer, Arthur Atwell, and Bill and Prudence Forsythe. Just after the third sip of that drink, Lane Stagg started in on how the neighborhood was changing for the worse. And Hamilton, already seeing the Staggs as future in-laws, agreed. He was not drinking. And neither was Bill Forsythe. Prudence had quietly come upon Bill two weeks before looking out their bedroom window at Amanda Bennington collecting toys from her front yard. Prudence watched him for more than five minutes before going to see what had captured him. Bill had a drink in his hand and Amanda was wearing the tight blue jeans she would have on the day of the fracas and it was not even one thirty. "Nice day," Bill said to his wife, already drifting toward happy land and so unable to compose something better. "I'm fucking tired of you getting ideas," Prudence said. "I'm fucking tired of you and your ideas." "Honey," Bill said, "keep your voice down. The neighbors, honey. The neighbors." Meaning not the Benningtons on one side, but Arthur and Beatrice Atwell on the other side. She took the drink from Bill, and Prudence did it in such a way that the ice cubes did not clink against the sides of the glass.

Lane Stagg, pained about his Terence, was as eloquent that evening as he would be at the last meeting of the neighbors years later. He said that though the prior neighbors in the Bennington house had not been in the same league as those sitting now in his living room, the good neighbors of 8th Street could live with them. But he had to admit that the building had really not housed the proper sort of folk in years. "What," he asked, "does that white man across the river in Arlington care about our neighborhood?" He had been the captain of his debating team in high school when the schools had such things. He would have made a good lawyer, everyone said. But the son of a coal and ice man rose only so far. His wife, whose father and mother were lawyers, married him anyway.

It was not a long meeting, but before it ended, they agreed that they would raise the money to buy the house from the white man who lived across the Potomac River in Arlington. The white man and his family had been the last whites to live in that neighborhood. "Come on over to Arlington," his white former neighbors kept saying, "the blacks are all off in *that* neighborhood so you hardly ever see them." The white man and his wife had a son, deep into puberty, and the son was growing ever partial to blondes, which 8th Street didn't grow anymore.

So the good neighbors of 8th Street decided to raise the money and buy the house and rent it to more agreeable people. "Let's drink to that," Lane said and stood up. About then Sharon Palmer came down from upstairs where she had been comforting Terence. The medicine had finally overcome him and he had fallen asleep. "Thank you, sweet Sharon, thank you, thank you," Lane said and he sat his drink on the table beside his chair and put his arms around her. "It was the least I could do," she said. "It was the very least."

After everyone had left, and his wife had gone to bed, Lane sat beside his son's bed. He had enjoyed that house for a long time, and it saddened him, beyond the effects of the liquor, to think that he would not see his grandchildren enjoy it. He loved Washington, and as he sat and watched Terence sleep, he feared he would have to leave. He was hearing good things about Prince George County, but that place, abutting the even more redneck areas of the Maryland suburbs, was not home like D.C. He had heard, too, that the police there were brutes, straight out of the worst Southern town, but he had come a long way since the boyhood days of helping his father deliver coal and ice throughout Washington. Dirty nigger coal man and his dirty nigger coal son, children had called them. And that was in the colored neighborhoods of maids and shoe shiners and janitors and cooks and elevator operators. But he was a thousand lives from that now, even though he wasn't anybody's lawyer. With his reputation as a GS 15 at the Labor Department and a wife high up in the D.C. school system and a bigger Maryland house and a son on the way to being a doctor, the police in Prince George would know just what sort he was.

The good neighbors were helped by one major thing—the white man and his wife across the Potomac who owned the Bennington house had been thinking for some time about moving to Florida. Their son, who had no interest in real estate in Washington, was now off to a great start nevertheless—he owned two used car lots, one in Arlington and the other in Alexandria. He had a lovely wife and two children in Great Falls, and he had a mistress in both cities where the car lots were. Of the three blond women, only one had been born blond.

Lane Stagg, Hamilton Palmer, Arthur Atwell, and Prudence Forsythe met with the white man on the highway in Arlington named for Robert E. Lee, in a restaurant that had been segregated less than two years before. They offered him $31,000 for the Bennington house. The white man whistled at the figure. Arthur Atwell was silent, as usual. He was semi-retired and liked to think he had more money than he really did have; his widow, Beatrice, was to discover that when he died not long after that meeting. The white man, Nicholas Riccocelli, whistled again, this time even louder, because the $31,000 sounded good—he really had no idea how much the house was worth. For several moments, he studied a cheap print of a Dutch windmill on the wall beside the table and thought about how many days on a Florida beach $31,000 would provide. That plus the money from some other property and his investments in his son's businesses.

Riccocelli said give him a week to think it over, and he called Lane Stagg in four days and said they had a deal. The white man had never had any trouble with the Benningtons and so felt he owed it to them to tell them himself, formally, that they would have to move. He came late one Saturday afternoon in early February, and when Derek told him his mother wasn't home, Riccocelli wanted to know if she would be gone long.

"If there's something important," Derek said, "you can tell me." And when the white man told him that they would have to be gone in two months, Derek turned from his spot in the middle of the living room to look at Amanda and Neil standing in the doorway to the dining room. "Can you believe this shit?" Then to Riccocelli, he asked, "Why? Ain't we always paid rent on time? Ain't we?"

"Yes, but the new owners would like to start anew."

"Who are they?" Derek said. "You tell em we good tenants and everything'll be all right."

"I'm afraid," the white man said, "that will not work. The new owners wish to go in another direction altogether."

"Who the fuck are these people? What kinda direction you talkin about?" Derek came two steps closer to the man.

"Why . . . why . . ." and Riccocelli seemed unable to complete the sentence because he had thought their neighbors would have somehow let the Benningtons know. "Why your neighbors around you." The man sensed something bad about to happen and backed toward the front door. Where, he wondered, was the mother? She had always seemed so sensible.

"Get the fuck out!" Derek said and grabbed the man by his coat collar. The man opened the door and Derek pushed him out. "You sorry motherfucker!" The woman who always wore sunglasses, seated between two children, began to cry, and the children, following her, began crying as well.

"Derek, leave him alone," Amanda said. "Leave him be."

Out on the porch, Derek still had Riccocelli by the collar. He pulled him down the stairs. "Derek!" Amanda shouted. "Please!"

"Don't hurt me, Mr. Bennington." The ride over from Arlington had been pleasant enough. Riccocelli was a small man, and his eyes only came about thirteen inches above the dashboard, but he enjoyed driving. There had been gentle and light snow most of the way from Arlington, and a few times he saw lightning across the sky. Snow and lightning, and then the thunder. How could a day go wrong that quickly? He would miss the snow in Florida, he had thought all the way across Key Bridge. Now, as the two men stumbled and fell their way down the steps to the sidewalk, there was rain, also gentle, but the sky was quiet. "You mustn't molest me, Mr. Bennington." Riccocelli had parked behind Derek's Ford, and Derek pushed and half carried him to the car and slammed him against it. "You come back and you dead meat."

After the man was gone, Derek went up and down both sides of the street, shouting to the neighbors to come out and confront him. "Don't be punks!" he shouted. As he neared the middle of the other side of 8th, Grace came around the corner, and she and Amanda and Neil, who had been standing in the yard, went to him. "We got babies in that house, man! It's winter, for Godsakes!" Sharon opened her door and came out on the porch, but she was the only neighbor to do so. "We got sweet innocent babies in that house, man! What can yall be thinkin?" They were able to calm him but before they could get him across the street, the police came.

Arthur Atwell died of a heart attack not long after the Benningtons moved at the end of February, two days before Derek got out of D.C. Jail. Arthur's widow, Beatrice, found that despite all Arthur had said, there was not much money, and she had to back out of the Bennington house deal. She moved to Claridge Towers on M Street, into an apartment with a bathroom where she could hide when the thunder and lightning came. Everyone was sad to see her leave because she had been a better neighbor than most. Those still in on the Bennington house deal did manage to buy the house, but the good neighbors rarely found their sort of people to rent the place to.

Sharon Palmer Stagg's car had been in the shop two days when she finished her shift at Georgetown University Hospital one Saturday night in March. It was too late for a bus, and she thought she would have a better chance for a cab at Wisconsin Avenue and so she made her way out of the hospital grounds to P Street. She was not yet a nurse, but did have a part-time job as a nurse's assistant at the hospital, where she often volunteered on her days off. Just before 36th Street that night, she saw a small group of young men coming toward her, loud, singing a song too garbled for her to understand. She was used to such crowds—Georgetown University students, many with bogus identification cards they used to buy drinks at the bars along Wisconsin Avenue and M Street.

She had been married for nine months. Terence Stagg was in medical school at Howard. His maternal grandparents, the attorneys, had been killed in a car accident by a drunken driver who was himself an attorney, and they had left their only grandchild more money than was good for him. Terence and his wife lived more than well in a part of upper Northwest Washington where the Benningtons could only serve and never live.

Just before Sharon reached 35th Street, the group of young men came under a streetlight and she could see that two of them were white and the third was black. The black one, six or so feet from her, said to the white ones, "I spy with my little eye something good to eat," and the three spread out and blocked her from passing. "I always have these fantasies about nurses and sponge baths," the black one said. She was wearing a white uniform and that had told them all they needed to know. They came to within three feet of her and one of the white ones held his arms out to Sharon, while the other two surrounded her. She did not hear the car door behind her open and close.

The black one touched her cheek and then her breasts with both hands and one of the white students did the same, and both young men breathed sour beer into her face. Sharon pulled away, and the two looked at each other and giggled. The third student gave a rah-rah cry and came up and slapped her behind twice. As the black student inhaled deeply for another blast into her face, something punched him in the side of the face and the black student fell hard against a car and passed out. "Hey! Hey!" the white student who had had his hands on Sharon said to the puncher. "Whatcha do to our Rufus?" The puncher pulled Sharon back behind him and she saw that it was a face from a long time ago, and her knees buckled to see it. He may well have been a ghost because she had not seen him in that long a time. "They spoil the best nights we have," Derek said to her.

The white student who had not touched her pulled out a knife, the blade more than three inches. Derek reached into his own pocket, but before his hand came out, the white student had stabbed him in his left side, through his leather jacket, through his shirt, into the vicinity of his heart, and Sharon screamed as Derek first faltered and then pulled himself up. In a second his switchblade was out and the blade tore through the student's jacket and into his arm, and the student ran out into P Street and down toward his university. "I wanted to keep this clean," Derek said. "But white trash won't let me."

"Hey! Hey!" the second white student said as he sobered up. "We didn't mean anything." He raised his arms high. "See, see . . ."

"Oh, you fucks always mean somethin," Derek said, holding his knife to the man's cheek and flicking it once to open a wound in the cheek, less than two inches from his nostrils. The man crumpled, both hands to his face. His black friend was still out, and the man with the arm wound was shouting as he ran that they were all being killed by niggers. Derek sheathed his knife and returned it to his pocket and then pulled Sharon down the street to his car.

Within moments he had driven them down P, slowly, across Wisconsin and to a spot before the P Street Bridge, where he stopped. He turned on the light and inspected his side. "Shit!" he said. "Bad but maybe not fatal. Damn!"

"Let me help you," Sharon said.

He started the car up, and after looking in the sideview mirror he continued on down P Street, again slowly. Two patrol cars sped past them, and she watched him watching them go away in the rearview mirror. "Dead or alive, the black dude won't matter," he said to the mirror, joining the traffic moving around Dupont Circle. "But them white dudes are princes and the world gon pay for that." He became part of the flow going up Connecticut Avenue. "And it happened in Georgetown. They'll make sure somebody pays for that. But they were drunk and so describin might be a problem. Real drunk." He seemed unaware that she was there. "Thas why I never went to college, Derek. Black people gotta leave all their common sense at the front door. College is the business of miseducatin. Like them people would ever open the door anyway." She feared he might pass out, and in the near darkness of the car, she was comforted by the fact that she could not see blood creeping around to the right side from the left. Two more police cars passed them, screaming. "They gonna pull that one patrol car they have in Southeast and the only one they got in Northeast and bring em over here to join the dozens they keep in Georgetown. You watch, Derek," he said to the mirror. "You just watch."

"Derek," she said. "Stop and let me help you."

They had crossed Calvert, they had crossed Woodley, and he looked at her for the first time since they entered the car. "I lied," he said. "I lied. Red wasn't a bad color. It was way good anough for you. Any color you put on is a good color, didn't you know that? You make the world. It ain't never been the other way around. You first, then the world follows." They were nearing Porter. Two blocks from the University of the District of Columbia he stopped, not far from her condominium building, which had one of the few doormen in Washington. "You can walk the rest of the way home," he said. "All the bad thas gonna happen to you done already happened."

She moved his jacket aside and saw where the blood had darkened his blue shirt, and when she touched him, the blood covered her hand and began to drip. "Come with me and let me help you." And as she said this, her mind ticked off the actual number of years when she had last seen him. Three days later she would have the time down to weeks. She took a handkerchief and Kleenex from her pocketbook and pressed them gently to his side. "It's bad, but manageable, I think. We need to get you help, though."

He took her hand and placed it in her lap. "Let me be," he said. "You best get home. You best go home to the man you married to."

"Come in. You helped me, so let me help you."

"You should tell that glorious husband of yours that a wife should be protected, that he shouldn't be sleepin while you have to come home through the jungle of some white neighborhood. Tell him thas not what bein married should be about."

She took the bloody handkerchief and Kleenex and returned them to her pocketbook. She did not now want to go home. She wanted to stay and go wherever he was going to recover. She snapped the pocketbook shut. Her father had walked her down the aisle, beaming all the way at the coming together of his two favorite families. The church had been packed and Terence had stood at the end of the aisle, waiting, standing as straight as he could after a night of drinking and pals and two strippers who had taken turns licking his dick for half of that night.

"You best go home." "Please," she said. "Let me stay." He reached across her and opened the door. "And one last thing," he said. "Neil been at me for the longest time to have me tell you it was never him. He was always afraid that you went about thinkin he was stuck on you, and he always wanted me to set the record straight. Now the record is straight." How long can the heart carry it around? How long? The answer came to her in a whisper.

She got out and shut the door, and he continued on up Connecticut Avenue, his back red lights, throbbing and brightly vital, soon merging with all the rest of the lights of the Washington night. Her BMW was in the shop. The man had promised that it would be ready by the end of the week. Terence's Mercedes had never seen a bad day.

As soon as she locked the door to the condominium, she heard the hum of the new refrigerator, and then the icemaker clicked on, and ice tumbled into the bucket, as if to welcome her home. The fan over the stove was going and she turned it off, along with the light over the stove, the two switches side by side. In the living room she noticed the blood on her uniform; if the doorman had seen it, he did not say. In the half darkness, the spots seemed fresh, almost alive in some eerie way, as if they had just that second come from Derek's wound. Bleeding. Bleedin. She had emerged unscathed. The overhead fan of grand, golden wood in the living room was going, slowly, and she considered for the longest whether to switch it off. In the end she chose to stop the spinning. Her family had moved away from 8th Street when she was in college. And so had the Forsythes and the Spoonhours and the Prevosts and all the people she had known as she grew into womanhood. We are the future, her father-in-law Lane Stagg had proclaimed at a final dinner party at the Sheraton Hotel for the good neighbors. Who was left there now? Bad neighbors, her father had called those who came after them. Bad neighbors. Before the whites came back and planted their flags in the new world. The motor on the fish tank hummed right along; the light over the tank was on and she turned that off. The expensive tropical fish swam on even without the light. The stereo, which had cost the equivalent of seven of her paychecks, was not playing but the power light was on and she pushed the button to put the whole console to rest. She placed one finger against the fish tank, and all the fish in their colorful finery ignored it. Her father had risen at that hotel dinner and given the first toast, his hand trembling and his voice breaking at every fifth word. And he was followed by Lane Stagg, who was as eloquent as ever.

Terence was sleeping peacefully, one foot sticking out of the covers, the exquisite German clock's dull red numbers shining down on him from the bedside table with the reassurance of a child's night-light. Her father hated such clocks, the digital ones that told the time right out; he believed, as he had tried to teach Sharon and her brother, that children should learn to tell time the way he had learned, with the big hand and the little hand moving around a circle of numbers. Possibly a second hand, but that was not needed to know what time of day it was. She stood in the doorway and watched Terence and the clock, and for all the time she was there he did not stir. A burglar could come in, she thought, and he would never know it. She could stab him to death and end his world and he would never know it. She could smother him. The whole world could end and he would not know that either. The insurance they paid on all that they owned—not including the cars and their own lives, which had separate policies—came to $273.57 a month. It is worth it, the white insurance man had said as he dotted the final *i*, "because you will sleep better at night knowing you are protected." Knowing. Knowin.

She got out of her clothes in the bathroom, took off everything she had on, even her underwear, and found that the blood had seeped through all the way to her skin. She held her uniform up before her. She stared at her name tag and found it hard to connect herself with the name and the uniform and the naked person they belonged to. Am I really who they say I am? The blood reminded her of someone that had a name but the name escaped her. Bleeding. Bleedin. None of Derek's people had ever used the *g* on their *ing* words; one of the first things she herself had been taught early in life was never to lose the *g*. The *g* is there for a reason, they had told her. It separates you from all the rest of them, those who do not know any better. Sharon did not shower. Another Sharon in another time might have been unsettled by him appearing from nowhere, by the thought that he had been following her. But the idea that he had been there, out there in weather of whatever sort, out there in the dark offering no sign and no sound, out there for months and perhaps years of her life, seemed to give her something to measure her life by. But she did not know how to do that. After she turned out the bathroom light, she stood in the dark for a long time. In their bedroom she decided against putting on underwear and so got into bed the way she came into the world. Terence stirred, pulled his foot back under the covers, but beyond that, he did nothing. Almost imperceptibly, the rightmost red number on the fine German clock went from two to three.

TAPESTRY

Were it not for the sleeping car porter, she might well have grown old there. And then—for her people were people of long lives—she would have grown older still. The case could be made that Anne Perry would have married Lucas Turner, for though she had gone off him after Lucas told her she was not as beautiful as she made herself out to be, she was fast maturing and was coming, day by day, to sour on Ned Murray, who told her endlessly how pretty she was. Ned promised that he would marry her and hang the moon and the planets and star-jewels around her pretty neck. ("I'll wring your damn neck!" Ned was to say to the woman he would marry within two years. "I'll wring it all to hell and back again.") "Oh, Ned," Anne's mother found her saying late one Saturday morning, smiling into the mirror at her face. A face with a past of few tears that mattered. The same mirror her father used to shave. "Oh, my sweet Ned." "Anne, honey, I needs to confess to you that many's the woman in the world done been bamboozled by nothin," her mother said, straightening her bonnet without once looking into the mirror. Anne's mother opened the back door, took the one step down into the yard, turned and then stood, one foot still in the doorway and one foot in the yard. She held out her open hand, palm up, and slowly raised it until the hand seemed to be floating. "I needs to confess to you, honey, thas the weight of pretty."

So, yes, were it not for the sleeping car porter, Lucas Turner, the second son of Maize and Ozell, would have become Anne's husband. Lucas would have come back and said to her words that would have been as close to an apology as a young man like him could manage. "You is beautiful, and I shouldna said you whatn't. But sometimes you make it hard. . . ." Lucas's father, Ozell, had been a deaf-mute all his days, so many people just naturally thought his nine children would not be able to manage so much as a "hey" or a "linger here." Lucas would have made Anne Perry a good husband. He wouldn't have told her every day how much he loved her or how beautiful she was, but on those rare days when he could force himself to get that out, she would know he meant it with his whole heart, and just maybe his saying it would have carried her up the mountain until the next time he said it. And Lucas would never have hurt her, was not raised that way. The world could not say that about Ned. And if Lucas had, in some insane moment, deviated from a sound upbringing, his father would have thrashed him to know he could bring something like that into the world. Then Anne's father would have torn him asunder and cast his parts to the winds.

Yes, were it not for the sleeping car porter, Lucas Turner it would have been. He had large hands, strong hands to work the acres his father would have passed on to him, wordless. Her own practical father would have perhaps bought them many more acres, maybe even a piece of that haunted but fertile section of land owned by the white man Hooper Andrews, a generous soul who woke up one cold morning and found that during a night of sound sleep all his perfect teeth had fallen out and were lying in a special, bloodless pile on his pillow. God, people said, did more mysterious things in Mississippi than he did anywhere else on Earth. The land from Lucas's father and the land bought from Andrews might have been enough for Anne and Lucas Turner to make a good life—some little of this, a whole lot of that, enough of a living raising crops so that they could put more and more distance between themselves and the legacy of slavery. The children would have helped to do that, too. They would not have had less than five children, given the kind of people they came from. The first boy would have been called Roger, named for Lucas's grandfather, who had been lynched, just the opening act of the entertainment for an Independence Day celebration. Just before the white people's picnic and five hours before the fireworks, which had been imported cheap that year from New Orleans.

The first girl might have been named Maize, after Lucas's mama, but Anne would have wanted to honor her father's mother, Clemie, the one who taught her how to make tapestries, that long and arduous process of creating something giant and wonderful enough to put up in a church or a palace, or even on a family's wall to replace the wallpaper of magazine and newspaper covers. "Anybody can crochet," Clemie said to the ten-year-old Anne and her older sister on the day of the first lesson, spreading out on the kitchen table a large thick cloth and spools of yarn. The blue river of one spool especially caught and held Anne's eye. That blue and the other colors would ultimately not be enough to hold her sister, who would eventually lose herself to crocheting. "Well," Clemie sighed to Anne the day the sister wandered over into crocheting, "a body can be happy there. I been there. It ain't so bad. But me and you will have to settle for somethin that will stay round for a hundred years. Maybe even a thousand. You think you gon like that? You think you gon like that many years?" Anne nodded sure, her hands resting on the table's edge—one hundred, two hundred, three hundred. It didn't matter, as long as she could keep touching that blue. And the green, the green was nice, too, lush and warm as a thick blanket of grass after a hard day's work. And the yellow so hypnotically bright, as if John Henry had taken the sun and whipped it up in a cake-making bowl and laid it out in streams of gold across the table end to end.

Some of Anne and Lucas's children would have been farmers and married other farmers, but there would have been others who would go off to St. Louis or Chicago or Detroit. And many of their farming grandchildren would have followed their relatives north. Anne and Lucas would grow old seeing their world thinning out. A house where some child or grand of theirs first lived as a married soul would come to stand empty or be inhabited by other people—good folks maybe, but nevertheless unrelated to the Turners; and so she would tell Lucas as they went about in their wagon, then in their car, to take another route because while that married child was fine and happy in St. Louis, that didn't help her inconsolable heart traveling down a bumpy Mississippi road. During the summers and some holidays, their world would repopulate again with children and grands and great-grands coming home in big cars and with presents and the city ways of people who lived in places where saying no to white people was an every-other-day thing. Back home, back in Mississippi, the grands especially might not even know how to act. "It's a free country" didn't translate in Mississippi. There was a strain in both Anne and Lucas that would have produced a teenage grandson with a hat cocked Chicago-style who would have had to cut short his two-month summer vacation after three days. Or end up at the bottom of the river, anchored there with a seventy-pound cotton gin fan tied to his neck with barbed wire.

Lucas would have died first, for that was just the way his people were. A heart attack as he stepped out of the field to get a drink of water. And then, way later on, it would be Anne's peaceful turn, far into the night after a good meal and after some grandchild or great-grandchild had read something to her from a schoolbook or from the Bible, and after one more dream about Lucas going off to the fields and never returning. All her kin would come back to bury her, from Chicago, St. Louis, Washington, New York, the county next door. To praise her good name at a funeral preached at Everlasting Light Baptist Church, where the funerals of her parents had been preached, where they would have had the funeral of one or more of her own children, dead of whooping cough or dead of falling down a well or dead of just not having been born with enough life. "We're jealous of God this mornin," the preacher would begin at her funeral, "cause He's sittin with our Anne and we won't be able to sit and talk with her again until nine and a half minutes after we step through them Pearly Gates. We're jealous of You this mornin, yes, but we must thank You for all the livelong days we had with her, O Lord. We're thankful for every single minute, but still we can't help but be jealous this mornin. . . ." So Anne Perry Turner's life would have come to an end. And God would lick the tip of His forefinger and turn the page. Ashes to ashes. Dust to Mississippi dust.

B ut Anne Perry had a cousin, a sleeping car porter, and he came to the October homecoming at Everlasting Light with his friend, another sleeping car porter, George Carter. Anne's cousin had set off a year before to make a new life in Chicago, but on the train just before St. Louis, a man in a gray suit and purple tie and wearing tiny black-and-white, two-tone shoes told him about Washington, D.C. "They treat colored people like kings and queens in Washington, cause thas where the president lives. Would they treat colored people anything but good in a city where the president hangs his hat and pets his dog and snores beside Mrs. President every night? Now would they?" Being who he was, Anne's cousin took too long in answering, so the man in the gray suit gave him the words, "No. Course not. They wouldn't do such a thing to us." Anne's cousin got off the train in St. Louis and exchanged the rest of his ticket to Chicago for one going to Washington, where he didn't know a soul. The cousin never once wondered why—if D.C. was the Promised Land, "a place where," as the purple tie man had said, "men dying in the desert dreamed of"—why the man on the train, as he himself had confessed, had never actually seen the city but had lived all his life in Gary, Indiana.

Anne's cousin and George Carter were good friends, lived on the same floor in a house on Corcoran Street, N.W., and though George was born and raised in Washington, he usually had the humility of a patient farmer who had worked his whole life behind a mule. He had seen New

York and Chicago and Philadelphia and he knew that while his D.C. was fine for him, it did not rise up and command the sky the way other places did. Anne's cousin—returning home for the first time since leaving—and George got off the train the first day of the Everlasting Light homecoming and got a ride the few miles to the church after they bought just about all the soft drinks at a little store near the train station. "I don't wanna go home with just the presents in my suitcase," the cousin told George, informing him that at such gatherings everyone brought something for everyone else to share. "They call these sodas up in Washington," the cousin bragged to his great-aunt at the homecoming, "and we drink em all day long." The aunt was blind and nearly toothless and she took two slow sips of the orange soda George had handed her. "Taste just like the soft drink they got over to the white man's sto," she said.

The cousin came in his blue wool suit, and George had on his brown wool suit. The suits were too warm for Mississippi in October, but the young men got points for looking good, even as the sweat rained down their faces through the long day, their coats resting on their arms or over their shoulders most of the time so people could see their pants matched up real nice with the coats. The cousin introduced George to just about everyone at the homecoming, which was held to the right of the church. The cemetery was over to the left, where Anne's dead were resting.

At about three that afternoon, the cousin got around to introducing George to Anne, who was not impressed for many reasons, but partly because she had Neddy around and Lucas wasn't too far away. Her mother's remark about pretty weighing nothing had been one month before, not yet long enough for Anne to know that Neddy might not be the one. There was even someone named Hayfield just waiting to come onstage. And Washington, unlike St. Louis or Chicago, was a universe away. Too far for a young woman still used to adoring her face to have dreams about. George, with his fancy wool suit, was sweating from doing no more than saying, Hi you doin, Hi yall doin this afternoon, not a sign of a man used to hard work. Anne thought as she took him in with one hurried glance, If he sweats with just this much work, how much work could he ever manage behind a plow? Years and years later, George Carter, speaking into a cassette-recording machine, would say to the grandson named for him that he wanted to walk away, walk all the way back to the train station, because in her eyes he had seen how limited his life on the rails had been.

As Anne shook his hand and told him welcome to Picayune, she spied Ned over his shoulder saying something to Clarice Tilman. At one point Clarice threw her head back and laughed to the sky. "Hope you have a good time here, Mr. Carter," Anne said without thinking, still shaking his hand. Clarice wasn't a fast girl; she was a good girl from a good family, raised to know right from wrong. She had some lemonade in one hand and after she laughed, she drank a long time from her mason jar, not seeming to care that Ned had to wait for her to finish before he could say something else that would make her laugh. And wait he did. Anne did a quick look around to see where Lucas was, but she could not find him in the crowd of people standing and sitting. She couldn't find Hayfield, either. George said after she pulled her hand from his, "It's a hot day but I think I'm gonna make it." Anne, with her mind elsewhere, did not hear him. She had already seen how perfect the day was, if a mind was in a state to enjoy it. Years and years later, she would describe for her grandson, talking into the cassette-recording machine, the dress Clarice was wearing, the way her free hand hung limply out in front of her, the way her other hand went halfway around the mason jar. "Yesterday is a hundred years ago," she would say to him, "but the look and the pattern and the color of that dress, they're with me right now. I could paint it in extreme detail like I just saw it this mornin."

George stayed with the cousin's family that weekend. The young men had planned to catch the train to Jackson on Tuesday morning to get their new assignments. On Sunday morning George went to church with the family and saw Anne again. She waved at him after the service, a dark spirit in a long blue dress, and then disappeared on a road with some friends, with Lucas a few steps ahead of them. "I was afraid," George would tell his grandson and the recording machine, "afraid that God was tellin me somethin and I might not be smart anough to read the signs right." He had on the same wool suit and the weather punished him even more than it had the day before and he was still somewhat hobbled by what he had first seen in Anne's eyes. "I got separated from her cousin, my buddy, and just followed her and that crowd on up the road, hopin I wouldn't get lost."

When she happened to turn and see him walking alone, she came back and let him know he was going the long way to her cousin's place. He told her he figured that sooner or later the road would double back, and he'd be where he needed to be. The roads may work that way in Washington, D.C., she said, but by the time the roads in Mississippi double back, you could be in another state or in the river.

"Can I walk a ways with you?" he asked nearly half a mile from the church, wringing out his handkerchief again.

She shrugged. "Ain't that what you doin now?" He wasn't Neddy- or Lucas-handsome either. Too light as well. Dark had a way of touching the heart. Light, she had decided at seventeen and a half, only shook hands.

"Yes," he said, "but I'm doin it without none a your permission."

The rains came early that afternoon and he stayed at her place. Unlike other women up and down his railroad lines, she had surprisingly little interest in Washington, and he kept digging deep, trying to come up with some detail he felt would make him seem a man of the world. Women liked men of the world. They talked on the porch sitting on cane-bottom chairs, her mother sewing at one end of the porch, three of her brothers sitting on the floor in the middle, playing Old Maid with cards their father had bought in Jackson. The rain never letting up. At one point she turned her face and managed to cover her yawn with four fingers before asking where his people came from. She had not learned that colored people could actually be born in Washington. And when he could say no more than that his parents came from some forgotten place in North Carolina, her face saddened as if, in the end, she was talking to an orphan. He saw that look, because, unlike the one with the yawn, she failed to hide her face in time. Orphans are to be helped and not so much pitied, her father had taught her, but most of all try to make them feel like human beings. Remember, you your own self got a mother and father.

It might be that her father knew that his second daughter was destined for some place else, beyond where he could walk in a day or two to see her if all other transportation failed. He stayed away until George had left early that evening, did not even make it to supper, something that had not happened within the children's memory. Everyone else in Anne's household was fascinated by the fact that George lived in Washington, especially her mother, who wanted to know if he had ever met the president, whether colored people did not have to step into the gutter when a white person approached.

Anne was quiet most of the meal, and George figured correctly that she was bored with him. She was quite aware that he was trying too hard. She liked confidence to just roll off a man. Maybe, he thought just before the peach cobbler, it would have been different if he had been from Chicago or New York. Then he could have had something to poem about to her. But after the cobbler and before the coffee, he let it all pass, stopped trying to say something to impress her. Anne's mother placed a cup of coffee before him, and he thanked her. He turned to Anne while his coffee cooled and asked why she chose to work on something like a tapestry that took so many months, even years, when she could do a crochet and be done in a few days or weeks. On the way to the kitchen table he had seen the tapestry she was working on folded up in a corner of the parlor and had asked what it was. She had started it three weeks before. A winter scene that came almost entirely from her imagination, because snow had been rare in her life. It would be nine years before the work was completed. "I seen women turn out them crochets left and right in lil no time," he said. "My tapestry ain't a race, Mr. Carter." She had completed only three other tapestries in her lifetime, and the first of those had been with her grandmother's help. "I hope thas always the case," George said. "Them other women, they was mostly doin it to make a livin." "Well," Anne said, looking from her mother to her brother named after their father, "I do it cause I can't help myself." Her cousin came for George before sunset, having been told by someone who had heard it from someone else where he could be found. It was still raining, but the cousin had brought some clothes that George could wear to save his wool suit. Go-to-work-in-the-field clothes. On the porch, preparing to leave, he surprised himself and everyone else and asked Anne if he might see her tomorrow. She turned to look momentarily at her mother, who nodded, and then Anne shrugged for the fifth time that day and said to him, "Why not?" He was twenty-two, and she was a few months from being eighteen. The year was 1932.

Her father returned about seven and found her at the kitchen table with the new tapestry. She was inspecting a trail in the snow that a brown bunny had made on its way back home. Only one detail among dozens. So much white thread, so little gray. Because she had known next to no snow, she was working only from half-remembered pictures in books and from what her mind told her a snow world looked like. Her father stood in the doorway and said nothing, leaning against the doorjamb, his arms folded. When he spoke, she was startled and said, "Oh, I didn't see you standin there, Daddy," and he said, "No, I don't spose you did."

He came to her and sat at his place at the head of the table. He had even avoided George all the day of the homecoming. "Whas this one gonna be?" he said, picking up one edge of the cloth with one hand. She had made a few light pencil markings on it, but aside from the bunny heading home, it was a large and empty thing. The new calluses on her father's hand snagged on the material. He dropped the edge and watched it swing just a bit, then come to rest.

"I'm gonna try makin this snow scene work," she said. They could hear her mother and her five younger brothers in the parlor, laughing, talking about every little piddling thing, for they did not yet know that the world had changed just that quickly. His oldest daughter, the one who crocheted, had married a man from the Chatsworth family and settled with him within a short wagon's ride of where he now sat. Fifteen minutes if he could get ahold of someone's Ford and the roads weren't flooded. Not more than four hours if he had to walk. More than a day if he had to crawl.

He rose to leave. "You might have a time of it since you ain't seen much snow." He thought she had seen a snowstorm once when she was seven, but the snow he was thinking of had been in his mother's childhood, not Anne's.

"I'll just imagine it."

"You have a good evenin," her father said and stepped toward the door.

"You, too." Anne used her left forefinger to trace the pale gray trail the bunny had made. She came to the bunny and her finger hopped over him. Two inches from him she decided that that was where his home should be. The line he had made behind him was seven inches. Her eyes went back to the beginning of the trail and she realized for the first time that the work would not be complete without a diving hawk, a bird of prey more dominant than anything else in the sunless sky. A hawk with its talons exposed, glinting so that the killer might be portrayed in all its murderous and beautiful glory. Her right forefinger went up near the top of the tapestry, and when she knew where the hawk would be, she looked momentarily out the window into the yard, toward the east and beyond, and then she called out, "Daddy?"

"Yeah?" Her father stopped two feet beyond the kitchen.

"Want me to fix you somethin to eat?"

"No, baby," he said without turning around, "I done had all my meals for today."

❄

The rains did not let up and the train to take the cousin and George to Jackson could not make its way to Picayune. Anne saw him every day that week, the two sitting on the porch in the late afternoon and evening. By Tuesday he knew his way on his own to her place, and by Thursday, unlike the other days, a tad of her was looking forward to seeing him in the borrowed field work clothes, coming along the road from the left full of purpose and then stepping over the dog and his two duck companions lying in the mud at the entrance to her place. She didn't stand on the porch with her arms around the post, the way she had months and months ago, before Lucas Turner told her she was not as beautiful as she thought she was. More than anything, being with George gave her something to do with her afternoon and evening time. "The heart can be cruel, the heart can be wicked, the heart can give joy," Anne was to tell her grandson and the recording machine years later, "but it is always an instrument we can never understand." Neddy had already wandered over to Clarice's way. Lucas Turner's mother had asked him that Wednesday why he wasn't putting down time with Anne, and he told her what his heart had told him that morning when he woke at four: "We ain't twirlin like that anymore."

The rains eased to drizzle on Friday and George woke on Saturday morning in the guest bed several miles from Anne and knew the train was coming. All that metal, all that motion, the power of a million mules just to sweep him up and take him away. Even before he got out of bed he wondered if he would be happy as a farmer, for he had supped with her family the evening before and had felt her father's eyes peering into him the whole time. The eyes had not been charitable to a man who might take Anne away. So maybe he could live on with her as a farmer, for he knew now, less than a week of being in Mississippi, that he was capable of loving her that much. His grandfather had been a farmer, so perhaps farming was in his blood, a dormant something waiting for the soil to shake and awaken it. Could the blood that allowed farming in North Carolina permit him to make a life in Mississippi, with a woman who at that very moment did not even care if he came or went? But as he trembled to put on the work clothes and then looked out the window at the land that seemed to breathe as it went on forever, he knew how homesick he would be for Washington, where there was someone he knew around every corner. He looked down at his friend, Anne's sleeping cousin, and George knew that that homesickness might have the power to kill him in Mississippi.

The train came for them that Wednesday and he told Anne on Tuesday that he would be back to see her as soon as he could. "I will write," he added. Already, in that short time, she was not the young woman who had been talking to herself while standing before the mirror, but she was also not a woman who felt very much for him. "I won't expect any letter from you till I got it in my hands," she said. That hurt him somewhat, because it told him that she was capable of life without him, and clinging women were all he had ever known. He wanted her standing on the porch each day, waiting for the letter, dying just a little bit when it didn't arrive. "I will write, and you can count on it," he said. She said, "I'll write you back. Soon as I get your letter in my hands. But not before." They were again on the porch, and as if to emphasize what she had said, she raised her hands in front of her and looked at them. He reached to take them but she only took one of his and shook it, like two strangers meeting on a downtown street as the world flowed on about them. When sufficient time had passed, she withdrew her hand. They were alone on the porch. They had, of course, never kissed and they would not kiss for the first time until three weeks before they married more than a year later. In 1933. There were to be five more visits, including the month he took time off from the railroad and helped in her father's fields. The railroad people telegraphed him two days before that month was up: "Remember: Our calendar has but 30 days in Sept."

❖

The wedding was held in late October, when George and the cousin managed to get one week off. It was a large ceremony, held just to the right of the church, Everlasting Light. After the harvest, after the homecoming. Neddy and Clarice, doomed to marry, stood together on the steps that led up into the side of the church. Lucas was in Jackson that day. A young woman, Mona, sat in the crowd witnessing the wedding and thinking of Lucas, even as he, sitting in a lawyer's office three blocks from the Capitol with his father, was thinking of her. "Our babies may not be able to hear or speak," Lucas had told her earlier that month. "You got more to worry about," Mona said in reply. "We all crazy in my family. Cut your throat cause you burnt the biscuits crazy. You any good with the cookin, Lucas?" The first thing Anne and George did as newlyweds was go around to the other side of the church and stand for a few seconds at the graves of her people, ending at last at the place where her grandmother Clemie was sleeping. The tapestry teacher. Each night of the next few days, as they waited for the first train on their long journey to Washington, George slept downstairs, and she slept upstairs in the bed she had been in since she was seven years old. The rings on Anne's and George's fingers did not matter to her father, and they did not matter to her mother. When she returned a year and a half later with her first child in her arms, only then did her parents make a new place, one bed, for her and the husband.

In all the excitement of her new life, she had not worked on the new tapestry very much, and in packing for Washington, she was to forget it because it had been in a corner of the house she did not visit very much anymore. She completed two others in Washington in those first years, including a scene of Corcoran Street covered with snow and the children of that street village on sleds and throwing snowballs and her mother and father standing and watching it all, though they were never to see Washington in winter. The snow tapestry in Mississippi with the diving hawk ended up on a shelf in a closet on the second floor until one day her father came upon it six years after her marriage. He mailed it to her, noting in a letter he had his youngest son write, "You forgot this a long time ago." She would have by then grown into something else in Washington and had barely enough left of Mississippi in her to finish the snow scene. It took three more years, but it looked nothing like the world she had first imagined in Picayune. She unstitched it until the brown bunny was gone, though the hawk stayed, still dominant, still glorious. Not diving, not intent this time on ending the life of something, but just sailing past. A tourist. None of her descendants were ever to become tapestry women.

Just before the train with the newly married couple left Mississippi, it stopped at a patch of a place so small no one had bothered to give it a name. The entire train was full, and that first cabin, which got most of the smoke and soot from the engine, had only colored people. George, the sleeping car porter, would work most of the trip to Washington. Anne, settling into being Mrs. Carter, got to know many of her neighbors in her cabin. No one in that first leg of the trip, save her and George, was destined for lives in Washington; the other future Washingtonians would be picked up along the way—farther north in Mississippi and then in places east, especially St. Louis.

At that patch of nowhere in Mississippi, three colored people got off, and a pregnant Negro woman and a white man got on. They were married, though none of the Negroes knew that. Instantly, there arose in their hearts a disdain for the white man and a you-po-put-upon-thang attitude for the woman, who was some seven or eight months in the family way. They waited for the white man to leave, perhaps to go to one of the cars for whites, or, more likely, to leave the train altogether. After all, he had had his pleasure. But he followed the woman to a seat two down and across from Anne. He stored two suitcases above the seat.

When she was seated, he helped the woman take off her shawl and folded it and made a pillow for her head, then he knelt, unhooked her shoes, and began to massage her stockinged feet. The Negroes could see that they were not yet thirty. The train's engine snorted right and left, shimmied, and then started up. In five blinks of Anne's eyes, it was on its way. The seat of the Negro woman accompanied by the white man was facing Anne, who saw the woman with her head still leaning back, her eyes closed as the man worked her feet in his hands. The Negroes around the couple, some standing, some sitting, were silent and they, all but the smallest children, looked at one another. Maybe he was not really white. He took a pair of yellow slippers from his coat pocket and put them on the woman's feet. He stood and took off his hat and nodded to just about every Negro head in the car, and then he removed his coat. The man took the seat at the window beside the woman and disappeared from Anne's view. The Negro woman's head was still back and she opened her eyes before long and smiled at the older couple in the seats facing hers and the white man's, then she looked at the white man and smiled. The oldest person in the car—the woman of the couple facing the Negro woman and the white man—asked them in a voice many heard, "Yall goin far?" The pregnant woman nodded and smiled some more. "Yes, ma'am." They knew he was white when the conductor came in twenty minutes later and said in a loud voice, in a voice white people had for each other when they knew one was making a mistake in the presence of Negroes, "You sure this where you want to be?" "I'm sure," the white man said. Many of the adults in that car would live to see the first man on the moon, and a good bunch of those would never believe it had happened. That scene with the white man and the Negro woman was far more incredible; but those who believed would do so because the scene on the train had come to them unfiltered, without the use of some camera operated by the space people out to try to trick their eyes.

❖

Well after St. Louis, the car's population became more or less stable, with most of the people there going on to Washington, including the pregnant woman and the white man. The Negroes started calling him "Mr. Feet," and he never took offense. Anne continued to see little of her working husband, but she was content and busied herself with getting to know her fellow passengers. In the end, she became as at home with them as the people around Picayune. "My Picayune people," she thought at one point after finishing a piece of sweet potato pie from a man five seats down, "my Picayune folks who never even saw Picayune." They shared food, they shared stories about home, about Southern places that would be the foundation of their lives in the North. None of them could know that the cohesion born and nurtured in the South would be but memory in less than two generations. The one thing that Anne told her grandson and his recording machine about the trip was the story of the child who got on with her parents not long after they left Missouri. This honey-colored child of one year, she said, going up and down the aisle in her diaper as if she were at home, stopping at nearly every seat and conversing in her gibberish as she rested her hands on someone's thigh or knee. "People talked to her like every word of hers made sense. And she talked back the same way. She was my child, she was that woman over there's child. She was that man down there's child, that man that fiddled to her goin up and down the aisle. I've always wondered what happened to her. We could talk to her or pick her up when she fell and we could know things would turn out good for us where we was goin." All the people in that car would have said two generations was a long time. It was, and yet it was not.

Somewhere in Tennessee, after a somewhat quiet afternoon, she remembered the snow scene tapestry and longed to work on it to give her restless hands something to do. She had not seen her husband in many, many hours, and not knowing any better, full of the peace and joy she had gotten from being in the cabin, she ventured out beyond her own car, out there to where the white people were, thinking she might see George for a second. Let him know she was thinking of him. She knew she could never sit beyond her own place, but she did not think there was any harm in just finding her husband and giving him a little "Hi you doin?" It was in the third car of white diners that she saw the back of George. He was standing before the conductor, the same man who had asked if the white man from Mississippi wanted to come and be with them. George's head was not down, but it was not raised either. The conductor was talking somewhat loud to her husband. Certainly loud enough to disturb the digestion of the closest diners. His words were very harsh. The conductor was taller than George, and when he saw Anne, he indicated with his raised chin that there was one more thing George should attend to.

George turned slowly and his eyes widened to see his wife. He had already been shamed before all the white people, and now here was his wife. He was quickly before Anne and took her painfully by the shoulder and practically pulled her along back to the front car. He forced her down into her seat and shouted, "When I put you in a seat, I mean for you to stay there!"

"Now, George, wait here a minute—"

"I mean for you to stay where I put you!" He went back to work.

The car was silent, and they all felt for her because she was family. Why would he treat our Anne that way?

The experience was so completely humiliating that Anne wanted first only to cry. But she, her father's child, began to encase herself so that everything around her disappeared and she started making her way back to Mississippi. She stayed to herself for many hours, hearing and seeing nothing about her though her eyes remained open. George did not come back to her and that made it easier for her. People tried speaking to her, but she did not respond. She began to see that very foolish girl, saying foolish things into the mirror. That foolish girl had fooled herself into marriage and had been knocked straight on her way to her new home, even before she had consummated the marriage.

Along toward evening, as the car went on with its life, she felt that not a single person had anything in common with her. It was just before nine o'clock that she, with the clearest mind yet, knew that the marriage was in tatters and should never have happened. Whatever little bit of it there was at that moment would be dead before they reached Washington. It was better to know that now, before they had become a proper man and wife, better to have such a large mistake over and done with at nineteen than to carry it through in misery on into twenty-five, to thirty, to thirty-five. She had seen that with other women, but that would not be her: *I could not help myself. Lord knows. Jesus, why did You turn Your back on me? Why did You make me old at forty with this man?* There had been something in George's voice that she could not forgive. Her heart was breaking, but that was in the nature of hearts, she told herself as the car quieted for the night. It was also in their nature to heal for however long it took, six months, a year, two years. After consulting with the Picayune stationmaster four days before she left, Anne's father had given her $50 and her mother had sewn the money into the hem of her dress on a day when George was away from the house. "This will bring you home from wherever you are if you ain't abidin mongst angels," her mother said before breaking the thread with her teeth and finalizing the deed with a solid knot in the thread.

So she decided that at the next stop, wherever they were, she would buy a ticket back to Picayune, Mississippi. There was not anything George could say that would change her mind. *This the weight of pretty. I'm going home,* and that one thought eased her heart. *This the weight of me goin back home.*

As the evening went on, she saw her life after the next stop: Once the train dropped her off in Picayune, she would have a six-or-so-mile trip to her parents' place, to her home. If the weather was bad, she knew she would not have a problem getting a ride on somebody's buggy or wagon or in a car. White or black, they knew her father, a good man, a no-nonsense man, and no one would deny his daughter and she would reach home unmolested. But she had a feeling that God would have perfect weather when she returned, so she would leave her suitcase and trunk at the train station to be retrieved later, and then she would walk the miles. Besides, her heart would be broken and she would feel that the walk would do her good.

Her train rounded a corner and swayed and the people swayed with it.

In Picayune, she would take off her new shoes just beyond the station. She had lived barefoot most of her life in Picayune, and so that is what she would return to. The town of Picayune was a small place and the walk through it would take less than thirty minutes, depending on whom she would see along the way. The speckled dog that always lounged outside Moss's general store would walk beside her as always to the edge of town. Then it would turn back, afraid of leaving the known world.

It would be morning, and she would say "Good mornin" to all, white and black, as she went down the main street. And everyone would say "Good mornin" back. The newlywed come home so soon, they would whisper. What could be the matter? What did he do to our po Anne? Found a good girl just to lose her to his foolishness. She would not hang her head, for that was not how her people were. Outside of the town, with the dog gone, she would not see humans again until another half mile unless someone was on the road. At that half mile would be the farm of the Petersons, a white family of nine children. She had known quite well the third oldest girl. If someone there happened to see her pass, they might offer her a drink. That third oldest girl was dead now, died bringing her first child into the world, but the family would remember that Anne had been a friend. "Sit a spell and have a little somethin, Anne. Get out that sun. Linger here, child. Home can wait." And if her heart would allow it, she would do just that.

Thin smoke wafted through her train and the adults held their breath; the children didn't know enough to do that.

Unless a body was on the road outside Picayune, she would not see people again until she was a little more than a mile from the Petersons. The road would have turned just after their farm at nearly 90 degrees. The Elbow Road is what people for years had been calling it. "I meet you at the turn in the Elbow Road." "Bless her heart. She had that baby right there on Elbow Road." Just beyond the road was Patches' Creek, the swimming hole for Negroes. Some of her best memories were of Sundays after church when the family piled into her father's wagon with two baskets of food and went to Patches' Creek. The Negroes liked to call such Sundays "vacation." "You comin on vacation?" "He just up and died after his vacation. No sign of nothin bad. Just happy all durin his vacation." "The nerve of that little hussy shamin herself and her family right out there in front of everyone. Spoiled my vacation." Patches' Creek was on land owned by a woman, Deborah Kerrshaw, who fancied herself the richest Negro in Mississippi. She would die not knowing there were five undertakers and one insurance company founder who were richer. She never charged anyone to swim in her creek.

After the creek, the winding road went on for some two miles with only farmland on either side. Especially now, with the crops gone from the fields, it would be lonely there because the nearest house was just about invisible and the cows and mules and horses sunning in the fields usually kept to themselves, never bothered to come out to the fence unless they knew a person. That nearest house could only be reached by leaving the road and heading away for nearly half a mile. But people used the road all the time. She had first seen four-year-old Neddy on that road, playing tag with two white boys, one of them being the descendant of one of the men who had lynched Lucas Turner's grandfather. Lucas had taken her hand in his for only the second time on that road. And she had trembled even more than with the first time. If hunger took hold and she had not eaten at the Petersons or stopped for something at the Kerrshaw place, she would have to turn off the road and knock at a Negro door. The earth and its ground and its trees would have nothing to offer her because they were preparing for winter. But she would be welcome at any house.

The lights of her train dimmed and the adults pulled the children closer as the smoke cleared from the cabin.

Then, after the fields, the road would straighten as it neared Everlasting Light Baptist Church. If she had eaten, she would tarry at the cemetery, if only to tell her grandmother what had happened. Linger here. The time among the graves might tell her that there could yet be a life with Hayfield. Some land. Children. He could be taught to tell better jokes. She would know more and would take even more time before marrying. No matter how much he might plead with her. "We got time," she might say. And if he was any kind of man, then he would wait. And if he didn't, if she never married another living soul, then well . . . So be it. She had one aunt, near the center of the cemetery, who had never married. At eighty-two, to win a bet with a grown nephew she had raised from an infant, the aunt of slight build had done seventy-nine push-ups, four more than she needed to win the bet. Then she had stood and wiped her hands clean of dirt and waited for her nephew to count out the dollar he owed. "I's short one quarter, Auntie." "I don't care. I wants my money by tomorrow mornin or you'll have to find another home that ain't Picayune." Po thang, some had said of her aunt. Never married. Po thang. But Anne, mapping her journey in her train car, realized there were worse things in life than never having a man inside her.

She knew that the time at the cemetery would strengthen her somehow. And so if she met people on the final leg home, that would be good. But if she didn't, she would make it anyway. The stand of pecan trees that signaled the approach of the short road leading to her home would make her just about invisible to anyone on the porch until she was at the mouth of the path to the house. Coming from that side was different than coming from the other side, the way George had come to her those times from her cousin's place. Everyone could be seen coming from that side.

Her train began an awful shaking. She knew that when she had passed the last pecan tree, the person waiting on the porch would be her father. She felt that every second of her life had been leading to a dead marriage and a father who would come out to her without her taking even one step back onto their property, back onto where she had first known life. The dog and his duck companions would not rouse because she was old news. In some twenty-three long steps her father would be in front of her, having used the last two to step over the dog and the ducks. It would be about three in the afternoon. He was not really a man of touching, but if she wanted, she—now tired from her longest walk home—would be able to cry and fall into his arms, her wedding ring back there at the train station in the suitcase. But, no, she would wait to cry. With her mother. He would look down past the trees and ask, "How far back you leave your things?" "The train station." Her mother would now be on her way from the house. Running. Her father would ask, "Anything you need amongst them things that can't wait for now?" "No, I can wait, Daddy." "Tomorrow then. I get Billy to go get em tomorrow." Then she would be home.

The train did not stop for a very long time, after she had leaned her head against the window and fallen asleep about midnight. She was awakened a short time after the train left that station by a gentle shaking of her shoulder. She came to in a car of sleeping people. George was beside her. The train was all but dark. "Whatcha want from me, George?" There was no grogginess in her voice, only resolve. "Sayin I'm sorry." "I want only to sleep now. I'm goin back home. I have a home to go back to." "I know that, Anne. I know that bout you." "Then let me be." "Take my pology. I couldn't mean anything more." "I take your pology. Now let me sleep." He was silent and she leaned her head back against the window. She had made her decision and everything was easy now. But as she neared the house of sleep, she sat up and said, "Your next woman down the line should not be treated like a child, George. Take that little piece of somethin and make somethin of your life with a nice woman,

George. Try and do that. It won't be hard. But me, I ain't your child. I got only one father and he's waitin for me in Mississippi." "I know that, Anne. I know that. I'll get you a ticket for home." "I brought my own money, George." He had had more words, but her last ones silenced him because they had such utter finality. *I brought my own money.* I will count off the days until I have a little peace, he thought. She returned to sleep and he sat and listened to the silence that was her sleeping. He was tempted to return to work even though he was free until morning, but he was now paralyzed by her words. Anne had thought they were far from Washington. She did not realize that they were way beyond the middle of Virginia. George stayed at her side. He did not know what else to do. Another man, someone with a living marriage and a wife still loving, would have stayed there, if only to wake his wife from some trifle of a nightmare, a little reassurance to her as they built the foundation of their life together. But that was a sweet chore he would no longer have. About two hours before dawn, George, after nearly a day and five hours mostly on his feet, went to sleep. Immediately, he began grinding— "gritting" as Anne's mother called it—his teeth. More than an hour before dawn, Anne woke to find his head leaning softly on her shoulder. He could control many things about himself while awake, but sleep set him adrift. She pushed him away, back fully into his seat. His teeth began gritting again and he commenced talking almost in whispers in his sleep. *"I'll do it,"* he said, *"I'll clean every barn before I sleep, master. No need for that thing. No need for that again. I'll do it. I told yall I'd do it all."*

The sounds of the other sleepers now came to her as well, and there were many who were also talking in their sleep. Men and women speaking whole thoughts. A shout or two. A plea. Even the white man was talking as he slept, but not the Negro woman who was his wife. She, like all the children in the car, was dreaming in silence while the others talked. Sang. One sermon. Why, Anne wondered, had the previous nights been quiet? Why now, when the journey for many was nearing its end?

George began a gentle struggling, a man at the beginning of a job that would take far longer than he was telling the man in his nightmare. Anne turned and listened to him. *"I'll spic it and then I'll span it, master,"* he moaned. She shivered as she listened to him and the others in the car. *"Close eyes, wait by side of mule, child, and angel come down for us like promise,"* the man across from Anne whispered. She shivered again, the way she had as a small girl when her oldest brother told her and their siblings ghost stories way deep in the night forest. *"You done done it and you know you done done it,"* a woman far behind her hissed. *"Why crucify me with them lies?"* It was, in its way, like being on a train with talking dead people. So many times, her oldest brother had had to pick her up and carry her, shivering and crying, out of the night forest. "Please, don't tell Mama," he would say of scaring his siblings with his ghost stories. But she and her siblings had always gone into the dark of the forest of their own free will. "Don't tell Papa." *"Master, please . . . ,"* George said. She took his head and laid it in her lap. She closed her eyes but she did not return to sleep. That was over. A little more than a half hour before dawn, she reached up and touched the window with all the fingers of one hand, and the entire train seemed to stop its shaking and rattling. "There," she said as if the train could hear, as if it had granted some final wish. "There . . ." To get to where she was now in Virginia, it had taken three trains. She wondered how many it would take to return home, to arrive at a life without George.

Anne was not at all a morbid person, but it occurred to her quite simply that wherever it was she would die, it would not be in Mississippi. Within seconds of that thought, the train entered Washington, where she was to come to her end more than sixty-eight years later, a mother to seven living and two dead, a grandmother to twenty-one living and three dead, a great-grandmother to twelve, a great-great-grandmother to twins. George's teeth ceased their gritting and Anne brushed the back of her hand against his cheek. The train slowed. "Mama, I'm a long way from home," Anne whispered into the darkness and confusion. "Papa, I'm a long way from home."

ACKNOWLEDGMENTS

I am grateful—once more—to my editor, Dawn L. Davis (mother to Bijah), and to Rockelle Henderson and Jane Beirn at HarperCollins.

To Lil Coyne, Shirley Grossman, Marcia Shia, and Aslaug Johansen.

To Eric Simonoff (father of Henry and Lucy), my agent.

To Cressida Leyshon, Deborah Treisman, and David Remnick at *The New Yorker.*

I am especially thankful for the support and encouragement from the Lannan Foundation and the John D. and Catherine T. MacArthur Foundation.